THAT NIGHT

A DI Max Byrd &
DI Orion Tanzy Thriller

1

C. J. GRAYSON

'That Night' first published in E-book format by the method of self-publishing via Amazon (Kindle Direct Publishing) in 2020.

ISBN: 9798640098266
Print Edition May 2020
Version: First Edition

Books by C. J. Grayson

Standalones –
Someone's There

DI Max Byrd & DI Orion Tanzy –
That Night (book 1)

'Be the change you wish to see in the world.'
– Mahatma Gandhi

Prologue

After she heard footsteps enter the room, she clamped her eyes shut. She had no idea what time it was, but her little body clock assumed it was early morning. Next to her was a pile of old clothes that smelt like they'd been there forever. The musty smell reminded her of an attic or an old cupboard.

She'd used a fleece of some sort, at least that's what it felt like in the darkness, to keep her as warm as possible when the temperatures dipped overnight. She had no idea where she was. All she knew was that she was in a tight space surrounded by four walls.

There'd been no sound for hours - the person must have been sleeping. Near her, there was a box, about the size of a shoe box, maybe bigger, it was hard to tell but she knew it was locked. She'd already tried opening it the day before and nearly broke one of her little finger nails in the process.

She sighed, taking a long slow breath. The air in the cramped space was still and stale. Rancid in fact. Breathing became a chore after two days, but she'd taught herself to breathe slower. It had taken only three hours for her to urinate in her pants. Then two hours after that, she soiled herself.

That was the first day.

If her body clock was right, today was day four. Four days' worth of human urine and faeces was bad enough to turn the strongest of stomachs but somehow, her senses had got used to it.

There was no doubt she needed help. Badly.

She hadn't seen daylight or took a breath of fresh air for days.

Near her feet, the empty plate rested on top of the pile of musty, old clothes. She couldn't see it, but she knew it was there, because after she'd ate the sandwich that had been made for her, that's where she'd put it. As she thought about the plate, she thought about the sandwich. It was ham. Just ham. But she was starving, her insides rumbled and contracted. A bottle of water stood near the plate, too, and every few hours, she took a sip. When it was empty, she waited nearly half a day before someone came back to fill it up. Each day, that's all she got: a ham sandwich with a fresh bottle of water.

She thought about her mother making her a ham sandwich whilst she was sat down in the kitchen, watching cartoons on the television on the wall.

Oh God, she'd do anything to be there right now.

At home.

With her family.

Most of all, safe.

The footsteps came closer towards the cupboard. She could hear someone breathing on the other side of the door. Her body shivered as she quickly pulled the fleece up close to her face, the musty smell temporarily masking the awful odour of her wet, stained, filthy clothes.

The footsteps stopped just outside the cupboard.

Then the door slowly creaked open.

1

Wednesday Early Morning
Darlington

Ian Porter sighed into the phone and closed his eyes.

'Listen,' he said, 'I'm sorry. I should have reacted quicker. I…'

'What is it?' his wife, Julia, asked.

'I should have closed the gate and none of this would have happened.'

'It's done now - don't worry about it. We just have to make sure it doesn't happen again.'

Ian smiled. 'How's he doing?'

'He's – he's okay. The doctor said it's just a bump to his head, but he'll be fine.' Julia fell silent for a second. 'He's smiling at me, bless him.'

'Good. That's good.'

'I thought he'd be okay, but best to check.'

Ian physically nodded although his wife couldn't see him. 'Yeah, definitely.'

'How's the other two?' Julia asked.

'Fast asleep,' Ian said, 'I read them both a story. One of them is snoring upstairs, not sure which one. Where are you now?'

'I'm just leaving. It was so busy. The waiting room was packed. One kid had a cut on his neck, not sure what happened to him, but he was there before me, and I was there five hours. It wasn't the staff's fault, it's just too busy – they need more doctors there.'

Ian agreed.

'I'm starving,' Julia said. 'I didn't have any tea, did I?'

'Go get a McDonald's or something, just use my card, if you like?'

'Yeah… I'm passing there now. I might.'

Hours ago, their youngest son, Liam, who was almost one year old, had crawled halfway up the stairs and came cart-wheeling down. Their eldest, Jonah, had watched it happen, saying he'd smacked his forehead on the wooden floor at the bottom. It was awful. So Julia had rushed off to hospital to get him checked out.

'Okay, well I'll see you soon, Ju.'

'Wait, stay on the phone - I'll be going under the bridge soon.'

'Which bridge? Whessoe Road?'

'Yeah… it's dark. You know I don't like that bridge even during the day.'

'Of course it's dark, it's one in the morning.' Ian let out a laugh.

'Very funny,' Julia said, 'just turning the corner now.'

'Okay.' Ian readjusted his position on the living room sofa. 'You through it yet?'

'No… there's a car going really slow in front of me. It's just around the corner.'

'What car? Who's driving around at one in the morning?'

'Ian…'

'What?'

Julia didn't answer.

'Julia, what is it?'

'The car has stopped in front of me. I…'

'Go around it then.'

'I can't, it's too tight on the other side – there's a car parked opposite.'

Ian sat up on the sofa, felt his heartbeat starting to rise. 'What's happening?'

'It's just parked there.'

'Okay, okay,' Ian said, trying to remain calm. 'Just wait and see what happens. I'll stay on the phone.'

'Come on, all I want is a McDonalds,' Julia blurted out.

'Who's driving the car?'

'I can't – I can't see. I don't know – ahh, a woman is getting out of the passenger seat.'

'She's probably been out, got a lift home.' Ian's chest sunk and his breathing eased.

'Yeah. Short skirt. Skimpy top. She's definitely been out. He's moving now – the driver. Just put his hazards on as a thank you for waiting.'

'Get me a cheeseburger, please…'

'I thought you were on a diet?' Julia said with a hint of humour, aware of his daily struggles trying to keep his calories down.

'Just get me the burger… I'll start again tomorrow.'

'Yeah, yeah, whatever. Just going down the road then through the bridge. Stay on the phone.'

'Not going anywhere.'

'It seems darker than normal,' Julia said. 'Some of the streetlights must be off.'

Ian made his way to the kitchen, flicked the kettle on. The smell of lavender hung in the air from a plug-in near the high table as he grabbed a mug from the cupboard above the worktop. Then through the phone, he heard the high-pitched sound of brakes squeaking.

'What's that?' he asked.

Julia didn't answer.

'Julia?' Ian stopped still, frozen. 'What the fuck was that sound?'

'There's…'

'There's what? What is it?'

'…a man standing in the middle of the road. He's looking at me.'

'A man? What man?'

'He's – I don't know. He's just stood there looking at me. He's just staring at the car.'

'What does he look like?' Ian's pulse started to quicken. 'What's he wearing?'

'Black. Black jeans and a black fleece.'

Ian heard Liam cry in the back of the car through the phone.

'Hey buddy, it's okay, we'll be home soon,' Julia said in a forced delicate tone, trying to soothe him.

'Go around him!' Ian shouted.

'Okay…'

Ian clamped his eyes shut and waited.

'He's moved across the road. He isn't letting me passed.'

'Okay, is there anyone else in the bridge. Are there any cars nearby?'

It took Julia a second to check her rear-view mirror. 'No, no one.'

'Shit, you need—'

Julia let out a scream.

'Julia, what?'

'There was a bang at the back of the car. Shit. What the—'

She screamed again.

This time, Ian heard the sound through the speaker. 'There's someone behind the car, I see him in the mirror,' she cried.

'Fuck,' Ian muttered. 'Right, listen, listen. You need to run him down, the man in front. Just fucking go for it.'

'I can't, Ian, I—'

'Just fucking do it – get around him then, I don't care. Go!'

The Qashqai's engine revved, then the wheels screeched a little before it was drowned out by the sound of Julia's screaming which ripped through the car. The car door opened.

'He's in the back of the car – he's got Liam…'

Ian's breathing was rapid now.

'Get the fuck off him!' Julia begged, her voice almost breaking. 'Leave him alone!'

The sound of another door opening came through the speaker then a sound of a hard slap froze Ian to his core.

'Ian! Help me, please,' Julia gasped.

'Julia!'

Ian sprinted to the front door and put his trainers on. Within sixteen seconds, he was in the Astra. He didn't even think about his other children sleeping upstairs – he didn't have time to think. He put the phone on loud speaker and threw it onto the passenger seat, started the engine, forced the gear in first, and spun off the driveway onto the quiet, dark road.

'Julia?' he shouted to the phone resting on the seat.

All he could hear was her screaming and Liam's crying.

'Hold on, I'm coming,' he shouted. He was shaking with both anger and fear.

Ian reached the end of Brinkburn Drive, threw the car left onto Brinkburn Road, narrowly missing a parked car on the opposite side. He planted his foot and reached sixty-three miles-an-hour quicker than he ever had. The roar of the Astra echoed off the sleeping road under the inconsistent flickering glare of the orange street lights above. No one was around. He reached the end of Brinkburn road and took a sharp left, again, almost colliding with another car before he managed to straighten out.

'Julia?'

Julia didn't answer.

Ian saw the small road which went down to the bridge. 'Come on, come on.'

Slowing the car, he angled left, guiding it down the narrow road and entered under the bridge. It was dark, the only light coming from a poorly lit street light halfway down on the right. He stopped the Astra behind the diagonally parked Qashqai where he noticed both the driver's and rear passenger door were wide open.

Ian jumped out.

'Julia! Liam!' His voice echoed against the aging brickwork.

He glared wide-eyed inside the car, panting, desperate for air. Julia wasn't there. Liam wasn't in his baby seat in the back. 'Fuck.'

Then he heard Julia's scream.

Coming from behind him, somewhere higher than where he was. He turned quickly.

'Julia?' He galloped back through the bridge and took a sharp right onto a set of concrete steps, climbing them two at a time. Reaching the top of the steps, he entered a wide-open tarmac area in front of Hopetown Working men's club. He saw a white van quickly pulling away, the tires screeching on the tarmac.

Inside the back of the van, he heard his wife's muffled scream and his baby's stifled cry.

The van turned the corner out of sight up Brinkburn Road.

'Julia?' he whispered in desperation.

The sound of the van's engine faded in to the quiet, cold night.

He crumbled over, his lungs burning for air, his palms pressed on his knees. On the floor near his feet, he saw his son's blue dummy.

He picked it up, and watched it shake in his trembling hand. A sound buzzed from his pocket - a text message. He lifted his phone out and unlocked it.

It read:

Ian, this is all because of you. Because of what you did. I really hope you locked your door when you left your house, because we're about to surprise your other children.

2

Wednesday Early Morning
Darlington

Ian held his breath and read the text message again. He was in so much shock, he couldn't comprehend the words. Then it dawned on him – *I really hope you locked your door…*

The sound of the van had vanished, but the sound of his thumping chest remained.

'Fuck!' he shouted, his anger filtering in the quiet, cold air. He span around, and two at a time, he jumped down the stairs back down to the narrow road under the bridge. Never realising he'd left the car running as he made his way back to the open door, he pulled it open. As he climbed in, he heard quick footsteps behind him.

That's when he felt a sharp pain followed by a short wave of white heat run across his neck and shoulders. He lost consciousness, collapsed to the floor, and then everything went black.

He opened his eyes, blinked several times.

'Hey man, you okay?' a distorted voice said. It sounded like a robot.

'He looks badly hurt,' another voice said, sounding softer, more than likely a female.

'We should ring an ambulance,' the man said.

Above him, there was a man and a woman glaring down at him. The woman was on her knees with her hand on the side of Ian's shoulder. The man stood behind her, glaring down into the light of his phone. For a second, he thought the man looked familiar, but he couldn't place him.

Other car headlights filled the space under the bridge. There was a hum of concerned voices nearby as a little crowd gathered.

'Is he okay?' a distant voice asked.

The woman kneeling turned. 'I don't know – we found him like this.'

Ian grunted.

The woman leaned in closer. 'What did you say?'

'Where are they?' Ian tried but his voice was too weak, sounding more like 'waa-aa-da.'

'I – I don't know, where are—'

'Waa ma famyee?' Ian tried.

'Hey,' the man said calmly, 'you need to relax, you've been—'

'Lemme up!'

The man and woman carefully picked him up then took a step back, giving him some space, unsure what he was going to do. He could be disorientated, capable of anything.

Despite the cries of people telling him he needed help, Ian climbed in the Astra and slammed the door closed, the sound echoing under the bridge like an angry slap. With his head spinning, he did a three-point turn and raced back up the ramp, taking a right at the corner where the betting shop was, then planted his foot down to the floor, working his way up through the gears until the Astra hit seventy.

As he passed the Brinkburn pub on the right his head pounded. Shooting waves of intense pain bombarded the back of his head where something had hit him before he'd passed out.

He tried to ring Julia. It rang out.

'Shit!' he shouted, banging his palm off the steering wheel. He breathed light and fast, then felt something strange growing inside of him, something heavy on his chest. He was dizzy too.

He'd never had a panic attack but thought it might be the start of one.

Ian slowed the car a fraction and turned the corner of Brinkburn Drive, the car barely staying on four wheels as he rounded the sharp bend. Lucky it wasn't wet because he'd taken it far too carelessly and fortunate not to smash into the building of the care home. He put the car into third gear and whizzed through the chicane-like bend, barely avoiding the front bumper of a brand-new Mercedes with its nose pointed out.

'Come on, faster!'

In his head, he knew he was less than a minute behind them. He'll make it, he told himself. He'll get home to his children.

He saw the front of his house on his approach.

The hallway light was on.

He stopped the car next to the path, flung the door open, jumped out, and raced around the bonnet. He jumped up onto the step and pushed down the handle quickly. The front door he'd forgot to lock opened and he went inside.

'Julia?' he panted in the hallway.

The street behind him was absolutely silent. There was no sign of the white van in the street or on the roads.

There was no reply from Julia.

'Julia?' he said again.

The sound of his plea filled every wall of the house. He looked up the stairs at the dim glare coming from the night light positioned on the small table on the landing. There were no sounds. Using the handrail on the bannister, he propelled himself upwards.

His body was on fire, the pounding inside his head worsened by the second, almost to the point of being too much to bare. At the top of the stairs, he took a right towards his children's bedrooms.

He went to Jonah's room first.

Through the crack in the door, he could see it was in total darkness. He threw open the door with his shoulder, the hinges wailing loudly and found the switch on the wall to his left. Cold, harsh light filled the room.

'Jonah?' he cried.

Jonah shuffled in his single bed, slowly opening his tired eyes, wiping away the sleep with the back of his small hand. He glared up at Ian, confused.

'Dad… turn the light off. I was asleep.'

Ian turned off the light and went to Cameron's room. He turned on the switch, the space erupting in a bright light.

His heart skipped a beat.

Cameron wasn't there.

His bed covers were ruffled, his teddy bear was upside down on the floor. Ian stepped inside quickly, frantically searching for his son, his eyes darting around the room like a metal ball-bearing inside a pinball machine. He looked inside the double wardrobe where his son's aged-four clothes hung neatly.

'Cam? Cam? Where—'

'Dad, what's going on?' a voice said from Jonah's room.

'Ahh, nothing, Jo, go back to sleep.'

Ian left the room and jumped across the dipped step onto the wide landing. He noticed the bathroom door was closed. He stopped and grabbed the handle.

'Cameron?'

The sound of the toilet flushed.

Ian opened the door fast.

Cameron was pulling his pants up wearily and glared up at his Dad. 'Daddy?'

'Oh, Cammy!' Ian gasped, racing over to him. He picked him up and squeezed him so tightly, he almost hurt him.

'Daddy, let me go!' his young voice said, waving his helpless arms around.

'Sorry, just glad you're okay.' He put him down. 'Go back to bed now, okay?'

Cam yawned, nodded his sleepy head, then padded out of the bathroom. His little body moved across the landing and back into his own room. Ian let out a sigh of relief but the sickness in his stomach still churned with the absence of Julia and Liam.

'Where the fuck are they?' he whispered in panic.

He checked all the rooms upstairs. Apart from Cameron and Jonah, he found no one.

Back downstairs, the cold seeped in through the front door he'd left open. He closed and locked it.

In the kitchen, he pulled out his phone and tried Julia's phone again.

Nothing. The small digital clock in the top corner of the phone screen told him it was 1.59 a.m..

'Eh? I don't understand,' he whispered. Then it dawned on him the blow to the back of his head must have put him out for nearly forty minutes under the bridge. He didn't think about that. All he wanted to do was find Julia and Liam. The next step was ringing the police.

He typed in nine nine nine, pressed CALL, and put it up to his ear.

Leaning against the worktop in the silent kitchen, trying to steady himself, the feeling of dizziness returned. The call connected. After two rings, the emergency operator picked up.

'Hi, emergency services, what service do you require?'

He heard the question vividly, but he'd zoned out. The sound of something else grabbed his attention. The sound of—

'Emergency services, what service do you require?' repeated the operator.

Again, another sound.

A baby's cry.

It was familiar sound. Liam's cry.

Every hair on his body stood on end as he glared into the hallway, where he figured the sound was coming from. Ignoring the question that operator had asked for the third time, he lowered the phone and placed it on the windowsill above the sink.

'Where did…' he barely whispered.

The baby cry grew louder. It was coming from the dining room. Cautiously, he crept around the kitchen table, out into the hallway. The door to the dining room was closed. Grabbing the handle, he pushed it down, the sound of the crying spilling out into the hallway as he opened it further.

Inside, the room was almost pitch-black.

But he could see something. An outline of someone sitting in the chair near the table.

On the wall next to him, he found the light switch and turned it on. The room quickly filled with light.

Sitting on the floor near the table, was Liam. His little blue eyes flooded with tears and snot came from his nose as he sobbed, dampening his little grey sleepsuit. Liam looked up at Ian. When his little sore eyes saw his father, he cried harder.

Next to his son, slouched in the chair at the table, was Ian's wife, Julia.

Ian gasped, throwing both hands up to his mouth.

'Oh, God,' Ian panted, 'Jul...'

Tears formed in his eyes and spilled down his face as he dropped helplessly to his knees. Staring at Julia with wide terrified eyes, he couldn't help being sick on the laminate floor in front of him.

Liam continued to wail, desperate for his father's love, but Ian couldn't move, he couldn't function. Instead of picking up his distraught crying son, he clamped his eyes shut, and fell forward to the floor.

The sound of helpless cries filled the house as Ian started to wail.

What was in front of Ian was something he'd never forget – it was unlike anything he'd ever seen. It absolutely terrified him.

3

Wednesday Early Morning
Low Coniscliffe – Outskirts of Darlington

DI Max Byrd's phone rang on his bedside table, the sound disturbing him from his sleep. Wearily, he opened his eyes and angled his head in the direction where the noise was coming from. He slipped a hand out from under the covers, grabbed the phone to see who was calling.

His colleague Tanzy.

'The fuck does he want?' he muttered in confusion.

He accepted the call.

'Ori, what's going on?' He glanced at the bedside clock, a sudden panic enveloped him when he noticed it was 3.43 a.m.. 'You know it's only—'

'Where've you been, Max?'

Byrd frowned. 'What – I've been—'

'Get dressed, Max,' DI Tanzy told him.

'Ori, it's not even four in the morning.'

'Max, get your clothes on and come outside, I'm waiting in the car. The station have sent out urgent assistance.'

'What's going on?' Byrd asked, propping himself up, wiping his tired eyes. He'd only been asleep for two and a half hours. It wasn't unusual for Byrd to go to bed late. He'd always been the same. Whether it was out of having things on his mind or not being able to sleep, he always felt the effects of sleep deprivation.

'We are needed,' said DI Orion Tanzy. 'Come on, get dressed, I'll fill you in when you get down here. Bring your strong stomach with you, we're gonna need it today.'

As Byrd locked his front door, he gave DI Tanzy a confused gaze, but Tanzy wasn't looking, instead, his head was angled down, his face lit up by the gentle glow of his mobile phone on his lap.

After Byrd rounded Tanzy's Volkswagen Golf parked up on the kerb, he opened the passenger door and climbed in, closed the door gently, being mindful of the early hour when his neighbours would be still sleeping.

The inside of the car was hot, the blowers full blast throwing waves of heat out rigorously. Tanzy put his phone into his pocket and turned down the heat a few notches.

'Morning,' Byrd said, settling into the shape of the sporty seats. He pulled the seat belt down around his stomach and clipped it in. 'Ori, what on earth is going on?'

'Morning, Max.'

'What's going on?'

Tanzy turned Capital radio down so they could talk.

'There's been a body found. Have you not seen your messages?'

Byrd shook his head. 'I've not been sleeping well recently, was probably flat out when we got it.' Byrd checked his phone, noticed there were unread messages. 'Shit.'

'It sounds bad, Max,' Tanzy said. 'Harrison phoned me, she's there now.'

'Where we going?'

'Brinkburn Drive. Just near—'

'I know the place, one of my cousins lives near there,' Byrd said. 'Man. Woman?'

'Woman, mid-thirties, I'm led to believe.' Tanzy took hold of the steering wheel and put the gear in first. 'There's a small team there now. Forensics are there, too.'

'That was quick.'

'Darlington's finest.'

'Yeah.' Byrd looked forward through the clear windscreen as Tanzy pulled slowly onto the road.

'According to the first responder,' Tanzy said, 'the woman was taken whilst she was in the car with her son, under the bridge at the bottom of Whessoe Road. Whoever it was came from behind, opened their doors and took them. The husband was on the phone whilst it was happening.' Tanzy paused for breath. 'He'd jumped in his car and raced there as quickly as he could. He found the car parked sideways under the bridge.'

'Where's the car now?'

'Still there – I've sent a team to block off the road and set up a perimeter where they were taken.'

'Forensics?'

'Yeah. I spoke with McCabe and he said he'll get the new recruits and go down with them.'

'Okay,' Byrd replied, glaring out the window. The roads and paths were lined with frost that sparkled under the streetlights. It was minus two outside, according to the temperature on the dash board of Tanzy's Golf. Last night, the weather report had said there was a possibility it would hit zero, but it was colder than that.

'I bet your head is cold, Ori?' Byrd said.

'My own fault for having no hair though, Max.' They both let out a laugh as Tanzy pulled out on to the main road, leaving Low Coniscliffe to sit in the morning darkness.

DI Orion Tanzy was six foot, two, slim and had an unusually good posture. He'd shaved his hair off a year ago when his hair was starting to thin but instead of persevering with hair growth products and fancy shampoos, he bought some sheers and shaved it all off in one go. His wife, Phillipa, was so gobsmacked when she saw him, she dropped a pan of pasta in the kitchen. With his square jaw, nicely-trimmed goatee beard, and tanned skin, he could wear a tatty old rug on the top of his head and still be attractive to the opposite sex.

In the passenger seat, almost four years older, was Max Byrd. He was two inches smaller than Tanzy and didn't quite have the same wash-board stomach as his colleague did. More often than not, he'd like to indulge in takeaways and junk food and because of that, he sported a slightly more rounded build than Tanzy. Although his diet wasn't the best, he burned many of the calories off playing five-a-side football, but he was – and always would be – a long way off being athletic.

Byrd reached up, ran his hand through his thick head of black hair.

'I didn't realise how big some of these were,' Byrd said, staring out the window at the monstrous houses on Coniscliffe road.

'Massive, some of them,' Tanzy said. '*We* need to move. Our house is too small. We're under each other's feet all the time.'

Tanzy was referring to his wife, Phillipa, and his two children, Jasmine and Eric. They lived in a three-bedroomed house in Newton Aycliffe, in one of the new estates close to Tesco. It wasn't that it was too small right now, but they figured as the kids grew, it wouldn't cater for their needs.

'How's Pip doing?' Byrd asked.

Tanzy slowed the car down at the Elm Ridge roundabout, flicked the indicator on, took a left, and planted his foot. The car surged forward to just over forty. The road was empty, the surface of it glistened under the staggered street lights ahead.

'She's good mate. She's doing well.' Tanzy put the Golf into fourth and settled at forty.

'Bet you're proud of her, man,' Byrd said.

'Yeah, she's done brill.'

It took a further five minutes for the Golf to arrive at Brinkburn Drive. They spoke more about Tanzy's wife and Tanzy had asked about Claire, the woman Byrd had been seeing over the past eighteen months. After that, they fell silent for the remainder of the drive, both mentally and physically preparing themselves for what they were about to see.

Tanzy had received the heads-up that it was going to be a nasty one. He brought the Golf to a halt behind a red Tiguan and switched off the engine.

The car to Byrd's left, parked across the road, was familiar.

'Your boy's here,' Byrd commented. 'Cornty.'

Tanzy followed Byrd's gaze, seeing the blue Peugeot parked up on the kerb. 'How did he get here so quick?'

'He's keener than you, that's why,' Byrd mused.

'He didn't have to drive to the outskirts of town and wake you up, sleepy head, *that's* probably why,' Tanzy replied.

Byrd sniffed the air.

'Hope you're not getting a cold,' Tanzy said, pulling his keys out of the slot.

'I don't get colds.' Byrd pulled the handle of the passenger door and edged it open. The cold rushed into the car and Byrd shivered suddenly, wishing he'd worn a thicker jacket.

They got out. The time was nearly four-thirty. An eerie silence whispered in the air.

There were two street lights that didn't work, leaving certain areas of the path in almost complete darkness. Byrd made a mental note to report that to the council. Several lights were shining along the street, no doubt people being awoken by the arrival of the police car and the ambulance. Some of them were peeping out, others were more obvious by standing on their steps in dressing gowns.

Down the street, there was a barrier positioned at the front of the house in the shape of a square, covering the width of the house, coming out towards the road roughly eight metres. On the opposite side of the barrier, there was an elderly couple probably in their eighties, holding each other, trying to battle off the night frost, dressed in thick coats, desperate to see what all the fuss was about. Next to them, a woman in her forties to fifties, was dressed in a bathrobe, a cigarette hanging from her mouth, the smoke spiralling into the air as she exhaled.

Inside the barrier on the closest side to the detectives, stood a PC who they recognised. He was one of the new recruits, although neither Byrd and Tanzy had spoken with him yet.

There was a slight shift in wind direction and the smell of cigarette smoke hit Byrd's nose. A long time had passed since he made the decision to quit, but strangely enough, the smell right now was pleasant; pleasant enough that if he was offered one, he'd probably give in.

They stepped up onto the path, making their way towards the barrier. The PC standing at the barrier was making sure no one got inside. Byrd tried to remember his name but realised he'd never known it. The PC offered the detectives a smile, lifting up the tape to allow them in.

'Forgive me, what was your name?' Byrd said, stopping and offering his hand.

'PC Leonard, Sir.' He took his hand, shook it.

Byrd followed Tanzy under the rope. Ahead of them, glaring down at his phone, was PC Phillip Cornty. He was thinner than a pencil and had the face of a mouse; his pointy little nose, for some reason, annoyed Byrd more than it should have. Byrd didn't have a lot to do with him because Cornty was in Tanzy's team, but whenever Byrd saw him, he annoyed him in some way.

PC Cornty, after hearing the footsteps of the detectives, angled his head to the left and made eye contact with them.

'Hey, boss,' he said to Tanzy, who replied with a courteous nod. He glanced past Tanzy, his eyes falling on Byrd. 'Hey, Max.'

'Morning, Phillip,' Byrd said. His tone showed similar enthusiasm to how he felt when he was awoken half an hour ago by Tanzy's call.

'Why you here, Phil?' Tanzy asked him, stopping by his side. Tanzy was tall but Cornty had a few inches on him. He must have been six foot, four. Maybe six foot, five. His towering height didn't help his very slim frame.

'I'm working…' Cornty frowned at his superior when the awkward silence followed. 'I don't understand…'

'You're on days this week, why are—'

'I'm covering Mac,' Cornty explained. 'He's on holiday.'

'Again?' Byrd chipped in, shaking his head. 'When is that man not on holiday?'

An amused nod from Cornty. 'Yeah, I was asked to leave yesterday at dinner time and I started last night.'

'Who asked you to do that?'

'DCI Thornton,' he countered.

'Okay, when you finish,' Tanzy said, 'make sure you have enough rest. I can't be arsed giving Thornton any excuses to throw at me. Okay?'

Tanzy, as a Detective Inspector, knew the actions of these individuals came under the supervision of him, so it was important he kept them in check.

'Yeah, okay,' Cornty said, then looked away from both detectives, feeling like he'd done something wrong. His gaze fell on to the front door of the house where the bright light in the hallway spilled out.

Byrd looked past Cornty.

In front of the house, away from the perimeter of the plastic barrier, there was an ambulance parked across the road with its rear doors open. PC Kim Harrison was standing with a man who was wrapped in a blanket. She was talking to him about something, but Byrd couldn't hear what was said, but it was obvious from the man's body language how upset he was.

In front of the ambulance were two police cars, intentionally parked sideways to prevent any traffic access. Two officers were standing near the cars; one of them spotted Byrd, gave him a wave before continuing their discussion.

'What have we got?' Tanzy asked PC Cornty.

'It's bad,' he said without hesitation.

'How bad?' Byrd asked.

Cornty let out a long sigh, briefly glanced down onto the concrete path below before collecting himself and met Byrd's gaze. 'Bad. I think you better go see for yourself.'

Tanzy and Byrd both nodded and moved away from him.

'Hey, wait,' Cornty said. The detectives stopped, looked back. 'Put these on.' PC Cornty handed them both a pair of plastic disposable overshoes. 'I'll be just out here – there's no way I'm going back in there.'

'That… bad?' Tanzy asked, frowning.

Cornty briefly looked past them in to the bright hallway. 'Worst I've seen.'

DI Max Byrd and DI Orion Tanzy carefully digested his words, then moved past him onto the driveway. At the front door, Tanzy stopped, and turned to Byrd.

'After you,' Tanzy said.

Byrd sighed lightly, then stepped up into the house.

4

Darlington
Wednesday Early Morning

Inside the house, they both picked up the horrific odour seeping down the hall.

'Jesus,' Tanzy gasped, cupping a hand over his nose to mask the smell. 'That's foul.'

Byrd inhaled it without a fuss and said nothing. At the end of the hallway under the harsh, bright light of a ceiling pendant, PC Anne Tiffin was standing near the doorway. A walky-talky was in one hand and a notepad in the other. Her head was tipped forward, reading her notes. Hearing the detectives footsteps on the laminate floor, she pulled her attention away and glanced towards them.

'Morning, Anne,' Byrd said quietly.

'Morning,' she said in a gloomy tone. She waited till they were by her side before she continued. 'Have you been given the brief?'

Tanzy and Byrd nodded.

'We have,' said Byrd. 'Cornty said he's not coming back in here.'

'Cornty is weak,' Tiffin said.

Tiffin had been in Byrd's team for nearly two years. She was fresh, eager, and almost beyond keen. Her diligence and attention to detail was something that Byrd hadn't seen on the force at Darlington. She'd be climbing the ladder very soon, Byrd had no doubt. A hard-working, straight-talking, motivated young woman at the age of only twenty-three, he'd do his best to help and guide her the best he could. Her level of focus reminded him of a younger female version of himself when he was that age.

She was the only PC in the house. This was because she was the first one at the scene: the first responder. The call from the operator had been radioed and she was the first to pick it up. When she'd arrived at 2.09 a.m., she cautiously opened the door and heard a man wailing and a baby crying somewhere down the hallway. To her right, standing on the stairs, were two young terrified children. They'd heard their father crying and came downstairs to see why. He'd shouted at them, telling them to stay away, to go back upstairs. After seeing the body of Julia Porter sitting in the chair, she'd made the call for emergency assistance.

'Forensics are inside doing their thing,' she continued. 'Give 'em room, okay?'

'Who is it?' Tanzy asked. He had an idea it would be the senior forensic team, Jacob Tallow and Emily Hope, but the forensic team had recruited two new members, but neither Byrd nor Tanzy had really spoken with them much.

'Hope and Tallow,' Tiffin confirmed.

Byrd bobbed his head. He knew them well. The two of them were the total opposites but worked well as a team. After five years of working with anyone, sooner or later, you started to develop a bond and an understanding. Their first few months together didn't go so well; but they moved on and made it work.

'Has McCabe been yet?' Byrd asked.

Tiffin shook her head. 'Not yet.'

'Okay.' He sighed, glanced towards the room for a moment. Today, no doubt, would be a long day, and he knew by what he was about to see, it would take a turn for the worst.

'Let's do it,' Tanzy said.

'Whenever you're ready,' she said, standing at the door of the dining room. Taking a step back, she allowed them enough room to pass.

Byrd, who was in front of Tanzy, nodded and slowly entered the room. Tanzy followed. The horrendous smell was much stronger in the dining room: the pungent, stomach churning odour took their breath away. Tanzy gagged a little but managed not to make a scene – he never quite got used to the rancid smells associated with some of the crime scenes they had to endure. Not wanting to distract the duo of forensics, Byrd and Tanzy stopped a few feet inside the room and observed the scene in front of them.

'Jesus,' Byrd said just above a whisper.

Tanzy, staying silent, glared at the woman sitting motionless on the chair.

Byrd turned back to PC Tiffin standing at the doorway. 'What's the story?'

'The husband said he was on the phone to her when she went under the Whessoe Road bridge. Said there was a man standing in the middle of the road. Then it sounded like there was more of them who came up from behind and grabbed her and their baby. Ian Porter raced out of the house but when he got there the car was empty. He then said he heard a scream coming from outside of Hopetown club and ran up the steps. By that time, he was too late, the van was almost around the corner.'

'Is this the bottom of Brinkburn Road?' Byrd asked, finding his bearings, trying to visualise exactly what'd happened. Ever since he was young, he analysed everything. According to others, he seemed obsessed, but it was how his brain worked things out, how he processed new information. Even if he looked at something simple like a tree, he would think about the outer layer of bark, the way it had matured over the years, the inside of the tree, the structure and strength and what held it up, the roots, how far they went under the ground, how much moisture it held.

She nodded. 'Alliance street, it's called.'

'Then what happened?'

'He came home. Then he realised he'd left his other two children asleep in bed, so went up to check on them. Back in the kitchen, he made a 999 call, then heard his baby crying in the dining room.' Her eyebrows raised a quarter of an inch. 'He then… came in to this.' She physically opened her palms in the direction of Julia Porter who was slumped in the chair.

'Where was the baby?'

'Right next to her…'

'God.' Byrd let out a concerned sigh. 'Horrible.'

'He'll be too young for any influence – he'll be okay,' Tanzy reassured Byrd, having dealt with similar cases in the past.

Byrd looked away from his partner back in the direction of the door. 'Did the husband really make the call?'

'Yes, we checked.' She glanced down at her notes for a moment. 'The call was made at 1.59 a.m., but the operator said he'd hung up after a few seconds without saying anything. Ian said he'd left the house just after one, and when the van had drove off as he got back to the car, he felt something hit the back of his head and reckons he must've been out cold for over thirty minutes. After checking the kids, he came downstairs. That's when he heard the baby cry in here. He then phoned back and told us about his wife.'

'Where are the children now?' Byrd enquired.

'Ian's mother collected them. They are safe. She left her contact details should we need to reach her.'

Both detectives gave the police constable a grateful nod and returned their focus back at the scene, watching the two forensics dressed in thin white overalls position yellow markers in different locations that they deemed to be relevant. The tall, thin guy, Jacob, took a couple of photographs and placed his camera slowly down by his side.

'I think we are about done for now, Detectives,' he said, knowing they were standing behind watching. 'Don't touch anything. We're taking a short break. We need to come back.'

'Okay, thanks,' said Byrd. 'Good job, guys.'

The detectives watched them leave the room, then Tanzy turned to PC Tiffin who was standing at the door.

'Where are her clothes – do you know?'

'No clothes have been found, Sir.'

'Okay.'

'I'll be outside if you need anything. I need some air,' she said, turning, and heading for the door.

'I've never seen anything like this in my life,' Byrd said to Tanzy.

'Me, neither, Max.'

5

Wednesday Morning
Darlington

The dining room was square shaped with a table against the centre of the back wall. Above the table, there was a wide rectangular mirror, making the room appear bigger than it really was. The wall opposite the table and mirror - the wall to their right - was lined with a huge shelving unit jammed with toys, ranging from cuddly baby toys to jigsaws to more complex figurines such as transformers and battery-operated remote-controlled cars.

The detectives looked straight towards the table.

Julia Porter was tied to a black leather chair, which had been pulled away and angled facing the door, so it was the first thing that the person walking in would see.

Byrd shivered.

On the floor, her bare feet rested in a pool of dark, congealed blood about two and a half feet in diameter. Above the pooling of blood, her bare legs were flaccid and awkwardly twisted open, revealing her hairy vagina. Her drooping breasts were misshaped by a thin blue rope that was tightly wrapped around her body and tied at the back of the chair preventing her from falling forward. Her head was angled back with the nape of her neck resting on the top lip of the chair. The detectives took a small step forward, concentrating on her bloody face.

'Who the fuck has done this?' Tanzy said.

Byrd, staying silent, absorbed the scene in more depth. After a minute of silent assessment, he itched his stubbly chin. 'The question is… why?'

'Why, what?'

'Why this, why this set up?' Byrd turned to Tanzy. 'It's like a stage show. Whoever has done this is sending a message.'

Tanzy glared back at Julia Porter, unsure what Byrd meant. He knew one thing for sure: her eyes were missing. The deep empty sockets were the frightening focus of her pale face, pooled with deep, crimson clots. There was a thick trail of blood that had ran down her face like red slugs; over her breasts, stomach, vagina, the inside of her thighs, then finally, on to the wooden floor where it had pooled.

Switching their attention to the table next to her, they saw a message on the surface, written in what looked like a red crayon.

She didn't see it coming.

'See what coming?' Tanzy said, thinking out loud. He noticed Byrd edge a little closer to inspect the words carefully. 'Are you seeing anything?' he asked, angling his head toward Byrd.

'It's a message, Ori.'

'A message?'

'Yeah… and this message could mean absolutely anything.' Byrd sighed heavily and physically sank into himself for a second, taking a few steps back and letting his shoulders drop. The smell of Julia Porter was horrific, but they'd got used to it now and each breath seemed to become more bearable.

The room went quiet for a while as both detectives analysed the scene before them, until Tanzy broke the silence.

'What meaning would you give it?'

'I'm speculating here, Ori… so bear with me,' Byrd said.

Tanzy patiently nodded, waiting.

Byrd went on: 'This was meant for her husband, Ian…' Byrd opened his palms in the direction of Julia and the scene before them. 'Her nakedness could identify with her being vulnerable. The trail of blood from her eyes down to her vagina could signify a trail, maybe to that particular place on her body – to somewhere personal. The missing eyes could tell Ian she's seen something that she shouldn't have, or maybe that she won't be able to see anymore.'

'Meaning what? You know I'm not one for riddles, Max. And, it's too early in the morning for one of your complex intellectual explanations.'

Byrd half-smiled before becoming serious again.

'What about the writing?' Tanzy added. 'You've told me what you see… but what do you make of the writing?'

'What do *you* make of the writing – what's your thoughts, Ori?'

'Perhaps it's a message intended for Ian about somebody else. Maybe Ian knows what the words mean or can think of the significance.'

'It could mean anything.' Byrd shrugged hopelessly. 'Why is it written in red? Does that mean danger to Ian… to his family?'

'Or maybe it was the closest colour they could find?'

'Anything is possible here, Ori.'

'Where are your eyes?' Tanzy asked Julia Porter. 'Where are your clothes?'

'Come on, let's go outside. If I stay in here any longer, I'll throw up and contaminate the room with last night's Amaretto and pizza.' Byrd stole one last look at Julia Porter and the table next to her, scanning the words in red crayon before turning and leaving the room.

In the hallway, he slowed, rotating his head back to Tanzy. 'We'll speak to Ian Porter. If we ask the right questions, we'll hopefully get the right answers.'

They left the rancid smelling house and headed through the front door out into the darkness where the air was clean and fresh. Tanzy snatched a lung full. They stepped off the drive way, headed over the road in the direction of Ian Porter who was leaning on the back of the ambulance wrapped in a blanket, accompanied by PC Kim Harrison.

Byrd took the lead. 'Mr Porter?'

He leaned forward, placed a gentle palm on the outside of Ian Porter's left shoulder. 'I'm Detective Inspector Max Byrd of Durham Constabulary, and this is my colleague, Detective Inspector Orion Tanzy. We are very sorry for your loss. We can't imagine what you're going through.' He paused for a few seconds. 'Can we get you a drink?'

Ian Porter shook his head and didn't glance up at Byrd, instead, he remained looking at the floor near his feet.

'If it's okay,' Byrd went on, 'we'd like to ask a couple of questions down at the station?'

Porter jerked his head up quickly. 'I – I never did this!'

Byrd slowly raised his palm. 'Mr Porter, no one is saying or suggesting that you did. At the station, we can get you warmed up, get you a drink, get you comfortable. Maybe we—'

'Where's my children?'

'Your mother has them. One of my colleagues has spoken with her – your children are safe. Your children are fine, Mr Porter.'

'Are they?' Porter asked anxiously.

'They are,' reassured Byrd confidently. 'There's a car outside of your mother's house. Don't worry about your children.'

Porter finally lifted his head, making eye contact with Byrd.

'Will you be willing to come to the station, see if we can figure this out?'

Porter, reluctantly, agreed.

That Night

6

Wednesday Morning
Brinkburn Drive, Darlington

Once PC Kim Harrison had slowly helped Ian Porter into the back of her police car, she closed the door and turned to Byrd and Tanzy, who were standing a few feet from her.

'Are you coming back with us now?' she asked them.

'We need to see where they were taken before we head back,' Tanzy said. 'See what's happening down there. You take Mr Porter back, get him a coffee. We won't be long, okay?'

Harrison turned, but Byrd gently grabbed her forearm.

'Get a sample of his DNA as well, please. It could be vital.'

Harrison smiled and nodded, making her way around the back of the car to the driver's door and lowered herself in. To their left, beyond the plastic barrier, a crowd started to gather. The woman in her dressing gown was still smoking away.

Behind the small number of interested parties, were a couple of people further down the street, watching intently. A man and woman were standing in front of a bush belonging to the third house down. They kept their gaze on both Tanzy and Byrd.

Byrd narrowed his eyes at them before turning and heading back to Tanzy's car. On their walk back to their right, they noticed Tallow and Hope head back inside. PC Anne Tiffin could be seen through the open door as they passed the house, peering down at her notepad in the hallway.

Byrd smiled at her commitment and dedication.

'She'll make it one day,' he muttered.

'Huh?' Tanzy said.
'Ah, never mind.'

At the bottom of Brinkburn Road where it joined the corner of Alliance Street, Tanzy slowed and came to a stop. The police officer standing in the middle of the road held up her palm and squinted into the darkness to see who it was, ready to divert the driver of the car down one of the streets away from the scene. It didn't take long for her to recognise Tanzy behind the wheel. She lowered her arm, smiled and waved him passed.

He followed the bend to the left, slowly veering around the Astra that the PC had parked intentionally to prevent access to the bridge and brought the Golf to a halt.

After turning off the engine, they both stepped out into the cold.

A long stretch of plastic barrier tape had been tied halfway along the wall of Hopetown Men's social club, running diagonally to the metal railing that met the corner of the street just before the road dipped down under the bridge.

Standing at the tape, was PC Josh Andrews.

'Morning, Sir,' he said to Byrd.

He'd worked under the supervision of DI Max Byrd for nearly a year. He was of average height, with hair that always looked like it was a month overgrown.

'How you doing, Josh?'

'Good, Sir, I'm good, thank you,' he replied. One thing Byrd had always liked about Josh Andrews were his manners. He spoke correct English and carried himself like a gentleman. He'd told Byrd about his father and uncles being officers in the British Army and had taught him how to stand, talk, conduct oneself etc., so Byrd understood his almost unusual – but admirable - behaviour.

'What do we have?' Tanzy asked.

'Morning, Sir,' Andrews began. 'The car is still down there. Forensics are here.'

'McCabe?'

'Yeah. He's here.'

Byrd this time. 'He alone?'

'No, he brought the two new people with him. The new girl, Forrest, and that new guy, Beech. He thought he'd leave the scene at the house for Tallow and Hope. Let the new guys check out the car to see what they could find.'

'They could do with the experience,' Byrd said in agreement. 'Come on, Ori, let's have a look.'

As they crossed the open concrete area in front of the club, on the floor, they saw tyre marks, stretching about four metres in total. Byrd stopped for a moment and glanced down.

'That's where the van had pulled away after they'd grabbed them,' Andrews said loudly, projecting his voice, still standing at the barrier.

Byrd nodded at him and turned back, continued to the concrete steps. Once they descended them, they stepped onto the road under the bridge and glared at the diagonally parked Qashqai.

On the floor next to the Qashqai, a briefcase belonging to the forensics was open. As Byrd and Tanzy rounded the rear of the car, standing on the kerb with his hands tucked deep into his pockets, they saw Tony McCabe, the Crime Scene Manager.

'Morning,' he said to them as they wandered over, but he kept his attention on the two assistant forensics that were working inside the car.

'Morning, Tony,' Byrd said, extending his hand. 'Trusting them already I see?'

McCabe shook it. He was just over six feet tall and a carried a broad set of shoulders. Word was he used to do boxing in his younger years. His large, slightly crooked nose was a testament to that, no doubt broken several times.

'They need to learn somehow.' He smiled at Byrd, who agreed. 'How's it going at the house?' he asked.

'Tallow and Hope are on it,' Byrd replied. 'As we left, they were heading back in. How's it going here?'

'We've checked the car for prints, found some on the door handles, but I have the feeling that whoever did this had the intelligence to wear gloves. They looked like small prints so most likely, it'll be their children – they do have children, other than the baby?'

Tanzy nodded. 'Yeah, three children in total.'

'Jesus,' he replied, realising the children would be motherless for the rest of their lives. He let out a sad smile, and glanced away from Byrd, back towards the car.

McCabe had been the crime scene manager for three years. In total, he had over seventeen years' experience dealing with forensics. He'd done the majority of his time down in Birmingham, starting as an assistant forensic for nearly four years, then as a forensic for another four years, then he joined the Durham division as a senior forensic and held that role for nearly eight years, until three years ago, there was an opening for the role of Crime Scene Manager.

He had a passion for his job but at the same time, it upset him, because it meant someone had often died or a serious crime had been committed. Dealing with situations that involved finding dead children was something that brought a lump to his throat because in the past he'd thought about his own children, how they'd be safely tucked up in bed when he was figuring out cases that were truly scenes from nightmares.

'How they doing?' Byrd asked. 'They getting up to speed?'

McCabe winced a little. 'These things take time. I've been doing the job over fifteen years and I still miss things. They are… doing okay.'

'Okay, good.'

To their right, in the direction of Whessoe Road, a car had stopped at the opening and beeped several times, the driver obviously annoyed about having to take the diverted route, sticking his two fingers up before he sped away. Byrd and Tanzy glanced for a second but after ignoring the man's frustration, looked back at Beech and Forrest who were both standing at the back door, leaning in, doing something with the baby's car seat under the help of a bright torch. It was still dark.

Amanda Forrest was twenty-seven, short, a little on the chunky side and carried a warm smile. Her straight blonde hair sat just on the top of her shoulders and radiated a shine which made women envious. She'd done a degree in Forensic psychology, finishing her course six months ago. McCabe, when interviewing her, had read the majority of her very impressive, detailed dissertation on the effect of blood when it came into contact with the air.

Next to her, was Paul Beech. At the age of thirty-five, he was late starting his degree when he took the plunge five years ago. He'd worked in the IT industry as a technical cable installer, travelling up and down the country. His wife missed him too much and suggested he tried something else. He'd always said he had an interest in Forensics, so took out a loan and hit the books hard. After finishing his degree in Forensic Scene Science, he'd recently moved back to Darlington nearly a year ago when there was a job opening for a trainee forensic practitioner. He'd moved away from Darlington a decade ago and had spent the last ten years in London due to a promised spectrum of opportunities in the IT world, which like most things, hadn't turned out as brilliant as promised, spending much of his time away in hotel rooms.

'We need to head back, Tony,' Tanzy said. 'Keep us updated.'

'Of course,' he replied. 'We'll be in touch.'

Byrd and Tanzy crossed the quiet road. Before they climbed the steps, Byrd paused and followed the curved footpath, glancing up in to the sky.

'What you looking for?' Tanzy asked.

'Cameras.' There was none. Typical.

They climbed the steps and glanced around again, looking at the tops of buildings but again, saw nothing.

7

Wednesday Morning
Police Station

Byrd and Tanzy used a small training room down at the station. They felt using an interrogation room was a bad idea, agreeing it would make Ian Porter feel like he was being accused of something. They needed him to open up and be honest, not to feel pressured.

Painfully and slowly, Ian ran through the events that had happened hours before, starting with being on the phone to Julie then coming back to the house and finding her and Liam.

'Someone hit you from behind?' Tanzy asked.

'Yeah.' He raised his palm and touched the back of his head.

'What happened when you woke up?'

'A couple were kneeling down over me, asking me if I was okay.'

'Did you recognise them?'

Porter switched his focus to Byrd. 'No, I mean… I don't think so. I've never seen the woman, but the man looked a little familiar. Darlington is a small town, I suppose.'

'The words on the table – She didn't see it coming – does that mean anything to you?' Tanzy asked.

Ian shook his head, raised a hand to wipe away the tears from his eyes. 'No, nothing.'

'Has your wife seen something recently, something she shouldn't have?'

'What do you mean?' Porter's tone turned a little sour.

'Anything in her life – or both of your lives – that has taken her by surprise recently. It could be anything. A person, an image, anything.'

Ian shook his head again.

'What does she do as a job?'

'She works at Lloyds bank. As a cashier.'

'Okay… that's good. You're doing great, Ian.' He paused for a second. 'Would you like a coffee?'

Ian nodded. He was tired. Dark semi-circles lined the bottom of his eyes. It was nearly six in the morning and due to obvious reasons, he hadn't slept yet.

Tanzy turned towards Byrd. 'Would you mind getting us a coffee, Max?'

Byrd bowed his head, slid his chair out, and found his feet. 'Yeah, no problem.' He opened the door, stepped out into the well-lit hallway, and walked away towards the canteen.

'I sent Max because he really does make the best coffees. I'm hopeless,' Tanzy said. Ian gave half a smile.

'Ian, can you describe the van you saw near the bridge?'

'It was a big van.'

'What colour was it?'

'White, I think – yes, white,' he confirmed.

'Slim chance, I know, under the circumstances, but can you remember the registration plate?'

Ian thought hard for a moment, but his stare seemed lost, as if he was thinking about something entirely different.

'Ian?'

'Huh?' he said, snapping out of it.

'The reg plate of the van?'

A hopeless gaze appeared on his face. 'No, I – I don't remember. It all happened so fast.'

'I understand.' Tanzy nodded and fell silent for a second, then: 'So, when you go—'

'Listen, I just want to go see my kids,' Ian said sharply. 'I don't really want your coffee. I don't want to be sitting here talking to you. No offence, Detective. You're trying to help me… but I want to go. I need to get out of here, now.'

Tanzy could understand his frustration. The last thing he wanted to be doing was sitting in the station when his wife had just been murdered. It was horrible.

With an understanding, courteous nod, he said, 'Any information you have – even the smallest grain of information – could help us identify exactly what's happened and give us more hope catching who did this. You do want to find out who did this, don't you, Ian?'

'Of course I do!' he shouted, the sudden anger echoing around the room. His eyes widened for a moment before they returned to normal, focusing back down at the table. Tanzy mentally noted the flash of frustration but moved on without commenting.

As Tanzy let the silence fill the room, Byrd walked back in, carrying two plastic cups, steam twirling from both of them. He leaned over, placed one in front of Ian. 'There you go.'

'Thanks,' he said, but never reached for it or made eye contact with the detective.

Byrd glanced down at his watch. It was six-thirty. 'You're probably tired and you'll want to go back and see your kids, no doubt. What's their names?'

Ian Porter frowned at him. 'What?'

'Your children, what are their names?' Byrd asked.

'Jonah, Cameron, and Liam,' he whispered. He glared up. 'I need to see them. I need to see them - they only have me.'

Porter's emotional words found their way to the hearts of the detectives. They'd seen relatives of victims crumble before their eyes - it never got any easier. In fact, it got worse, because every time it happened, it reminded them how bad this world could be, how cruel life could turn on you in a second.

'Nice names,' Byrd commented.

A thin smile appeared on Porter's face.

'Before you go to see Jonah, Cameron, and Liam,' Tanzy said, 'can you try to think again if there's anything your wife may have seen – something you've maybe missed. I know we've touched on this briefly but it's so important to helping us. Had she seen you do something that she didn't expect, something out of the ordinary? The message on the table may have been for you?'

Porter pondered the question with furrowed eyebrows, and finally, he nodded. 'She caught me cheating four years ago – that's the only thing I can think of.'

Without being judgemental, the detectives both bowed their heads in silence, waiting for Porter to add to it.

He didn't.

'Okay,' Tanzy said.

Byrd this time. 'Did you get a good look at the van when it pulled away near Hopetown club?'

'Detective Tanzy has already asked me this. The answer is the same, I—'

'There was a lot going on, I appreciate that,' Byrd noted.

'I wasn't really in the right mind for memorising letters and numbers, Detective.'

'I understand, Mr Porter,' Byrd countered with a soft palm, knowing Tanzy asked the same questions whilst he was out getting the coffees. It was a tactic they'd used over the years to see if the person told the same story.

Silence grew around them until Tanzy said, 'Well, thank you for your time, Ian. You can go and see your children. One of our colleagues will drive you to your mother's house, okay.'

'Thanks.'

Without touching his cup of coffee, Ian stood up and headed for the door. Outside in the bright corridor, PC Kim Harrison waited for him, offering him a sympathetic smile.

'Come on, I'll take you home,' she said to him and guided him out of the building.

Back in the room, Tanzy made eye contact with Byrd, who was slouching a fraction in his seat.

'No good sitting like that all the time, Max, that's doing your back no good what so ever.'

Byrd shuffled up a little. 'My back is fine.'

'It won't be when you're fifty.'

Ever since knowing Byrd, Tanzy had attempted to guide him to be healthier, whether it be eating right or doing more exercise. Byrd claimed that playing football a few times a week kept his weight off.

Tanzy laughed every time he'd said it because he knew that Byrd was forty-one. Things would only get worse. Compared to Byrd, Tanzy was mega fit. He led a healthy lifestyle and had been doing Judo since he was six years old. He'd mastered almost every throw and hold ever invented, a handy asset if you were backed into a corner. Byrd would never forget the time they went out for a drink, maybe going back four or five years, when a careless drunk knocked into Byrd so hard it knocked Byrd's pint on to the floor. The smash of the glass on the floor echoed around the bar and everyone stopped to look.

As the situation developed, it turned out that it had been done on purpose. The man had recognised Byrd as one of the detectives linked to a trial where the man's brother had been sent down for drug dealing. The man and two of his associates had started on Byrd, backing him into the corner.

Tanzy, when he returned from the toilet, saw Byrd was on the floor covering his head as the men were kicking him. Tanzy lost it. Went crazy. Within half a minute, he'd dismembered all three of them laying them out on the floor. He'd helped Byrd up and told the manager of the bar that he would personally cover the damage to the stud wall of the disabled toilet where he'd thrown one of the men through.

They'd always kept that mishap between themselves.

As Ian Porter's footsteps disappeared down the corridor, Tanzy sniffed the air, thinking for a moment. 'Do you think he did it?'

Byrd shook his head. 'No, but forensics will hopefully come back with some prints, telling us what we need to know. We need to check for cameras in the nearby area - specifically Brinkburn Road, as we know they drove that way back to Brinkburn Drive.'

Tanzy nodded.

'I do know one thing, though…' Byrd added.

Curiously, Tanzy raised his gaze. 'What's that?'

'Ian Porter knows more than he's letting on.' Byrd was known to be a fantastic judge of character. 'He's lying about something, that's for sure.'

8

Wednesday mid-morning
Police Station

'So, what do we have?' asked DCI June Thornton, sitting on her chair behind her very large, tidy desk. Behind her, lining the walls, were several certificates that she'd been awarded over the years, which she'd always kept polished and proud. Byrd not once had seen the glass framed credentials with a speck of dust on them.

She knew the basics of what'd happened – it didn't take long for the news to get around the office. She leaned back, raising one leg over the other, and delicately placed her palms down on her thighs.

On the other side of the desk, sitting in the two chairs, was DI Byrd and DI Tanzy.

Byrd coughed before he spoke.

'Julia Porter was tied to a chair naked with a blue rope. Her eyes were missing. There was a note written in red crayon, "She didn't see it coming!" She was taken whilst she was in her car with her youngest son, Liam, who's almost one. A man was standing in the middle of the road, so she had to stop. Then it sounded like – according to her husband, Ian Porter – that others came from behind and opened the back-passenger door and grabbed them.'

DCI Thornton stared for a second, absorbing his words.

Just bordering on the age of sixty, Thornton was an attractive, petite woman, who kept herself in fantastic shape. She divorced her husband, Mike, a decade earlier and had spent her spare time, outside of the office, at the gym and fitness classes. Her bronze skin tone was testament from the three holidays she took every year. Other women her age were envious of her, with her perfect white teeth and her neatly cut short, blonde hair that was always pristine.

Another trait of the Detective Chief Inspector was that she didn't take shit from anyone. She never had done. You didn't rise through the ranks by being soft and accepting a rejection when someone told you no. You stood your ground. You spoke the truth, even if it meant rattling a few feathers in the process. If something needed to be done, she'd get it done.

'I see,' she said, calmly. She turned to DI Tanzy. 'Orion, what's your thoughts?'

Tanzy stared for a short moment, mentally collecting them. 'Erm… I think it's a message. I think by removing her eyes, whoever did this, doesn't want her to see any more. And –'

'Have you located the eyes?' she asked.

'No,' Tanzy replied.

'Forensics never came across them,' Byrd added. 'They're carrying a full investigation and will be getting back to us soon.'

She nodded.

When she spoke to Byrd and Tanzy, it was clear they had a good relationship. They'd been working side by side for nearly sixteen years. Byrd had joined the force when he turned eighteen. His father, Alan, was an army man in his earlier years and when a young Max Byrd had told him he wanted to do the same, his father told him no. He said he should go in the police force instead, so it meant he didn't have to travel the world. At the time, some of Byrd's friends had joined the army and his father figured that had something to do with it. Byrd had agreed, although a little reluctantly, to give it a shot. Twenty-three years later, not once had he looked back or regretted the decision he'd made.

Tanzy had been on the force for sixteen years. Now the same level as Byrd, both being detective inspectors, Tanzy originally wanted to do forensics. At sixteen, he'd left school and went to university to study forensic psychology after watching countless episodes of Law and Order and the early episodes of Silent Witness. His father, Andre, who lived with his mother, Claudia, down in York, still watched them relentlessly. After Tanzy had gained his degree, he joined the police at age twenty-one as a police constable. He wanted to veer into forensics but at the time, he enjoyed his team, enjoyed the relationships he was building. Now thirty-seven, having moved up the ranks respectively, the dream of being a forensic had faded away, but he still occasionally watched Silent Witness and wondered how different his career could have been.

DCI Thornton nodded. 'What else?'

Byrd said, 'First impressions are that he never killed his wife. That story wouldn't add up with how—'

'Add up?' interrupted Thornton.

'With how the position of how the Qashqai was found under the bridge. The tyre marks on the road where the car skidded. Also one of the first things that PC Cornty checked on his arrival was the bonnet of the Astra. It was warm, meaning Ian Porter drove it a little while before.' DCI Thornton agreed with him by bobbing her head and continuing to listen. 'Forensics have taken prints from the steering wheels of both cars. Chances are, that both Julia and Ian drive both cars, so we can expect them on both, but if we can pick up another fingerprint from the Qashqai, maybe on the door handles, we may have something.'

'I read in the report that Ian was on the phone to Julia when she was attacked?' Thornton probed.

Tanzy and Byrd both nodded.

'Have the phone records been checked?'

'Yes,' Tanzy said, 'we have cross referenced the phone call to the time that Ian said, and it matches up.'

'Do we have Julia's phone? Have you taken it as evidence?'

Byrd shook his head. 'No. Her phone hasn't been found yet.' He paused for a moment, then: 'My gut tells me this isn't a random attack on Julia Porter and that her killer – or killers – know her. I personally don't think that Ian killed Julia, but I certainly do think he knows more than he's letting on.'

'Why do you think that, Max?' she questioned.

'Because I'm a very good judge of character.'

'That's a fair comment.'

It was true. DI Max Byrd had the ability to judge the situation better than most, especially about people. Seldom was he wrong about a hunch or someone lying about something. He observed their reactions and the way they moved; even the slightest eye twitch spoke volumes and told its own story.

'Thanks for your time. Keep me updated,' she said before she diverted her attention to her computer screen. The detectives stood up and left her office, then headed towards the canteen in desperate need of coffee.

'She's hard work sometimes,' Tanzy whispered, glancing at Byrd as they took a seat at their back at their desks. Their desks were next to each other. Behind them, was DCI Thornton's office so they had to be mindful saying too much about her, or too much in general. Not every story made it to her level.

'Yeah, tell me about it.'

Byrd pulled his desk chair in, the wheels rolling along the carpet until his padded stomach hit the edge of his desk. He placed his coffee down and wriggled the mouse to wake up the standby screen.

The office was a large rectangular space.

A central walkway ran from the double glass entrance door to the other end where DCI Thornton's office was located. Either side of the central walkway were pairs of desks running parallel down the length of the room. There were six rows, four desks in total, two either side. Eighteen of the twenty-four desks were being used, the other six were vacant, two of which contained piles of paperwork which Thornton demanded be cleared by the end of the day.

If you walked through the entrance door, you'd see Tanzy and Byrd sitting on the last row, on the left-hand side.

'Gonna be a long day,' Byrd sighed. His eyes were tired, the lack of sleep already taking its toll on him. He was looking forward to getting a hot shower and climbing into bed later.

'You're not kidding,' Tanzy said, taking a sip of hot coffee.

Over the next hour, they caught up on emails and filed a personal report on the Julia Porter scene. DCI Thornton wanted each individual, whether you were a DI who'd been there twenty years or a PC who'd just stepped through the door, to file their own.

After the morning meeting with their individual teams, Byrd and Tanzy went down the hall to see Tallow and Hope, hoping there was an update on the murder scene at Brinkburn Drive. Both of them were in the middle of something and asked if they could pop by later. Both detectives complied and left them to it.

The morning ticked on and the time approached twelve. The level of activity was starting to dip as people made their way out for lunch. Some went to the canteen, which was located on the first floor, while others liked to get out for half an hour, going to Greggs or McDonalds or whichever convenient fast food establishment tickled their fancy.

Tanzy was focused on the report in front of him, about the seven-year-old, Evelyn Jones. She'd been missing for a week now, but no body had been found yet. He'd been in contact with her parents who'd been ringing constantly. Tanzy couldn't blame them. As a father, he'd do exactly the same. Bloody hell, he'd move heaven and earth for his own kids. He'd promised the girl's parents that he and his team, were doing everything in their power to find her, but the trail was going cold.

Evelyn was last seen eight days ago around three-thirty in the afternoon. It was a Wednesday. One of the parents, after picking their children up at the local primary school, had seen her on the corner where Conyers Avenue met Barnes Road. The woman said Evelyn had taken a left onto Barnes Road, but the woman and her own children had taken a right, so after that, she couldn't assist the police in relation to her next move.

After knocking on nearly every door in the Mowden area, which took nearly two full days, Tanzy and his team were left with nothing. The corner of where Conyers Avenue met Barnes Road was her last known location. It was as if she'd vanished like a ghost.

Tanzy hated it.

The only positive that came to Tanzy's mind was that the little girl hadn't been found dead. And to him, that meant there was hope. Every day, that hope decreased but there was still a possibility she was alive.

9

Wednesday Afternoon
Forensics lab – Police Station

Jacob Tallow and Emily Hope were in the lab. Byrd and Tanzy had popped in earlier but they were in the middle of something and asked them to drop by later. After they'd secured some evidence, they had returned to Brinkburn Drive. In the short time they were there between the hours of 3.30 a.m. and 7 a.m. earlier that morning, they'd taken forty-nine pictures of the scene, all different angles, the majority of the shots focused on Julia Porter.

Tallow had also taken a video of the room before a tired looking DI Byrd and DI Tanzy had arrived just after four a.m.. It helped them looking over things when analysing later. It was as if they were there. Once the detectives had left, Tallow and Hope went back inside to collect more evidence. They knew Byrd and Tanzy were experienced enough to keep a safe distance whilst they were in the room; they both knew the importance of what a forensic would look for, so contaminating the scene was something Tallow and Hope weren't too worried about. They also made sure the detectives, who knew the correct protocol, had been signed in on arrival and signed out as they left. An imperative process.

Back inside the house when they returned, they checked the room thoroughly. Sometimes leaving a scene to take a quick break allowed them to look at something with fresh eyes, enabling them to see things that may have first missed. They rarely made mistakes, but everyone did at some point.

The crime scene manager, Tony McCabe, entered the room just after 11 a.m.. He'd been occupied under the bridge where Julia and her son, Liam, had been taken. Whilst he was there and not at the house, he'd made sure Tallow and Hope had cordoned off the area and ensured that any law enforcement that entered were wearing cover shoes and had been signed in and out. Tallow confirmed he'd already set this up and would continue to do so until the job was done – it was the basics.

'Hey, guys,' Hope said through her face mask, first glancing at McCabe, then at Forrest, then Beech, who all appeared in the doorway of the dining room where the rancid smell still lingered.

'Morning,' McCabe said, his eyes immediately falling on Julia Porter. They were finished under the bridge and ordered the car to be taken back to the station for further analysis. Apart from the fingerprints on the door handles, they didn't expect to find much but a thorough search using more adequate equipment needed to be carried out.

The road was now open for the good people of Darlington to use normally.

Examining a scene outside was completely different compared to a scene inside. A closed room would last longer in its original state. The air was still. The humidity was even. Outside, if a body was found, the wind and rain can alter the aspects of a scene making it very challenging to collect accurate evidence, so determining how the body reacted during the time after death is altered and needed to be considered.

The fresh-eyed forensic assistant, Beech, stepped forward a little. Although he'd been doing it a year, each crime scene amazed him. Firstly, how someone could have been so cruel in the first place, and secondly, his excitement about the process of carrying out the work - how they'd look for things, collect the evidence.

'Ahh, wait,' McCabe said to him, holding out his palm.

Beech stopped, glanced at his superior.

'I know you're keen,' McCabe said, 'but let Tallow and Hope talk you through some things first, okay?'

Beech nodded. McCabe glanced towards Amanda Forrest, who was standing next to Beech, so she knew this applied to her too.

'Have you found anything unusual here?' McCabe asked the senior forensics.

'You mean apart from a dead woman with no eyes?' Hope asked him with elevated eyebrows. She knew what he meant but he appreciated her humour.

McCabe offered a smile. 'Yes…'

'Hundreds of fingerprints. Everywhere.'

'Have you guys found anything near the bridge?' Tallow asked, looking up from his electronic tablet.

'Fingerprints,' Beech said.

'Nice.'

'Hey, I need to go guys,' McCabe said. 'You guys work together, and I'll catch up with you later. There's some place I need to be.'

'Don't forget to sign out, sir,' Tallow said, smiling at his superior.

'You got it, boss,' he said with a wink and left.

They found several hairs around the room and bagged them for DNA analysis. Blood samples from the congealed pool on the floor directly under the body of Julia had been taken. Countless finger prints on the dining room table and on the floor were found with the assistance of a powerful UV light. Some of them were smaller fingerprints, implying they probably belonged to their children, who were most likely sat at that same table when they had breakfast, lunch, and dinner the day before.

But then they found something strange.

There was only one set of footprints in that room.

Because of the nature of the crime, one would assume there were several people involved. That's a fair assumption to make. Due to the moisture outside and the damp conditions on the ground, one would also think that whilst murdering someone then taking out their eyes, tying them to a chair, the last thing you would think of is cleaning the floor with a bleach to get rid of footprints.

Sure, you might not see them with the human eye. You wouldn't normally, unless they were wet or dirty. But under the light of UV, you'd expect to see something.

There had been no smell of bleach lingering in the air, or any sign of any cleaning products anywhere in the house. It would appear that only one person had been in that room. That person wore sized ten footwear.

Chances are, judging by looking at her feet, it wasn't Julia Porter. The single set of footprints would be checked and cross referenced with Ian Porter as he was the likely source. And most likely, the set of foot prints were his.

It was clear to Hope and Tallow that they weren't dealing with clowns here. These people were smart. These people knew more than the average Joe. The scene was very clean from a forensic point of view.

When they finished examining the room under UV light, they'd switched the ceiling light back on. Deciding they'd collected all they could, they moved out into the hallway and carried out the same process. It was a tedious task, but they loved their jobs and took pride in doing their best.

Out in the hallway, they found several fingerprints on the top surface of a radiator cover and dozens of footprints near the door. As an entry and exit point of the property, it was expected.

'Brilliant,' Tallow said sarcastically at the time, staring down at the uncountable prints on the wooden floor.

They asked who lived at the property and were told there were two adults and three children. It was important to get samples of their DNA so if there were any samples that were analysed and didn't match, that could point them in the direction of something extremely important.

Back in the lab, on the computer screen in front of Hope, were several pictures of Julia Porter. Beech and Forrest had both gone to McCabe's office for a meeting. Every time they'd been to a crime scene, he wanted to speak to them to see what they'd learnt, to see how their training was going.

'It's very neat, isn't it?' Hope said, keeping her curious eyes on the screen.

Tallow, who was looking through the video the Porter's dining room, pressed pause on the remote, the screen showing a still shot of the side of Julia Porter's bloody face and glanced over to her. He knew she was referring to the method used to remove the eyes from Julia Porter's face.

To a trained eye, it was obvious that a very sharp instrument had been used. She'd seen this procedure carried out in the past, but she'd never seen this precision, not outside of a medical or pathology lab. It was almost mind boggling, considering the time frame that the individual or individuals had to do it.

Ian Porter claimed he was unconscious for forty minutes under the bridge. He said when he'd woken, there was a couple standing over him asking if he was okay. He then left the bridge and raced home. Taking that into account, would leave fifty to fifty-five minutes for Julia Porter to be brought back home.

In that time, she was tied to a chair, killed, then someone removed her eyes. All traces of footprints, apart from one, who was most likely her husband, Ian Porter, who lived with her, had vanished.

'Yes, it is,' Tallow agreed, frowning. 'It's quite impressive, isn't it?'

'It's worrying,' she replied, 'that's what it is.'

Unless the footprints they found belonged to the single person who was responsible for the murder of Julia Porter. Unless it wasn't a stranger at all.

10

Wednesday Afternoon
Police Station

'You heard anything on Evelyn yet?' Byrd asked Tanzy.

They were sitting at their desks eating lunch. Byrd had popped out to get them both a sandwich from somewhere in town. Said he needed to stretch his legs. Tanzy had told Byrd that whilst he was gone, he would check in on his team, see if they had anything more on the missing seven-year-old, Evelyn Jones.

There were no more updates. Tanzy finished a mouthful of the ham and cheese sandwich, then took a sip of Pepsi from the open topped bottle next to his keyboard. It had been a week since her disappearance, but nothing had come back yet. There was a nationwide missing person's search that had been first broadcasted four days ago, making it three days after she was last seen. The article, written by reporter, Steve Allan, had his own section on The Northern Echo website and his own column in the paper. Each day, he provided an update, a public appeal, begging people to stay vigilant and stated that Evelyn's parents needed their help. His column in today's paper said that Evelyn was *One of our own and needed to be found ASAP. We are praying for her.*

There was a ping from Byrd's phone. He leaned forward and unlocked it. It was from Claire:

Looking forward to seeing you tonight. X x

A smile ran across Byrd's face. He ran his fingers across the screen and replied with:

You too :) Love, M x x

'What you smiling at?'

'Nothing.'

'Maxi in love?'

Byrd leaned over and punched his arm, causing Tanzy to sway to the left nearly falling off his chair. They had a great relationship, inside and outside of work. They told each other about their personal life, about what was going on, about their families.

Byrd knew Tanzy had two kids: Jasmine and Eric. He knew what school they went to and he knew how old they were. He knew what things they liked to watch on television and what food they liked to eat.

Tanzy knew that Byrd didn't have any children. He'd never really had the inclination of starting a family just yet, never felt like he'd met the right person whom he thought would be a good mother to his future children. Tanzy also knew that Byrd had just pipped over the hill of forty, and becoming a parent, in his opinion, would only make life harder. Byrd had been with his partner, Claire, for nearly eighteen months. Tanzy liked her. She was educated, had her wits about her. She was good for Byrd, just what he needed, someone to take his mind off the job when he got home, otherwise he'd just stay in the office day and night.

Often, Tanzy, Phillipa, Byrd, and Claire, would go out for meals. A few weeks back, they went to Al Fornos on Skinnergate in town, then went around a few of the pubs afterwards. Nothing too heavy.

At their desks, they both finished their food and sat back, letting it digest.

'What do you think they'll find?' Tanzy said, referring to the forensics at Julia Porter's house on Brinkburn Drive.

Byrd cocked his head. 'They could find anything. They are the finest forensics I've ever worked with.'

Tanzy agreed.

DCI Thornton's office door opened.

'Hey, you two,' she said quickly.

Byrd and Tanzy both turned.

'What do we know?' DCI Thornton asked. 'He was on the phone.' By *he*, she meant Superintendent Barry Eckles. 'He's looking for an update. I said I'll ring him back ASAP.'

'Not much to add when we spoke with you earlier. We'll chase up with McCabe and his team shortly.'

'Okay.' She turned, returned inside of her office, and closed her door. She seemed flustered, unsure about something, which was unusual because she was normally as cool as ice.

Eckles was on her back constantly, making sure she was doing things right. Not only right, but fast. He wanted everything done yesterday which was always an impossible task.

Byrd and Tanzy turned, focusing on their own screens.

It was then when Byrd's mobile phone rang on the desk near his keyboard. He stopped typing, picked it up, and put it to his ear.

'Hello?'

'Max Byrd?'

'Speaking?'

'Hello, Max, I am a nurse from Darlington Memorial Hospital, my name is Amanda Horne. I'm sorry to tell you this, but we have some bad news. Your Mother and Father have been involved in a serious road traffic collision.'

The words ran over Byrd like a cold shiver.

'Are they – are they okay?'

'Please come to the hospital,' she said clearly, 'they're both in a very bad way.'

11

Wednesday Afternoon
Darlington Memorial Hospital

It took Byrd just fourteen minutes from receiving the call to arrive at the reception of the Darlington Memorial Hospital.

'Good afternoon, how can I help you, sir?'

Byrd leaned forward, his stomach against the rounded edge of the high desk, glancing down at the blonde in her mid-fifties dressed in white sitting on a swivel desk chair. She wore stylish rectangular glasses.

'My parents were in an RTA a short while ago. Name's Byrd.'

'Hold on a second, Sir,' she said, diverting her attention to the screen in front of her. On her right breast pocket, the name Angela was sewn on. He watched her eyes reflect the screen's dim glare. 'Yeah, found them,' she said.

'Which floor?'

'Ground floor, ICU.' She glanced to the left, raising her arm down the corridor. 'If you go down there, then take a right, you'll–'

She fell quiet, realising Byrd had already left the desk and now out of sight, running down the corridor towards the Intensive Care Unit.

His hurried, heavy footsteps pounded the floor and echoed down the hall, causing everyone to slow a beat as they stared at him fearfully. He quickly passed an elderly woman hunched over in a wheelchair, almost taking her kneecaps out in the process. He muttered an apology under his breath but didn't wait for a response from her or the angry younger man who was pushing her.

Taking a left, he narrowly missed a pair of young doctors, who were forced to halt their strides to avoid the collision. This time, he didn't apologise. He needed to get there. His heart pounded through his chest as he slowed down in front of the double doors. Through the door, to the right, there was a wide, low desk with a sign indicating the Intensive Care Unit Reception.

The handsome-looking man behind it lifted his head, glancing up over the top of small, square glasses.

'Can I help you?'

Byrd rushed over. 'Yes, yes. My parents were in an RTC. I was told they were in here. Name's Byrd. B. Y. R. D.'

The time it took the man to do the search was merely seconds, but it felt like hours. Byrd anxiously glanced down at his wrist watch, breathing light and fast.

'Are they here?'

'Just a second…'

'I was told they—'

The man lifted his head a fraction of an inch. 'Yes, they're here. Take a seat, I'll get a doctor to come and speak with you.'

'But I—'

'Sir, if you just take a seat, a doctor will come and see you as soon as possible – I'll tell him you're here.' The man behind the desk held a palm out in the direction of the two remaining seats behind Byrd. He sighed, went over and took one of them.

He tipped his head forward, letting his face fall into his wet palms. A few long minutes passed before the double doors to the left opened. Byrd craned his neck. A slim Asian man of average height stepped through the threshold, wearing a tightly fitting pale blue shirt accompanied by a thin black tie. Byrd guessed he was close to sixty, although it was hard to tell.

He appeared to be looking around and it wasn't long before his stare found Byrd. Standing to his feet, Byrd met the doctor halfway between the doors and the small seating area.

'I'm Dr Ching,' he said in a soft voice.

'Are they okay?' Byrd asked quickly, frantically, looking past him through the doors.

'Are you a family member?'

'Yes – their son. I'm their son, Max. Are they - are they okay?'

Dr Ching let out a small sigh. 'Please follow me – they're in a very bad way.'

The doctor turned, padded a few steps then leaned to the right side of the door, using his key card to gain access. After the beep, the doors opened automatically away from them, then Byrd followed the doctor down the dimly-lit corridor.

12

Wednesday late afternoon
Police Station

Tanzy's phone rang in his pocket as he walked through the exit door of the station, feeling the cold air outside. After the stressful day, he was glad it was over. He flashed a courteous smile to the female colleague walking past him and she thanked him for holding the door open for her.

Plucking the phone from his pocket, the ringing growing louder, he checked the caller. Byrd.

'Hey, Max.' Tanzy slowed his walk to the car so he could give Byrd his full attention. 'How are they doing?'

Byrd sighed through the phone. 'Not good, Ori. They're both in a coma.'

Silence hung in the air as Tanzy stopped dead at the edge of the car park and raised a hand to his head. 'Max, I'm so sorry.'

Byrd coughed and Tanzy could hear the emotion climbing up his throat. 'Yeah.'

'Do you want me to bring you anything?'

Byrd fell quiet. This time, Tanzy gave him a few more seconds.

'Max, do you ne—'

'No, it's okay mate, thanks, I'll be alright. I'm meant to be seeing Claire tonight. She might drop by.'

Tanzy started moving again, dawdling towards his car. 'I can if you want, Max, I'm not doing anything.'

'No, Ori, it's fine – don't worry about me, honestly.'

'If you're sure. Ring me if you need anything, okay?'

'Will do,' Byrd said, before he hung up.

Tanzy sighed, feeling the burden of his friend's pain, and put the phone back in to his jacket pocket. Using the key, he opened the door, climbed in, and sat for a moment. What a day. He stared out the window, watched a grey Kia Sportage pass and turn for the exit. The car park was thinning. The sun had long gone, the sky now smothered by huddling grey clouds.

He itched his goatee for a second and thought about his brother, Daniel, who lives down in York with their parents, Andre and Claudia. He renovates houses and does most of the work himself. Tanzy spoke with him on the phone – usually once or twice a week – but he was usually in the middle of something. Which was good; it kept him out of trouble and at the same time, he was earning money renovating houses.

Tanzy glanced at the dash board. Almost six. His judo lesson started in fifteen minutes. A part of him couldn't be bothered today. He sometimes had them days. Finding the body of Julia Porter early this morning and finding out his best friend's parents were now in a coma after a car crash. For a second, he thought about ringing his wife, Phillipa, and picked up his phone.

Staring at the screen, he decided not to, and placed it back down on the passenger seat. They'd had an argument last night and went to sleep on bad terms, which was something that hadn't happened in a while. Due to the early start this morning, he hadn't seen her or even spoke to her all day.

After his class, he showered, then put on his spare clothes and made his way outside. It was dark. The air was filled with a moisture implying it was about to rain.

Along the path away from the entrance door of the Dolphin Centre, a group of teenagers were sitting on the bench. On his approach, their mumbles fell silent as he felt their stares fall on him. Noticing the sudden quiet, Tanzy looked up. Five of them. Three of them on bikes, the other two sitting on the bench, leaning forward with phones in their hands.

'You have a spare fag?' one of them asked. He was young. Sixteen maybe.

'No, sorry,' Tanzy replied, ambling past, his kit bag hanging over one shoulder, resting off his hip.

'Dickhead,' the lad said.

Tanzy, after passing them, stopped and turned slowly.

'Problem like?' The lad stood up and took a few steps towards him. 'Eh, dickhead, you have a problem?' He had a skin head and thick chains around his neck.

Tanzy smiled, and calmly asked, 'Excuse me?'

'Do. You. Have. A. Fucking. Problem?' The lad was tall but not quite Tanzy's height. At six foot, two inches, Tanzy had a couple of inches on him but the lad stood taller than boys his age, which Tanzy guessed was maybe fifteen or sixteen. The young brave man was thickset, too, his arms were big, and muscles protruded from his neck.

'I don't have a problem, no,' Tanzy said.

The lad wandered over and stopped a few inches from Tanzy's face, then glared deep into his eyes. He raised his hand to his mouth, smoking the last of his cigarette, then lowered his arm and quickly blew the smoke in Tanzy's face.

Tanzy didn't flinch or move an inch. 'Bad for you that, you know?'

'Fuck off eh, dickhead.'

Tanzy understood the situation the young lad had found himself in. He'd challenged someone in front of his mates, someone much older. Someone he didn't know had done judo for twenty-two years. He'd have to follow through now because his reputation was on the line.

'Okay, sir. You have a pleasant evening.' As Tanzy attempted to move around him, the muscular lad reached out quickly, grabbing the arm of Tanzy's hoody. As he did, he felt the solid muscle of Tanzy's forearm.

Tanzy turned slightly, smiling at the boy.

'Your call, son…' he whispered, leaning closer.

The lad eyed him wearily for a long moment and decided to let go of his arm. He backed away a few inches, giving him a stare that suggested he'll let Tanzy off this time. Tanzy's smile widened as he turned and walked down the angled path back towards his car.

'Pussy,' one of the lad's friends said to him as he sat back down.

'I'd have knocked him out,' the lad claimed. 'I didn't want to, though.'

Tanzy climbed into his car. He put the bag on the passenger seat and plucked the phone from his pocket. He found his wife's number and called it.

'Ori…' she said when she answered. Her voice was weak.

Something was wrong.

'Hey, Pip, you… okay?'

'Ori… I'm so sorry,' she said.

'What's – what's happened?'

'I've done it again. I've ruined everything. You need to come home… now.'

Her words crept into his heavy heart as he dipped his head into his chest, knowingly. He ended the call and threw his phone into the passenger footwell.

Then he tipped his head back and screamed.

13

Wednesday Evening
Darlington

The man sat down on the large sofa, plonking himself next to his wife, and glanced down nervously at his watch.

It was nearly time.

'It should be on any minute now,' he said, a tinge of excitement creeping into his voice. Their eyes met for a second before she offered him a sad smile. Finding her hand, he squeezed it.

'They're going to wish they never did what they did.'

'They deserve all they get,' she replied with a determination in her voice.

On the television attached to the opposite wall of the room, the ten O'clock news had started. He exhaled heavily. According to the reporter, who sported a dark blue suit and matching tie, a body had been found.

His hand tightened around hers.

'We have a report confirmed that the body of a woman has been found in a property on Brinkburn Drive in Darlington. Let's go to Colin Chalmers who was there in the early hours this morning.'

The screen suddenly changed from a studio setting to footage recorded of a man standing in a dark street, dressed in a padded black coat, a microphone clutched in his hand close to his chest. Below the clip, there was a headline: *Woman found dead in a house in Darlington.*

'Here we go,' he whispered, squeezing his wife's hand, who for a brief moment, glanced at him before she returned her focus back at the screen.

'I'm here outside a house in Brinkburn Drive in Darlington,' Colin Chalmers said, standing directly in front of the camera light, 'where the body of a woman has been found. It's unclear what the cause of death is at the moment. We have information to believe that the victim's life was taken in a malicious, unlawful act. It's confirmed her identity is thirty-seven-year-old, Julia Porter. A wife and a mother of three young children. It's believed that her husband found her in the dining room in the early hours. Police were informed and attended the scene to find the woman in a condition they described as sickening and horrific. More information to follow once we know more in the coming hours. You can see behind me,' Colin turned slightly, glancing behind him, raising his padded arm. The camera followed his finger and focused on the house that was maybe thirty to forty metres behind him, 'That a team of forensics are here investigating the crime.'

On the screen, a tall man dressed in white plastic overalls walked out of the house, down the drive, opened the boot of a car and returned back into the house.

A shivering Colin turned back to the camera. 'Once we know more, we'll be updating the public. I have no doubt that the police will do everything they can to determine the reason behind this malevolent act. Until then, this is Colin Chalmers of ITV news.'

Once the screen switched back to the studio, the man on the sofa took hold of the remote and turned off the television. A deathly silence filled the living room quickly.

The woman on the sofa stared at him. 'You okay?'

He slowly smiled, giving her a light nod. 'I am.' He paused a beat. 'He'll be sending a picture of Julia Porter very soon. I can't wait to see her blood.'

14

Wednesday Night
Low Coniscliffe

Byrd stopped his black BMW X5 on the driveway, applied the handbrake, and dropped his head back into the headrest for a moment. He felt the tears well up in his eyes, then allowed them to trickle down his face. After stifling a short cry and feeling the salty taste in his mouth, he wiped them away with the back of his hand.

The time was just after 11 p.m..

He was starving. His stomach begged for food but that was the last thing on his mind. He needed to get inside where he could find peace and quiet.

And a drink.

God, he needed a drink.

What a day it had been. He'd been at the hospital for hours, watching his mother and father lying on their individual beds, surrounded by the continual beeping equipment and the pitter-patter of the doctors and nurses moving around them, assessing what they could do to fix them.

Alan and Jackie Byrd had been driving northbound on the A1 at seventy miles-an-hour when a car had stupidly undertaken them on the inside lane. As Alan pulled across into the slower lane, he'd clipped the back end of the passing car throwing their vehicle to the right, causing them to collide in to the central reservation before their Honda Civic flipped twice and landed on the roof. Instantly, they'd fallen unconscious. It took fourteen minutes for emergency services to attend the scene. The fire service had carefully pulled them both out of the car and the paramedics had cautiously put them in the back of the ambulance where they were given an oxygen supply and taken straight to Darlington Memorial Hospital.

They didn't wake.

The first thing Byrd had questioned was the whereabouts of the car that had undertaken them. Where was the person responsible for this? The report had said that the car wasn't at the scene by the time of emergency assistance, and there was no way of asking his parents because they were unconscious. He'd speak to Highway patrol, see if it could be located and tracked down.

Dr Ching, who'd walked through the door when Byrd had been waiting at the reception of the ICU hours ago, had told Byrd what damage his parents had suffered. Severe head trauma from the impact had caused their brains to swell and the fluid had pushed against their skulls, forcing their brains to push down on their brains stems, damaging their Reticular Activating Systems. Their injuries were almost identical, which was rare in situations such as this, because the possibilities of what could have happened were almost endless.

The only thing that was on Byrd's mind now was: Are they going to make it?

Byrd was aware of their ages. He was also aware that his mother, Jackie, had COPD from years of heavy smoking.

When he asked Dr Ching the question, the doctor's eyes narrowed. 'Due to their ages, and taking in to account your mother's condition, I pray that they'll awaken. If, or when, they awaken, we don't know the severity of the damage until we can assess them in a conscious state. At the moment, we've assessed them and will know the severity of the damage using the coma scale. You should be aware the chances of recovery are deeply affected by their ages and their health – it's important that you understand that.'

'I understand that,' Byrd had told him.

'Your father is in good health,' the doctor continued, 'surprisingly good health. However your mother, not so good. What I can tell you is that they could be in this state for up to two weeks, and if I was you, I'd go home and rest, because chances are, this won't be an overnight fix.' Dr Ching gave him a sad, sympathetic smile. 'We'll update you every step of the way, okay, Mr Byrd.'

Byrd opened the door of his X5 and stepped out into the darkness of his driveway. The street was stone-dead quiet. Across the road, Mrs Lovell was standing at her bedroom window looking out at him. When she noticed his stare, she closed the curtains quickly.

Making his way up the short drive, he could faintly smell fire in the air. No doubt caused by the kids earlier at the river, where they'd sit round a fire with their friends, telling ghost stories or smoking cannabis. It was cold but they did it most of the year. It was only a few minutes' walk down to the river opening. Byrd and Claire had been down there walking a few times.

As he reached his front door, his phone rang. He glanced down at it.

Claire.

He'd texted her earlier, informing her what'd happened to his parents. She told him she'd drop by to see him when he got home. She didn't ask to visit the ICU because she hadn't known Alan and Jackie all that well, not well enough to warrant being there when they were fighting for their lives.

He answered the phone whilst he fumbled with the key inside the front door that badly needed replacing. 'Hey.'

'Hey, Max.' Her voice was soft, caring. 'Are you home?'

'Just,' he said. 'What are you doing?'

'At home.' She fell quiet for a moment. 'You want me to come over?'

He closed the door, locked it and hung his long black coat on the post at the bottom of the stairs. 'If you like, I won't be the best company mind, but it'd be nice to see you.'

'Give me fifteen minutes,' she said.

Byrd put the phone back into his trouser pocket and walked into the long rectangular-shaped kitchen. At the far end, he flicked on the kettle and stood there as it boiled. Then he thought, fuck it, and reached up and grabbed a glass and the bottle of whisky from the cupboard above. He poured himself a healthy measure and knocked it back. He filled it halfway up again. Knocked that back, too.

He sat down at the square table, staring blankly at the surface of the wood, his mind running over the day.

The body of Julia Porter.

His parents in a coma.

Then he cried louder than he had done in years.

15

Wednesday midnight
Darlington

Tanzy pulled onto the by-pass and floored it in second gear. The engine of the Mercedes CLS 350 roared as the torque pulled the vehicle into the night.

With determined, focused eyes, he could see that for the next mile the road was empty. No one around. Just him and his busy thoughts to deal with.

Often, he did this when he needed to get out. When he needed to be alone. Fire up the Merc and waste some fuel. Normally, Phillipa drove this when he was at work using the Golf. But it was his car. His pride and joy.

He'd always liked his cars from being young. He remembered, although he doesn't like to be reminded of it, when he was seventeen and he passed his test. He bought a 1.1 litre Peugeot 106 and spent over a thousand pounds on modifications. He'd put a new exhaust system on it and changed the air induction system. He bought some shiny new alloys, which in hindsight, looked ridiculous – he had a photograph somewhere to prove it. He even talked about putting NOS in it but after his friends had laughed at him, he changed his mind. Before the Merc, he'd gone through the whole section of young cars, ranging from his first Peugeot to a Clio to a Civic Type R. The Honda was his favourite – he loved it. One of the reasons was that he owned it when he met Phillipa. They used to go through to Teesside park and go for meals and spend nights at the bowling alley.

They were the good times. The happy times.

Now it was different. Very different.

When Tanzy had screamed in the car earlier after being on the phone with Phillipa, he knew what she meant when she said she was sorry and that she'd ruined everything again. He couldn't believe it. All the hard work.

For what?

For fucking nothing.

He'd raced home earlier and when he'd walked through the door, he'd heard her shouting at the kids. They were cowered in the corner of the living room holding each other, scared. When Tanzy had walked in, he saw the Vodka bottle in her hand with only a third left in it. Eric and Jasmine had looked up and sighed with relief after seeing him enter the room.

They both got up from the corner, ran over to him, and hugged him tightly.

'That's it, go and fuck off to Daddy then!' she'd shouted. Her words were slurred as she waved the bottle around in mid-air. 'Same old fucking story, innit?'

'Listen, Eric, Jaz,' Tanzy had quietly told them, 'go to your rooms, I'll be up in a minute.' He held on to Jasmine's arm, but she winced a little. On her arm, he saw a dark bruise. It broke his heart. He pushed it to the back of his mind and kissed their heads before gently pushing them towards the door away from their mother. He stood up and faced her.

'What the fuck are you looking at?' she screamed at him. 'Don't you—' She stumbled a little, losing her balance. Then she pointed at him. 'Don't you fucking judge me, Orion fucking Tanzy. You don't know what it's like. What I've been through.'

Tanzy had breathed slowly, watching her sway side to side as she took another swig of the vodka, the upper half of her body swaying uncontrollably, threatening to topple at any second. Most of the vodka had missed her lips and fell down her chin, down on to her thin dressing gown that was almost falling off her. She wasn't wearing a bra either.

'You're a disgrace, Pip. Speaking like that in front of our kids. Eric is ten and Jaz is seven.'

She stared blankly at him as if she didn't even know who he was referring to. She was in such a state. Tanzy turned, walked out of the living room and when he was in the kitchen, he phoned Phillipa's mother, Elena. He'd told her what had happened, and Elena told Tanzy she'd come to collect the kids straight away. She lived on the other side of town and she'd be there within ten minutes.

When she arrived, she didn't even want to see her daughter. She just collected her grandkids and off they went.

Phillipa had been sober for nearly six months. She was so close to her six-month badge at AA. Tanzy had been so proud of her, until tonight anyway. He half expected it - it wasn't the first time she'd fallen back in to her old ways. It was the seventh, but she'd never got anywhere near the six months mark. Tanzy knew what she'd been through, what she had to cope with, but it was the same as Pip's mother. She'd dealt with the same issue.

Pip's dad, Peter.

What a horrible man he was. He used to hit Elena and Phillipa over and over again. He also used to visit Phillipa's room after he'd been out on the drink and force her to have sex with him. Elena, of course, knew what her husband was doing to her daughter, but she was terrified of him. They both were. He used to lock them both in the airing cupboard on the landing and urinate through the vent holes, then leave them in there for hours.

'I saw the bruise on Jasmine's arm, Pip,' Tanzy said. He glowered at her, stabbing a pointed finger in her direction. 'If you ever touch her like that again, it'll be the last thing that you do. I'll fucking arrest you and send you away for a long time. Do you understand me?'

She continued to sway for a few seconds until she backed away, falling on to the sofa. He knew it wasn't the right time to have this discussion. He needed to get out, away from her.

Tanzy took a right at the roundabout and headed in the direction of town. He passed Cummins engines on the left and reached the new roundabout near the new Costa and went straight over. Within a few minutes, at the bottom of Yarm Road, he passed the Hippodrome on the right-hand side then took a right at the lights. He decided to drive around the old route he used to when he was younger. Dozens of cars did it. They'd go down Duke street and take a right on to Skinnergate, then a left on the corner where Hoskins was, which at the time was called Humphrey's, then down the side of the Dolphin Centre.

The town was quiet.

Not many places stayed open later than twelve during the week – all the fun was at the weekends in Darlington. As he approached the rear of the Dolphin Centre, his phone beeped with a text message. He slowed the Merc and pulled over, stopping in the loading area behind the Dolphin Centre, and turned off the engine.

A text from Elena. He read it:

Eric and Jaz are asleep. Safe and sound. We'll sort Pip out tomorrow. I know what she's been through, but we have to move on. We all have to move past it and get on with our lives. I'll speak with her tomorrow. Love, E x

He sat in deep thought for a moment, then through the gap in window, he heard footsteps from across the road. He didn't see anyone initially, but the sounds got louder. Out of the dark alley, an elderly man stepped out and dashed across the road, passing the front of Tanzy's bonnet onto the path, and along the side of the car up towards Boyes. Through the passenger door mirror, the man seemed to be in somewhat of a hurry, as if something was bothering him.

Then Tanzy heard further sounds coming from the alley. Multiple footsteps. He turned his focus to the right, saw three men dressed in tracksuits step out from the alley and look around intently.

'There he is,' one of them said, pointing behind Tanzy's car towards the direction in which the elderly man went. 'Come on, let's see what he has.'

The men seemed to be in their early to mid-twenties and walked with a youthful bounce of energy and attitude. Carefully, Tanzy watched them pass the side of his car and heard one of them comment on his Merc. They obviously hadn't seen him sitting in the driver's seat.

'Hey, fuck the car,' one of them said, 'we'll come back for that later, let's go. That old bloke has a few hundred quid on him. Hurry up, he's gone up the alley where Pizza Hut is.'

Tanzy waited ten seconds and gave a heavy sigh, then slowly opened his car door and stepped out into the cold midnight air. Gently, he closed the driver's door then very quickly and quietly, followed the three men into the dark alley.

16

Wednesday Midnight
Darlington Town Centre

The alley was pitch black. Tanzy kept to the right, close to the wall, in case of any of the men turned and saw his silhouette against the orange glare of the street lights on the road behind.

'Where did he go?' one of the men said about half way up, his voice echoing back down the alley.

'Fuck knows,' muttered another. 'He was just here. We need that money? I need my fix.'

Tanzy's eyes started to adjust. He could see the outline of the three men up ahead. One of them pulled a phone from his tracksuit bottoms and turned on the torch function.

Shit, thought Tanzy. If they turned, they'd see him creeping along the wall, so he hid behind a large blue cube-shaped bin on wheels for a moment.

'Hey, what's this?' he heard one of them say. 'There's a wall on the right.' Their footsteps faded a little until one of them shouted, 'Hey, found him! He's hiding behind the wall!'

'Please,' begged the elderly man. 'I need to get home to my wife, she's waiting for me.'

'Give us your money, old man!'

Tanzy took a lung full of air before he crept around the side of the bin and moved back close against the wall, slowly making his way up the alley.

'I can't, it's all we have. My wife, she – she needs medicine,' pleaded the man, his voice quavering in the darkness. Tanzy edged closer, seeing the three men surrounding the old man who was cowered on the floor in the corner with no way out. 'Please, don't.'

Tanzy made his move.

'Hey!' Tanzy shouted, staggering towards them, purposefully appearing like he was drunk.

The three men shuddered a little then whipped themselves around at the noise. The man with the phone light shone it on Tanzy, the dazzling light was blinding, and for a second, he couldn't see anything, but he knew there was a gap of four to five metres between him and the nearest man.

'Fuck off, pisshead, stay outta this,' one of them said, before breaking out into laughter.

'Hey,' said Tanzy, 'I need some money.' Tanzy fell clumsily to his knees and put his hands together as if he was praying to them, then he started clapping slowly. His knees felt cold as they absorbed the moisture on the wet ground.

The man with the phone said, 'Hey, Craig, deal with the pisshead eh.'

'What should I do with him?'

'Whatever… knock him the fuck out if you have to, I don't care,' he told him. 'We need this old bastard's money.'

The elderly man cowered further into the corner, raising his arms in front of his terrified face, losing hope that Tanzy would be of any help.

Little did he know.

'Right, pisshead,' said one of the men in a tracksuit walking confidently towards Tanzy. 'You're gonna wish you never came down here.' Tanzy, who was still on his knees, glanced up with wide eyes so they adjusted to the dim surroundings. He knew exactly where the man was, and as he approached, Tanzy slowly moved his left leg up, planting his foot on to the floor to steady his body.

He was ready.

The man kicked a high leg towards Tanzy's head. Tanzy waited till the man's calf was just above his left shoulder and threw his arms up to grab it, trapping his shin between his forearm and the side of his head. Tanzy then jumped up from the floor with the man's leg trapped on his shoulder and lifted the man into the air, until he awkwardly crashed down on to the concrete with a sickening thump.

Wasting no time at all, Tanzy darted for the next man who was in mid-turn after hearing the sound of bone hitting concrete, but by the time he realised what was going on, Tanzy grabbed the material of the man's hoody with his tight grip and swept the back of his legs from underneath him. The man made a 'whoop' sound as he collided to the hard floor with a yelp.

The man with the phone turned towards Tanzy frantically. 'What the fuck? The fuck are you?' he gasped.

Tanzy didn't wait for the conversation to develop, quickly grabbing the outsides of the man's shoulders with both of his hands, and moving close into him, he placed his right leg across his body to the outside of the man's right foot and threw him over his hip in one swift movement. The man literally went upside down as Tanzy man-handled him down on to the concrete. He dropped the phone, smashing onto the floor in to a thousand pieces. The light went out and the alley fell into darkness.

Standing to his feet, Tanzy padded to the corner and helped the old man up, telling him it was okay, that he was safe. The man thanked him then left the alley quickly.

The men stayed on the floor groaning in agony as Tanzy casually strolled out of the alley, back to his Mercedes.

17

Thursday – Early hours
Darlington

Ian Porter was in the small bathroom of the Premier Inn, swallowing the remaining vodka in the glass in his hand. He went back into the room, grabbed the bottle on the desk, unscrewed the cap, and filled it up again.

His eyes were sore; he'd been crying for hours.

It had been nearly twenty-four hours since he found his wife dead in the dining room of his home. The police and forensics had finished in the dining room and the coroner had been over to remove his wife's body, but he wasn't allowed to stay there. DI Byrd and DI Tanzy had told him, to increase their chances of catching whoever did this, he needed to stay away from the house so he didn't contaminate the crime scene.

The words written in red crayon on the table ran over in his mind in a constant loop.

She didn't see it coming.

He didn't know what it meant. He couldn't help the detectives yesterday because he didn't know himself. He wished he did. He wished he could come up with a reason why this had happened to his wife.

Peeling himself away from the desk with the glass of vodka, he went to the window, looked out on to a dark, wet Yarm Road. Across from the hotel was Cummins. All Ian knew was that they made engines. The place was huge and was made up of several buildings.

He froze, narrowed his focus.

'What was that?' he whispered, turning around, glaring at the room.

It happened again. A sound, a vibration.

'Hello?'

He glanced at the door, which was locked, the bar securely across the latch. A lonely silence answered him back as he gave his head a shake and drained the remaining vodka, then went back to the desk and placed the empty glass on it.

The sound again.

It was coming from behind him. He swivelled on the carpet, looked at the wide, low bed in front of him. Creeping out the bottom of the pillow near the headboard, was his phone. He went over, pulled it out, and noticed the little blue light flashing at the top of the screen, telling him he had a notification. It could be from WhatsApp. Or something from Facebook. Or a Twitter response – he'd started using that recently, to market himself to the world. Or it could be an email.

It wasn't any of those.

It was a text message.

Sliding the phone to unlock it, he clicked on his inbox. There, he found two messages. The first was a text message from an unknown number. It read:

She didn't see it coming, either.

His heart skipped a beat. Scrolling down to the next message, he noticed the sender's number was the same, but for some reason, the message wouldn't open.

Something was wrong.

Seconds of confusion filled his head before a 'download' bar appeared on the screen. Ian frowned, anticipating its progress as it slowly crawled across the screen. After a few seconds, it was complete, and the message finally downloaded.

A picture message. He clicked open.

His wide eyes zoned in on the contents of the picture. Time stopped when he felt a nauseating white heat slowly filling his feet, making its way up the length of his frozen body, then crawl up his back and across the top of his neck.

Dropping his phone onto the carpet, he threw his hands up to his mouth and gasped at the image.

'No, no, no…' he whispered.

He doubled over and vomited the contents of his stomach onto the floor.

It was now clear to him why his wife had been murdered.

18

Thursday Early hours
Darlington

On the workbench in front of him, there was a selection of instruments. A very sharp scalpel, a small pair of silver forceps, and some short-handled scissors with tips so sharp and fine, it resembled a pin head. Next to the variety of tools, resting on the surface of the high bench, was a black case, lined with various other surgical apparatuses. He took a seat on the leather swivel chair, pulled himself in, and let out a proud smile.

In the world of medicine, the importance of taking proper care of surgical instruments was vital. On a professional level, each instrument that had been used for a medical procedure, had to be cleaned properly. The man looking down at the tools knew there were three stages to this.

Cleaning. The first step was to remove all the dirt and biological matter. He did this using a small bowl of water mixed with cleaning fluid, wearing gloves so it didn't come in contact with his skin. It took him four minutes to clean the dark liquid off the three instruments.

The other two stages were disinfecting and sterilising. He knew how to do this inside out, but he wasn't going to tonight – he didn't need to.

He slid the chair back, stood up, and had one final look. He then placed the tools back into the pouch, rolled it closed, and placed it back on the shelf. High up. Out of the way. Smiling once more, he switched off the light and the garage fell dark.

Stepping into the kitchen, he closed the door, locked it, and headed over to the kettle. The watch on his wrist told him it was after 1 a.m.. Another late one for him.

'Hey… have you seen this?'

He jumped when he heard the voice and frowned looking down the hallway. Normally, his wife would have been in bed hours ago, but tonight, it was anything but normal. She'd been busy doing designs for a new school that the council were building across town. An architect by trade, she also involved herself with the interior aspects of a building too – it flaunted her inner creativity.

The kettle started to rumble. 'Seen what?' he shouted.

'Come here,' she said. 'It's the news, come see.'

He let out a short sigh and padded across the tiled kitchen floor. 'Coming.'

'Here, come watch…' Her arm was extended in mid-air with the television remote fixed to the end of it. 'I can't believe it.' She tapped the seat next her left, indicating for him to sit down. He did.

'What is it?'

'It's the ten o'clock news. I've recorded it. Watch.'

She pressed play and the people started moving on the screen. There was an ambulance, a police van, and two police cars parked on the street. The house the camera was looking at was cordoned off with yellow tape in the shape of a square. A police officer was standing at the end of the driveway.

'What is it?' he asked, impatiently.

'Do you recognise it?' she said, pointing at the screen. 'The street?'

Frowning to aid his concentration, a few seconds passed before he gave a slow shake of the head. 'I – I don't. Where… is it?'

'Brinkburn Drive. About half way down, on the left. I was there the other day, seeing a client who lived across the road. What are the odds?' Her tone was both sad but curious about what was about to follow.

His eyes narrowed a little, almost like slits. 'Erm, yeah, I guess it looks familiar.' He eased back a little, letting himself fall into the soft back of the sofa. 'What happened?'

On the bottom of the screen, the headline was: WIFE FOUND DEAD.

'A woman found dead.'

'Jesus!' he said, giving her a concerned look.

They watched the report for the next four minutes. The reporter said he'd spoken to one of the detectives, a DI Max Byrd from Durham Constabulary, who claimed no leads had been found yet, and that it was an ongoing investigation. Forensics had taken everything they could, and everything that could be analysed, would be analysed using the best resources available over next few days. The reporter claims the detective said, 'No matter what, we'll find out who did this, it's only a matter of time…' before thanking the viewers for watching and that any updates will be aired as soon as there was any progress.

'What's the matter?' she said, seeing something in his face.

He glanced at her. 'What?'

'Do you know him?'

Frowning, he said, 'Who?'

'The detective – the man on the screen?' She watched him curiously.

He shook his head. No, it's just it doesn't happen very often.'

'Alright… hey, what time's your shift start tomorrow?'

'It is *tomorrow* already,' he laughed peeping down at his watch.

'You know what I mean.' She gave him a thin smile.

'Twelve till twelve, tomorrow.'

'A long one?'

He nodded. 'It's going to be like that for the remainder of the week, unfortunately.'

A look of sadness enveloped her face. It was tough being the wife of a man who worked long hours like he did.

'I'm used to it now – we're short staffed,' he added, 'especially this time of year.' He turned and walked away. Just as he reached the door, she said, 'Pick up your stinky underwear before you go in the morning. Lena is coming tomorrow.'

Lena was their cleaner, who'd just started working for them. She went twice a week, keeping the place clean and tidy. It was hard work working all the hours they did and fit in the time to keep the house nice too.

'You know me,' he said, leaving the living room.

'I do – that's why I'm telling you.'

He headed back to the kitchen, making a mental note about needing to give an update on Mrs Connor.

He found the number, pressed a few buttons and put the phone to his ear. Although tired, his body relaxed a little, the bottom of his back resting against the worktop. As it started to ring, he pulled out the high chair under the worktop and sat down.

'Yeah I heard about it,' he said into the phone. 'We've just been watching it on the news, it's awful,' he explained. 'I don't know how anyone could do such a horrific thing.'

'I hope they catch them,' the man replied. 'They could do it again, and probably will, if they're not stopped.'

'Yeah me, too. It's awful, especially being so local to us.'

'I need to go - Mrs Connor has pressed her assistance button.'

'Yeah okay, give her my best. I'll see you tomorrow.'

'See you then, Doctor.'

19

Thursday Morning
Darlington

Ian Porter hadn't slept since he saw the picture message come through on his phone. His eyes were red and sore, his breathing still light and fast. Glaring at the image on the screen in front of him, he sat rigid on the hotel bed and managed to peel his eyes away from it.

The sound coming from the phone startled him, the ringing disturbing the silent room. It was his mother calling. He answered.

'Mam…'

'Hi, Ian, how you holding up?'

Ian didn't answer.

'Love? Are you there?'

'I – I need to go…' he panted and hung up.

'Shit, shit, shit!' he shouted.

He rubbed his face hard, sighed heavily, and thought for a moment. Bending down, he picked up the phone and found the number he needed. Pressed CALL. After three rings, it was answered.

'Ian… this is unexpec—'

'Listen, James,' said Ian, straight to the point, 'listen very carefully… I received a picture message hours ago.'

'Okay…' replied James.

'Do you remember that night?'

'Which night?'

'The night when… when - when she was killed?'

James didn't respond.

'Do you remember?'

'Of course I remember, Ian. It was what – fifteen years ago?'

'Yeah.'

'I was there. I remember. How could I forget that night? It was horrific. Wait – you said you received a picture message. What picture?'

'It's her… it's a picture of her.'

'She's dead, Ian…'

'I know she's dead, God dammit!' Ian sighed, hopelessly.

'What's she doing on the picture?'

'She's just how we left her in the garage that night.'

James didn't reply for a moment, then: 'Who sent the picture?'

Ian physically shook his head, although James couldn't see him. 'It's an unknown number, but I can't reply or phone it.'

'Just hold on for a second, Ian, just take it easy – let's think for a moment here.'

'Who was there, that night?' Ian asked. 'There was me, you, Greg, Stu…'

'What you going to do?' James asked.

'On the message, it said: *she didn't see it coming either.* It's the same message that was written on my dining room table when I found my wife, Julia, yesterday.'

'I heard about that, I'm so sorry, Ian.' James fell awkwardly silent.

'Yeah. I think my wife's murder had something to do with it.'

'Wait – what? You think he did it? He moved abroad, last I heard.'

'Maybe he's come back home…'

20

Thursday Morning
Police Station

Once he got home after saving the elderly man down the alley near Pizza Hut in town from the three men dressed in tracksuits, Tanzy noticed the time was nearly 1 a.m. on the dashboard of his Mercedes when he pulled up on his driveway. Entering the house quietly, he found Phillipa asleep on the sofa in the living room, her dressing gown open, her breasts shamefully hanging to the side.

He'd left her there.

She was in no fit state to carry a civilized conversation and he didn't have the energy or patience to try. He'd wait until the following day to discuss things with her. He didn't want to speak to her so he'd left the silent house first thing without saying a word, assuming she was still asleep.

'Morning, Ori,' he heard from his left, stepping into the warm office.

He offered the man sitting at a computer screen in the second row next the window a smile. 'Good morning.'

'Cold one, isn't it?' the man commented, rotating his head to follow Tanzy's movement.

'You're not kidding.' Tanzy smiled and looked forward.

At his desk, Tanzy took off his long grey Parker coat and put it on the back of his chair, then pulled it out and lowered into it. He couldn't stop thinking about his wife and the state she was in last night in front of the kids. Embarrassing. But he also felt sad, because she'd done so well; almost six months. She was so close.

The door behind him opened, almost silently but loud enough to be heard.

'Morning, Ori,' DCI June Thornton said, stepping out of her office.

He turned one-eighty and looked up at her. 'Morning, boss. How you doing?'

'I'm okay – cold… but okay.' She stopped near him, a cup of coffee in her hand, steam twirling upwards from it. She was wearing a white blouse, covered by a dark blue suit jacket and a knee-length pencil skirt. A scent of perfume enveloped her which was very sweet yet pleasing. 'You heard from Max this morning?'

He gave a sympathetic smile and shook his head. 'I haven't. I sent him a text him before I left the house, but he hasn't replied yet. He'll no doubt have—'

'Good morning,' said a chirpy, upbeat voice.

Tanzy looked right.

Thornton looked left.

'What – what are you doing here, Max?' DCI Thornton asked, shocked to see him.

Byrd took off his long black coat, hung it over the back of his chair and pulled it out. 'I'm working,' he said, smiling. He sat down, turned towards his computer, and dragged his chair in.

'Max, your – your parents are in a coma. You need to go home. I think it's—'

Byrd swivelled quickly, raising a sudden palm. 'I appreciate your concern. I do. And to be honest, if anyone else was in my situation, I would totally agree with you – I would advise it. But the truth is, I've already been to the hospital this morning and nothing has changed. I was told by one of the doctors that the likelihood of anything changing this morning is very unlikely. So if it's okay with you, I'd rather keep my mind active and be here. I'd only be sitting at home over thinking things. And I – I don't want to do that.'

Tanzy threw a tight smile his way, knowing his colleague and understanding his point. Byrd was a driven individual and needed to be focused on something – it kept him going.

Tanzy, on the other hand, would happily sit on the sofa, watching some Chinese martial art film if he had the chance to.

'Okay, Max…' DCI Thornton said slowly. 'I understand. Just – just take it easy, okay? If things at all are feeling too much, just go home, Max.'

Byrd nodded at her in appreciation. 'Okay.'

'Have we made any progress on Julia Porter?' she asked, moving to the left and grabbing a chair from the desk on the other side of the walkway.

Tanzy and Byrd remained quiet for a few seconds. Thornton took a sip of her hot coffee as she pulled the chair back, sat down, and waited for an update. They both turned towards the contents on their desks. Byrd soon hit a wall, realising he wasn't there much of yesterday due to his parent's accident and glanced towards Tanzy, who was currently stifling through unorganised paperwork.

'Em,' Tanzy began, 'we haven't received anything back yet from forensics – it's too soon but I'll chase it up today.'

Nodding, she got up. 'Okay, I've got the superintendent on my case so let me know when you have something.' Then to Byrd: 'I appreciate you coming in, Max, but if at any time today, you need to go, don't hesitate.'

'Understood.'

Tanzy waited for Thornton to close her door before angling his body towards Byrd. 'Hey buddy, you alright?'

For a second, Byrd didn't reply.

'Max?'

'I have to be, don't I?' he said, without looking in his direction, fighting back the tears. 'The doctors said they'll get in touch if there's anything I need to know. No point in me just sitting there, getting all upset over it. I can't physically do anything – it's up to them now.'

Leaning across on his chair, Tanzy placed a palm on the side of Byrd's shoulder, who acknowledged it with a tight smile. Tanzy could see he was holding back his emotions, so lowered his hand from Byrd's shoulder and returned his focus back to his computer.

'I was up late last night,' Tanzy said. Byrd, hearing a certain tone, and knowing him well, knew there was a good reason for it.

'How come?'

'Pip… she – she nearly went six months, Max. Nearly fucking six months.' Tanzy dropped his head. 'So disappointing.'

'How was she—'

'She was a state. Out of it. I got in and she was swaying around the living room. The kids were there. I thought she'd cracked it this time, Max, I really did.' Tanzy fell quiet for a moment, unsure whether to say the next part. Byrd knew there was something else and waited. 'There was a mark on Jasmine's arm…'

'A mark?'

Tanzy bobbed his head, making eye contact with Byrd. 'A bruise.'

'She never?'

'She did, mate.'

'Awful,' Byrd commented. 'It's awful what drink can do to good people. I hope she really digs deep and sorts—'

'I think I want a divorce,' Tanzy said, almost surprising himself with his words.

It would break his heart ruining the family he had at home. His kids, Eric and Jasmine, would be devastated. But if he wasn't happy, his sadness would only rub off on them, and that's the last thing he wanted. He couldn't leave them with her though, he didn't trust her anymore. Even after all the promises she'd made, all she'd done is let them down time and time again.

'Big decision, Ori.' This time it was Byrd's turn to place a palm on Tanzy's back. After a few seconds, he pulled it back.

'Yup.'

'Where are the kids?'

'At her mams – she doesn't want to talk to her either. She's had enough.'

Byrd digested his words. 'I hope you get things sorted, mate. It's not healthy for the kids.'

The office was warm and smelt of coffee. Tanzy stood up, made his way over to the office door after asking Byrd if he wanted one. Stopping near the doorway of the office, he had a short conversation with one of the admin girls who was holding a pile of paperwork close to her chest, looking nervous but there was a confident sparkle in her eye.

Byrd tipped his head back, looking over the top of his computer screen, watching him. To his knowledge, the girl, Charlotte, if Byrd remembered correctly, was in her early twenties. She always seemed on cloud nine when she saw Tanzy, which was fair enough; Tanzy was a good-looking man. Byrd could appreciate that. There were only four years between him and Tanzy, but Tanzy dressed a decade younger, no question about it. Byrd wasn't the biggest fan of fashion. He had nice clothes, but he'd choose comfort over fashion any day. Smiling, he glanced back to his computer screen, clicking on the tab titled reports. Once it opened, he read the report on Julia Porter.

Minutes later, Tanzy returned to the desk and sat down. He rattled the mouse to awaken the computer screen, logged on and waited for the system to boot up.

'Anything with the missing girl yet?' Byrd asked, angling his body towards Tanzy. It had been eight days since she was last seen.

'Not yet, Max.' Tanzy gave a sigh and shook his head. 'There will be, though, I made a promise to her parents. It seldom happens in this town and I'm going to find her – I promised them.'

Byrd gave a thin smile, returned his attention to his own screen.

The office started to fill with the low drone of activity from fellow colleagues readying themselves for the day. Every Thursday at 9 a.m., there was a meeting with DCI June Thornton in the conference room. All the DI's gave updates to the whole team on current investigations and told them of any updates or strategies that were in place. Although some members of the team weren't personally invested in certain cases, everyone came together as a team and suggested ideas or anything they deemed helpful. Some of it was used, some of it, ignored. All a part of the process.

The door opened behind them.

'Orion,' DCI June Thornton said. Tanzy turned.

'Yeah?'

'A word please?'

Tanzy stood up, stepped into her office, and closed the door.

21

Thursday Morning
Darlington town centre

High Row in the centre of town was busy. Small markets were being set up. Men and women moved around their own stalls, pinning up advertising banners and arranging their merchandise, telling passers-by about their daily offers. There was E-liquids, socks, t-shirts with rock bands on, double glazing, you name it.

The man selling e-liquids and vape accessories shouting about the three bottles of liquid for the price of two fell on the deaf ears of Mary Richards, who was walking along with her four-year-old daughter, Mia. One hand was holding the phone to her head, and the other, had tight hold of her daughter's hand, as they weaved in and out of the early crowds.

They passed Post House Wynd on their right and continued, heading towards Binns. In the window of Greggs, Mia saw a fairy cake covered with orange icing under a green coloured butterfly with big eyes. She slowed and tugged on her mother's hand.

'Mia – what?' Mary sighed.

'Mama, I want,' her little voice said.

'Mia, come on,' her mother replied, her attention mostly on the phone call.

Mia stopped, causing Mary to come to a halt. 'I want.'

'Let me call you back,' she said into the phone and placed it back into her bag. Mary lowered down to her daughter's height. 'Mia, I said no. We'll get something a little later, it's not even ten o'clock yet. Okay?'

Mia pushed out her bottom lip and it didn't take long for that to pull on Mary's heartstrings.

'Mia wants,' her daughter said softly.

'Okay, baby,' said Mary, rising to her feet. 'You can't eat it now, though. You have to wait until after lunch.'

A dull glisten appeared in Mia's eyes. 'Okay.'

'Is that a deal?'

'Okay, Mummy. Deal.'

Mary took her daughter's hand and they stepped up into Greggs. The heater above the door kept the place warm and the smell of freshly baked pastries spilled over the top of the counter.

'What do you want?' Mary asked, looking down at her blonde-haired four-year-old.

'The one in the window!' she pleaded.

Turning away from Mia, Mary peeked over the glass counter and caught the attention of a lady who was wearing a smile and an apron and told her what she wanted. The woman nodded and walked away, then moments later, handed her the cake.

'Mammy, can I—'

'No, Mia,' Mary said firmly, 'I told you. After lunch.' The assistant smiled at Mary knowingly, and watched them leave the shop. They turned right in the direction of Binns when they heard a coarse voice behind them.

'Excuse me, excuse me.'

Mary slowed, turning with Mia. A man approached them dressed in an old grey tracksuit and looked to be in his forties, possibly older. He carried an old carrier bag in one hand, and a white Greggs packet in the other.

'Me?' Mary asked, pointing at herself.

'Yeah,' the man grunted. 'Are you Mary?'

Mary, subconsciously took a short step back, placing an arm across her daughter, an automatic reaction a parent would do when speaking to a stranger. 'Yes, I'm Mary?'

The man stopped a few feet before them. 'You left this?' He pointed behind him in the direction of Greggs.

The man held out his arm, handing her the Greggs packet. Frowning, she was confused. She'd only ordered the butterfly cake for Mia, didn't she? Unless she—

'Here,' the man said, leaning forward, encouraging her to take it.

Mary took the packet and thanked him. The man smiled, gave them both a nod and turned. Within seconds, he was lost in the crowd.

'What is it, Mummy?' Mia asked. 'Is it another cake for me?'

'I – I don't know.' Mary let go of Mia's hand and used her fingers to open the packet. She tilted her head forward and peered inside.

Her eyes widened as she dropped the bag on the floor. The contents of the bag rolled out onto the pavement as she threw her hands to her mouth.

Everyone glared at her when she screamed.

22

Thursday Late Morning
Police Station

Byrd headed back to his desk with a glass of water. His choice would usually be coffee but he felt a headache coming and he knew from past experience that coffee only made it worse. He noticed Tanzy at his desk glaring at his screen. It was just before lunch time, according to the clock near the door of DCI June Thornton's office.

As he sat down, Byrd noticed a box of salad in front of Tanzy. 'Ori, why are you eating salads – there's nothing on you?'

'I know but—'

'How much do you weigh – wait, let me guess… thirteen stone, give or take a few pounds.'

Tanzy raised his eyebrows to a valiant effort. 'Good guess.'

Byrd smiled. 'Not just a pretty face, you know. But seriously, why the salad?'

'I'm trying to keep trim.'

'You have a six pack. You're six foot, two, with nothing on you but muscle. You can't get any trimmer than that. Unless you're modelling for Men's Health next month or something?'

'They couldn't afford me.' Tanzy and Byrd shared a laugh. 'How much you weighing nowadays, Max?'

'I apologise but Max Byrd isn't available right now. If you could leave a message and he'll get back to you on his return.'

Tanzy smirked, focused back on his screen, his fingertips typing away on the keyboard.

Byrd took a sip of water, leaned in towards Tanzy. 'What was the meeting about with Thornton, Ori?'

Tanzy stopped typing. 'It was about you.'

'Me?' Byrd placed his glass of water on the desk. 'What about me?'

'About how stable you are?' Tanzy said, slowly turning towards him.

'Are you serious?' Byrd said, narrowing his eyes.

'Yeah.' Tanzy said. 'She asked me, with what's happening with your parents, are you in a stable enough condition to be at work.'

'Stable?'

'Yeah, mentally stable.'

Silence grew between them for a long moment as the concerned look swept across Byrd's face. 'What did you say?'

'I said absolutely not. I told her you're the worst DI I've ever worked with. That you've never been any good.' They both smiled. Tanzy added, 'I told her I'd never worked with anyone more capable and focused in my life. I told her if anything, it would give you more focus because you know how to channel your concentration.'

Byrd nodded admiringly. 'Appreciate that.'

'Have you heard anything from the hospital?'

Byrd shook his head, told him he hadn't. 'I'll ring on my break to see if there's an update.' Byrd had been away in a meeting for an hour in the room along the hall, room 102, with his team, discussing ideas to crack down on shoplifting in and around Darlington.

Tanzy's mobile phone rang from inside the pocket of his trousers. He pulled it out and answered it.

'DI Orion Tanzy speaking… Oh hi … When? … Okay … thanks for telling me … okay… …I'll be right there.' He put the phone on the desk.

'Who's that?' Byrd asked. 'You're frowning - it's something serious when you're frowning. Why are you frowning?'

'Cornty. He said he's in town on High Row. Apparently it's important and I need to be there. Are you coming?'

'Yeah, why not, I wouldn't mind stretching my legs anyway.' Byrd stood, grabbed his long coat from the back of his chair.

'What's he found?' Byrd asked.

'He said a woman has found something in a Greggs' packet.'

'Greggs packet – what is it?'

'Cornty said it could be just what we're looking for.'

They pulled up in front of Timpson's near the town clock. Byrd applied the X5's handbrake. Up on the steps near Post House Wynd to their right, they could see a small crowd gathering. PC Cornty had informed Tanzy the area had been cordoned off and that other PC's were at the scene securing the perimeter. With the buzz of people around, it was perhaps the worst location for this to happen.

'Looks serious,' Byrd commented as they climbed the steps.

'Serious enough for people to stop their busy schedules and have a look anyway.'

'If everybody could just keep back, please,' they heard a voice say up ahead. 'Thank you, thank you.'

They reached the back of the crowd and slowed, scanning the people, trying to locate PC Cornty. It didn't take them long. He was an easy find. He was standing at the far side of the perimeter talking to a man. At the scene, there were four officers and someone inside the perimeter. That someone was Jacob Tallow, the senior forensic. He was close to the floor down on one knee, leaning over something. The perimeter was squared-shaped, covering the front of the Mountain Warehouse shop.

Byrd and Tanzy veered around the crowd and headed towards PC Cornty.

'Cornty,' Tanzy said.

The PC looked to his left, and almost stiffened, as if standing to attention. 'Hey, Ori. Hey, Max.'

They both nodded. Tanzy said, 'What do we have here, Phillip?'

'Hey, is this going to be much longer – I'm waiting on a phone call about a delivery,' a voice said from behind them.

Byrd and Tanzy turned, noticed a gentleman dressed in a dark blue jumper with a Mountain Warehouse logo on.

'Listen, Sir,' PC Cornty said, stepping forward with a raised palm, 'we're doing all we can, I can assure you of that. If you kindly could keep your patience, we'll be able to complete this task more efficiently and be out of your way sooner.'

Byrd heard the frustration in Cornty's voice but admired his professionalism, assuming it wasn't the first time the frustrated man had posed the question.

'Come on, I'm losing customers, they can't get into my shop,' he pleaded, glaring past Tanzy directly at Cornty.

Byrd gave a tight smile and took over, edging forward a few inches. 'We can only apologise for this, Mr…?'

'Mr Fortley.'

'Hi, Mr Fortley,' Byrd said. 'I'm Detective Inspector Max Byrd of Durham Constabulary. This is my colleague, Detective Inspector Orion Tanzy. We can only apologise for the delay and I can assure you, that we are doing everything we can.'

Mr Fortley gave a reluctant nod, then stepped backwards, now realising he was outnumbered. 'Fine!'

'So, Phil, what do we have?' Byrd said, turning back to PC Cornty.

Cornty pointed to the other side of the tape, where PC Kim Harrison was talking with a red-haired lady standing with a small blonde-haired girl. 'Go and see Kim over there, she's speaking with the woman you need to talk to.'

Tanzy and Byrd followed his finger and headed under the tape, crossing the front of Mountain Warehouse. To his right, he watched Tallow carefully place the evidence which was found in the Greggs' packet into a small clear plastic bag. Tallow glanced up at Byrd and gave him a courteous, professional nod.

On the other side of the perimeter, they ducked under the plastic barrier.

'Morning,' PC Kim Harrison said.

'Hey, Kim,' Tanzy replied.

Byrd smiled.

'This is Mary Richards,' Harrison started, and then pointed to the small girl in front of her, 'and this is her daughter, Mia.'

'Hi, Mary.' Byrd smiled. He then lowered to Mia's height and grinned. 'Hi, Mia, how are you?'

Mia was nervous but managed a shy smile, tucking herself into her mother without saying anything. Byrd rubbed the side of her small shoulder softly, then stood, switching his focus to Mary.

'So, Mrs Richards, would you mind explaining to us what exactly happened?'

Mary pulled a face, suggesting it was an inconvenience to her, as if she'd explained it over and over. 'Yes. Okay, then.'

Byrd and Tanzy waited.

A small number of people stood nearby. Byrd directed his attention away from the Richards and signalled to one of the PC's to move them backwards, so they couldn't hear what was being said. The PC nodded and used his authority to shift the crowd back a few paces.

'We came out of Greggs,' Mary Richards started, 'and a man called my name – I don't know how he knew my name. I didn't recognise him when I turned. Then he handed me a Greggs bag and told me I've left it. I was sure we only bought one item. The cake for Mia'— Mary squeezed her daughter's shoulder slightly–'but I took it anyway, thinking I'd maybe made a mistake.'

'Okay,' Tanzy said.

'I opened the packet and that's when I saw…' she trailed off, not wanting to discuss it with her daughter present – she'd already seen enough to scar her for life.

'Okay. Would you mind coming to the station to answer a few questions? It would be very helpful if we could get an official statement from you – it would assist us in finding this man.'

Mary sighed impatiently, glancing down at her wrist watch. 'Will it take long? I was meant to be dropping Mia off and going to work.'

'Not at all,' Byrd said, 'thirty minutes at the most. We need to find this man – with your help, we'll be able to. And considering the situation, I'm confident your employer would understand.'

'That's okay with you honey, isn't it?' Mary said, leaning forward, directing the question directed at Mia, who bobbed her head three times in response.

'Okay, good.' Byrd turned to PC Kim Harrison. 'Kim, could you take Mary and her daughter, Mia, to the station?'

'Sure, boss.' Harrison stepped forward smiling at Mary and Mia. 'You two want to follow me?'

Mary and Mia Richards left the scene and headed towards the car which was parked outside of the Indoor market.

Tanzy watched them leave, then turned back to Byrd. 'Let's go see Tallow.'

'Yeah.'

Jacob Tallow stood near the entrance door of Mountain Warehouse. A camera hung from his neck. He held an iPad in his right hand and by his feet, there was a rucksack, and inside, the evidence he'd just placed there. He lowered to the floor, looped the camera off from around his neck.

'Tallow,' Byrd said. Tanzy, a step behind him, watched the crowds start to disperse; there was nothing left to see. Show was over.

Tallow glanced up. 'Hey, Max, how are you on this fine morning?'

'Living the dream. Is it bagged up?'

'Yeah,' he said, pointing down to his rucksack.

'Would you mind if I…?'

'Be my guest,' he said, lowering down to the bag, placing the iPad carefully onto his folded jacket. He unzipped the bag and cautiously pulled out the small clear plastic bag. 'There you go.'

Byrd turned his body away from the crowds, hiding what they were looking at. 'Jesus,' he gasped.

'Do you think they belong to Julia Porter?' Tanzy asked, leaning in.

Byrd sighed. 'It's possible. It's likely under the circumstances. Same town. There's not many eyeballs go missing very often. The question is, why were they specifically handed to Mary Richards in a Greggs packet?'

'Let's go find out.'

23

Thursday Late Morning
Brinkburn Drive

Ian Porter put down his phone, dropped it on the sofa to his left. Thinking about the picture message he'd received, he threw himself forward and raised his trembling palms up to his face.

'Fuck,' he cried, his weak voice muffled through his cupped hands. He'd came straight home after checking out of the hotel. His mother was dropping the kids off soon. It would be their first-time home since their mother was murdered. The last thing he wanted to do was tell his children what had happened to her, but he had to; it was his job.

The hurt would be unbearable, he knew.

Porter ambled to the kitchen and stared at nothing. He didn't move. Frozen against the free-standing worktop, his hand was firmly on the wooden surface to steady himself. The thought of his kids walking through the door not knowing what had happened to Julia sickened him to the core.

After forcing himself to make a cup of coffee to distract himself from the horrible thoughts swimming around in his head, he drifted back into the living room and sat down. To his left, the door through to the dining room was closed; he had no intention of opening it just yet. He placed the hot drink on the windowsill and picked up his phone.

The picture that the unknown number had been sent stared up at him. It repulsed him. He felt it coming but couldn't stop the sick from climbing up his throat and projecting from his mouth, landing on the rug near his feet.

There was a knock at the door.

'Fuck, fuck.' He wiped his mouth quickly with the back of his hand and stared down at the sicky bile on the floor, the smell immediately filling the room.

He opened the door. 'Hey, kids.'

Jonah and Cameron were standing on the front step. Liam was behind, in his nana's arms. A cool breeze seeped into the house from outside. The sky was grey and the street was dim. Winter was truly on its way. His children – even Liam - all smiled at him with an excitement that crushed every part of his body. His eldest, Jonah, stepped over the lip of the door and hugged him tightly.

'Hi, Daddy.'

'Hey, Son,' Ian replied in almost a whisper, kissing the top of his head.

'Where's Mum?' he asked.

The question hung in the hallway until Ian let out a sigh. He exchanged a brief glance with his mother, Irene, who knew this wasn't going to be easy.

Cameron then stepped inside and hugged him. 'Where's Mammy? Me want to see Mammy?'

'Come in…' he said, his voice almost breaking, 'I need to have a little word with you. In there.' He pointed towards the living room.

'Can I play on Fortnite, Dad?' Jonah asked, eagerly shuffling on the spot. He hadn't played on his Xbox since he was last there. Ian looked sadly at his son for a moment: Dressed in a blue Adidas tracksuit, his hair swept neatly over to one side, the innocent face of an eight-year-old staring up at him. He didn't know the horrors his father was about to tell him.

'Where's Mammy?' Cameron repeated, clutching at his leg. 'Me see Mammy.'

Ian winced a little, feeling the tears form in his eyes but fought them back as he placed his hand softly on his head. 'Come on, in here. Daddy needs to tell you all something.'

'Erhh, what's that?' Cameron said, pointing to the sick on the floor in the living room. He brought his hand up to his mouth. 'Smelly.'

'Ahh, sick. Daddy, are you sick?' Jonah asked, his little face adorably concerned.

'Don't worry – Daddy is better now. Please - please sit down all of you.' He motioned with his palm towards the sofa. Jonah sat down. Cameron reached the sofa but remained standing with his back resting against it. Ian's mother took a seat on the single swivel chair to the left and placed Liam on her knee.

Taking a deep breath, Ian lowered to his knees in the middle of the floor and faced them all. He stared at his children, particularly Cameron and Jonah. 'I… I –'

Liam made a sound which silenced him for a moment. It sounded like he said 'Maaaam.'

'I need to tell you something,' he began. 'I don't really know how to say this.' His eyes fell to the floor for a moment.

'Daddy, what is it?' Jonah asked, seeing the concerned look on his father's face.

'It's about your mum.' He took a few slow breaths. 'She… she died. She erm—' he expelled a sudden breath, stopping himself from bursting into tears. 'She - she isn't coming home.'

The silence that followed was deafening. It lasted for three seconds until Jonah's face changed and he threw himself into the sofa and balled his little eyes out. Cameron, turning to watch Jonah, turned back to Ian, not fully understanding at the tender age of three, the severity of what was going on.

'Mammy not here?' he said.

Ian slowly shook his head at his son.

Out of the corner of his eye, he saw his mother wiping the streams of tears cascading down her face. He held everything back for the sake of the kids but watching and hearing Jonah wail on the sofa, broke him.

Finding his feet, he let out a cry and sat down next to Jonah, scooping his quivering body up in his arms. Cameron, seeing his big brother cry, started to cry too. He buried himself in between Ian's legs and held him tightly.

Ian's mother, Irene, watched her son and two grandsons on the sofa, clutching each other closely, floods of tears between them. In her arms, Liam sat nicely, oblivious to the news his father had just told his brothers. He didn't know, but soon, he'd grow up without a mother.

And it was all his father's fault.

24

Thursday Afternoon
Darlington Town Hall

Jennifer Lucas, the tall, thin well-dressed woman sitting at the desk in the control room of the Town Hall, heard the phone ring to her right. She picked it up.

'Hello, Jennifer in the DBC control room, how can I help?'

As usual, her voice was lovely, carrying the calm, confident warmth it usually did, making Tanzy all soft as he melted into the phone. She had a slightly different accent, as if she was raised somewhere closer to Durham or Newcastle.

'Good afternoon, Jennifer, it's—'

'Detective Inspector Orion Tanzy?' she said.

For a second, he was lost for words. 'How – how did you know?'

'I can tell by your accent,' she said, letting out a quiet giggle.

Considering he moved from South Africa when he was four years old, he still carried a slight accent. Often, people never noticed but others did when he pronounced some of his words a little different.

'I need your help, Jenny.'

'What's up, Ori?'

'We had an accident earlier today on High Row – I need to see the footage.'

'What's the time?'

Tanzy didn't reply straight away. Then: 'It's just after two.'

She laughed. 'Not now, Orion, what time frame do you need?'

'Oh… sorry.' Tanzy fell silent, feeling stupid. 'Between ten and half past ten, please.'

'What part of High Row are you needing to see?'

'I need the camera closest to Greggs.'

'Okay, I'll send it over ASAP.'

'Thank you – hey, do—'

She hung up and Tanzy curled his lip. In hindsight, he was glad she did because he wasn't sure what he was going to say. Probably something stupid. He put the phone down and focused on the computer in front of him.

'Have you heard back from forensics?' A voice said from behind him. He turned to see DCI Thornton standing at her door, her hand resting on the handle, a look of impatience on her tired-looking face. 'Any updates?' she asked eagerly.

'Not yet. Guna chase it up very soon. Just looking over the CCTV on High Row.'

'We need results, Orion.'

'I know… I'm on it.'

She nodded firmly, retreating back into the office and closing the door without saying anything else. Tanzy understood the pressure she was under from the superintendent. If you looked in the Dictionary for the word arsehole, you wouldn't be surprised to see the name, Barry Eckles. There was simply no way of dressing it up. Thornton, Byrd, Tanzy, and the rest of the good folk sitting in this office were lucky his office was located on a different floor. He usually only showed his face a couple of times a day and even that was too much. Tanzy had seen him in her office earlier, heard him raising his voice about something he wasn't happy about. When he left, he wasn't shy about slamming the door either.

A 'ping' sound came from the computer. An email. He opened it up. The footage from High Row appeared in the corner of the screen. Tanzy double clicked it open. The time in the top corner informed him it was 10.00 a.m.. The camera angle was positioned five shops along from Greggs, close to the House of Fraser, covering the width of the pavement all the way down to Barclay's bank.

Leaning forward, trying to block out the background hum of the office noise, Tanzy squinted in concentration. Beyond

Greggs, he noticed a man sitting cross-legged on the floor, just past the cut of Post House Wynd. The camera picked up on the vivid colours, his tracksuit a shade of light grey.

For the next fourteen minutes, Tanzy watched people walk up and down, in and out of view, people walking across the screen, people stopping to talk and people sitting on the benches on the right-hand side.

Until he saw them.

Walking towards the camera from the distance. Mary and Mia. Although far away, he saw the man in the grey tracksuit glance up briefly as they walked by. Mary and Mia passed Post House Wynd and Mia tugged on her hand. Mary seemed to finish her phone call and turned back to her daughter, who was pointing at the window of Greggs. After a short discussion, she led her daughter into the shop.

'Ahh, what's that?' Tanzy whispered.

Using the mouse, he scrolled the time frame back ninety-four seconds.

As Mary and Mia stepped into the shop, a man that was sitting on a bench on the right side of the screen, wearing a black fleece and dark blue jeans, stood up and made his way over to the man in the grey tracksuit. He bent down, spoke to the man for around ten seconds, then pointed towards the direction of Greggs. The man in the black fleece nodded several times at the man on the floor, reaching inside his of pocket and then handed him two objects.

One of them looked like a small white bag; the other, Tanzy couldn't quite make out. He scrolled the time line back and tried to zoom in but whatever it was, was too small to be seen.

Standing, the man turned and started walking, unfortunately for Tanzy, away from the camera. As Mary and Mia came back into view, the man in the grey tracksuit climbed to his feet and followed them. They turned, and the man handed her the small bag. The camera didn't show it very well, but it did match up with the events which Mary Richards had told them.

'Who is the man in the black fleece?' he asked himself.

25

Thursday late afternoon
Darlington Memorial Hospital

Byrd checked in with the ITU receptionist who instructed him to take a seat on the chair behind him. He turned slowly, ambled over, and dropped into one of the empty chairs. A clinical smell floated in the air, familiar to a usual hospital smell.

In the seat, he glanced around; the waiting room was empty, but the usual pitter patter of feet filled the corridor to his right.

The door to his left opened.

Byrd craned his neck. Dr Ching walked through the door and half-smiled at him.

'Good afternoon, Mr Byrd,' he said.

Byrd stood, extended his hand. 'Hey, Doctor, how they doing?'

'Follow me, please, Sir.'

Byrd went to say something, but Dr Ching turned before he had the chance to, and they both walked through the door into a short corridor and angled round to the left. There was an open door to the right-hand side with 'Dr Ching' written on a white plate in thin black letters.

'In here,' he said.

Byrd entered the small room and stood awkwardly, unsure where to sit. They were three chairs, a high bed, a shelving unit, a window with blue curtains draped down either side, and a desk to the left of the room in the corner. To the right, a shelving unit containing files and plastic boxes filled with medicinal equipment and bottles stood tall and proud. A pleasant smell of deodorant lingered in the small space, but Byrd couldn't see any deodorant lying around; probably tucked away in one of the three drawers under the desk.

'Please, take a seat.' The doctor motioned with his palm towards the two seats located to the right. The doctor lowered into the other seat, next to the desk.

Byrd sat down. 'How are they?'

For a moment, Dr Ching didn't reply until he was fully settled and focused. He gave a gentle sigh and let his eyes fall on Byrd, who sat patiently, leaning forward in his chair with his eyes locked on the doctor.

'Mr Byrd… things aren't going as well as we'd hoped unfortunately.' He paused for a moment to let that sink in. Byrd nodded lightly but waited for more. 'Our first assessment of your parents,' the doctor went on, 'was that your father seemed in a healthier state in comparison to your mother, but unfortunately, your father isn't recovering as well as we'd hoped. He—'

'What do you mean not as well as you'd hoped?'

'His body isn't recovering as quickly. He—'

'What do you mean, Doctor?' Byrd's heart rate went up a notch.

'Your father's score is similar from when I first saw him.'

'You mean on the Glasgow Coma Scale?'

The doctor smiled inside at the detectives awareness of the term. 'Yes,' the doctor said sadly. 'The good news is that your mother is showing signs of improvement. Her score from the three categories are seven, which is an improvement from the original three.'

'What's my fathers?'

'Four, detective Byrd. He's improved only one I'm afraid.'

Silence grew while Byrd pondered his thoughts. He started to feel hot in his long coat and placed his fingers between his throat and collar to allow a little air in.

'Do you want to see them?'

Byrd nodded twice. 'Please.'

Dr Ching stood up. 'Follow me.'

Along the brightly lit corridor, they took a left, passed a nurse who was sitting on a chair writing something on the clipboard which rested on her knee. She glanced up and gave Dr Ching a courteous smile. He stopped beside her.

'This is Janine, the nurse who's monitoring your parents, Mr Byrd.'

She smiled, placed her pen on the clipboard and extended her hand towards Byrd. 'Hi, Mr Byrd.'

'Hi, Janine,' said Byrd, leaning down and taking it. 'Thank you for your care and everything you're doing for them.'

'Please, call me Jan.'

Byrd nodded.

They walked further until Dr Ching opened the door on the right and stepped inside. 'Take as long as you need,' he said, before turning and leaving the room.

Byrd entered the space and took it all in again, like he'd done before on his last visit. The two beds, side by side, the equipment, the flashing lights, the constant regular beeping. Standing between them at the foot of their beds, he glanced left and right.

'Hi, Mam. Hi, Dad.'

For the next few minutes, he spoke to them individually, telling them how much he loved them and how important it was for them to wake up. He informed his father specifically that Newcastle were needing their number one fan back and told his mother that Silent Witness was in desperate need of their number one viewer.

After ten minutes, Byrd decided to turn and leave. He passed Janine in the corridor who glimpsed up at him.

'You going?' she asked.

'Yeah. Is Dr Ching around?'

'He just left before. He took an urgent call and had to leave.'

'Okay, tell him I said bye.'

'I will,' she said. 'We'll keep you updated with anything, Mr Byrd.' She smiled, showing her perfectly white teeth. Byrd guessed she was around forty but could pass for thirty if you didn't look too closely at the crow's feet lining the corners of her eyes. Her blonde hair, although quite short, was kept and maintained. A very attractive woman.

'Thank you. I'd appreciate that.'

In the wide corridor outside of the ICU, he angled a right, joining the traffic of people heading towards the exit. In front of him, a man was hunched over pushing an elderly lady in a wheelchair.

'It won't be long, Mam, they need to do more tests on you,' he heard the man say to her.

'I'm sick of this, I need to get out,' she replied, her voice deflated.

'Soon, Mam, let's get some air.'

Byrd moved around them and walked down the centre of the corridor until he reached the end where he took a left. As he rounded the bend, something collided hard into his right shoulder and knocked him off balance, causing his left shoulder to impact the corner of the hard wall.

'Jesus!' he shouted, confused, not knowing what had happened.

'Shit,' he heard a voice say to his right.

Crouching down, holding his left shoulder with the opposite hand, Byrd glanced up at the man. It was Dr Ching.

'Are you in a hurry or something, Doctor?' Byrd asked, a touch of anger in his voice, still feeling the roaring pain where he'd hit the wall. 'Slow down a little, will you?'

'I am so - so sorry, Mr Byrd, I—'

'You need to watch where you're going, Dr Ching,' Byrd said, finishing his sentence. 'If that was a little girl or boy instead of me, you'd have really…'

The doctor raised a palm. 'I do apologise, truly. Please accept my apology.' He looked flustered, as if not quite with it, his eyes darting left and right.

Passers-by came to a halt and watched the minor altercation, as did the man pushing the old lady behind them.

'Come on, we haven't got all day,' the lady in the wheelchair said in frustration.

Placing a palm on to the outside of the doctor's arm, Byrd said, 'Hey, don't worry about it – no harm done. Not this time anyway.' A smile crept across his face, but the doctor just nodded and walked away with the small black case clutched in one arm.

Strange, Byrd thought to himself. How he went from being so polite and professional, to this.

'Show's over folks,' he told the people who'd stopped to watch, then headed towards the exit.

The fresh, cold air hit Byrd like a slap in the face. To his right, an Ambulance slowed and let him walk the crossing. Byrd thanked the driver with a palm.

'I'm coming, I'm coming,' Byrd heard a voice say to his right.

Along the path near a small fenced grassy area, Byrd saw doctor Ching marching down the side of the car park. Through years of training on human behaviour, Byrd had acquired the talent of reading people's body language. He could recognise lying, truth, frustration, love, all by the way that someone moved their body. The doctor stepped off the curb down into the carpark and hurried across towards a blue Skoda Octavia. He pressed the fob and got inside.

'There's definitely something on his mind,' Byrd whispered, looking away and angling to the left towards his own car. He picked out his phone and rang Tanzy to check on the latest cases.

It had been another tough day. Little did they know, tomorrow would be even worse.

26

Thursday Late Afternoon
Darlington

'Hello, Mrs Ching,' said Lena, the cleaner, who'd just emptied the bin in the kitchen.

'Please, call me Marie,' Mrs Ching said, walking past her in the direction of the kettle. 'Would you like a coffee?'

Lena, who was somewhere between thirty and forty, shook her head. 'Not while I work – it distracts me.'

'You've been working for over an hour already without a break. Come on, you could do with a drink.'

She pondered the question for a few moments. 'Okay.' She opened the back door and disappeared for a short while with the bin bag and returned a minute later.

'You don't take sugar do you?'

Lena shook her head. 'No, thank you, Mrs Ching – I mean, Marie. Sorry.'

Marie smiled, stirring the coffee. 'Anything planned for the weekend?'

'Not really,' Lena said. 'I'll see what my husband fancies doing.'

'Have you got any other family?' Marie asked, then raised a palm. 'Sorry, I'm being personal, you've only just started cleaning for us recently.'

It was only her second month cleaning at the Ching's house, which she did twice a week, without fail. It would normally last around two hours, sometimes three, and she charged them by the hour. They didn't mind – she did a fantastic job. Marie wanted her there all the time, but doctor Ching said it was an unnecessary cost. She did the hoovering, kitchen, and bathroom mainly but sometimes, Mrs Ching would ask her to polish the kitchen cupboards and the wooden furniture which normally took her into her third hour.

'Hey, don't worry,' she replied, 'if you're meaning children, no, we don't have children. My husband and I tried many years ago, but it just didn't happen for us. I'm not exactly a spring chicken anymore so I'm guessing it's too late now.'

'How old are you if you don't mind me asking?' Marie shuffled across the tiled floor and handed Lena her coffee, who accepted it gratefully.

'Thank you. I'm thirty-six.'

'Plenty of time to have children. Your husband, is he—'

'Older?'

Marie Ching nodded then took a sip of coffee.

'Only by two years,' Lena said.

'Loads of time for you, don't worry. I'm sixty-three and it's true what they say about the body changing but trust me, you have time, that's if you change your mind – you should talk to your husband about it.' Marie glanced towards the circular table near the wall. 'Hey, take a seat, we'll have a little chat while you drink your coffee.'

'I shouldn't, the bathroom upstairs needs—'

'The bathroom upstairs can wait,' Marie countered. 'Please, Lena, have a seat. Relax a little. It'll give me time to get to know you better.'

Marie Ching had hired her, not only because she didn't like doing housework herself, but because she had a challenging, time-consuming job and the last thing she wanted to do at six or seven in the evening was to come in and start cleaning. She wanted to get a bath and put her feet up. Life was too short for housework, so she decided two months ago that it was time to get a cleaner in. After Dr Ching and Marie had discussed it, he'd walked in one evening with a recommendation from Jason at the hospital, one of the pathologists who works along the corridor. Jason had told Dr Ching about Lena and how good she was.

Between themselves, the Ching's decided to give her a trial run of a month to see how things went. They originally left a key under the plant pot near the front door which Lena used to gain access, then placed it back under when she left.

As Marie Ching entered the house after the first afternoon that Mary had cleaned, the smell of lavender hanging in the air and the freshly-bleached bathrooms was so satisfying. Everything else was neat and tidy.

'Yes, yes, yes, this is what I need in my life,' Marie Ching had said two months ago. That same evening, she picked up the phone and told her how pleased she was, and could she come over twice a week. They agreed on a Monday and a Thursday.

'So, Lena, have you lived in Darlington long?' Marie asked, raising the mug to her mouth.

'Almost a year and a half. I was born in Durham and lived there until we decided to move to Darlington.'

'It's nice Durham,' the doctor's wife commented.

'It's lovely. I might move back there one day.'

'What tempted you to move here?'

'It wasn't out of choice. My husband Arthur works in Aycliffe. We live near Cockerton and he said it's easy to get out on the A1. Plus, he's lived here all his life. I met him two years ago.' A look of embarrassment washed over her face. 'Online dating, as it happened.'

'Wow… so them sites do actually work?'

'Did for me…'

They both shared a smile.

Lena drained her coffee and stood up. 'Right, I'll clean the bathroom and your en-suite and then I'll have to make a move.'

'Okay,' Marie said, also finding her feet. 'I need to get these plans done. I've been working from home today. If you need me, I'll be in the dining room.' Marie carefully placed her empty cup in the sink and left the kitchen.

Lena gathered her box of cleaning sprays, gloves, wipes, and selection of bleaches, and made her way along the hallway, then taking a right, she climbed the stairs. At the top, she stopped, turned around, and listened carefully.

After thirty seconds, she realised that Marie was getting on with her work report in the dining room. She smiled to herself, snuck past the bathroom and entered their large master bedroom.

She glanced around looking for it.

It wasn't the first time she'd done this. It was the third. She got quicker each time, becoming familiar with the layout. Her eyes widened when she saw the object resting on the surface of Dr Ching's bedside drawer.

With the box of cleaning stuff, she padded around the bed, her feet cushioned by the soft carpet. At the bedside drawer, she stopped and glanced down at the object next to the base of the lamp.

A smile ran across her face as she bent slightly to pick it up. Very quietly, she placed it in between the cleaning sprays, so it wouldn't be seen—

'What – what are you doing?' she heard a voice behind her.

Lena stiffened slightly and turned quickly. Feeling her face warming, she said, 'Hey, Marie… I was… seeing if the bedside drawers needed a dust,' she explained.

Marie's eyes narrowed a little. 'It's okay, just do the en-suite like normal. I'll ask if there's anything more, okay?'

Lena smiled and gave her a nod. 'Okay, no problem. Sorry.'

With the object hidden in the cleaning box, she made her way passed Mrs Ching and entered the en-suite. Marie left the bedroom and returned back downstairs, leaving Lena to wonder why she'd come upstairs in the first place.

In the confines of the en-suite, Lena sighed heavily.

That was a close call.

27

Thursday Evening
Darlington

Mary and Mia Richards stepped through their front door into the dimly-lit hallway just after seven. Mary closed the door, shutting out the uninvited cold that seeped in, and placed her keys on the table next to the base of the thin lamp. The heat coming from the radiator was nice.

'God, where have you been? I've been worried sick,' said a voice from the kitchen.

'We had to go to Sainsburys – I did text you to let you know,' Mary replied.

She took off Mia's small purple coat and hung it on the post at the bottom of the stairs. After that, she did the same with hers, then made her way to the kitchen, following her daughter's little footsteps.

'My phone died, I've been meaning to charge it – I'll do it now,' the man said as she entered.

Mia ran up to her Dad, throwing her arms out. He stopped looking for the charger, bent down and gave her a hug. 'Hey, Sweetie.'

'Hi, Daddy.'

Mia let go and turned to Mary. 'Mammy, can daddy read me a story? Please, please?'

Mary, leaning down, kissed her daughter on the head. 'Yes, but not a long one, Mia, you have nursery tomorrow. Go get your pyjamas on and I'll send daddy up.'

She smiled and nodded, then trotted up the stairs towards her bedroom.

Stuart found his charger and plugged it into his phone, then went back near the table and stood in front of Mary.

'Hey, I can't believe what happened, are you guys okay?' he asked, pulling her close to give her a hug. 'You're freezing, I've just put the heating on – hey, sit down, tell me what happened.'

They took a seat at the small wooden table.

Her eyes started to glaze over but she stayed silent.

He said, 'I'm sorry, I couldn't get away from work, I got your text and asked to leave. My boss said I had an important meeting and when you said it didn't matter, I kinda left it. I feel bad now knowing what had happened. Sorry I wasn't there for you.'

She smiled, reached for his warm hand. 'It's okay…'

'So, what happened?' he asked, desperate to know.

'Someone called my name on High Row. I turned. He asked me if I was called Mary. I said yes. And then he handed me a small Greggs packet, then walked away. I looked inside. At first, I thought it was a wind up, but then I saw the dried blood and pieces of flesh stuck to the eyes.'

'God.'

'So I screamed and dropped them on the floor. The eyeballs rolled out onto the pavement. Oh God, Stuart, it was awful. Mia was devastated.'

'Bloody hell!' He edged back in awe. 'I can imagine, bless her – who was the man?'

Mary shrugged. 'Think he was a tramp, I'm not sure – he wasn't dressed very well.'

'What was he wearing?'

'An old faded tracksuit, I think.'

Stuart nodded, raised a finger to his face to push his glasses back up his nose. 'Why did it take so long at the station?'

'You know what these things are like,' she confessed, 'some detectives wanted to speak to us about it. Had us waiting for ages. I wasn't happy at all.'

'They probably thought you had something to do with it.'

'It wouldn't surprise me.' She looked past him and sniffed the air. 'Have you made tea? Something smells nice.'

'I put some pasta bake in before, nothing fancy.'

'Thanks.'

'Even put cheese on it for you,' he said with a smile. 'Just needs warming up.'

'Thank you.' She stood up and headed to the kettle, flicked it on. 'Nah… I need wine.'

'You look sexy in that suit.'

'I do, don't I,' she replied, grinning.

'Don't tease me…'

They heard a hurried pitter-patter of feet coming down the stairs, then along the hall. Stuart turned, seeing his daughter walk in, her face a little worried.

'Mia?'

'Daddy, I heard something in my room.'

'What was it? It must be a monster,' he teased, raising both palms up in the air as if he was playing a role in an old Frankenstein film.

'Stop it, Stu!' said Mary. 'Don't wind her up.'

'Okay, okay, let's go see your room. Daddy will go beat up the monster.' Stuart stood up and patted his daughter's head, then turned back to Mary. 'Hey, if you're having some pasta, put some on a plate for me, too. I'm starving.'

'Okay.' Mary reached up and opened one of the top cupboards, pulled out two plates, and placed them down onto the granite worktop.

'What were the sounds, Mia?' he asked, trailing his daughter slowly up the stairs.

She came to a halt halfway up. 'You go first, Daddy, you go first.'

'Okay, Mia, I'll go first.' He stepped past her and reached the landing. Inside her room, he turned on the switch near the door and watched the room flood with light. 'See Mia, there's no monster in here.'

Standing at her open doorway, she peeped inside cautiously. 'I heard something in the corner.'

'Mia, there's nothing in here, I've been home for a few hours now. No one is here, okay?' He dropped to his knees in front of her. 'Go to bed, it's getting late. I'll be up soon to read you a story.'

Reluctantly, she nodded, and did as she was told, climbing into bed. She then leaned over, grabbed her pink dinosaur teddy off the floor and dragged her pink covers up to her small chin.

'Good girl, I'll be up soon,' he said, flicking the light switch near the door, the room plummeting into darkness.

'She's a worrier, that one,' he said to Mary back in the kitchen who was sitting at the table with a plate of pasta bake and a full glass of wine.

'Gets it from you, Stu,' she mused.

He sat down opposite Mary. 'Was gunna say before, but thought it was nothing. A man passed the house four times within half an hour before. Thought it was a bit strange.' Mary acknowledged his words with a raised frown. He continued: 'He looked like he glanced through the window every time, too. I stood up and went to the window and watched him cross the road, but he never looked back. I haven't seen him since.'

Mary finished her mouthful of pasta. 'When was this?'

'An hour ago, maybe.'

'Well, we do have the house up for sale - maybe a potential buyer wanting to know the area.'

'It's possible, I suppose.' He paused a beat. 'But to wear a hood up in the darkness is a little strange.'

'Trust me, it's cold outside,' she countered, 'if I had a hood, I'd wear it up, too. Anything else?'

'What do you mean?'

'You look like you're going to say something else?'

'You know me well.'

'I've been married to you for eight years. I should know you well.'

He made a 'fair enough' expression. 'When I was in the shower, I heard something out the back, rustling, that kind of thing. I turned off the shower and looked out into the garden. Next door where out in the garage, figured it was nothing. I don't know, I've got the creeps tonight. Especially you finding them eyeballs today. Some crazy cats out there.'

She inhaled another mouthful of pasta as if she hadn't eaten for days.

Stu found his feet. 'I'll go tell her a story, she's waiting for me.'

He took the stairs very slowly, his legs tired from his day at work, although he hadn't done much, nothing physical anyway. He reached up and flicked on the light in Mia's bedroom. She was sitting up in her bed, looking down at something in her hand.

He frowned. 'Mia, what's that?'

It was a lollypop.

'He gave it to me.'

Glaring, Stu lowered to the bed and sat next to her. 'Who – who gave it to you?'

'The man…'

'Which man – someone at nursery? You shouldn't really be having lollies at your age, I've seen some nasty things where children choke on them. Give it to Daddy, please.' He held out his hand.

She unwillingly handed it over.

'Who gave this to you, Mia?'

'The man in the hood,' she explained softly. 'He told me not to tell you.'

Downstairs in the kitchen, he heard Mary stand up, the sound of the chair scraping across the tiled floor, then a moment later, a plate was lowered into the sink. He craned his neck towards the door. 'Mary?' he shouted.

When she didn't reply, he returned his focus back to his daughter. 'When did this man give you this lolly, Mia?

'When you went downstairs. He was standing in my room.'

A chill enveloped his whole body, the icy fingers crawling up his spine. 'Mia, don't joke with things like this…'

Her little face filled with sadness at his tone.

Stuart bolted up and checked the wardrobes and under the bed. 'Mia… there's no one here. You can't make things up like this. It scares Daddy, okay?'

'He told me it was a secret. He said—'

'Stop it, Mia!' he shouted, pointing a finger at her.

She started to cry as she lowered her gaze towards her lap. Dropping to the bed, Stuart wrapped his arms around her and apologised for shouting.

'What is it, Stu?' they heard Mary's distant voice from downstairs.

'Doesn't matter,' he shouted, angling his head towards the door. He turned back to Mia. His voice went quiet. 'You need to go to sleep now, Baby, okay. Go to sleep, get some rest. I need to speak with mammy. We'll see you in the morning.'

At the door, he watched Mia get comfortable for a moment, holding the dinosaur close to her little chest. Smiling, he turned out the light and went to the bathroom next door. He popped his head in a few minutes later to check on her and found her sound asleep.

Making his way downstairs, he took a left at the bottom and pulled the lolly from his trouser pocket, ready to show Mary and explain what Mia had said. 'You wouldn't believe what Mia had in bed with her.' He noticed there was no one in the kitchen, so peeped into the living room. She wasn't there, either. 'Mary?'

No reply.

He went back to the kitchen.

'Mary?'

Noticing the bin had been pulled out away from the wall and was empty, the lid open, he figured she was out the back emptying it. At the kettle, he flicked it on and leaned over, pulling the charger wire from his phone. While it boiled, he checked his social media profiles. One of his friends tagged him in a meme funny enough to crack a smile but there wasn't much else. As time went on, he glanced at the open back door, feeling the cold start to creep in, wondering what was taking Mary so long.

He placed his phone down on the side, walked to the back door, and stepped out on the decking. 'You out here?' He rounded the brickwork of the extended kitchen to where the bin was.

He froze.

On the floor, near the open bin in the darkness, he saw something.

'What the fuck?' he whispered.

He backed into the house quickly, retrieved his phone then went back out. Using the torch function, he directed the brilliant beam towards the base of the bin.

It was her shoe, resting sideways on the floor. Next to the shoe, there was a small pool of blood.

'Jesus…' He leaned down, picked up the shoe. On the bottom of it, there was a message written in red marker pen:

She didn't see it coming.

A chill shot through him. 'What the fu…'

He angled the phone light along the path, noticing a trail of blood droplets, until he reached the gate, which he saw was wide open.

Then he heard his wife's scream rip through the air before there was a metallic bang. The screaming suddenly stopped. He raced to the open gate, galloped out onto the driveway, and the screech of spinning car tires resonated somewhere down the road.

Frantically, he stared in both directions, but he saw nothing.

Mary had gone.

28

Friday Morning
Low Coniscliffe

Byrd walked into the kitchen. Although he'd been showered, he looked shattered, the dark semi-circles sitting under his eyes made him look like he was knocking on the door of fifty.

'Hi, Max,' said a chirpy Claire, who was sitting at the table sipping her coffee, leaning over her Kindle. 'You look handsome in that.'

He was wearing a light blue shirt with a dark blue tie, and black trousers.

'Good morning.' He bent over and kissed her forehead. 'You smell nice.'

'My natural skin,' she replied, grinning.

'How'd you sleep?'

'Better than you,' she said. 'You were tossing and turning all night long.'

'*I was?*'

She nodded. 'Yes.'

'Sorry if I disturbed you.'

She waved it away as if it was the norm. 'I made you a coffee,' she said, pointing to the mug on the opposite side of the table, then half turned her upper body, pointing towards the worktop. 'There's also croissants in that packet over there. I've been out already.'

'Early bird catches the worm. Where did you go?'

She smiled. 'I didn't want to wake you. Just popped to Mowden. Is there an update with your mam and dad?'

'The doctor said my mother is getting better, but my father isn't showing the signs of improvement which he expected to see.' A look of sadness swept across Byrd's face. Claire moved her chair back, stood up, ambled over to him and wrapped her arms around him.

'I'm sorry, Max.'

He smiled into the side of her neck but didn't say anything in return. There was nothing to be said. Her familiar scent of Dolce and Gabbana perfume brought a needed comfort to him.

'I'll warm up your croissant for you,' she said, peeling herself away from him.

Byrd grinned appreciatively, turned and took a seat at the table. Watching her pad towards the worktop, he admired her slim physique, realising how lucky he was. On the table next to her half-filled coffee, he laid his eyes on her Kindle. 'What you reading on there?'

'Chris Carter's new one… erm… Hunting Evil.'

'Chris Carter – never heard of him. Is he good?'

She closed the door of the microwave. The plated croissant inside started to turn under the dim light and whirring sound. 'Some of the crime scenes would even make you feel queasy.'

She opened the microwave door, grabbed the plate then placed it down in front of Byrd, the smell of the warmed pastry rising to his nose. 'You should read it after I've finished, it's really good.'

'I might just do that, I haven't read fiction in a long time. And don't worry, I have a strong stomach,' he countered.

'What was the last book you read?' she asked.

'God knows. The Da Vinci code maybe?'

'It's good – I've read that, too.'

'I can't remember what happens in it really.'

'What time you going to work?'

He glanced down at his watch. 'Not long, I'll have this and get a move on. What's your plans for today – anything interesting on your day off?'

'I need to see my Mum, she's putting up some flat-pack furniture she got delivered from Ikea. I say she's putting it up.

She isn't. I am. Anyway, I'm going to make a move myself. Need to pop into town and get some bits.'

'Okay, have a good day – I'll ring you on my dinner,' Byrd said.

'If you get one?'

Byrd smiled at her humour and nodded in agreement. 'If I get one, yeah.' There were days, as a DI, where there wasn't even time to go to the toilet but that was the nature of the job.

She leaned down and kissed him, grabbed her bag from the floor and her black fleece from the hook above the radiator, and walked out the front door. Silence filled the house quickly whilst Byrd sat at the table finishing his croissant when he received a text from Tanzy. It read:

Get here, Max, the post mortem is back from the pathologist. You need to see it.

29

Friday Morning
Police Station

Byrd parked his X5 in the third closest bay to the entrance door, which was usually occupied by DCI Thornton but for some reason, she hadn't arrived yet. Byrd could probably count on his hand the amount of times he'd beat Thornton into the office and felt a small sense of victory on the days that he did. She usually liked to get there early, get a head start on the day so when the superintendent, Barry Eckles, traipsed in, she could give him the lengthy explanation for her daily agenda that he demanded.

The thick, grey sky started to throw down heavy rain. Byrd watched it bounce relentlessly off the windscreen then cascade down the angled glass out of sight. He unbuckled his belt, grabbed his phone and opened his door, then made a dash towards the entrance door. Inside, he gave himself a shake.

'Morning, Max,' said Charlotte, the twenty-something admin girl who seemed to have the hots for Tanzy.

'Good morning.'

'Hey, have you seen Orion?' she asked, clutching several thin A4 files close to her large chest.

'I haven't, not yet. When I do, I'll tell him you're looking for him.'

'Thanks,' she said, smiling. She pivoted and strutted off with the youthful energy Byrd remembered he used to possess at that age.

Before going to his desk, he went up to the canteen and made a coffee. For some reason he put two spoonful's in this time. He felt like he needed the extra caffeine boost. As he approached his desk, he saw Tanzy sitting at his computer.

'Morning, Ori, how are you today?'

Taking his eyes off the screen, he glanced up at Byrd. 'Hey, Max.'

Byrd placed the coffee on the desk, pulled out his chair, and dropped into it. 'Charlotte is looking for you…'

'Is she,' he said, keeping his eyes on the screen. 'Did she say what it was about?'

'No. Anyway, what's this email you said on the text?' Byrd asked, turning to his computer and shaking the mouse to wake it up. The log-in screen replaced the black screen and Byrd typed his username and password in, then pressed ENTER.

'I'll let you read it for yourself.'

'Fair enough.' Byrd sipped his coffee, found the email titled 'PM – Julia Porter' sent from the Pathology department, and clicked open. For the next few minutes, he scanned the report.

'Interesting,' Byrd whispered.

'Yeah…'

'So the pathologists think what's been done to Julia Porter, in terms of her eyes being removed, was carried out by a medical professional?'

'That's what they're saying,' Tanzy replied. 'They haven't seen work so fine in a very, very long time, especially outside of a lab.'

30

Friday Morning
Cemetery Lane, Darlington

The morning traffic along Carmel road was no different to what it was like yesterday or what it would be like tomorrow.

Scott Anders turned left into Cemetery Lane with his dog, Milo, an eight-year-old Labrador, who, as usual, was trying to go faster than Scott allowed him to.

'Take it easy, boy,' Scott said, holding the lead with a solid grip.

He glanced up after hearing footsteps in front of him, noticing a woman around the age of sixty, also with a dog, walking towards him. They made eye contact and exchanged a brief smile.

'Morning,' she said. The dimples on her cheeks were the cutest thing Scott had seen since his wife died last year. It had been a rough year for him, but he was managing, taking every day in his stride. Now retired, he spent a lot of his time walking Milo, often, for miles a day. Around this time of day, he strolled down Cemetery Lane; he had done for nearly four months now. Most mornings, he passed this woman walking the opposite way. Sometimes, he missed her, but he tried his best to time it right, so he could see her attractive smile – it was often the highlight of his lonely day.

To say that he wasn't missing his wife would be a lie, of course he was, but he was ready for something more, even companionship would lessen the painful solitude he felt on a daily basis. Over and over in his head, he'd played out the conversation with this woman, trying to imagine how it'd go, but he'd never got beyond saying 'Good Morning'.

Today was going to be different, he decided.

'Good morning,' he replied, smiling, but not going over the top.

Just as they crossed, she looked back down at her dog. Some type of poodle, Scott guessed but wasn't too sure.

'Erm – em…' he stuttered.

'I'm sorry,' she said, slowing and angling her body towards him.

'Sorry?'

'Did you say something?' she asked, awkwardly.

Oh my God, she was even more attractive than he realised. He felt his face warming, knowing it wasn't going as well as he'd visualised.

'I… I did,' he admitted.

'What did you say?'

'I said good morning.'

'After that, you said something?'

'I did?' He knew he did.

'You did,' she said quietly.

A smile swept across her small face, her thin lips arching.

'Hey, I was wondering,' he started, 'please don't think I'm a creep or anything here, but do you fancy a cup of coffee or something?'

A cold silence grew between them and her smile faded very fast. 'I…' she fell quiet.

He raised a soft palm. 'Hey, it's okay, I didn't mean—'

'…I'd love to,' she said, cutting him off. 'When?'

Scott's eyes widened and a warmth he hadn't felt for nearly a year filled him. 'Whenever you like. I'm free this morning?'

She nodded. 'Sounds good to me.'

An awkward silence hung in the air as he racked his brains thinking about what to say next. 'Good. Erm…'

'Where you going now?' she queried.

'Just home, I walk this way. My house is down the lane. Only a few streets away.'

She followed the direction of his arm and glanced down the lane for a brief moment.

'Your house, then?' she suggested.

'If you're free, that would be nice.'

'Okay then.' She pulled back the small dog and came to his side.

'I'm Scott.' He offered her his hand. She shook it. 'And this,' he said, pointing down, 'is Milo.'

'I'm Elaine. This is Edgar.'

They looked away from each other, a grin lining both of their faces as they started to amble down the lane towards Scott's house. Moments later, Milo stretched the lead, tugging Scott towards a wide, low bush to their left. Then Edgar seemed to have picked up on the same scent, dragging Elaine to the same place.

'Steady Milo,' grunted Scott. 'What have you found?'

Milo dug his face into the bush and immediately started to bark, the deep howls disturbing the quiet lane. Edgar joined in, before both dogs backed away and growled, showing their sharp teeth.

'What – what is it?' Elaine said, suddenly concerned.

'Here, can you take him?' Scott handed Milo's lead over to her. She steadied her grip on both of the dogs and wrapped the leads around her wrists several times.

Leaning down, using his cold hands, Scott spread the leaves and branches apart, squinting down into the base of the bush. That's when he saw it. He froze.

'What is it?' she asked

'Jesus.'

'Sc – Scott, what is it?' she muttered.

He didn't speak, just stared.

Trying to find words, he managed only a whisper. 'It's a hand.' This time louder: 'It's someone's fucking hand.'

He turned to her quickly, seeing the fear intensify in her face, the colour of it sheet white. Scott edged back a touch, glancing nervously up and down the lane.

They were alone.

The sound of the dog's barking continued to pierce the icy air but resonated beyond his focus, his eyes fixated on the bloody hand.

'It's – it's a what?' she mumbled, the words clogging in her throat.

Then he felt it.

Something on his face.

Raising his hand to the tip of his nose, he touched the cold liquid with a fingertip, then lowered his hand to have a look.

It was bright red.

'Blood?' he whispered.

'Is that… blood?' Elaine asked confused.

He tilted his head back and peered up to the sky. A frosty shiver of fear enveloped his body when he saw her. Elaine, following his gaze, glared up, and instantly let out a blood-curdling scream that rattled the air.

The dogs barked even louder.

In the tree directly above them, hanging by a blue rope attached around her neck, the body of a woman hung silently. From the open cut where her hand once was, beads of blood dripped on the cold ground near Scott's feet.

31

Friday Morning
Police Station

Byrd carefully scanned the post mortem report sent from the pathologists about Julia Porter another three times whilst sitting at his desk. Tanzy came over with another coffee for him, placing it down to the left of his keyboard. Without taking his eyes off the report, Byrd said, 'Thanks, Ori.'

'No problem, Sir.' Tanzy sat down and leaned back, closing his eyes for a moment, waiting for Byrd to finish it again. He knew Byrd was meticulous and had the finest attention to detail.

In their earlier years, it annoyed him how long it took Byrd to process information and come up with an answer, or a solution. IQ wise, Tanzy probably had the edge, but after carefully piecing the missing parts of the puzzles together, it was usually Byrd who came up with the answers.

Tanzy topped his IQ, but Byrd worked harder, was more determined. Ever since his sister was murdered twelve years ago, Byrd had changed. Once a month, he went to see a therapist, had done for years. Neither Tanzy or Thornton knew about it, or anyone else on the force, no one apart from his best friend, Keith, who he saw every now and again. He'd been meaning to tell Tanzy about his meetings but as time passed, he'd left it and decided not to mention it at all. The therapy sessions lasted an hour, costing him around seventy pound for the hour. The therapist, Dr Alice Morgan, would use her techniques and over the time she'd seen Byrd, had noticed tremendous improvements in him. Actually, it was her that told him he didn't need to see her anymore, but he'd insisted, telling her it was the only way he felt he could unwind and be completely honest. She'd asked him about his current partner, who she learned was called Claire, about opening up to her, but he'd said about struggling to fully let his guard down with a partner, because of how bad it ended with a previous relationship.

'Okay,' Byrd said, peeling his eyes away from the screen and picking up the mug.

'So?'

Byrd scanned over the document on his screen again. 'Why the eyes?'

'Huh?'

'Why take her eyes? Why leave that message – I don't understand this, Ori.'

'You and me both, Max,' said Tanzy, itching his goatee.

'If they were going to kill her, why not just strangle her and that's it – done. Why go to the trouble of taking out her eyes and then somehow they end up in a Greggs packet, being handed to Mary Richards on High Row in the middle of town with her daughter?'

Following his trail of thought, Tanzy said, 'It's as if someone is showing off their skills, wanting to be appreciated for their work.'

'Or to appear they know what they're doing, as the pathologist stated, as if they are trained in some form of medical or surgical procedures.'

Tanzy pondered his partner's words for a moment. 'So, apart from the missing eyes which appear to have been taken out in a meticulous way, and the strangulation, there isn't really anything to go on.'

'Not yet. The footprints came back as Ian Porter's, matching the prints on the bottom of a pair of trainers he has.'

'So, the people who did this were wearing overshoes?'

'Likely.'

'Seems a thorough job,' said Tanzy.

'Very thorough – someone who knows what they are doing.'

'I – I need to go see Ian Porter, tell him that no other traces of DNA have been found on his wife's body.'

'Okay – I'll chase up with PC Cornty about the cameras on Brinkburn Road.'

'I'm surprised he hasn't come back with them yet,' Byrd commented. 'He's normally quick.'

'Me and you, both,' Tanzy replied, 'I'll go see him now.'

'I'll let you know how I get on with Ian Porter – I still feel like there's something he's not telling us.'

Tanzy stood and walked away from the desk. 'I'll be back soon.'

'You're not going anywhere,' a hurried voice said behind them. Tanzy stopped and turned. Byrd swivelled on his chair, seeing DCI June Thornton standing at her open door.

'You're both going to Cemetery Lane just off Carmel Road,' she told them.

'What for?' Tanzy asked.

'There's a dead woman hanging in a tree.'

32

Friday Morning
Cemetery Lane

Byrd and Tanzy stepped out into the cold and closed their doors. They waited for a gap in the traffic on Carmel Road and crossed over when it was safe to do so. Up ahead, at the metal gate at the start of Cemetery Lane, a crowd of people had gathered. Tanzy squeezed through the people and showed his ID to the PC's manning the gate; they moved aside, allowing the detectives through.

'Where the fuck they going?' someone shouted, scowling at Byrd and Tanzy.

Byrd glanced back at the growing crowds for a second, then turned to Tanzy. 'The smallest thing in this town gets everyone out, doesn't it?'

'It's an area that's been cordoned off. Most don't care, but for some people, they need to know why. It's the same anywhere. People are nosy. People have got nothing better to do with their time.'

They walked on towards the forensic team ahead, who were dressed in their usual whites. Byrd clocked Jacob Tallow standing next to PC Kim Harrison. He had a large clear plastic bag in his gloved hands. Compared to Tallow, Harrison looked like a dwarf, although she wasn't particularly small. To Tallow's left, his partner, Hope, was crouched down near what seemed like a bush.

As they drew nearer, Byrd and Tanzy both absorbed the scene. Tallow said something to PC Harrison, then turned, taking a step back, diverting his attention on what his partner was doing. The detectives approached Harrison.

'Morning, Kim,' Byrd said to her.

She turned. 'Morning, Max.' She switched her focus to Tanzy. 'Morning, Orion.'

'Hey,' Tanzy said, giving a shiver.

Byrd stopped at her side, looking beyond her. 'What do we have?'

'A couple found her – turns out they're not actually a couple.' She turned, pointed to the cut that led to Netherby Rise. Both detectives swivelled around, laid eyes on a man and woman standing on the narrow path, dogs sitting beside them. Beyond them, a police car was parked purposefully blocking pedestrian access to the lane.

At one of the houses behind, a woman stepped out of the green door of a semi-detached house dressed in a dark red dressing gown to see what all the commotion was about. She glanced in the direction of the lane; it didn't take her long to let out a scream and throw her hands over her mouth.

The detectives diverted their attention back to Harrison.

'They found her hanging,' Harrison said, turning and pointing upwards.

Byrd and Tanzy followed her finger.

Tanzy swallowed. 'Jesus. It's Mary Richards.'

'It certainly looks like her,' she agreed.

'God.' Byrd winced.

'You don't seem fazed by her?' Tanzy said to Harrison.

'I was told last night.'

'What do you mean?' Byrd asked.

'Her husband, Stuart, called saying she'd gone missing – just disappeared from the house. He'd heard her scream on the street then heard the sound of screeching tyres. He didn't see the vehicle. He mentioned her daughter had told him there was a man in her room. Stuart thought she was being ridiculous and just being silly. He went down stairs and Mary was gone. On the decking near the bin, there was one of her shoes and drops of blood.'

'How the fuck are we just hearing about this now?' Byrd cried.

Harrison stared blankly at him.

'Was there a report filed for this?' Tanzy asked.

'I think so.'

'Who filed the report?' Tanzy demanded.

'Erm… DS Stockdale, I assume. He went out to their address and took pictures of the blood. He knew to file the report afterwards. I'm sure he did. I spoke to him last night – he mentioned he'd been over there.'

'Stockdale?'

She nodded at Byrd. 'Yeah.'

'How did he file it? Manually or through the new way?'

She offered only a hopeless shrug. 'I don't know…'

'Fuck sake!' Tanzy glared up at the sky and clamped his eyes shut for a second. 'He'll have done it the old way, that's why we weren't notified.' He opened his eyes, briefly glanced at Byrd, then his eyes fell on Harrison. 'That's why the auto filing system came in, so everyone knew what was going on.'

'DS Stockdale has just transferred over, though, maybe he didn't know?'

'It's basics, Kim,' Byrd replied.

Harrison heard the disappointment in his tone.

'Who attended the scene with Stockdale?' Tanzy asked.

'The what?'

'When Stuart Richards made the call, who went with him to their house?'

PC Harrison narrowed her eyes, thinking. 'PC Cornty, I think DS Stockdale said.'

A look of disgust swept across Tanzy's face and remained there for a while. 'Cornty?'

'Yeah, I think.'

'Why on earth has he not mentioned it to me yet?' Tanzy was raising his voice now, so much so that Tallow and Hope glanced his way for a second. 'Where is he?' he added quickly.

'He's not here yet.'

'Fuck sake.'

Byrd, looking away from Tanzy, scowled up into the tree. Mary Richards was wearing a black blouse with smart grey trousers. Her face was ghostly white, the colour of a porcelain doll. Due to the lack of blood flow that her once-functioning heart had pumped to her head when she was alive, the blood settled in the lower half of her body. The ambient frost wasn't helping her complexion either.

Byrd frowned. 'Where's her hand?'

'It's on the floor in the bush where Hope is.'

'What the fuck is going on in this town?' Byrd muttered to himself.

'Never a dull day in Darlington,' said Tanzy.

Both detectives drew closer, minding their footing on the muddy, slippy ground below. The smell in the air was a mixture between damp trees and mud.

'Morning, Jacob,' said Byrd, rubbing his hands together. 'Cold one.'

Jacob Tallow, in his white plastic overalls, turned to the detectives. 'Morning, Max.' He nodded towards Tanzy but said nothing, who returned the gesture in the same manner. Whenever there was a crime scene, and Jacob Tallow was involved, usually Byrd did the talking. Tanzy and Tallow had a falling out a few years back. Although both sides had apologised for their argument on the best way to preserve one of the crime scenes, there was still a tension between them that still lingered.

'Has McCabe been informed about this?' Tanzy asked him.

Tallow looked at Tanzy. 'Yeah, he's tied up somewhere he said. He'll be here soon with Paul and Amanda.'

'How long do you think she's been up there?' Byrd asked.

'My guess is as good as yours, Max.' He half turned, glaring up the hanging dead woman. 'We won't know until we get a closer look at her. Judging by what I'm seeing, anywhere between two to six hours. We'll know more when the coroner turns up.'

'Has Peter been contacted?' asked Byrd, grabbing Tallow's attention.

'He has – I made the call earlier. He said he also had a few ends to tie up, then he'll be straight over.'

Peter Gibbs was the lead Coroner for the Durham and Darlington Coroner office, which was based at Durham Miner's Hall in the city of Durham. It would take thirty minutes to travel straight from the office to Darlington on a good day with no traffic disruptions, so Byrd and Tanzy guessed it would be at least forty-five minutes before he turned up. Peter had files on every death that's been recorded in the district of Darlington for the past one-hundred years. Every crime scene which involved a death, Peter usually attended and worked with forensic investigators to establish the confirmation of death and collection of necessary evidence for further analysis. If his analysis suggested that the death wasn't crime-related, then he would allow law enforcement to leave the scene. Obviously in this case, a woman hanging from a tree with her hand missing would strongly suggest a crime had been committed.

'Has the fire department been contacted?' Tanzy said. Starting to feel the cold, he placed his hands deep into the pockets of his grey, long coat.

Tallow shook his head and frowned. 'Why – where's the fire?'

Tanzy smiled, understanding and appreciating his humour for a change.

'Yes, I've called them – they're on their way,' Tallow confirmed.

The fire department would have the necessary tools and equipment to access the body of Mary Richards, which, Tanzy judged, was at least fifteen feet in the air, or nine or ten feet above their heads.

'How on earth did she get up there?' Byrd whispered.

'What's that?'

Byrd turned to Tanzy. 'How did she get up there?'

Tanzy shrugged. 'Beats me. Let's go see Hope, see how she's getting on.'

'Don't go too close,' Tallow said, 'there's blood on the floor near the bush. Don't want you contaminating it, Orion.'

'We know the drill,' he said, grinning.

The detectives came to a halt, craned their necks and looked up at the woman hanging almost directly above them. Mary Richards was missing a shoe and they thought about that for a moment in their own individual minds. Tallow moved away from them towards Hope, who stood up carefully from a crouching position, then backed away from the bush, holding the severed hand carefully in her right glove. Very judiciously, she placed it inside of a clear plastic bag, then squeezed her thumb and index finger to slide it along the seal at the top. The detectives stood about four metres from her and decided to give them the room to work.

'How did this happen, Max?' Tanzy said quietly in Byrd's ear.

In silence, Byrd digested the scene in front of him; the tree, the rope, and the woman. A chill ran through him as he watched her motionless, white face. Her cold, still eyes stared off to the left. The rope wrapped around her neck went vertically up to a thick branch of what looks like an English Oak tree, then around the branch, running down the opposite side at an angle, securely wrapped at the base of the next tree.

'It points to a number of people, surely,' Byrd commented. 'One person couldn't have done this by themselves.'

Tanzy nodded firmly. 'Yeah… to throw the rope over, tie her up, and pull down on the other side. It's the work of three of four, in my opinion.'

'Maybe more. To have the strength to pull her up is impressive.'

They heard Tallow and Hope say something, but they couldn't quite hear what was said. In the distance behind them, the increasing siren of a fire engine rippled in the air. Turning to the increasing noise, they saw a truck pull up behind them, the brakes hissing as the large red machine came to a halt. Out stepped four cautious firefighters who frowned as they looked over; Byrd noticed their gazes fall on the woman in the tree and noticed one of them lipread 'Jesus Christ' before saying something to another fireman.

They turned back to Hope who was standing there. Hope was mid-thirties, with short blonde hair that sat on top of a moody looking face. Her blue eyes were piercing through her stylish square black-framed glasses.

'Hey, Trish,' Tanzy said.

Byrd rolled his eyes. He remembered Tanzy once mentioning he found her very attractive in the past. He adored her tattoos. She had a sleeve on her right arm and a half sleeve on her left. Seldom did he see them, but he cherished the times he did when she took her coat off.

'Hey, Ori, how you doing?'

He nodded, looked into her gorgeous eyes, then focused down on the hand inside the bag. 'What's your first thoughts?'

'Well apart from her being dead, the cut to the hand is interesting.'

Byrd this time, stepping forward. 'Interesting how?'

'A very sharp tool has been used here.'

Byrd again: 'A surgical tool?'

She bobbed her head confidently, then glanced to her right when Tallow appeared. 'A surgical tool, similar to the one from Brinkburn Drive where Julia Porter's body was found.' She paused for a moment, then added, 'and a very steady hand. Pardon the pun.'

33

Friday Late Morning
Darlington

Marie Ching entered her bedroom and stopped in the doorway. She glanced to the side of her bed and remembered their new cleaner, Lena, standing there the day before.

She went to where Lena had been standing and stopped. For a few seconds, she felt silly, not really knowing what she was looking for, but there must have been something. Something that Lena was interested in. All that was on her husband's bedside unit was his electronic alarm clock, his hair brush, a pack of mints, and the thin charging point of his phone charger wire.

'Weird.'

Or was she genuinely going to clean the surface of the table? Marie ran her finger along the surface, then lifted it to her face and noticed there was no dust whatsoever.

Or was it something inside the drawer.

She felt bad doing it, but she bent down and opened it, then had a look inside. There was more in there than she'd imagined. Money. Receipts. Chewing gum. Batteries. An old phone that hadn't been switched on since 2016 – God knows why he kept it, she thought. A diary from last year which looked brand new and unused. She put her fingers in and lifted a few of the items out, so she could see the hidden objects underneath.

A notepad, a few pens.

Four bookmarks and a small paperback that she hadn't seen him read in months.

The small paperback was titled: CSI – real stories.

She plucked the phone from her jeans and phoned his number. Within five rings, he picked up.

'Hey,' she said. '… Yeah, I'm okay… listen, something is playing on my mind… it's…. well, you know the cleaner, Lena… well, she's… Yes, I know she is but she… okay, it doesn't matter… I know, I understand… I'll tell you later… Okay, speak then.'

She lowered her hand, dropped the phone on the bed, disheartened by his dismissal. He'd told her he was busy and didn't have time to speak to her.

Then she started thinking. Thinking about Lena. Lena… what was her second name? She sat up, frowning, trying to think, hard.

'Keeton,' she whispered, remembering she'd told her in the first week.

She grabbed her phone, unlocked it and opened up social media. She typed in the name Lena Keeton and pressed ENTER. A long list of profiles came up, all with various unique profile pictures. Some colourful, others dull. Some smiles, others miserable.

Meticulously, she scrolled down the list searching for the familiar face.

She didn't see it.

After opening up another social profile, she tried again, searching for the name and clicking GO this time.

Again, nothing.

'Weird.'

Everyone and their dog were on social media nowadays, weren't they?

It was as if Lena Keeton didn't exist.

34

Friday Afternoon
Darlington Memorial Hospital

The man behind the desk looked up and offered Byrd a smile. 'Can I help you?'

'Here to see my parents, Alan and Jackie Byrd, please.'

'Of course.' The man glanced down, switched his focus to his computer screen, and moved the mouse. 'If you want to go straight through.'

'Thank you.'

Byrd left the desk of the ICU reception, making his way through the open double doors into the dim corridor. He angled right and walked down the short corridor then took a left. It was unusually quiet in the department today. From previous visits, murmurs were heard coming from open office doors or idle chatter from the small canteen towards the left.

But today, there was nothing.

At the end of the corridor, on the wall in front of him, his eyes fell on a large poster. The title of the poster was: Struggling with the loss of a loved one?

Not yet, he hoped. Not yet.

Reaching the closed door of the room where his mother and father were, he paused and courteously knocked twice, before pushing down the handle and edging it open. The room was dark, the blind halfway down the window to the left, which he noticed was open a few inches, a slight chill hanging in the air with the smell of damp from outside. Glancing out the window briefly, he looked out on to the car park, which was full to the brim with cars, people moving back and forth on the paths under a sky thick with grey clouds.

The beeping of the machines quietly filled the room.

Watching the wires and hoses linked to his parents, he couldn't help but feel heartbroken, seeing the people who'd brought him in to this world, the same people who looked after him, guided him, then to see them like this, was truly a horrible experience.

A strange feeling grew within him. As if he wasn't in the room alone. He glanced to his right.

Jan, the nurse, was watching him.

'Jesus,' he gasped, throwing his hand to his chest. 'You scared me.'

'Sorry,' she said, sitting on the chair in the near corner, one leg over the other, a pen in one hand, the clipboard in the other. 'How you doing, Max?'

When his heartrate lowered, he managed a nod. 'I'm okay.' He pointed towards the beds. 'How they doing?'

'Sorry… no change yet, I'm afraid.'

Byrd nodded at her then focused back on Alan and Jackie. 'From your experience, what do you think?' Pondering his question, she sat in silence for a moment; Byrd recognised her hesitation. 'Just your opinion, that's all, nothing official,' he added.

She winced, knowing she couldn't be one-hundred percent truthful – it wasn't her place. Also, it wasn't ethical giving someone hope when she believed there wasn't any. 'I can't say, I've been told—'

'Please,' he begged desperately. 'I need to know, be honest.'

She mulled his anxious words over. 'Okay… in my opinion, and from my experience, I think both of them will not wake up.' The silence was deafening. 'But time will tell.'

As her words crushed him internally, he felt tears well up in his eyes, and glared back at the beds, the sound of the beeping machine suddenly magnifying in his own mind. 'Okay,' he whispered.

'I'm sorry, I was being—'

'It's okay,' he said without looking at her, 'at least I know what to expect.' He took a step back towards the door. 'I'll pop back tomorrow. Let me know if there's any changes – or improvements.'

Giving a sad smile, she nodded. 'Of course.'

As Byrd opened the door and stepped out onto the corridor, Jan stood and placed the clipboard on the side, and waited for a few seconds. When she heard nothing but silence, she popped her head out into the corridor. The coast was clear. She left the room, closed the door, the sound of the monotonous beeping disappearing behind it.

She felt sorry for Byrd. She could see the pain in his eyes when she spoke to him, as if he'd experienced a loss in the past and was readying himself, but hoping, that he'd never have to go through it again. It was getting close to lunch time, she could feel her stomach twisting in knots so decided to knock on Dr Ching's door to see if he wanted anything getting from the canteen.

His door was closed. She leaned into it, tried to listen, but there were no sounds coming from inside.

She knocked twice, waited a few seconds, then edged the door open.

Dr Ching was standing on the right side of his office, in front of the cupboard, leaning over a case of surgical tools which were placed on the worktop. When the door had opened, he slammed the lid of the small case closed, but there was enough time for her to see the type of tools that were inside.

Surgical instruments.

'Jan – how – how can I help you?' he stuttered.

She frowned at him for a second, wondering why he was acting so strange, then asked, 'I'm heading out for dinner… is there anything I can get for you?'

He shook his head quickly and dismissed her.

35

Friday afternoon
Brinkburn Drive

Byrd was sitting in his warm car with the heaters blowing. The sun had yet to come out and the afternoon was bleak and depressing. He pressed a few buttons on his phone, put it to his ear, and listened to it ringing as he stared out onto the dark street.

'Hello,' the voice said.

'Cornty, hey listen, I need to ask you a question.'

'Go on,' said Cornty.

'Did you check for cameras on Brinkburn road when Julia Porter went missing? Tanzy told me he'd asked you?'

'Yeah,' he said, 'I had a look – checked with the council's CCTV and there were no matches in that area. I checked outside the perimeter as well, near Cockerton, West Park, back into town, but no sign of the van. Sorry, I thought I'd told him.'

'Okay, good work.'

'Thanks. Speak soon,' the PC said before disconnecting.

Byrd let out a sigh, put the phone back into the pocket of his coat and stared at Ian Porter's house. He watched the house for a few moments, noticing the silver Astra and dark grey Qashqai on the road directly in front of it. A dim light shone from the large bay window upstairs, which Byrd assumed was his bedroom.

He glanced around the street.

He thought about knocking on a couple of doors to see if the neighbours had anything to say or if they'd seen anything unusual late Wednesday night or early Thursday morning, but he recalled that had already been done.

He pulled the key from the ignition, opened the door and stepped out into the late afternoon. Opening the gate, he stepped onto the driveway, and when he reached the front step, he knocked firmly on the door.

On the other side of it, he heard a muffled voice and through the glass, he saw a figure appear. The lock clicked, the handle came down, and the door slowly opened.

'Detective?' Ian Porter said, slowly. 'How – how can I help?'

'May I come in, Mr Porter?'

'Sure, sure, come in.' Porter moved back a little, allowing Byrd space to enter.

'Thanks.'

'Can I offer you a coffee, I've just boiled the kettle?' he asked, closing the door.

'Yes, please.'

'Sugar?'

'I used to but not anymore. Just milk please.' Byrd followed Ian Porter down the short hallway into the kitchen. On his left, he passed the room where Julia Porter's dead body was found two days ago. He remembered the scene so vividly: Tied up, naked to the chair, her eyes missing, the pool of blood beneath her.

He shuddered past the sickening thought.

'How've you been, Ian?'

Porter flicked on the kettle. 'It's been hard, Detective. The kids are struggling to come to terms with it.'

'I can imagine, it must be extremely difficult for you all. *Where* are the children?'

'Upstairs. I'm just about to make them something to eat.' He bent down and pulled some chips and chicken nuggets from the freezer and put them onto a metal tray. 'I never was a great cook.'

Byrd could hear the genuine sadness in his tone. 'Don't mind if I sit, do you?'

Porter turned. 'Not at all.'

Byrd dropped his weight onto one of the high chairs at the worktop.

'What is it I can help you with, Detective Byrd?'

As the sound of the kettle started to take over the kitchen, Byrd said, 'We have the post mortem results back for Julia. I thought I'd speak to you in person about it.' Byrd noticed Porter froze half a second after absorbing the news.

'I see,' he said, closing the oven door and turning the nob round to the desired temperature. He stood, faced Byrd with glassy eyes. 'What happened to her?'

'She was strangled. I'm sorry.'

'What – what about the eyes, how did that happen?'

'It appears they were removed using a sharp surgical tool.'

Porter digested his words in silence, then: 'Like a doctor's tool?'

Byrd nodded only once. 'We believe so, yes. We are trying to determine the registration plate of the van but so far have struggled to pick it up on the town's CCTV system. No cameras have picked it up.'

A thought came to Porter's mind.

'What is it, Ian?'

'Next door,' he said, frowning.

'What about next door?'

'The lady next door,' Porter said quickly, 'she has a camera above her driveway. Maybe that picked it up?'

36

Friday Late Afternoon
Darlington Town Hall

Tanzy passed through the automatic doors, stopped at the counter, where his eyes fell on the dark-haired receptionist sitting behind it. After she finished what she was eating, which looked to be a chicken sandwich, she glanced up over the top of her square-rimmed glasses.

'Can I help you?' she asked.

'You can,' Tanzy started, 'could I please see Jennifer Lucas. She works in the—'

'Control room?'

Tanzy smiled and nodded.

'I'll see what I can do,' she said, picking up the phone quickly.

'Thanks.'

To the right, there was an open area in front of two lifts which took the space of the back wall. In front of the right one, a woman was standing with an impatient child who repeatedly tapped the elevator-call button over and over again. Tanzy grinned and briefly thought about his own son, Eric, who used to do the same thing at that age.

'Go straight up, she's on the first floor,' the woman behind the desk said, raising her arm towards the lift. 'Take the lift – or the stairs. Come out on the first, take a right, walk about twenty metres and the door is on the left. There's a sign on it saying Control Room.'

'Thank you for your help,' Tanzy said, stepping away.

At the lift, Tanzy stopped next to the woman and the little boy. She was telling him to stop being silly as he hit the lift button for the umpteenth time. She turned to Tanzy, gave him a quick smile.

Tanzy returned the gesture, then glanced down at the kid, who glared up at him mischievously, half of his small face hiding behind his mother. It wasn't long before there was a 'ding' sound coming from the lift and the doors opened. They stepped inside. Tanzy watched the little boy press the button for the first floor. Then floor two. Floor three—

'Jackson!' she shouted, reaching forward and pulling him back. She glanced at Tanzy, her cheeks warming with embarrassment. 'Sorry about that - where are you going?'

'First floor,' he said.

'Good job,' she sighed.

'Mine did the same at that age, don't worry about it.'

Tanzy turned and faced the front, and in his mind, briefly thought back a couple of years when he entered a lift. There must have been ten people inside at the time; it was pretty full. The lift doors opened, and a man stepped in. Tanzy had courteously half-smiled at the man but then something strange happened. The man didn't turn around and face the door. Instead, he looked towards the mirror at the back of the lift. For the other nine people, it was probably the most awkward thing they'd ever encountered.

'Nice name,' Tanzy commented.

'I'm sorry?' the woman said, curling a few strands of her behind her ear.

'Your son's name? Jackson?'

'Ooo right, yeah,' she said, now understanding.

'I don't know many Jackson's,' Tanzy said.

'Different, isn't it?'

'It is.'

The lift doors finally closed, and the lift started to move upwards.

'I chose it. My husband is useless.' She laughed, then diverted her attention away from Tanzy back to Jackson who had pressed another button. The lift stopped at the first floor and the metal doors pinged open. He held out his palm towards them, indicating for them to go first.

'Not only good-looking but manners too?' she said as she stepped out and took a left.

'Have a good day,' Tanzy replied, stepping out after them. 'Bye, Jackson.'

'Bye, Man,' his little voice countered.

Down the wide corridor, the dark grey carpet felt soft and a faint smell of fresh paint lingered off the high bright, white walls.

At the door with the sign on, Tanzy knocked twice and opened it. The room was darker than the hallway with a haze of light coming from the left side of the room. At the small desk in the centre of it, a woman was sitting facing the monitor. She heard Tanzy enter, turned her head towards him, and smiled widely. His heart melted. It was the first time he'd visited the control room and only the second time he'd ever seen her. Everything else was done through emails or over the phone.

'Hi, Orion,' she said, softly.

Her accent alone filled his insides with a warm fuzz. In front of her, there were three rows of screens, eight screens on each row, each picture impressive in a vivid colour. The light coming from the screens gave her face a gentle glow as she stared at him with the nicest eyes he'd ever seen.

'Hi, Jennifer, how you doing?' Tanzy stopped near the desk, grinning down on her. He didn't know if it was the mild glare from the CCTV screens, but he couldn't stop staring at her face; she was beautiful.

'I'll be better in forty-five minutes when I finish,' she replied.

'Going out in town?'

'I am actually,' she said, 'I have a date tonight.'

Although Tanzy was married, he felt a little stab to the heart. 'Oh?'

'See what happens, it's only a date. Some Pizza, maybe a movie, a few drinks.' Her eyes drifted away from his as she focused back to the screens. At the far side of the room, a lady entered through a door and asked her if she'd like a coffee. Jennifer nodded at her then turned to Tanzy. 'You want one?'

'Please. Coffee. Just milk, no sugar,' Tanzy told the short, stumpy woman, who turned and disappeared through the door.

'So, Mr Tanzy, how can I be of service?'

He took his time answering, his mind going places where, as a married man, it really shouldn't. 'I need to see a few cameras, please. You remember the footage you sent over from the camera on High Row?'

She bobbed her head.

'Well, I found something, but I need to see more, I need to see other angles.'

'Sure.' She stood up, told Tanzy to come over to the large control panel directly in front of the twenty-four screens. He followed and dropped down into the seat next to her. 'So, if I remember correctly…' She typed in the date of when Mary Richards was handed the small Greggs bag. 'This should be it - what time was it?'

'Around 10 a.m.. If you could find the same camera angle that you sent me, and I'll see if I can see him first, then we can go from there.'

She clicked the mouse on the desk and tapped away on the keyboard. 'Here, watch that screen.'

They both glanced up, watching the familiar scene in a frowned concentration. It took Tanzy seconds to spot the man in the black fleece.

'You see this man?' Tanzy said, standing up, leaning towards the screen with a pointed finger.

'Yeah?'

'I need to know where he goes. Stay on this angle until he goes out of shot.'

For the next four minutes, the man remained on the bench, until he got up and walked north.

'Can you get the next camera?'

'Sure.'

The smell of her perfume pleasantly hit Tanzy's senses. He took a long, slow breath.

'What?' she said.

'Huh?'

'You sniffed?'

'Did I?' His cheeks started to warm. The next screen that came up was near Barclays Bank and clocked the man turning up a narrow alley which Tanzy knew led to the carpark behind High Row.

'He went down the alley – have you got access to cameras in the car park?'

'Sure.'

The door to their right opened and the short woman padded over with two coffees and placed them down on the desk where they're sitting. 'There you go.'

'Thank you,' said Tanzy, glancing up.

'No problem.' She turned and walked away, then stopped. 'Oh, Jenny…'

Jennifer craned her neck in her direction.

'Leave on time today please, there's no gold medals for stopping back, you know.'

They both shared a laugh.

'What was that about?' Tanzy asked, picking up his coffee. It burned his throat. 'Fuck,' he whispered harshly.

'Language, Orion… this is a professional establishment.'

He couldn't tell if she was being humorous so apologised anyway.

'I often work back late,' she explained. 'I don't get paid any extra – there's no overtime here. But,' she paused for a moment, unsure about her words, '…I enjoy my job.'

'Isn't a bad thing, I suppose, enjoying your job.'

She smiled, glancing back to what she was doing. 'So… yes, here.'

On one of the screens, an image of the carpark came up showing a shot of the opening of the alleyway that the man had disappeared down. Tanzy leaned forward an inch, squinting. He didn't see it, but Jennifer sneakily rolled her eyes in his direction, watching him closely for a few moments. It seemed they shared a mutual attraction.

Her focus was disrupted suddenly when he rasped: 'Ahh, there he is.'

On the screen, the man paced casually out of the alley into Abbott's Yard carpark with his hands in his pockets. Passing a couple going the opposite direction, he angled towards the right near the first row of cars out of camera shot.

'Where'd he go?' Tanzy asked.

'I'll find the next one, hold on.' She moved the mouse of the pad near the keyboard and tapped away again. Next to her, Tanzy nervously rocked his right leg side to side as he waited impatiently.

'Shit,' she said.

'What is it?'

'The next camera is missing, I can't seem to—'

'Where's the one after?'

'Hold on,' she muttered. Tanzy fell silent, observing her work her magic. It wasn't long before she told him there were three exits – other than the one that the man used to access the car park – that he could have possibly gone down. The camera on Skinnergate picked up the small road that vehicles used to leave the car park by the side of Tanner's pub and a camera on Bondgate covered the two alleyway entrances.

'Right…' she said, changing the screens in front of them.

'You see him yet?'

'Not yet,' she replied.

The camera on Skinnergate picked up twenty-seven cars leave the car park in twenty minutes. The driver of each car could be seen clearly on the camera but none of them matched the profile of the man they were looking for. Jennifer changed the angle and picked up the camera on Bondgate. After she scrolled along the time bar to the time they needed, she resumed it.

Another twenty minutes passed.

'I don't understand,' she said, feeling defeated.

'What – what is it?' he asked, frowning.

'It's weird.'

'What is?'

'I can't find him at all. It's as if he's just vanished into thin air.'

37

Friday Early Evening
Brinkburn Drive

Through the obscured glass of the white front door belonging to the house next to Ian Porter, Byrd saw a dim light at the end of the hallway. The light became brighter, and out of the room, appeared a small figure, slowly moving towards the door.

'She's coming,' he said, turning to Ian Porter, who was standing to Byrd's left down on the block paved driveway.

The sound of the key being inserted could be heard, then a click when she unlocked it, then the door creaked opened a few inches.

'Can – can I help you?' she asked, peering nervously out.

Byrd, aware that Porter had used the word 'old' when describing her minutes before, would guess she was between seventy-five to eighty. Her frail, tiny figure was wrapped in a thick black bath robe which looked far too big for her.

Byrd firstly apologised for interrupting her then introduced himself. When he saw her frown in confusion, he reassured her there was nothing to worry about. He stepped back, pointed up to the camera positioned above the garage.

'Does that camera work?'

'Erm, I think…' Her eyebrows furrowed as if she didn't quite understand him. She leaned forward and glanced to the right, then nodded, remembering she had a camera. 'I think it does. Why?'

'Would it be possible to see the footage from late on Tuesday night?'

'What is this about, Detective, Burg?'

'It's Byrd,' he said, correcting her.

She let out a laugh. 'Sorry my hearing isn't what it used to be.'

He gave a sympathetic smile, briefly remembering what his own mother could be like at times.

'That's okay, no worries.'

'The camera works but I don't know how to use it. My son set it up for me a while ago – six months maybe. Could have been a year. We have some not very nice people come around and try ripping people off.' Byrd could see her mechanical cogs turning, trying to think. 'There was a few break-ins, too, and he said it needed to be a safe place for me. And that if anything ever happened, then I'd have the camera to send to the police. He did something with my computer, so it's able to record it - I don't how to do it.' There was a lost look in her eyes.

'It's always a good idea,' Byrd agreed with a nod. 'Can never be too careful. Could I see the camera? Potentially it could help us with what happened with Ian's wife, Julia. Maybe the camera picked up something that could help us with our inquiry.'

'Oh, just awful, Ian,' she bellowed, switching her focus to him. 'I'm so sorry for your loss, if there's anything I can do…'

Porter gave her a tight smile as she trailed off. It was a common yet courteous line which was used when someone lost a loved one. Whether they actually meant it was a different matter. He glanced down at the floor as his eyes filled up.

'Come in, Detective Burg.' She moved aside, letting them both into the warmth of the house. Byrd stepped in, not bothering to correct her this time about his name. The heating had probably been on all day since she got up. Byrd loosened the buttons on his coat and pulled the zip down to allow some air to enter. The hallway smelt of lavender, but there was nothing obvious in his sight that gave away the source.

'Where's your computer?' Byrd asked, following her slow, measured steps.

'Follow me.'

Byrd and Porter did as she asked. They passed the living room and took a right into the dining room. In the corner, beside a tall lamp, sitting on an old-fashioned brown desk, was a flat screen computer. Byrd could tell it was dated and hadn't been used in a while. The lady pulled the desk chair out, and lowered herself down slowly, wincing as if suffering some kind of pain.

'Right, how do I do this?' she asked no one in particular, methodically looking at the side of the screen for the ON button.

Byrd rolled his eyes, perhaps thinking this could be a lost cause. If she couldn't turn it on, what chance had they got in finding footage from a specific time two nights ago. He stayed positive regardless and offered her a patient smile.

'How do I—'

Byrd leaned forward and pushed the ON button. 'There you go…'

'Oh, thank you – I've never been any good with these things,' she said. The sound of the computer starting up was like an old plane coming out of a rusty old air hanger after spending years of collecting dust.

Byrd, standing directly behind her, glanced to his left, noticing Porter had taken a seat on the small fabric sofa. He offered him a quick smile, but Porter was staring at something in the other corner, which Byrd had clocked could be the set of framed photographs he noticed when he first entered the room. He was continuously scanning and observing, taking note all the time of everything around him. He rarely missed much.

On the wall next to him, there was a sofa facing the fireplace. In the left corner, a plant which looked like it needed a hefty dose of water. A set of white French doors were positioned on the left wall, but Byrd saw very little through them because of the early sunset, leaving it dark outside.

Next to the computer there was a small box with a wire dangling from the rear of it that draped behind the desk.

'If it's not turned on, does it record?' Porter asked, showing a similar level of doubt that Byrd did.

She sighed, unsure. 'I think – you see this black box?' Byrd and Porter focused on it. 'My son said even if the computer is turned off, it still records and collects the data, or something.' She frowned, unable to provide a solid explanation. Byrd nodded, knowing that was possible.

The computer screen turned blue for several seconds before the desktop background image appeared. It was a stock image of a yellow flower on the bank of a shallow river.

A folder named 'Camera' was located at the top of the screen. She used the mouse to slowly navigate over to the folder and clicked several times, more times than needed. 'I think this is it,' she said to Byrd.

Through the door of the room, a pleasant smell seeped in from the oven in the kitchen.

'Ooo excuse me you two, I'm baking cakes. I have family coming over tomorrow. Do you mind if I go and take them out? I don't want to burn them. Jeremy won't be too happy.'

'You do your thing,' Byrd replied, waving her off. She found her feet, shuffled across the soft carpet and left the room. The camera folder, after a lengthy wait, finally opened. Nearly seven months of files were saved inside the folder. Almost two-hundred items. Luckily, each file name was dated, so Byrd right clicked and sorted the files into date order to make things easier for himself. After the reshuffle, the file they were looking for was second from the top – he assumed each day covered from midnight to midnight.

Byrd clicked. The windows media player opened and the time in the corner showed 00:00.

'Ian, what time did you go out?'

'Julia called me at quarter-to-one. I left around one,' Porter informed him. Byrd skipped an hour and let it play at 1.02 a.m.. It wasn't long before he saw the Astra shoot past two minutes later. By this time, the elderly lady entered the room with three cups of coffee and a plate of biscuits, which she placed on a low-level table near Porter's knee.

Byrd, trying to distract himself away from the smell of much-needed coffee, mentally recalled how long Porter had told him he was unconscious under the bridge for and scrolled the time bar forward to 1.20 a.m..

From the camera angle, logically thinking if the van came from the right, he'd see it immediately; if it came from the left, then it would take longer as they'd be at Porter's house for a while with Julia Porter before they left.

At 1.46 a.m., the white van drove past. Almost so slowly, it took a good five seconds to crawl across the screen. Byrd used the mouse to scroll the time bar back and paused it. He leaned forward and squinted. In the darkness of the street, the light from a nearby street lamp truly served its purpose.

'Bingo!'

'What is it?' Porter asked, his body physically tensing.

'I have the plate,' Byrd told him. 'Here, you can just see it from that angle.' Porter placed his coffee down on the table and leaned in, following Byrd's finger. 'I'll run it through the system.'

Byrd plucked his phone from the inside pocket of his coat, tapped a few buttons and put it to his ear. It wasn't long before it was answered.

'Yeah, I need a check on a plate.'

'Sure,' said the voice. 'Reg?'

Byrd told the operator.

'Okay, I'll check now, bear with me.'

'Yeah, no problem.' Byrd squeezed his tired eyes shut for a second. The past few days had taken its toll on him.

Moments later: 'Detective Byrd, you there?'

'I'm here, I'm here, go ahead.'

'It's registered to a self-drive hire place on Whessoe Road in Darlington.'

38

Friday Early Evening
Police Station

DI Orion Tanzy, sitting at his desk facing his computer screen, nearly jumped when his phone rang in his pocket, the vibration sending a buzz down the side of his leg. Earlier, he'd asked Jennifer Lucas at the Town Hall if she could email him the footage they were analysing before, so he could check it again. He knew she was very competent at her job but maybe if he double-checked, something might stand out that she perhaps missed.

He edged forward, pulled his ringing phone from his trousers, and glanced away from the paused camera footage showing the two exits to the car park on Bondgate.

'Max?' Tanzy said.

'Ori, I've got a plate on the van that took Julia Porter!'

'What – how?'

'Old dear next door to Ian Porter had a camera fixed above her garage,' Byrd said. 'Was just at her place. I got a plate.'

'You ran it?'

'Yeah, turns out it's registered to a self-drive place on Whessoe Road.'

'I know the place,' Tanzy replied. 'You checking it out?'

'I'm there now. It seems like it's just closing so I'll catch them before it does. What's happening your end, Ori?'

Tanzy sighed heavily in his chair before he began. 'Two things, Max. One, I have the footage of the man in the black fleece on High Row. He goes into Abbott's yard carpark behind it but there's no shot of him coming out on the other three cameras. He didn't drive out nor did he walk out. We watched it for half an hour.'

'We?'

'Me and Jennifer, she's the—'

'I *know* who she is. How many exits are they?' Byrd asked quickly.

'There's four, Max. He came in through the alleyway into the carpark and there's another three. One on Skinnergate and two on Bondgate.' Tanzy paused a beat. 'No sign of him.'

'Have you got the full half an hour for all four cameras?'

'Yeah…?'

'You remember the surveillance training we did about seven years ago?' Byrd said.

'The one where there was that strange looking tall fella sat in the back who kept taking his shoes off and itching his feet?'

Byrd laughed. 'Yeah.'

'Yeah, I remember it, why – Oh…I get you now, you mean check the first camera, right?'

'Yes, Ori, check the first camera, he's probably doubled backed on himself. If he knows where the cameras were, he'd expect us to check the three exits and disregard that one.'

Tanzy absorbed his idea, knowing it was not likely but possible. 'Okay, yeah, I'll check,' he said quietly.

'Maybe I'm talking shit, but it's worth a shot, just in case. What's the second thing?'

'Huh?' Tanzy said.

'You said there were two things?' Byrd reminded him.

'Oh, the second thing about the missing person's report from last night that Stuart Richards made about his wife, Mary. He made a call, told the operator that he thought his wife had been taken. There were drops of blood on the path by the side of his house.'

'Okay…?'

'I originally thought it hadn't been entered on the system correctly. You know, entered the old manual way, so that's why we weren't informed about it.'

'Yes, we know this, Ori, what are you getting at?'

'Turns out it wasn't even reported, Max…'

'What?' Byrd's voice was harsh. 'How the fuck is that possible? Who – who went to the house?' He sighed heavily and said, 'You spoke to either of them yet – Stockdale or Cornty?'

'Tried calling them – they're not picking up. I need to go, ask around.'

'Okay. I'll go in here, see who hired the van two nights ago. See what comes back. If we get a name, we could be on to something here, Ori.'

'Okay, ring me soon,' Tanzy said then hung up. He placed his phone back into his trousers. He stood, left his desk and made his way down the walkway in between the rows of desks, scanning the people that still remained. He knew it was getting late.

Often on a Friday, people left a bit earlier to get a jump on the weekend. At the desk near the door, he stopped and glanced down at PC Amy Weaver, a young twenty-something attractive woman, who was typing away on her keyboard. Noticing him out of the corner of her eye, she stopped typing and looked up at him over the top of her thin, narrow glasses. Short blonde hair dyed with a touch of silver sat on the top of a tanned face.

'Detective Tanzy,' she said with a smile. 'You okay?'

'Hey, Amy, have you seen PC Cornty or DS Stockdale?'

'DS Stockdale has gone home, but Cornty is in the canteen – or he *was* five minutes ago.'

'Okay, thanks.'

Tanzy picked up his pace, climbed the stairs, made his way down the corridor and within forty seconds, he entered the canteen. At the large circular table in the middle of the canteen, under the hanging light, PC Phillip Cornty was sitting, reading a book. He hadn't noticed Tanzy enter behind him.

'Cornty?'

He rocked his head upwards and glanced over his shoulder. 'Hey, Boss.'

Tanzy, with a stern face, made his way over to the table, pulled out a chair next to him and sat down. 'Listen, I need a word.'

'Sure.' Cornty placed a long, green bookmark into the page he was reading and closed the book, placed it down on the table and gave the detective his full attention. 'What's up, Boss?'

Tanzy noticed the front cover of the book he was reading: How to deal with a Crime Scene – Forensics 101.

'Interesting read?' asked Tanzy.

'You know, it's quite informative,' Cornty said, his eyes peering over his geeky glasses.

'Good.' Tanzy composed himself. It was part of the job he didn't like. He hated questioning people and asking questions that implied they'd done something wrong. 'Why was the missing report of Mary Richards not put into the system correctly?'

Cornty frowned. 'I don't understand.'

'It's pretty simple, Phillip. Stuart Richards made a call last night to one of the operators, saying his wife had been taken and that there were drops of blood on the path outside his home. Also said he found a missing shoe. As you know, when we found her this morning at the crime scene, she had the other shoe still on her foot. I did some checks on the system, and I originally thought that one of you had entered the report wrong on the system - manually processed it instead of doing it the new way. That's why I thought it was Stockdale first. I know you know how to do it properly, you're a good PC.' Tanzy paused for a second, seeing the frown across Cornty's brows deepen. 'Then I checked the file and it turns out that the report hadn't even been entered either way – it wasn't on the system. That's how we didn't know she was even missing.'

'Wait a second, I have no idea what you're talking about?'

'You and Stockdale went to the Richard's house last night, spoke to Stuart, her husband, and reported him finding the missing shoe and blood. The question I have is why you didn't process the report correctly?'

'I didn't go to the Richards' house last night,' he said, still looking confused. 'I went home at six, I had things on.'

'What things?'

Cornty's cheeks flash a colour a red for a moment. 'I had a date.'

'A date?'

He nodded confidently.

'With who?'

'I really shouldn't be—'

'With who?'

Cornty could sense his serious tone and straightened his face. 'I – I don't think I should—'

'Tell me!'

'Okay, okay.' Cornty broke eye contact for a second then focused back on Tanzy. 'PC Amy Weaver, Sir. I promised her I wouldn't say anything.'

Tanzy absorbed his words in silence. He knew that Cornty was a little on the odd side, but he'd worked with him a while now, had the feeling deep down below that slightly strange persona, he was an honest man and certainly one he could trust. 'Why was I told that you went to the Richard's house then?'

He offered a hopeless shrug. 'I don't know, who told you this?'

'It doesn't matter, my mistake, sorry to bother you.' Tanzy stood and walked away. 'Have a good weekend, Phillip. Stay outta trouble.'

'Okay, I'll try.'

In the corridor, Tanzy stopped halfway down when a thought entered his head. Why would he have been told that Cornty attended the scene when he never? Back in the office he saw PC Amy Weaver still sitting at her desk, typing away.

'Hey,' Tanzy said, stopping beside her. 'What did you get up to last night?'

'I went on a date,' she said.

Tanzy nodded, appreciating her honesty. 'Who with?'

'Cornty.'

'Okay. When was the last time you saw PC Kim Harrison, I need a word with her?'

39

Friday Evening
Van hire Self-Drive

Byrd opened the door and stepped into the warmth of the small office. The man behind the desk was folding several pieces of A4 paper, then stopped, glanced up and squinted towards Byrd. There was activity in the room behind, which seemed half the size of the reception area, judging by how far the back wall went. A man was talking on the phone, slowly circling the room, his expression as if something was concerning him.

'Sorry, Sir, we're closed now,' the man behind the desk said to Byrd, hoping he would apologise, turn around and leave. Instead, Byrd moved closer towards the man, maintaining eye contact.

'Oh? I'm hoping you can help me?' Byrd said, stopping at the high desk. 'I'm Detective Inspector, Max Byrd.'

'What… can I do for you?' The man placed the paper down on the desk and gave the detective his full attention, figuring the quicker this was done, the sooner he could go home. Byrd had years upon years of experience speaking to people. Knowing how to speak to people respectfully determined which way a situation would go. If you were asking for help, being rude did absolutely nothing, regardless if you were the police or not.

Byrd plucked his phone from his jacket pocket and found the registration plate of the van that he saw from the camera belonging to the elderly lady next door to Ian Porter. 'I need to find out who rented a van on Wednesday night.'

After the man heard what Byrd had to say, he frowned in thought.

'What's the matter?' Byrd asked, not understanding the man's response.

'That's the van that was stolen on Tuesday night.'

'Okay…'

'Have you guys not found it yet?'

'I – I don't follow?' Byrd said, frowning.

'I made the call on Wednesday morning. Spoke to a woman down at the station. That van – the one you've just told me the registration of – was stolen sometime between us closing on Tuesday night at five to Wednesday at seven the following morning. When I turned up, there were four vans, not five. I checked with Ronny'—he pointed behind him towards the small room, indicating the man on the phone was Ronny—'and another lad, Karl, but they said it wasn't rented out. Someone was meant to be picking it up at eight a.m. Wednesday morning. Luckily, we had another van, so they took that one – would have been very embarrassing for us.'

'I'm sorry, I'm wasn't aware of this. So unfortunately, I don't have an update on that. Who did you speak to?'

'It was a woman. She was sent over an hour after I made the call.'

'Who came, do you remember?'

'A woman. She had blonde hair. I forgot her name. Mid-thirties. She took some notes. Told me she'd keep me updated.'

40

Friday Late afternoon
Police Station

DI Orion Tanzy walked back to his desk, sat down in the seat and sighed. He'd been looking for PC Kim Harrison. He'd checked her desk, the canteen, the locker room, the gym. Finally, he'd bumped into one of their colleagues who'd told him she'd already left and wouldn't be back for at least a week – she'd booked time off work last minute for an emergency.

Tanzy glanced to the right, and up on the wall, the clock told him it was nearly five-thirty. The office was quiet. There were a few people dotted around at their desks, tapping away on their keyboards. A man sitting in the corner, who Tanzy didn't recognise, was talking on the phone with someone regarding a smashed window.

One of the new recruits, Tanzy assumed.

There'd been three new DC's taken on over the past three months, a strategic plan from higher up to balance the teams and improve the overall statistics of this station in comparison to the ones in the area. Tanzy hadn't met them yet, but they'd soon be finished their initial training and will be paired up with experienced detectives.

He plucked the phone from his trousers, dialled her number. As he was about to press on the CALL button, an incoming call came in.

Byrd.

'Max, how'd it go?' Tanzy asked, leaning back, staring at the ceiling. He frowned when he noticed one of the polystyrene tiles was out of place, not quite sitting in the allocated ridged slot.

'Ori, the van that took Julia Porter has been stolen,' Byrd replied.

'Come again?'

'I checked with the rental place,' Byrd said, 'one of their vans – that specific van – was stolen sometime between Tuesday tea-time and Wednesday morning. There's no name attached to the rental.'

'Shit,' sighed Tanzy.

'Yeah.'

'What about cameras?'

'The cameras at the rental place?' Byrd asked.

'Yeah, did they see anyone take the van?'

'No, I checked with them after he'd said it had been stolen. There were four vans. The camera fixed to the side of the building was looking down on them from the side. Unfortunately, the wrong side. The van that was stolen was the one on the end. The angle is obscured. I didn't even see anyone on the video.'

'Nothing of the driver?'

'No, nothing.' Byrd sighed through the phone.

'I see. Listen, I've been looking for PC Kim Harrison. You know the issue with the missing person's report?'

'Yeah.'

Tanzy lowered his voice. 'Do you trust Cornty?'

'He's your guy, you know him more than I do,' Byrd said. 'You know me, I barely trust you, Ori, and I've known you for years.' He followed that statement with a laugh.

'On a serious note, though, Max, do you trust him?' Tanzy said, his tone serious.

'He's a little weird but I do think he has potential. And apart from this job, I don't think there's much else going on in his life. My gut tells me I'd trust him.'

'Okay…'

'Why?' Byrd noted. 'Why you asking?'

'I've spoken to him, asked him about filing the missing person report. When we were at the scene of Mary Richards, you remember PC Harrison telling us that Cornty and DS Stockdale had been to their house, then filed the report.'

'Yeah.'

'Well, she said that Cornty had told her that he'd personally filed the report and that it was on the system. Turns out the report was never there. And guess what?'

'What, Ori?'

'According to Cornty, he was on a date with PC Amy Weaver. He didn't even go to the Richards' house. My conclusion is that one of them is lying, Max… and I'm struggling to decide which one.'

Byrd didn't respond.

'Max, you there?'

'I'm here, I'm here.'

'I – I think—'

'Funny you should say that, Ori,' Byrd said, cutting him off. 'The guy in the rental place said that an hour after he made the call about the van being stolen, an officer came and took a statement. Said it was a woman in her mid-thirties, blonde hair.'

'Sounds like Harrison.'

'Yeah, it could be Harrison.'

'He said the woman had told him that she'd take care of it. Funny how it wasn't on the system though, Max.'

'I checked with Amy Weaver a little while ago. She confirmed she went on a date last night, confirmed it was with Cornty.'

'Shit,' Byrd said. 'If Cornty is the one who was lying, that means Amy is lying too.'

'I don't like how this is looking, Max.'

'You're not the only one.' Tanzy paused a beat. 'I need to phone Harrison, ask her what's going on. PC Leonard told me she'd left because of a family emergency. Said she'll be away for at least a week.'

'You didn't know about this?' Byrd asked, confused.

'I didn't know about it, no,' Tanzy admitted, shaking his head. 'I should have known, she's in my team. Every leave request from my team is ran through me first. You know how these work. It's the same in your squad.'

'Yeah,' agreed Byrd.

'Unless with it being an emergency holiday, it went straight to Thornton. I don't know – it doesn't happen very often. That might be a possibility.' Tanzy sighed through the phone, Byrd could hear his frustration. 'I need to speak to both Thornton and Harrison,' Tanzy went on, 'either way, I should have known about this.'

41

Friday Late Afternoon
Police Station

In the large meeting room on the ground floor in the corner of the police station, nine people were seated waiting for DI Max Byrd to come back. Tanzy was the man at the front, standing with his back against the table and the door. Minutes earlier, he'd just been on the phone to his wife, Pip, who was at home. She told him she was missing the kids and was ready for them to come home. She promised Tanzy she'll start again and that she'll beat the six months mark to get her badge from AA.

DCI June Thornton was seated to Tanzy's right, just near the window. Her face was blank but showed signs she was impatient. She'd just came back to the station and said the traffic had been a nightmare.

At the table in front of Tanzy, PC Cornty and PC Weaver were talking quietly between themselves. Next to them, were DS Stockdale, PC Josh Andrews, PC Anne Tiffin, and some other DC's, a couple Tanzy didn't recognise but assumed they were some of the new recruits. They were discussing their weekend plans. One of them was going on a stag do to Blackpool and had shocking plans for the stag. It would be a weekend he'd never forget. Apparently.

'Where is he?' DCI Thornton asked Tanzy, referring to Byrd.

Tanzy glanced down at his watch, then over to her. 'He won't be long, Boss.'

She nodded, said nothing more and looked away.

The sound of shoes smacking off the hard floor were heard outside, getting louder, until the half-open door opened fully and in stepped Byrd. He took off his jacket quickly and placed on the surface of the desk near Tanzy.

'You made it,' Tanzy said.

'Traffic,' he said. 'Bloody nightmare.' Looking around the room, he offered sympathetic smiles to everyone. 'Right, where are we?'

Tanzy reached down to his right and picked up the small black remote, then handed it to Byrd. 'Do your thing.'

Byrd took the remote like a baton and took a few steps back, turning to the large screen behind them. All the eyes focused on it as silence filled the room. Everyone was keen to hear the update, not only because they were interested, but to get things wrapped up and get a start on the weekend.

'This won't take long,' Byrd began, 'but it's important we all keep up with what's going on.' He did a quick sweep around the room. At first, he hadn't noticed DCI June Thornton sitting over to the right. When their eyes met, he held his gaze for a second.

'Most of you are aware that Julia Porter was taken in a van late on Tuesday night going into Wednesday morning. Her husband, Ian, was knocked unconscious under the bridge at the bottom of Whessoe Road, then forty-five minutes later, he woke up, and headed home. He found his naked wife tied to a chair in the dining room, her eye balls missing.'

He paused, allowing it to sink in.

'At first, Orion and I were thinking Ian Porter was involved with his wife's murder. However, we don't think that, but I do have a feeling he's not being one-hundred percent honest with us. He's acting—'

'How would you act if you found your wife dead in the house?'

Byrd glared over at PC Cornty, who was staring at him over the tip of his glasses.

'I'd be very upset, PC Cornty. Why do you ask?'

Byrd did well to remain calm.

PC Cornty always had an unusual way of communicating with people. Byrd put it down to being keen and having his say in group meetings. A way of standing out to his peers. He wanted his voice to be heard. If you spent longer than five minutes with Cornty, you'd know he was aiming for the top. So whenever there was a senior member of the department in his presence, this time being DCI Thornton, Tanzy and Byrd both expected it.

'Maybe that's why he's acting strange?' Cornty replied.

'Maybe,' Byrd countered. 'From a camera positioned from the elderly neighbour living next door to Porter, I managed to take note of the registration of the van that Julia Porter was transported in. After speaking to the rental place on Whessoe Road where the plate was registered to, I was told that the van that transported Julia Porter to her house was in fact stolen sometime between Tuesday tea-time and Wednesday morning.'

'They not have CCTV?' PC Amy Weaver this time. Her date with Cornty must be rubbing off, Byrd thought.

'From the angle of where the camera was, it didn't show anyone getting into the van. It's either bad security planning, or the person who took the van knew how not to be seen.'

'Hold on a second,' DS Stockdale said, holding up his hand. 'If the van was stolen, did they not report it?'

The question hung in the room for a while. Both Tanzy and Byrd had discussed this less than an hour ago. The description of the officer who went out was female, had blonde hair, and was aged around her mid-thirties, had very much matched the description of their colleague, PC Kim Harrison, who'd conveniently left for seven days for an emergency matter. The last thing either of them wanted was a hint of blame to be put on anyone in the department, especially a member of their own team.

'There was no report of any stolen vehicles recorded,' Tanzy said with a shrug.

Byrd glanced to his left, nodding at Tanzy, their eyes meeting and understanding each other.

'What's the latest on Evelyn Jones?' DCI Thornton asked.

'Evelyn's parents are doing another press conference tonight,' Tanzy said. 'I'm going to meet them later. I'm in touch with them daily. We decided it was time to release another one. We haven't had much luck so far.'

'Where are we on the Mary Richards case?' Thornton then asked, changing the topic suddenly.

Everyone in the room glanced over at her briefly, then returned their gazes to Byrd and Tanzy, interested to know their answer.

Tanzy glanced at Byrd.

'If you haven't seen the update, we found the body of Mary Richards this morning hanging from a tree by a rope,' Byrd said. 'Her right hand was missing, and her left shoe was also missing. We had forensics at the scene - Tallow and Hope. The body has been sent for examination, under the request of an emergency priority. We're waiting to hear back on that one. I'll update–'

'Was hanging the cause of death?' Cornty asked.

Byrd thought for a moment. 'Like I said, I'll update you guys when forensics have more sustainable evidence.' Byrd's focus fell onto DS Stockdale. 'You want to enlighten the group about the situation regarding Mary Richards?'

'I went to the Richards' house last night,' Stockdale started, 'her husband, Stuart, phoned, saying there was someone at their house – according to his daughter anyway. Personally, he said he never saw anyone. He said his wife went out to empty the bins and never came back inside. There was a small pool of blood and a missing shoe by the side of the house. We took pictures and returned to the station.'

'Thank you, DS Stockdale, for—'

'Did you file the missing person's report?' DCI Thornton said, interrupting Tanzy.

Stockdale turned his head, frowned, then looked back to Tanzy.

'The report was there,' Tanzy told her.

Byrd, standing beside him, said nothing.

'I never saw the report?' she said.

Tanzy looked away from her, back to the group. 'Yesterday, if you have read the earlier update, you will know that Mary

Richards and her daughter, Mia, were on High Row in town. They came out of Greggs and a man stopped them. He handed her a small Greggs packet and when they opened it, a pair of eyes fell out on to the floor. After DNA analysis, they were a match with Julia Porter. It seems there's an obvious link here.'

'Seems like Mary Richards was a target?' PC Amy Weaver suggested.

'Seems so,' Byrd replied.

'Julia Porter, too.'

Tanzy nodded. 'It's possible.'

On his watch, Tanzy noticed it was approaching six. 'Right, that's the end of the meeting. I'll stay back and handover to the other shift, let them know what I've just told you, see if we can make progress here. For the ones who've been kind enough to stick their hands up for overtime over the weekend, I'll see you in the morning. For the ones with a life outside of this place, have a good weekend.'

Most of them stood up and made their way to the door. Remaining in the room, were Byrd, Tanzy and DCI Thornton.

'Before you two go,' Thornton said, 'I need a word.'

42

Friday Early Evening
Police Station

Byrd and Tanzy both gave their full attention to DCI Thornton.

'Orion, why did you ignore my question?'

'Which one?' A wave of confusion washed over his face.

'You know which one – about the missing person's report. I checked myself. I didn't see it on the system. I know there's something you didn't want to share with the group, isn't there?'

Tanzy sighed lightly, then glanced at Byrd.

'Go on… spill the beans, don't look at Max.' she said. 'Don't be shy.'

He glanced at Thornton. 'When Stockdale came back to the station, he said that Kim Harrison had got the photos off him. She told him she'd file the report herself as Stockdale had mentioned he had plans for the evening, and as Stockdale was new, he wasn't sure how to do it yet. When we saw her this morning, I'd asked her specifically why Max and I weren't made aware of the missing report on Mary Richards.

'She'd said that Stockdale had returned back to the station and filed it. At first, I wondered if it was done manually and it hadn't updated yet. I checked, and it turns out that the report was never put in. Harrison told me that Stockdale had told her he'd processed it. According to him, he told me that she had done it. One of them is lying.'

'Hmmm?' she said.

'What is it?' Byrd asked, leaning forward.

'She came to me earlier,' Thornton said, 'told me she needed to take an emergency holiday. Something had come up.'

Tanzy this time. 'Did she say what?'

'She said she had a family emergency. Needed a week off to sort out whatever it was that needed sorting. Did she not come and ask you first?' she queried.

Tanzy shook his head. 'No. At least she mentioned it to you. I'll give her a ring. It's obvious we need to speak to her about this.'

'Yes, definitely. But she told me she'd cleared it up with you first and that you sent her to me.'

Tanzy shook his head. 'No, she never.'

'I'll leave it in your capable hands, Orion.'

Tanzy plucked his phone from his trousers, unlocked it, and dialled her number. Byrd and Thornton watched him as he raised the phone to his ear.

'Straight to voicemail,' he sighed.

'You need to get hold of her, Ori,' she told him harshly.

'I'll go to her house, see if she's there.'

43

Friday Evening
Darlington

In the small room at the back of the house on the first floor, the man was sitting at his desk, his body slightly slouched as he stared down at the document in front of him.

He wiped away the last of the tears and breathed heavily.

Through the open door behind him entered his wife, Grace.

'Hey,' she said quietly, fully aware of what he was looking at.

Sniffing, he wiped his face with both palms and collected himself, then propped himself up in the seat. 'Hey, you okay?'

She came up behind him, placed her arms loosely around his neck, and gently kissed his cheek. He smiled but his focus remained on the A4 paper document down on the desk. For the next minute they both concentrated on the words in front of them. His sadness was replaced by a burning desire of anger and revenge.

'That's two down, Grace,' he said, 'two to go.'

'How do you feel?' she asked, now staring up at the items on the wall.

Following her gaze, he did the same.

'I'm feeling better, a little better each time. There's more work to do, though.'

'There is. I'm here till the very end.'

'They look good up there, don't they?'

Grace kissed him on the cheek and let go, slowly unwrapping herself away from him. She turned and left him alone in the room to gather his thoughts. After her footsteps faded down the stairs, he picked out his phone.

For a moment, he was still, his eyes closed, envisioning what would happen next. He opened them, and with his phone still in his hand, he searched for a number. Once he found it, he pressed CALL.

After four rings it was answered.

'Hey, Cuz,' the voice said.

'Hey,' said the man, 'how did it go with Mary Richards? I haven't seen the report yet.' Excitement filled his voice.

'Easy stuff mate,' the man on the phone said. 'Your pals were a good help, they did everything I asked. We couldn't have done it without them. What's happening next?'

'I'll tell you tomorrow, I'm coming up with a plan. There's another two on the list.'

'It's unforgiveable what they did to her. They deserve all they fucking get.'

'I couldn't agree more.'

'Give me a call tomorrow, let me know what you want us to do.'

'Okay, speak soon.'

The man hung up the phone, placed it down next to the paper on the surface of the large, brown desk. He leaned back in his chair and glared at the wall behind his computer screen.

On the wall were two pictures. A4 sized. Full colour.

One was of Julia Porter. Tied to a chair, naked, blood running down her stomach. Her eyes were missing.

The other was of Mary Richards hanging from a tree. A rope wrapped tightly around her neck. Her right hand missing.

'Perfect,' he whispered.

He'd positioned them to the left side of the wall, leaving space for two more. Once he'd finished switching focus from both photos, he stood up and pushed the chair under the desk. Near the open door, he hit the switch on the wall and the room fell into darkness. He plucked his hand into his right pocket, pulled out a key and locked the door.

44

Friday Evening
Police Station

Tanzy sighed heavily at his desk, trying to think. He knew soon he'd be doing the press conference with Evelyn Jones' parents and thought about what his answer would be when the reporters asked if the police had made any progress.

The answer was no.

But they didn't want to hear that – nobody ever did.

Most of the people who waited for the meeting had now gone home. DCI Thornton was finishing up some paperwork in her office behind him. Byrd had gone out.

He took a deep breath and logged off his computer. As the screen went black, he pushed himself out, stood up, and put his long coat on. The office was warm, heat was blasting from the fans positioned high up on the wall behind him.

He pushed his chair in and left his desk.

Then he remembered something and stopped suddenly. As he squinted, angling his attention up to the ceiling area, directly above his desk, a ceiling tile was slightly out of place. Somehow, unknown to him, it wasn't quite sitting in the correct slot. He padded back a few steps until he was underneath it and glared up at it. It was too high to reach up whilst standing on the floor.

Deciding he couldn't leave it, he glanced around him, noticed a stool tucked under one of the vacant desks across the other side of the office. He remembered the maintenance man was in earlier, changing light bulbs, upgrading them. On one of the newsletters, he recalled reading something about energy saving methods, not that he took the time to sit and actually read it. Usually, he'd tell the man not to leave his shit around but in this case, it had aided him, so directly under the dislodged tile, he placed the stool and carefully stepped up.

Reaching up, he pushed the tile upwards and placed it nicely back where it should be, so it sat flush with the rest of the ceiling. Then his mind started to think: why was it like that?

He angled his head, noticed the nearest light was three metres away. Could it have been something to do with the electrical wires that fed the lighting system?

Maybe.

But he hadn't seen any electricians in, just the maintenance man, Jerry. And when electrical work was carried out, it was usual approved qualified electricians, not Jerry, the maintenance man.

He slowly pushed the tile upwards, moving it out of the way. He pulled his phone from his pocket and opened the camera app. After making sure the flash function was switched on, he leaned up, placed his arm through the open space and took a picture. The flash lit the space in the ceiling for half a second. He lowered the phone, had a look at the shot.

Just an empty void. At the back end, he saw the flat wall.

He tried again, this time, turning ninety degrees and took another shot. He checked again, squinting, now seeing something. At the back of the shot, he saw a collection of pipework running horizontally along the side wall. Four of five pipes maybe. On the same wall, he noticed two central heating pipes running vertically up from a radiator near one of the desks, figured it was them and the rest of the heating system.

He swivelled slightly on the stool, careful not to unbalance it, and was now one-hundred degrees from where he took the first snap. He pressed the button. On the picture in front of him, if he hadn't looked as carefully as he did, he would have missed it.

Something small. Black.

'What is that?' he whispered.

Reaching up, feeding his hand through the gap, he used his fingers to feel where he thought it was. There. It felt plastic.

He pinched it deftly between his thumb and fingers then slowly lowered his hand back down.

Straight away, he knew what it was. He'd seen dozens of them.

It was a listening device with a built-in high-spec microphone, the type you'd hide somewhere so you could hear people talking if you didn't want them to know.

Somebody had been listening to them.

45

Friday Evening
Darlington

After Tanzy jumped into his Golf and closed the door, he pulled the phone from his trousers and rang Byrd. The sky was full of rain and the car park was dark. Not many cars remained but it gave Tanzy a clear view of a small group of teenagers who were pondering around the front entrance of the flats opposite, looking like they were up to no good.

'Hey, Ori,' answered Byrd into the phone.

'Listen,' Tanzy said quickly, 'I found something at the office, Max.'

'What – what is it?' Byrd could hear the urgency in his voice.

'I found a bug, Max, just above where we sit, in the ceiling.'

Tanzy turned the engine on and let it idle. The lights, which were set to Auto, flicked on and cut across the cold, shadowy car park with brilliant xenon white beams.

'How on earth did you find that?'

'One of the tiles were dislodged above my desk. I stood on a chair, had a look. A little black bug, standard device.'

'Fuck!' Byrd shouted through the phone. 'What have you done with it?'

'I've left it there,' he told him, 'I don't want whoever did it to know that we know. We need to watch what we're doing and saying from now on, Max.'

Byrd sighed heavily and said nothing.

'I've just left the office. I'm meeting Evelyn Jones' parents for the media appeal very soon. On my way, I'm going to Kim

Harrison's house, see if she's there. I've tried ringing, but she isn't answering.'

'Where on earth is she?' Byrd said, frustration clearly filling his voice.

'God knows, I'll get hold of her.'

'What time will you be on tonight?' Byrd asked, referring to the media appeal.

'Be on the ten o'clock news, Max.'

'I'll stay up for it,' Byrd replied, knowing he hadn't gone to bed earlier than 10 p.m. in the last ten years. 'Let me know what's happening with PC Harrison, too.'

'Sure thing, I'll keep you updated. Have a good night, mate.'

'Speak soon, pal.'

Tanzy slipped the phone back in his pocket. Across the road at the edge of the carpark, he noticed the dodgy-looking youths had disappeared. He put the gear in first and rolled across the tarmac until he hit the exit, then pulled out, taking a left and headed towards Yarm Road.

It took him less than four minutes to reached the house of PC Kim Harrison. It was a semi-detached house on Neasham Road, set back from the road, giving the property the attribute of a little privacy and a long driveway. The front garden was big and square. Along the fence that separated the house and the place next door, a plethora of flowers and plants stood tall and colourful, even in the dark.

On the drive, there was only one car. It wasn't Harrison's, which made Tanzy wonder if she was at home. Assuming the other car belonged to her husband, he thought it wouldn't cause any harm asking him about her whereabouts. If Tanzy was being honest, he was starting to worry about her. She'd never gone that long without responding to phone calls or messages.

Tanzy switched off the engine and stepped out. The whistling wind sent a chill through him as he rounded the bonnet of the Golf and made his way down the driveway until he reached the door. He knocked three times, then took a step back.

The living room light was on, a dim, red glow fighting against the other side of the curtains. Through the glass in the front door, a figure came into view and gradually got bigger as it drew closer. The locked clicked and the door opened.

'Can – can I help you?' said the man, a frown on his face. There was a tea towel wrapped over his right forearm and the smell of cooked chicken seeped down the hall.

'Jack?' Tanzy asked.

'Yes?' The neutral expression on his face was replaced by worried look.

'Hi,' Tanzy said, extending his hand, 'I don't think I've had the pleasure of meeting you before.'

Harrison's husband shook it wearily.

'I'm Detective Inspector Orion Tanzy,' he pressed on, 'I work with your wife, Kim. I don't see her car here but I'm wondering if she's at home. I need to speak with her. I've tried calling but she isn't picking up.'

'She isn't here, I'm afraid, not yet, anyway,' the husband said.

'Not yet?'

'No, she hasn't come in from work yet,' he said. 'I figured she was staying back, working overtime.'

A look of confusion enveloped Tanzy and his eyes narrowed. 'Are you sure? She left a little while ago.' Tanzy mentally calculated it must haven't been nearly three hours since he'd been told that Harrison had left the station.

'I'd know if she was here, Detective.'

'I see.' Tanzy thought for a moment. 'Have you been in contact with Kim today?'

The man nodded twice. 'She spoke to me on her dinner. Mentioned about going to the shop after work to get some Mint Sauce for the chicken dinner I said I was making us.

'Have you spoke to her another time?'

'She rang me around four, I think'—he tipped his head, squinted—'yeah around four. She told me there was an issue at work and she wasn't sure how to handle it.'

'What was the issue?'

'She didn't get into it, just said that it could get complicated. That she didn't fully trust one of her colleagues. At the time, I had the tele on watching a football game I'd recorded earlier in the week so I wasn't really listening to her.'

'Could you do me a favour, please? Tanzy asked. The man gave a slight nod. 'Could you phone her. I need to ask her something regarding work. I've tried but she isn't answering my calls.'

'Sure,' the man said. 'Come in for a second, keep the heat in.' The man moved back and allowed Tanzy to enter, then found her number, pressed CALL. 'Straight to voicemail. Her battery must have died. She shouldn't be long if you want to wait?'

'Is your family member okay?' Tanzy asked.

'I'm sorry, Detective?'

'I was told Kim had left work and had put a week's holiday in for a last-minute family emergency?'

The man shook his head slowly. 'You must be mistaken… unless she hasn't told me about it. As far as I'm aware, there's no family emergency.'

'Okay,' Tanzy said. 'Could you try phoning her again?'

'Sure.' The man repeated the same actions moments ago and raised the phone to his head. But again, no answer, the call going straight to voicemail. 'Must have no battery left, it goes to voicemail when that usually happens.'

'Okay. When you see her, can you tell her to call me, it's important.'

'Sure thing, Detective Tanzy.'

Once Tanzy had stepped down on to the driveway, the man closed the door. Back inside the car, he tried calling her again.

Same result. Voicemail.

He found Byrd's number, pressed CALL. Tanzy told Byrd about what Harrison's husband had said, that there was no family emergency according to him.

'Well, where is she then?' Byrd said. 'What the fuck is going on?'

'I'm sure there's a logical explanation, Max.'

Tanzy started the car, turned the blowers on full. It was freezing outside now. The rain, which was light before, had suddenly got heavier, now pelting against the windows of the car.

'Shit, I need to go, Max, I'm seeing the Jones' soon.'

'Keep me updated,' Byrd said. 'I'll call around, see if anyone has seen Harrison. If I hear anything, I'll let you know, Ori.'

'Thanks.'

46

Friday Evening
Darlington

Tanzy placed the phone down on the passenger seat and edged out onto the road. A couple of minutes later, he pulled up in the carpark of Business Central Darlington and found one of the remaining spots near the entrance. The car park was half full, most of the cars had piled towards the spaces near the entrance, minimising their time out in the cold and rain, leaving the rear half of the carpark empty. Tanzy knew most of the vehicles would belong to media reps and local reporters.

As he walked across the tarmac, he glanced around, noticing the Jones' car over to the left. There was a colourful sticker in the rear windscreen that made him feel sad about Evelyn. For over a week now, he'd stared at her photograph on his desk, promising her little face on the picture that he'd find her.

Through the double doors of the building, Tanzy felt the warmth of the heating system instantly. The reception area was bright and well lit. The walls were white, and every surface and shape carried that quality of a modern-day interior design. A man was standing near the desk and raised his palm towards Tanzy as he approached.

'I.D, Sir?'

Tanzy showed him. The man nodded and let him passed. On the other side of reception, behind the desk, there was a small crowd of people. He recognised the parents of Evelyn standing with a man dressed in a black, tight-fitting suit. The man seemed to be consoling them, offering them some emotional support. He was tall and slim, almost four to five inches taller than Ray Jones. Next to Ray, was Evelyn's mother, Jane. She used a tissue to wipe her tears away and nodded several times at the man. Maybe he was advising her what they should say in the upcoming media interview, Tanzy wondered.

'Hi, Mr Jones.' He then glanced towards Jane and nodded. 'Mrs Jones.' They both turned. Ray gave Tanzy a brief smile, but Jane stayed straight faced and fed up. She had been disappointed so far by the help that the police had offered.

'Have you heard anything yet – how's the investigation going?' Ray asked quickly, edging forward a fraction.

It was another question that Tanzy would have to answer in a negative light because there hadn't been any updates or progress yet. If there had been, Tanzy would have already notified them. He understood their desperation. He'd be the same if either Jasmine or Eric had been taken. Usually, after the forty-eight hours had passed, the parents of missing children started losing hope. After that time, the chances of finding a missing child alive are massively decreased.

'Nothing yet, Mr Jones,' Tanzy said, 'but this is why we're here, we need to ask the good people of this town to help us, to keep an eye out for her.'

'It's been nine fucking days!' Jane gasped. 'Nine days, Detective Tanzy! Why is this taking so long?'

Ray Jones digested his wife's anger and gave a beaten sigh. The tall man standing next to them gave a thin smile and put his hand on her back.

'We'll find her, Jane, just hold this together for now,' the man said softly.

Ray Jones gave a thankful smile to the man and looked back at Tanzy with tired lost eyes. The man lowered his hand, faced Tanzy, then stepped forward, extending a hand.

'Hi, Detective, I'm Neil, Neil McMahon. I'm Evelyn's teacher at school.' Tanzy took the man's hand. It was firm. 'We're absolutely devastated at the school about Evelyn's disappearance. Her class friends are very upset.' The man spoke with a northernly accent, but it carried a certain level of education that you would associate with a respectable teacher. His face was kind, too, giving the impression he'd have the patience and aura to educate younger children. If Tanzy was to guess, he'd say he was late forties, maybe early fifties.

'I'm Detective Inspector Orion Tanzy, nice to meet you.'

Neil smiled, lowered his hand, and took a step back.

'Good of you to support them, Mr McMahon,' Tanzy said.

'Absolutely, Detective. It's a dark cloud hanging over the classroom – and the school - every day,' the teacher said. 'The children have been doing some colourful drawings for Evelyn.' He faced Jane and Ray. 'We've put them up on the drawing board for everyone to see. We are all praying for her.'

Jane raised a finger to her eye and wiped away a tear. Ray stood still fighting back obvious rising emotions.

'We're nearly ready,' a voice said behind them. Evelyn's parents turned to the direction of a small, thin woman dressed in a dark blue suit with a clipboard. 'If you'd like to follow me, please.'

Jane used her soggy tissue to dab her eyes one last time before she shoved it back into her pocket. She was attractive, probably mid-thirties. Long dark hair sat straight, shoulder length. After she turned, side by side, they followed the petite woman. Neil, Evelyn's teacher, trailed them. Tanzy hung back a few feet and followed them into the conference room.

It was rectangular. At the right side of the room on one of the narrowest walls, there was a long desk with a metre gap between the edge of it to the wall, the space between lined with a handful of chairs. On the table, small microphones were positioned equally apart, the same distance as the chairs. There was a jug of water and five empty stacked glasses next to a small box a tissues which Tanzy knew would come in useful over the next fifteen minutes.

The focus of the room, being the table, was lit up with two large lamps supported by their own flimsy-looking metal tripods that were positioned two metres back. Behind the lamps, were several lines of chairs occupied by reporters, members of the public, council officials and photographers.

Tanzy took a deep breath as they stepped into the spotlight and found their seating positions. Ray and Jane were in the centre, Tanzy on their left nearest to the door, and Evelyn's teacher, Neil, seated to their right near the wall.

The well-presented woman in the dark blue suit with the clipboard introduced herself to the camera then introduced Evelyn's parents. She then explained, although most of the people there knew, the reason for this, and that Ray and Jane had something to say.

The room fell silent, all eyes fell on Ray as he slowly rose to his feet. His cheeks blushed under the attention.

'Thank you everyone for coming here tonight,' he started. 'It's been… It's been an emotional week for my wife, Jane, and I. As you know, our daughter, Evelyn Jones has been missing for nine days now.' He stopped and fought back his emotions and the crowd respected that, giving him time and staying quiet. Behind the bright spotlights, cameras clicked constantly. 'I beg you for your help, I beg you all to help us find our beautiful little baby girl. She – she needs to come home. Please help us.'

When Ray had stayed quiet for a little while, it was clear that that was all he was going to say, and his body language gave the impression he was open to questions.

'Are things at home okay? Was Evelyn troubled at all?' one reporter shouted first, coming over from the right.

Ray scowled in the direction of the sound, matched her gaze but said nothing in return. Jane glared, becoming tense; all she wanted to do was jump over the table and rip the woman's hair out. But a moment later, her body seemed to relax when Ray placed his settling hand on her left shoulder, although he too, was livid inside. Typical reporters, he thought, always out to get the story without caring what damage it has on others. Ray and Jane were told prior to this conference to be mindful of responses if they felt angered. Everything said would be recorded and documented, so for them to persuade the public and get them on their side, they needed to be liked and their story needed to be relatable and mean something.

Ray looked like he was going to answer but another question was fired from the left: 'Is it true that Evelyn Jones has ran away?'

Where on earth were these reporters getting this information from? He started to feel wound up, his skin now growing hot, his heartrate going up a few notches, but he remembered what the police said about people asking difficult, sometimes, humiliating questions. They were looking for a reaction to sell to the papers, that was all.

'Do you think you will see your daughter again?' another reporter asked over the buzz in the room. Ray followed the voice as it was the first question that Ray had considered answering. It belonged to a man who was standing to the left. He was of medium height, had short black hair, was neither chubby or slim. He had a long, thin face with eyes that were as black as the night.

'My wife and I sincerely hope so. We know with every day that passes…' He paused a beat, choosing his next words carefully, changing what he was going to say: 'I believe in the police.' He glanced unexpectedly over to Tanzy, who met his gaze. 'I believe they'll do everything they can to find our daughter. We are distraught. We're broken. We can't cope without her.'

Looking away from Tanzy, he looked straight into the light of the cameras and the eyes of the eager reporters.

'As I mentioned in our last appeal a few days ago, Evelyn was wearing her school uniform and a red coat. She had a bright green bag with her school books, pencil case, and a pink teddy inside. If anyone has seen anything that could help, please, please get in touch with the police and get in touch with us.'

The woman in the suit with the clipboard, who was standing to the right of the long table, raised an attentive palm and told everyone that was enough questions for Ray and that Evelyn's teacher, Neil McMahon, had a few words to say.

Ray sat down, happy the questions had ended, that he was finally out of the spotlight. Next to him, Neil found his feet and nodded at the crowd. The cameras continued to click, and flashes hit the back wall like stabs of lightning.

'Hi everyone, I'm Neil McMahon,' he started. 'I'm Evelyn's teacher at school.' Everyone's focus fell on him. 'All I really want to do is add on from what Evelyn's father, Ray, has said and thank everyone for coming. Evelyn Jones is such a beautiful little person. I've had the chance to teach her for a few years now. At our school, we start with the kids in reception and move up as they progress through their school life. She's an absolute joy to be around and the other children love her. Today, we spent the afternoon drawing pictures for Evelyn and we are all going to show her them when she is found.' He fell silent and wiped a tear from his eye.

Ray and Jane angled their heads, watching him with emotional expressions. Jane, too, wiped away her tears and Ray watched him with admiration of what the man was trying to do, to send this heart-felt message across to people, hoping someone somewhere knew where she was. After he said his bit, he sat down, his body almost deflating. Ray patted his back as a thank you for his words.

It was Tanzy's turn to stand up. Raising to his feet, his heart beat multiplied when he realised everyone was looking at him. Although he was a confident guy, public speaking wasn't one of his specialities. He'd often let Byrd do the public speaking if they needed a DI to do any press talks.

The first question: 'Why has Evelyn Jones not been found?'

Tanzy swallowed the query and took a breath. He knew this question would be the most important question that the public wanted to know. He explained what the police had done so far, how his team had knocked on doors, relentlessly searched the local area she was last seen and devoted a small team to find her, making calls and searching for any potential leads. He told the crowd they would not stop until she was found.

'I promise you that,' he said, lastly.

After the conference was over, Tanzy walked outside. Immediately, the cold hit his face and calmed him. The rain had stopped but it had dropped a couple of degrees compared when he went in. Ray and Jane finally walked through the sliding doors, followed by their daughter's teacher, Neil.

Neil said something to them before he glanced towards Tanzy, gave him a wave, and made his way towards his car.

Jane and Ray padded sluggishly towards Tanzy, their bodies physically exhausted. The life was being drained from them before his eyes. Ray looked up at Tanzy and half-smiled, whilst Jane stared vacantly at the floor, visibly empty.

'I think it went okay,' Tanzy said, encouragingly.

Ray nodded. 'Yeah. Hopefully something happens now.' He wrapped his arm around his wife and squeezed her close.

'I just need to see her,' she gasped, then curled up into Ray's chest. 'I need to see my baby.'

Tanzy gave a hopeless sigh, wishing he could tell them it was going to be alright. It had been nine days since their daughter was last seen and not a single piece of information had been put forward so the police had nothing to go on. If Tanzy was being honest, he'd almost lost hope, but he had to believe that somewhere out there, Evelyn Jones was alive.

To their right, they heard the sound of an engine. They looked over to see Neil McMahon in his dark blue Ford Mondeo crawling along slowly, mindful of the layer of frost on the tarmac. He gave the Jones' a soft wave as his passed.

'He was very passionate about Evelyn,' Tanzy noted.

'He is, he's lovely,' Jane said, looking up. 'He knows how we feel. He's seen her five days a week for over three years. And obviously, because of what happened to him.'

Tanzy frowned at her, unsure what she meant.

'His own daughter went missing many years ago. She was playing football with him in the local park. She kicked the ball. Neil went to get it, just going out of sight and when he came back, she was gone. He hasn't seen her since.'

Tanzy digested the story with a sad smile.

'He wants to find Evelyn just as much as we do.'

'I understand,' Tanzy replied.

'Come on, Jane, let's get you home, it's freezing,' Ray said. His eyes met Tanzy. 'Please, find our daughter, Detective Tanzy, we can't go on without her.' They angled away from him and shuffled over to their car.

Tanzy carefully walked across the glistening tarmac to his Golf and climbed in. He turned it on, then put the heating on full blast to clear the misty windows. The Jones' car edged out from a space on his right, and slowly crawled past him. In the passenger seat, was Jane, who glanced at Tanzy and waved sadly.

In the back window of the car, there was something resting on the parcel shelf. It was a teddy. It was dark to see under the overhead lights of the carpark, but Tanzy was sure it was pink. The same colour of the teddy that Ray had told the media that Evelyn had when she went missing.

47

Friday Evening
Darlington

Ian Porter closed the door to his son's bedroom, leaving it open an inch, so the lamp on the table near the top of the stairs would prevent his room from falling into complete darkness.

'Good night, Daddy,' said the little voice inside.

'Good night, Cameron, sweet dreams, little man.'

Jonah and Liam were already asleep in their own rooms. Jonah had been very emotional today, getting used to life without his mother, Julia. He'd crashed out about 6.30 p.m. and Porter hadn't heard a peep since then. Liam was given his bottle of milk and had been put down just before that.

Once downstairs in the kitchen, he cracked open the bottle of Amaretto, placed it down on the worktop. He reached up, grabbed a glass from the cupboard, and positioned it next to the bottle. From the freezer, he picked up a handful of ice cubes and threw them into the empty glass. He watched the thick amber liquid crack the ice cubes and filled the glass until it was nearly full. He was going to wait until the drink was cold, but impatiently, he picked it up and took a mouthful, feeling the marzipan tasting liquid seep down his throat.

He topped up the glass and made his way to the silent living room, where he closed the curtains then padded over to the lamp near the window and switched it on, letting the warm light illuminate one side of the room, then he dropped down on the sofa.

The past two days had been the worst of his life.

Losing his wife.

Losing his will to live.

The people knew Ian Porter knew that Julia played the role of main parent whilst he went to work, which was understandable, because most people did it that way, unless both parents worked and used childminders and after-school clubs to watch them.

The television came on. Channel three. The ITV news was on very soon. It wasn't something Porter spent much time watching but he couldn't be bothered looking through the assortment of boring channels to find something which was probably half way through it by the time he'd found it. All he wanted to do was sit, do nothing, and stare. And so when the ITV News at Ten started, that's what he did, sipping on Amaretto.

The man sitting behind the desk in the studio told the viewers that a body had been found hanging in a tree on Cemetery Lane, just off Carmel Road, in Darlington. The woman identified as Mary Richards, was found earlier that morning by dog walkers. The television switched to a photograph of Mary Richards for a short period of time before switching to footage that was taken earlier, showing the scene – minus the body - and the tree where she was found.

It switched to an interview from a local reporter who was standing with a detective from local police, a DI Orion Tanzy, at the end of Cemetery Lane, explaining briefly what they'd found and if anyone had any relevant information, could they ring the number that rolled along the bottom of the screen.

'Jesus!' Porter gasped.

The name, Mary Richards, sounded very familiar to him. He'd heard the name before.

'Richards, Richards,' he said quickly, his eyes darting around the living room, trying hard to establish the connection.

A long time ago, he knew a Stuart Richards that he went to school with. He hadn't seen him in a while but last he heard, he'd met a woman called Mary.

He plucked his phone from his jeans and opened up social media. He wasn't sure if he was connected to Stuart as a 'friend', but he searched his name. Without typing his full name, a profile for Stuart Richards came up. After recognising the man in the profile picture, he clicked on it. Yes, it was definitely him.

He scrolled down his profile.

'Shit,' he whispered after seeing it.

There was a post on his page wall, saying, 'Omg Stu! I'm so sorry for your loss.' Along with the picture, there was an image of Stuart and Mary at some kind of dinner party, both of them dressed smartly with smiles on their faces.

Another post underneath was something similar, letting Stuart know to just call if there was anything his family needed.

'Shit, it *was* her,' Porter muttered in the silence of his living room. Porter sat back, thinking about Julia, then about Mary. Why was this happening?

Knowing he didn't have Stuart's number, he clicked on Messenger and started typing. Then after a minute, he re-read the message and pressed SEND. In the corner of the message, he saw an icon of Stuart's picture come up, indicating to Porter that the message had been read.

Three dots appeared, hovering at the bottom of the screen, telling him that Stuart was replying. Porter waited patiently but nervously. He hadn't spoken to Stuart since he was around the age of nineteen.

The message Porter had sent was asking Stuart to call him.

Stuart replied: What the fuck do you want?

Porter: Please ring me Stuart, it's important.

He pressed SEND.

It wasn't long before the ringtone disrupted the serenity of the living room. He took a breath and pressed ANSWER, then raised his arm, putting the phone to his ear.

'Stuart.'

'What the fuck do you want, Ian?'

'I need to talk.'

'Be quick about it, I'm in the middle of something,' Richards said, 'I don't know if you know, but I've just watched the ITV news report about my own wife. She was found dead this morning hanging from a fucking tree and—'

'I know, I know,' Porter admitted, 'that's why I'm ringing. I've just watched it, too.'

Richards never replied but managed a beaten sighed through the phone.

'Listen,' Porter went on, 'I don't know if you know, but my wife is dead, too.'

'Julia?'

'Yeah.'

Silence grew between them for a moment, then Richards said, 'Jesus – when?'

'Wednesday night.'

'Two days ago?'

'Yeah,'

'Fuck – what happened?

'She was… she was murdered,' he told him, 'I found her naked, tied to a chair with her eyes missing in our dining room next to our son, Liam, with a pool of fucking blood at her feet.'

'Fucking hell,' Stuart muttered, 'I'm… sorry, Ian.'

Porter never replied for a short while, then: 'I think they're connected, Stuart.'

'You think what?' His voice sharpened.

'I think there's a connection,' Porter explained. 'Because of that night. You know which night I mean, don't you?'

Silence.

'Stu, you know—'

'Ian, I know what night!' he barked.

'I think he's found out what happened. Found out what really happened to his sister.'

48

June 14th, 2004
Darlington
15 years ago

The house was filling quickly, most of downstairs now occupied with people ready for a good time, chatting in their little groups with drinks in their hands. Music blared from the CD-player inside the house spilling through the open back door that led to the decking area. A couple of steps led to the rest of the garden, where there was a pond on the right and the rest was made up of a patio which included a wide rectangular table and six chairs around it.

Sarah, leaving a small group of her friends, walked up from the bottom of the garden towards the house, stepping up onto the decking. She glanced to her left, half-smiling at Stuart Richards and Ian Porter, who were sitting on two plastic chairs, both of them with a cigarette and plastic cups filled with the cheap lager that they'd brought with them. They watched her fade into the loud house to refill her wine.

It was nearly 9 p.m.. Sherina Barker, or Shez, as her friends called her, was one of Sarah's best friends. Shez's parents owned the house, but they were away. What better way to spend a birthday than to host a party whilst your parents were away. All of the people who she'd invited, plus more, had turned up. It was looking like it would be one of the best parties of the summer. Another girl, Alison Thorne, threw one last month. Sherina never liked Alison. She thought she was up her own arse. In all honesty, she probably was. But her party was an event people spoke about for weeks.

That was a few months ago. This was now. Shez would make sure this would be a night to remember.

Sarah, after filling her plastic cup, came back outside and flaunted across the decking wearing a short skirt, a low-cut top, and black high heels. Her legs were tanned and muscular and her bum was something that every man at the party would have a peek at some point during the evening.

She was beautiful.

Long, dark straight hair fell on to her shoulders and her face carried the kindness of someone so innocent, it almost contradicted her physique and the way she moved back down to the garden.

Ian and Stuart were watching her closely.

'Would ya?' Stuart whispered.

'I wouldn't hesitate for a second,' Ian replied, smiling.

Ian Porter – and most of the other male teenagers there – fancied the arse off Sarah. The majority of the people at the party went to school with her and had felt something similar at some point during the five years of knowing her. In fact, the party was pretty much a school re-union. It had only been three years since they'd left, but everyone kept in touch. When Sherina knew her nineteenth birthday was coming up, what better way to spend it than get all of her old class mates together and get drunk, play loud music, and dance like they had no cares in the world.

At nineteen, you didn't. You thought life was tough and you were old enough to be considered an adult, but you knew nothing back then. People were naive at that age.

Sarah returned to the bottom of the garden.

'Hey, Sarah,' Sherina said.

'Hey, Shez,' she replied.

'You might wanna slow down,' Shez said, noticing another full glass. Not that she was counting, but she thought Sarah was now on her fourth glass of wine. The night was still young, and she didn't want to be looking after her best friend all night if she was being sick at the toilet.

'Don't worry about me, I'm in control,' Sarah said. Her tone was playful but there was a hint of annoyance in her reply, Shez could tell. It hadn't been the first time Shez had told her to slow down a little, and she knew it wouldn't be the last.

'I know, Sarah, I'm just saying you don't—'

'Don't worry about it,' she said again, this time more sternly. She took a big gulp and laughed.

Shez glared into her glassy eyes and said nothing more about it. 'Hey, where's your brother?'

'He told me he isn't coming.'

'Why?' Shez's pet lip came out. She fancied her brother.

'I don't know to be honest, he never said.'

Shez nodded, raised her hand and had a drink of the wine. 'It's strong stuff this.'

'It's only thirteen percent, no harm can be done…'

They both broke into laughter, and drank some more, then turned to the small group of friends and joined in a conversation about what had happened to a singer who'd been found dead in a hotel room over in America.

Back up on the decking, Stuart and Ian were watching them. 'I'm going to fuck her,' Ian Porter said quietly.

'What?' Stuart jerked his head towards him. 'Are you for real?'

Porter nodded confidently. 'Yes.'

'Mate, you tried that in year eight. She was having none of it.'

'Stu, we were thirteen back then. We're nineteen now, it's different.' Porter took another long gulp of cheap lager, swallowed it with a smack of his wet lips.

'It makes no difference, Ian. She's stunning and you're a hungry little pup wanting a bit. I guarantee it doesn't happen.'

'You wanna bet?'

Stuart Richards laughed out loud. The people closest to them turned and stared for a moment. 'How much, Ian?'

'Twenty quid?'

They shook hands quickly and smiled at each other. Porter turned away, glancing back down at the garden, watching Sarah laughing with Shez. Stuart knew Ian had tried his luck in the past with Sarah and had failed miserably. He knew he had no chance.

But glancing towards him right now, he saw something different, something dark in his eyes.

Determination.

Power.

A desire to get anything that he wanted.

So maybe tonight would be different.

49

Friday Night
Darlington

Neil McMahon turned on the television and took a seat on the large sofa. He leaned to his right and picked up his mug of coffee from the low table then leaned back and took a sip.

To his left, his wife Judith, was sitting comfortably in the corner with her legs tucked under her bum, her eyes focused on the screen. She'd been there most of the night, catching up on programs she'd missed over the past few weeks.

'How are they?' she asked him.

'They are a wreck,' he said, sadly.

'Bless them. It doesn't get any easier, does it?'

'No. it doesn't.'

The ITV news at ten had started moments ago, but Judith had paused it whilst Neil was tidying the kitchen. The first story was about the discovery of Mary Richard's body which was found in Cemetery lane just off Carmel Road. They had heard about it vaguely from colleagues and friends, but the details of the scene were harrowing. The shot went to an interview where a local member of the police, a DI Orion Tanzy, spoke into the camera asking people if they'd seen anything to come forward.

'That's the detective helping Ray and Jane,' Neil said, 'he seems a nice chap. I spoke to him at the media appeal.'

Once the report about the body had finished, it switched back to the studio, where the smartly dressed reporter told the camera about the update on the missing seven-year-old, Evelyn Jones.

'We go to Darlington Business Centre where the parents of Evelyn spilled their hearts out to the public, asking for their help to find their missing daughter,' he said.

The screen changed to a shot of the wide table in the conference room. Ray and Jane were sitting behind it in the middle chairs. The lights on them were so bright, it almost made their skin appear hollow. They looked exhausted.

'There you are,' Judith said, seeing him next to Ray.

Ray Jones spoke into the camera for a short while, whilst his wife wiped away her tears. Then Neil stood up and said his part, then DI Orion Tanzy filled the reporters in on how the investigation was going from a police perspective.

'I'm proud of you,' she said to Neil. 'Takes balls to stand up there doing that in front of all them cameras.' She leaned over and squeezed his hand.

He waved it away modestly. 'I just hope they find her soon. I know what Ray is feeling, I know how he—'

She squeezed his hand again, this time tighter. 'I know, Neil, I know. It's a pain that never goes away. I think about Casey every single day. She's left a hole in our hearts that will never be filled.'

When their daughter, Casey, went missing all them years ago, after a month went by, they'd lost all hope. At the time, they were told that after two to three days if she wasn't found, chances were that she'd never be found. Not alive anyway. When they finally accepted that they wouldn't see their daughter again, they tried for another child. Months went by, but Judith never felt pregnant. They even tried IVF, which proved a pointless effort.

'I still miss her now,' he said, 'I think about what she'd look like. What she'd be doing. What she'd have studied at University. What job she'd end up having. You remember she used to dress up in a little white nurse outfit and walk around with a plastic stethoscope?'

She nodded, absorbing his heartfelt words with tears in her eyes.

'I wish I never went to get that football…' he trailed off and leaned back, resting his head on the back of the sofa. 'She'd still be here.'

'I know, Neil,' she said softly.

'If Evelyn's not found, at least they'll have the money.'

'What money?' she asked, frowning.

'The life insurance money,' he said. 'Ray told me they took out life insurance for her in case anything bad happened. He said if anything ever did happen to her, they'd be too heart-broken to work anymore.'

'How much money will they get?'

'I'm not sure exactly,' he said, 'sure I heard it was over half a million.'

50

Saturday Morning
North Road, Darlington

James Whittaker had popped into work to get a holiday form on his day off. He knew he'd have to grovel to get the dates off he needed because of how much of an arsehole Colin Tapper was. Aldi stated that their holiday request policy was fair, but depending on staffing levels, it was up to the line manager.

His wife, Janice, and his daughter, Emily, were waiting in the car which was parked towards the back of the carpark. Inside the car, they were both occupied. Janice was deeply engaged on her phone, checking her social media updates – which recently, had started to get on James' nerves - and Emily was playing with her talking doll. He told them he wouldn't be long. All he had to do was go into Colin's office, grab a form, fill in the dates and very nicely ask Colin if he would agree and authorise it there and then.

He stepped down off the kerb, minding the slow-moving traffic coming towards him; the road was too narrow, and the spaces were proved difficult to park in due to their slight width.

The car park was beyond busy and James wondered why. After turning side-on, he crept down the narrow space between a Range Rover and his own car. The driver of the Range Rover, obviously an arsehole who thought they were above everyone, didn't possess the ability to keep the car between the white lines.

'Prick,' he muttered as he reached for his car door, edged it open and carefully slid in, mindful not to scratch any paintwork.

Once he put the key in the ignition, he put on his seat belt and smiled, looking forward through the front window. He knew that Janice would be watching him closely, sitting in the passenger seat, waiting to hear what his boss had said regarding the last-minute holiday request. He kept his focus through the windscreen, purposefully avoiding all eye contact with her.

He turned on the engine and put his hand on the gear stick. Before he had the chance to put the gear in reverse, he felt a palm on top of his hand. He smiled but never looked her way, knowing she'll be eager for an answer.

Then his smile faded. Fast.

Something was wrong.

The hand felt bigger than his wife's did. After glancing down, he realised it definitely wasn't his wife's hand.

51

Saturday Morning
North Road, Darlington

James snapped his head to the left and gasped out loud when he saw a large figure sitting in the passenger seat, wearing a white Michael Myers mask that the character did in the John Carpenter film, Halloween. He could see the man's dark brown eyes through the holes of the mask, glaring intently at him.

He felt every single hair on his body stand on end and almost shuddered when he felt a chill shoot through him from head to toe.

'Jesus,' he gasped. 'Who – who the fuck are you?'

He glared into the back seat searching for his daughter.

She was gone too. Instead, there was another man, also wearing a white Michael Myers' mask. James couldn't be sure looking at the mask, but he was sure the man was smiling at him.

'Where's my wife and daughter?' he whispered.

The men said nothing. James switched his focus between them. 'Listen, if you even hurt then, I'll—'

'Do nothing,' the man in the front passenger seat said. His voice was very calm and collected. 'You'll do absolutely nothing.'

'If you fucking touch them, I'll kill you.' He glared into the back of the car. 'You as well, I'll fucking kill you, too!

'You have a choice to make, Mr Whittaker,' the man in the front seat said. Again, his voice was even and composed.

'How – how do you know my name?'

'That isn't important, James. What's important is that you have a choice to make.'

'A choice?' Whittaker shook his head wildly. 'What choice? Where are they?' He stared out the windows, all around the car, trying to locate them somewhere in the car park.

The men stayed silent, both fixated on James Whittaker, watching the sweat run down his forehead and his body tremble in a terrified confusion.

'What – what choice do I have?' he finally asked, returning his focus on the strangers.

'Many years ago,' the man in the front seat said, 'when you were nineteen, you made a terrible decision.'

James frowned. 'What?'

'A decision that caused a lot of hurt to others. A decision that took someone away from me. A decision you're now going to really, really regret.'

'I don't understand,' he pleaded. His eyes started to well up with tears and his body started trembling.

'If you had to choose either your wife or your daughter to survive, who would you pick?'

'I don't understand what you're saying?'

'Let me simplify this for you: if one of them is going to die, which one would you save?'

He absorbed the question, staring into the man's eyes but he didn't have an answer.

'Look in the boot of the car,' the man said to him.

'Why?' James asked, wearily.

'LOOK IN THE BOOT OF THE FUCKING CAR!' the man screamed, causing James to flinch a little. Once the car fell quiet, the silence was deafening.

James slowly opened the door and slid back out, leaving the men inside of his car. After sliding between the narrow gap between his car and the Range Rover, he took a breath, staring nervously down at the boot of his car.

He reached down, pressed the button and lifted it open—

'Hey, James… James… you okay?' a distant voice said.

James' eyes flashed open a few times until they stayed open. He couldn't work out what was happening. It didn't take him long to realise he was in a small room. Bright lights shone down from the ceiling and the air was ice cold from an air conditioning unit someone near him. It was his supervisor's office, and on the other side of the desk before him, was Colin, the line manager.

'Huh?' James muttered.

'You were asleep, Jimmy. Sorry, I just had to deal with something downstairs,' he said, as he sat down and moved some paperwork on his desk.

James Whittaker blinked and came around. 'My apologies, I didn't sleep well last night.'

'No worries, Jim. Do you need me to sign that?' He nodded down to the holiday request form in Whittaker's hand.

'Ah, yeah, please.' James handed it over the desk and Colin signed it with – surprisingly – very little fuss.

'I'll get that processed immediately,' he told him.

James thanked him and left the office. On his way out, he waved at a few of the cashiers and told one of them who'd asked when he was next in that he'd be in on Monday.

The carpark was still as full. The sky was dark, filled with a plethora of dense, thick clouds that cast a haze of grey down on the town. He couldn't stop thinking about the dream he'd just had.

Back at the car, he was excited about telling Janice that Colin had signed the form. This time, there was no Range Rover, in fact, no car was parked there, so he didn't need to squeeze in. He opened the door, and climbed in.

The car was empty.

His wife and daughter had gone. On the back seat where his daughter was sitting, was a Michael Myers mask.

52

Saturday Morning
Low Coniscliffe

Byrd was sitting at the table in the kitchen, his eyes focused on his laptop. Next to it, was an empty plate containing only the crumbs left from the bacon sandwich that he'd demolished. He took a gulp of coffee, washing the remnants away.

Outside the window, a thin layer of frost covered the grass and a chill hung silently in the air. Several birds occupied the bare branches on the tree but they didn't hang around for long, coming and going all the time. It was 8.30 a.m.. Byrd woke at seven and came straight down stairs. Claire followed him after her shower and made them breakfast.

Claire was on the opposite side of the table, reading her kindle, cosy in her dressing gown. The kitchen was peaceful and warm. The heating had been on a while and she enjoyed reading Chris Carter. She loved Chris Carter. Every so often, she sighed at a point in the book where she read one of the lead detectives, Robert Hunter, finding a body or analysing a crime scene.

'What are we doing today?' Claire asked, peering over her Kindle.

Byrd glanced up. 'What do *you* want to do?'

She shrugged.

'We'll do that then,' he said, smiling. 'Give us half an hour on here then we can go out if you like?'

His eyes fell back to the screen.

'Where?'

He sighed, focused back on her. 'Wherever you like? We can have a drive into town, get some coffee. I can even buy you a dress if you're good.'

She grinned, joyfully lifting her shoulders for a moment. 'Sounds good. I need to finish this chapter anyway… oh, have you heard from the hospital?' she asked.

'No updates yet. I'll pop in later this afternoon after we've been into town. If you don't mind?'

'Of course I don't mind, Max, don't be silly. Did you think I would mind?'

He smiled. 'No, I didn't, but I did say that this Saturday would be our day and here I am'—he pointed down at his laptop—'doing work, again. Sorry.'

'Max, don't be sorry. This is your career. It's important. And seeing your parents at hospital when they're in a coma is certainly nothing to apologise for.'

He half-smiled, appreciated her understanding on both matters.

His phone rang in his pocket. Picking it out, he looked at the caller. It was Tallow, the lead forensic.

'Jacob?'

'Hi, Max,' he started, 'I didn't tell you the other day but when we examined the Qashqai that belonged to Julia Porter, we found a hair on the passenger seat. We've ran the DNA. It doesn't match any of the Porters.'

'Whose is it?' Byrd asked.

Claire looked up from her Kindle.

'We don't know. We don't have a match on the database, Max.'

Byrd digested his answer. 'Okay. Is there any update on Mary Richards?'

'Funny you should say that, because we found a very short strand of hair stuck in her finger nails. It was a different colour to her natural hair. Just hold on a sec.' His voice became quieter, as if he leaned away from the phone, speaking with someone else: 'Yeah, I've told him. Okay, no… no sugar. Thanks.' He brought the phone closer: 'Sorry, Max, I have Amanda and Paul here, showing them the analysis on the hair.'

'Say hi from me,' Byrd said.

'Will do.'

'When will the results come back from the hair found under her fingernail?' Byrd asked. Across the table, Claire frowned at him, listening to one side of the conversation. It was a world away to what she was used to in her line of work.

'Within a day, Max.'

'Thanks, Jacob. Speak soon.'

'Oh, before you go mate,' Tallow said, 'we're going out for a few drinks tonight in town. Amanda, me, and Paul. Tony said he'll try and get down, but he said he might have other things on.'

Byrd considered the response, flicking his attention on Claire, who'd focused back on her Kindle again. He'd told Claire that he'd devote his day to her. Would it be rude to go out tonight with work colleagues for a couple of drinks? Only one way to find out, he guessed.

'Yeah, okay. I'll bring Tanzy along, too.'

Now Claire glanced up, wondering what he was referring to.

'Yeah if… you like,' Tallow said, his tone a little grim.

'I thought you two had sorted things out?' Byrd asked.

'He's okay. We'll never be best friends, put it that way.'

'I'll drag him out, Jacob, you two can have a chin wag. Time you going out?'

Claire was frowning across the table now.

'I'll text you.' Feeling the heat off Claire's eyes, he said, 'Listen, I gotta go.' He placed the phone down on the table slowly.

'What was that?' she asked.

'Couple of the guys are going out tonight for a few drinks. Asked me to pop along.' He left that hanging in the kitchen, then finally they made eye contact. He could see she wasn't impressed. After all, he did say today was going to be their day. He leaned forward a fraction and grabbed his phone. 'I can tell him I won't bother. Sorry, I did say this was going to be our day, I'll message him and say I can't—'

'Just go, Max. We'll spend the day together and you can go out tonight.'

Byrd smiled and said nothing more.

53

Saturday
Darlington

James Whittaker, having not found his wife and daughter in the car when he returned, started to panic after when he saw the mask. First, he'd assumed that the dream he'd had was a fragment of his wild imagination, guessing they'd gone to another shop because they were sick of waiting. After all, he had been over twenty minutes when he said he'd only be five. Maybe that was it, maybe Janice needed something from Iceland or Poundland or Greggs.

He frantically glared around the busy car park. There were five shops, so they wouldn't be too much longer. But he knew his wife: she liked to talk. Perhaps she'd found a friend and started babbling about anything and everything.

She did that often. In the past, he'd always said no when she asked to go into town because she'd spend half the day talking to someone she knew. Their daughter Emily was the same, she could talk for England as well.

He opened his door, sat back in his car, leaving it open. From his coat, he pulled his pack of cigarettes and took one, then lit it up. The taste of the smoke in his throat calmed him and for a moment, he forgot about them, watching the passing cars and hearing the sound of idling engines. After another five minutes, he really started to panic.

'Where the fuck are they?' he said to himself, using the frame of the door to pull himself up to his feet. He took out his phone, he found his wife's number and pressed CALL. It rang and rang and rang.

'Fuck.'

He tried again.

She didn't answer. He sighed hopelessly and clicked on her mother's number. Janice had mentioned about wanting to go to her mother's house after James had got the holiday form signed. Maybe she was sick of waiting and starting walking with Anna. She didn't live far from Aldi. He found her mother's number and pressed CALL.

After three rings, her mother answered.

'Hi James?'

'Hey, is Janice and Emily there with you?'

'Here?'

'Yeah, are they at your house?'

'Not yet, you're coming soon though, aren't you?' she said. 'I've just—'

'We are, but I can't…' he trailed off.

'James, are you there?' she asked.

'I'll call you back,' he said abruptly, then hung up.

Standing next to him, was his daughter, Emily. There was a look of fear in her eyes that he'd never seen before.

'Where's – where's mammy?'

A tear fell from her eye down her cheek. 'They've taken her. She's gone, Daddy.'

54

Saturday Afternoon
Darlington Memorial Hospital

Byrd and Claire walked into the Intensive Care Unit. They'd been to town for a coffee at Costa and then to Next to buy Claire a dress. They pencilled in on the calendar to go out the following weekend. Nothing flash, just into town which they hadn't really done in a while. After Byrd had told her he was going out for a few drinks later, she suggested it and he couldn't really say no.

After checking in with the man sitting behind the reception desk, the button was pressed, allowing the double doors to slowly swing open.

As they entered the room where his mother and father were, Dr Ching was standing in between their beds, his attention focused mainly on his father but he turned when he heard the door open.

'Mr Byrd,' he said quietly. 'Nice to see you.'

'Hey, how they doing?' he asked stepping forward lightly, respectfully, anticipating the latest update on them. Claire trailed a step behind and absorbed the room: The white walls, the beeping of the machines, the lights, the wires, the cleanliness, the medicinal smell lingering in the air.

'Your mother is improving, Mr Byrd. I think she'll wake up in the next few days naturally.' The doctor stopped there.

'My father?'

The doctor's face changed, to something emotional, but he remained professional enough to prove he'd done this many times before. 'He's showing no improvements yet, unfortunately.' He paused for a second, thinking carefully about how to say his next words. 'If we don't see any changes in the next day or two, we might have to think about turning it off.'

Byrd didn't need to ask what he meant - he understood the situation. The longer his parents were in the room, the less bed space there was for other people to get the help they desperately needed. After all, they were both being kept alive in a hope their bodies would heal and fix themselves with aided medication.

His mother was improving, which was good. His father wasn't, which wasn't good. Apart from accepting what he'd been told, there wasn't much he could do. Staying silent, he watched his father closely. The way the mouthpiece was lodged in his mouth with the wire trailing down over the bed across to the machine. The drips placed in his arms. The beeping. The lights.

Suddenly, it got too much for him; he turned quickly and dashed out the room.

'Max!' Claire gasped.

The door opened, and he was gone, the sound of his shoes clapping along the hard floor like a frantic drum. Claire gave the doctor a sad smile and rushed after him.

'Max,' she shouted, 'wait!'

Once he was outside, standing at the metal railing with his palms across the top of it, Byrd took a deep breath of cold air. Then another.

'Max,' Claire said, finally catching him up. 'Are you okay?' She placed a palm on his back and noticed the tears in his eye; something she'd never seen before. It crushed her. She didn't know what to do.

'I'm sorry,' he said quietly, fighting the emotion that filled his voice. 'I'm sorry for doing that.'

'It's okay, Max, it's fine,' she said softly and quietly.

A smell of smoke tinkered in the air. Byrd looked up, saw a man smoking across the wide road, standing at the edge of the carpark.

'Wait here,' he told her.

'Max… what—'

He left the railing abruptly and marched over the road towards the man, who'd spotted him, but he turned away, assuming the anger on Byrd's face had nothing to do with him. As Byrd was halfway, the man's gaze fell on him and he frowned, watching Byrd heading straight for him.

'Hey, you!' Byrd shouted.

The man took a short step back. Byrd was tall and broad. If a man like Byrd charged at anyone with a face like thunder, they'd likely do the same.

'Me?'

'Yes. You.'

'What?' The man shrugged, took another drag of his cigarette, which Byrd noticed was nearly finished.

Byrd stepped forward, grabbed it from the man's hand and threw it down on to the floor, then stamped on it three times, the sound of his boot hitting the cold, hard concrete floor echoed around them.

'What the f—'

'You fucking listen to me,' Byrd said sternly, getting closer, his finger pointing in the man's face, 'there's no smoking in these grounds. Do you understand that? There are signs everywhere.'

After seeing the wrath in Byrd's eyes and reading his body language, the man knew he meant business, and nodded several times without saying anything.

'Good. If you want to smoke, go over there, behind that wall, where you're meant to. Don't let other people breathe in that shit!'

Byrd turned abruptly and made his way back over to Claire, who was still at the railing, her mouth slightly open, wondering what the hell had just happened. In the eighteen months she'd been seeing him, she'd never seen this side of him. It was as if a switch had been flicked.

'I'm sorry about that, come on, this way.' Byrd turned and headed in the direction of the car.

'Max… are you okay?'

He nodded. 'Come on, I need to get out of here. I'll come back and see them again tomorrow.'

Back in the car, Byrd turned on the engine and turned up the radio volume. Claire leaned over, turned it down. Byrd sighed, knowing she'd want an explanation for his random outburst moments earlier.

'What?' he sighed.

'Are you okay? Really?'

'Listen, Claire … I'm sorry about that. It's all – it's all getting a lot for me. I just need them to get better. I need them to wake up.' He paused. 'They're all I have in this world.'

She sympathised with his words but at the same time, felt a little hurt. 'You have me?' she consoled.

He realised what he'd said. 'I do, I know. I'm sorry, I shouldn't have said that. I *do* have you.' Their eyes met for a long moment.

She reached for his hand, interlocked her fingers into his and squeezed. She opened her mouth, ready to say something but Byrd's phone rang in his pocket, the ringtone disturbing the moment. She let go of his grip, dipped her head, and looked out the window.

'Fuck sake,' he said, leaning to his left and finding it with his right hand. He put it to his ear. 'Hello.'

'Max, there's been a call through from a man who claims his wife has been taken on North Road. I'm heading over there now.'

Byrd considered Tanzy's words carefully, thinking about the woman sitting next to him. She'd faintly heard what Tanzy had said.

'Just go, Max,' she said quietly, still staring vacantly out the window.

Byrd nodded at her although she wasn't giving him her attention, then said to Tanzy, 'When are you going?'

'Right now. Want me to pick you up?'

'No, I'll meet you there. What's the address?'

Tanzy told him.

'I'm not far from there. Be there soon.' Byrd hung up and shoved the phone back into his pocket.

He turned sheepishly to Claire. 'I'm sorry.' She didn't reply. 'Do you want dropping off or do you wanna go to mine?

When I'm finished, I could come home and then maybe we could—'

'Take me home, please.'

And that's what he did. On the way over, they never spoke. He wanted to apologise and tell her that he thought that the abduction of this woman Tanzy had mentioned had something to do with the previous two murders. That it was important. But he'd feel like it was something he'd already said, over and over again. She understood his job, understood that he would prioritise that over everything else.

Maybe she was getting sick of it.

When she got out, she never kissed him, nor did she say anything to him. Byrd watched her walk up her path, open the door and step into her house without looking back. He put the gear in first and edged out into the road, then headed in the direction of the address that Tanzy had provided.

55

Saturday Afternoon
Zetland Street, Darlington

It took him six minutes to arrive at Zetland Street. It was a narrow, terraced street, lined with cars and vans either side. Children were playing football halfway up, so Byrd drove carefully, tinkering along at fifteen miles-an-hour whilst keeping a close eye on them. After he passed them, he noticed Tanzy's Golf parked up on the right so found a space across the road and pulled in, applied the handbrake and switched off the engine.

The day was warm, much warmer than the morning had been. The early frost had dissipated, leaving the ground dry from the sun that shone brightly down on the street.

Byrd knocked on the door of number fifty-four.

A moment later, the door opened and standing there in his Parker coat, was Tanzy.

'Hey.' He stepped out of the way, allowing Byrd room to enter. 'Come have a look at this, Max.'

Byrd followed Tanzy through the small living room into the back of the house where the kitchen was. Halfway down the kitchen, the man standing there with a photograph glanced up after hearing multiple footsteps.

'Hey,' he said, extending a hand.

Byrd shook it firmly. 'I'm Detective Inspector Max Byrd.'

'James Whittaker.'

'What do we have?' Byrd asked, turning to Tanzy. Tanzy told him. Occasionally, Whittaker nodded, confirming Tanzy's version of the story.

'But look at this,' Tanzy added, holding his hand out towards Whittaker, who leaned forward and handed him the photograph. Byrd glanced down. There were four men on it. James Whittaker was one of them. Byrd, although they were young, recognised two of them.

Stuart Richards.

Ian Porter.

He didn't know the fourth.

The background was dark with a bright green light coming from the right-hand side of the shot. Ian Porter held a can of lager and Stuart Richards had a cigarette hanging from his mouth. Behind them, there were people in small groups in the background.

'How do you know each other?' Byrd asked, still focusing on the photo.

'We went to school together,' Whittaker began, 'then we were friends until we were around twenty, but we lost touch after that.'

Byrd absorbed the information with a nod, then glanced at Tanzy for a brief second.

'Did your wife say anything to you before you came back to the car? Anything at all?'

He shook his head. 'No, I had to go in to get something signed. When I came out, they were gone. I phoned her mother because we were going there after, wondering if she'd just walked with our daughter, Emily, but she said she wasn't there. That's when Emily came back, told me she'd been taken.'

'Is your daughter in?'

'Would you like to speak to her? She's upstairs.'

'Yes, please,' Byrd said.

'I'll go get her.' Whittaker left the kitchen, leaving the detectives by themselves.

They both stared at the photograph of the four individuals. On the reverse, it was dated, 14th of July 2004.

Fifteen years ago.

'Interesting, isn't it?' Tanzy said quietly.

Byrd nodded. 'Very. When did you get here?'

'Only minutes before you,' Tanzy said. 'I noticed a pile of photos on top of the microwave. I recognised Porter and Richards, so I asked him about it. He said he'd been sorting things out and needed to put them away.'

Byrd nodded.

'Strange though, isn't it? Ian Porter's wife. Then Stuart Richards' wife. Both within three days. Now Whittaker's wife goes missing. There's a pattern here.'

Footsteps pounded across the thin ceiling overhead then down the wall to their left. Moments later, Whittaker appeared with his daughter Emily. 'This is Emily. Emily, say hi to the detectives.' Despite the situation, her face showed a smile and her body displayed a youthful bounce, oblivious to the reality of the situation.

'Hello, Emily,' Tanzy said softly, lowering to his knees. 'How are you doing?'

'Good.'

'Hey, I like your dress, it's very pretty.'

She nervously shrugged, contracting her small, square shoulders, then glanced up at Whittaker, who smiled at her. Tanzy asked for his permission to allow them to ask her a few questions. He agreed.

'You say your mummy got into a van?' Tanzy asked.

Emily nodded several times. 'Yeah.'

'How many men were there, Emily?' Byrd this time.

'Three, I think…' she frowned, trying hard to remember.

'Good, that's good, you're doing great.'

Byrd and Tanzy were both down on their knees listening to the story unravel. It was important when talking to children not to talk down to them whilst standing, because subconsciously they'll feel inferior to the adult. Instead, when the adult lowered to their level, it made them feel equal, so they tended to open up more, improving the channel of communication between them.

She went on: 'They got into our car and my mammy screamed. I was playing with my doll, but I looked up. Two of them got into the back. One on this side and one on that side.' She pointed left and right.

'What did they look like, can you remember?' asked Tanzy.

'They had white masks on…' She winced at the thought.

'Were they a little bit scary?'

Exaggerated nods. 'Yeah.' She paused for a moment, screwed her face up; the detectives assuming she was thinking. 'The man in the front showed mammy something but I couldn't see it. He asked her did she understand. My mammy nodded. She looked scared. Then we got out of the car.'

'Where did you go?'

'To a big van. They put mummy in and then told me to come back to the car and wait for daddy.'

'Where was the van?'

'On the big road outside.'

'What colour was the van, can you remember?'

'White, I think. A big white van.'

The detectives nodded several times, then stood up. 'Thank you, Emily, that was very helpful. You can go play now. We need to speak with your daddy.'

'Go on sweetheart,' Whittaker said, 'go back upstairs to your room and play with your toys.' He placed a palm on her back guiding her back towards the stairs. Once she had disappeared, Tanzy stared at the photograph.

'Mr Whittaker, has anything happened to you four?'

Whittaker glanced down at the photograph. 'I don't follow?'

'Not sure if you're aware, but there's been two murders over the past three days in this town. Both women are wives to two of these men. Ian Porter and Stuart Richards. I find that a very strange coincidence…'

Whittaker frowned, then shrugged. 'Like I said, we were friends at school. We hung around a bit after, then lost contact when we were twenty.'

'Why?'

He shrugged again. 'Work I suppose. I went away down south. At the time, I was doing Joinery. That's where the work was. I think the others maybe stayed in contact for a bit, but I went away for nearly three years and kind of lost touch with them.'

'Have you spoke since?'

Whittaker narrowed his eyes and shook his head. 'I've seen them in passing, but nothing more. Darlington's a small town, people tend to see each other every now and again.'

'You haven't spoken to them any time in the last week? Has Ian or Stuart attempted to contact you?'

'No.'

That was a lie. Ian Porter had phoned him yesterday, telling him what had happened to his wife, saying the same had happened with Stuart Richards' wife. He thinks it could have something to do with that night.

'Okay. Who's the other guy in the picture?' Byrd asked.

Whittaker followed his finger and looked at the man. 'That's Gregory Timms,' he said.

'Does he live in Darlington still?'

He shrugged. 'He could live anywhere. I haven't seen him in years.'

'Have you got Gregory's number, by any chance?'

Whittaker shook his head. 'I don't. Like I said, I haven't actually spoken to Gregory in fifteen years.'

'That's a long time,' Byrd commented.

'Yeah.'

'We need to speak to Gregory Timms as soon as possible,' Tanzy chipped in. 'In the meantime, we'll process a missing persons' report for Janice. You need to contact all your friends and family, let them know she's gone missing. The more people who're aware, the better chance we have of finding her.' Whittaker nodded. 'Have you got a picture of her?'

'Yes.'

'We'll need that if that's okay, so we can inform the media. Get her picture out to the public, get them looking for her, too.'

He bobbed his head in understanding. 'I'll go get it – hold on.' He left the kitchen, went upstairs, his footsteps creaking directly above them.

Tanzy turned to Byrd. 'There's something wrong here, Max. This is beyond a coincidence. It has to be.'

Byrd agreed with narrow eyes.

Whittaker returned downstairs with a photo in his hand. 'Most recent photo of her. We keep most of them on our phones nowadays, but this is from four years ago. She has her hair the same on there as she does now, so…'

'Thanks.' Tanzy took it from him. 'If you hear anything, let me know.' Tanzy reached inside of his coat. 'Here's my card. I've got your details and will be in touch when we find her.'

Whittaker gave a thankful nod and walked the detectives out.

At Tanzy's Golf, Byrd said, 'Have you heard from Harrison yet?'

'No, I've tried and tried but she's not picking up. Her husband hasn't seen her yet, either.'

'Fuck sake.' Byrd sighed and sniffed the air, the smell of cannabis tinkering from somewhere caused him to turn and have a look around. All he saw were the children still playing football on the road. 'You don't see that very often, do you?'

Tanzy angled his stare towards the kids. 'See what?'

'Kids playing outside. It's normally iPads and Nintendo switches. Normally glued to them, most kids.'

Tanzy's kids weren't. 'Hey, I'll go back to the station with this, put it on the system. Then I'll go to Aldi, see if I can see the cameras. Might be able to spot something.'

'I'll come with you.'

'You not spending time with Claire today?'

'I was. We went to town, got a coffee. I bought her a dress. I'm all yours now though.'

'How romantic. Jump in,' Tanzy said, 'we'll come back later to get your car.'

They both got in the Golf and closed the doors. Once Tanzy turned on the engine, Byrd leaned forward and put the blowers on full.

'How's your mam and dad?'

Byrd turned his head. 'Overall, not good, I'm afraid. We went there earlier. My dad isn't getting any better, but my mam is improving a little.'

Tanzy didn't know whether to say that was good his mother was improving or bad because his father wasn't, so decided to say nothing. They took a left at the end of the road onto Haig Street then took another left onto Lansdowne Street. Half a minute later, they hit North Road.

'Fucking traffic's a nightmare,' Tanzy gasped, after counting fourteen cars that refused to let him out. Finally, some elderly gent in a red Micra slowed and flashed. Tanzy waved a thanks and joined the rush, heading towards Aldi.

Byrd plucked his phone from his coat, found a number and put it to his ear.

'Who you ringing?' Tanzy asked.

'Thornton.'

Tanzy slowed the car at the traffic lights.

Thornton answered. 'Max, you okay?'

'Hi, June, I'm good thank you. We've just been to James Whittaker's house, the husband of—'

'Janice Whittaker, taken from the carpark near Aldi a few hours ago?'

'No flies on you, is there?' Byrd mused.

'That's why I'm the boss,' she said. 'I'm at the office now reading up on the dispatch logs. What's the story?'

'Whittaker says his wife and daughter went missing briefly, then only his daughter returned. His daughter said three men told her to get in the van. She said they showed her mother something and then did whatever she was told.'

'Could have been a knife or a gun,' Thornton replied. 'If they were serious enough, Janice will have gone with them to save her daughter. Where are you now? You with Orion?'

'Yeah, he's driving. We're heading to Aldi to see we can have a look at the CCTV of the carpark. Might need to try the other shops there, depending on what we find at Aldi.'

'Okay,' she said.

'We found something else at his house,' Byrd added, preventing the phone call from ending. 'He had a photo. Four of them were on it. Ian Porter, Stuart Richards, James Whittaker himself, and a guy called Gregory Timms.'

'The four of them?' she asked.

'Yeah. He said they went to school together but haven't spoken in years. Lost touch around the age of nineteen or twenty, he claims.'

'How old were they in the photo?'

'They looked about that age,' Byrd said.

'Strange coincidence,' she said. 'Two wives of the men on there have been murdered, now another has been taken.'

'Maybe not a coincidence at all.'

'We need to speak with Gregory Timms then,' she suggested. 'I'll do some digging.' She thanked him and hung up the phone. Byrd put the phone in his pocket as Tanzy took a right into Aldi car park.

'Here we go.'

56

Saturday Late Afternoon
Aldi Car park

After explaining to the manager of Aldi that a wife of an employee had been taken, they watched the CCTV footage from earlier and found absolutely nothing. One camera picked up the entrance of Aldi, whilst the other, showed down the side of the shop. The one they needed, unfortunately, was down for maintenance. There was a guy coming to fix it tomorrow. The manager apologised profusely and made an urgent call in their presence to get it fixed as soon as possible. He started to explain about the difficulties of getting someone there today to fix it, that it would cost extra as it would be classed as an emergency call-out, so to save on expenditure, he had delayed it until tomorrow.

The detectives stepped outside, ignoring the man who was standing next to the sliding exit door asking him to buy a magazine. The car park was fairly quiet for half five on a Saturday. Although it had become mild, it was evident that rain hung in the air, then drops started to descent from the sky.

'Guna piss down,' Byrd sighed. 'I can feel it.'

'How can you feel it?'

'Just before it's about to rain, the temperature dips a few degrees, you can feel the moisture in the air.'

'We'll try over there, Mr Weather man,' Tanzy said, pointing in the direction of Iceland.

'Sure.'

Fifteen minutes later, they left Iceland feeling deflated. Their cameras only covered directly outside their shop and didn't even reach the second row of parking spaces.

Then they checked Poundland. They didn't even have cameras.

'Fuck sake,' Byrd said, getting back into Tanzy's Golf. They both closed their doors, happy to be under cover. The heavens opened, their hairs were damp, their skin cold and prickly.

'What you doing later, Ori?'

'Nothing,' Tanzy said, starting the car. 'Why?'

'Tallow is going for a few drinks with Forrest and Beech. McCabe said he might pop out later.'

'Are you going?'

Byrd nodded, putting on his own seat belt. 'Yeah, I'm going. You up for it?'

Tanzy mulled it over for a few moments. 'I've got nothing planned. The kids are at Pip's mothers anyway. What time?'

'They said seven. Meet down William Steads, take it from there. I won't be staying out too late. At my tender age, I can't handle the hangover anymore.'

'That makes two of us, then.'

57

Saturday Evening
William Steads, Town Centre

Standing at the bar, over the drone of idle chatter and careless laughter, Tanzy told Byrd he wanted a Coors Light. Byrd nodded and faced the smiling barman and told him the order. Next to them were Tallow, Beech, and Forrest.

Tallow was dressed in a long-sleeved, white Oxford shirt, dark jeans, and brown shoes. Beech was wearing a black t-shirt under a leather jacket and light blue, almost skin-tight jeans and white plimsols. Next to him, Amanda Forrest wore a black jump suit and black heels, and looked pretty sexy to nearly every man in there. Dangling by her side, was a gold-plated bag hanging from a gold chain looped around her shoulder. Around her neck, was a gold necklace which looked expensive and classy.

'Rule number one tonight,' Tanzy said to the others whilst Byrd was ordering the drinks.

'What's that?' Tallow asked, smiling, already feeling the buzz of a couple of drinks.

'No talking about work. I need a break from my life and my life includes work, so no talking about work.'

Tallow nodded, held up his palms. 'That's fine with me. I was wondering, where did you get that shirt from?'

Tanzy wore a black, tight-fitting long-sleeved t-shirt which hugged his athletic figure well.

'Next. Nothing flash,' he said modestly.

Tallow nodded his approval. 'Nice.'

Byrd turned away from the bar with the drinks and handed Tanzy his lager. 'So, have you had a good day at work?' he asked the forensics. Tanzy turned abruptly, about to cause a fuss then realised Byrd was grinning at him, overhearing what he'd said about not mentioning work.

'Dickhead,' Tanzy mused, then took a long sip. It felt good.

'You coming for a smoke?' Tallow asked the group.

'I don't smoke,' Byrd said, 'but I'll come outside with you for a little second-hand smoke.'

Tallow laughed and turned, leading the way through the crowds until he climbed the few steps, pulled the door open and stepped outside. The smell of cheap perfume and cigarette smoke hit them. Tallow stopped at one of the free tables, leaned over and pressed the button for the patio heater, then pulled a cigarette out of a packet and lit up. 'Anyone want one?'

Paul Beech nodded. 'Go on, just the one. I don't normally.'

'Anyone else?'

Byrd, Tanzy, and Forrest all shook their heads. Byrd had once tried smoking when he was sixteen and was sick. The way he felt was something he'd always remembered and hadn't touched one since. At the time, he wanted to be like his dad, who religiously smoked forty a day. Then his dad had a health scare and packed them in. His mother still smoked twenty a day, and there was nothing Byrd could do to stop her.

As the heat from the wall lamp started to warm them up, they talked about places they liked to go drinking, although Byrd and Tanzy never really got out much recently. They mentioned the names of the places they used to go when they were in their teens. Amanda Forrest hadn't heard of most of them. Then they talked about Football. Then rugby. Apparently, Beech used to play rugby in his earlier years, was playing in the Newcastle Falcons development team, but broke his ankle, his once ambitious idea of playing at a professional level now a distant memory.

'Is Tony coming out later?' Byrd asked.

'He said he was, but he's not answering his phone.' Tallow pulled his phone from his pocket. 'I'll try him again.'

Tanzy, Forrest, and Beech headed back inside to the bar. It was a nice, easy-going atmosphere. The heat lamps kept them comfortable and the buzz of the alcohol warmed their cheeks. Friendly, drunken conversations surrounded them as people came and went.

'How are they doing?' Byrd asked Tallow.

'Beech and Forrest?' Tallow asked.

Byrd nodded.

'They're doing well,' he said, 'Beech is a good guy, committed, hard working. He sees things how I used to see them when I first started. He thinks outside the box and asks the right questions, which as you know, is what you need in this game. Forrest is, well…' his face changed, as if he was about to say something less positive, 'She's—'

'Hey, hey!' The door opened to their left, Tanzy appearing with four jaeger bombs cupped in his hands with a cheeky smile on his face. The others trailed with an array of drinks.

'Here you go…'

'Just a quiet few tonight, eh?' Byrd laughed.

'Only live once I guess.'

They shared a smile.

They grabbed a shot each, clinked glasses and downed it. Forrest almost gagged but kept it from resurfacing, causing Tallow to laugh and Beech to spill some down his chin, which he dabbed with the back of his hand. Tanzy then washed the horrendous taste down with some lager; it had been years since he'd done shots.

'Who's up for Sambucas then?'

'Fuck that,' Beech said, 'not yet anyway…'

'Did Tony reply?' Tanzy asked Tallow.

'No, not yet, he—' He felt something in his jeans. 'Hold on.' On the phone screen, there was an incoming call. It was McCabe. 'Here he is.' He put the phone to his ear. 'Hello?'

Tanzy turned away, faced Byrd, said, 'Going straight to my head, this.'

'Mine, too, mate.'

They left William Steads and headed for The Green Dragon. It had loud music, flashing lights, a dance floor and the drinks were cheap. They got another round of shots in.

McCabe had told them he'd come out later after he'd finished doing something.

A few hours later, they were all worse for wear, standing in the Speedy Pepper takeaway shop holding themselves up on the shelf positioned on the left under the wide menu on the wall. McCabe had met them in Hoskins and started as he meant to go on, ordering three shots of Vodka. By the time they'd entered The Gate, he'd caught them up. In the Grange, they'd met up with one of Beech's cousins, Jason, who was out with his wife. They'd shared a few jokes before Jason and his wife left and got a taxi from the closest rank.

So far, they'd had a great night together. It was something they'd never really done as a group before. Usually, they'd socialise with their own teams, but it was Tallow's idea and was enjoyed by all. Him and Tanzy had had a laugh, settling their differences. Tanzy had apologised. He did the same.

Amanda Forrest was now leaning on the shelf, her forearm holding her unbalanced weight, her drunken gaze down on the floor, her eyes half closed. She was completely out of it.

'You okay?' Byrd asked her, concerned.

'She'll be okay,' McCabe said, rubbing her back softly. 'Some sleep and she'll be sorted.'

She let out an inaudible grunt in response.

'Number forty-seven,' a voice said from the counter.

Behind Byrd, Tanzy moved forward, stepping around a group of loud, rowdy teenagers, waving his ticket in the air. 'That'll be me.'

The takeaway shop was filling now, people piling in in groups, loud conversations and sullen name calling. Byrd glanced around, absorbing the people around him. The world had changed, and it wasn't until now, he realised how old he'd got. Not that forty-one was particularly old, but when surrounded by barely twenty-year-olds, it put things in to perspective.

'The fuck's your problem like?'

Byrd heard the voice to his right. He span round, frowned, trying to concentrate on who it was. A few feet along the shelf, Paul Beech was holding himself up and staring wearily at the young man who'd challenged him.

'The fuck you up to?' the young lad said again. He wore a tight-fitting top, almost skin tight, his muscles protruding through the material.

'Go on then, Trev, just hit him,' said his friend standing behind him.

Byrd turned fully and stepped forward, moving around McCabe and Forrest. 'Whoa, whoa, just hold on, what's the problem?' From what he saw, Beech was barely able to stand up, and whatever the lad's problem was, surely he'd made a mistake. Beech wasn't doing anything wrong.

'Fuck off, old man,' the lad snarled at Byrd. 'Go home and eat your pizza, fatty.' He glared back at Beech. 'Come on then, fucker.'

'Go on - hit him!' shouted one of the lad's friends again.

The pizza shop had become quiet now, the people inside realising there was a fight about to happen. All eyes fell on them. Tanzy, who just picked up his pizza, turned at the sudden silence and digested the scene. He watched the lad shove Beech hard into the shelf, his back colliding with the edge of it, then he screamed out in pain, and fell to the floor clutching at his side. Then the lad moved closer and kicked him in the back. Again, another scream from Beech. A women in the shop gasped and searched around for someone to step in and stop it.

'Hit him again!' a voice shouted from the front of the shop.

Tanzy placed his pizza on the side and dashed over to the front of the shop.

'Fuck do you want? You want some as well?' The lad screamed at Tanzy, his eyes full of alcohol-fuelled rage.

'You need to calm down, young man,' Tanzy said firmly, holding his palms out in front of him. He stopped a few feet from him, glanced down to his right, noticing Beech crunched up in pain. 'What was that about?'

Without answering, the lad swung a right hand towards Tanzy's face. Tanzy expected it and ducked, then quickly leaned forward, tucking his head under the lad's armpit and wrapped his right arm around the lad's neck, grabbing his hip with his left hand. Then in a sudden movement, he swung his own right foot forward and used it to sweep the back of the lad's legs, causing him to go down with a thud on the white, tiled floor.

'Calm the fuck down!' Tanzy shouted. He turned suddenly, glaring up at the lad's friends. 'Who's next?' There were two of them. Wearily, they eyed Tanzy up, calculating their chances. After a few seconds, they backed off, deciding they didn't fancy a go.

Minutes later, the lad had got up and left the shop with his friends without their pizza. Byrd and Tanzy checked on Beech after they helped him up. His ribs and back were both in agony.

'You should go to the hospital,' Byrd said.

'They're just bruises, Max, I'll be fine,' Beech said.

A group of women, who had watched what Tanzy had done, trailed past, staring at him. 'Call me,' one of them said, blowing him a kiss. Tanzy smiled and returned his attention back on Beech.

'You okay, man?'

'I'll be fine, thanks. I don't even know what their problem was.'

'Some idiots around this town,' Tanzy replied.

'No kidding.'

Once they were outside, they noticed the taxi rank to the right was at least twenty people deep. They took a left and wobbled down Skinnergate towards the other taxi outside of The Turk's Head pub which was usually a lot quieter.

'I'll take you home,' Byrd said to Beech, who nodded appreciatively, holding his own ribs. A taxi pulled up. They opened the doors and got in.

McCabe was holding Forrest up, who was hanging from him with her loose grip around his neck. 'I'll take her home, Orion, she won't make on her own.'

'Okay.'

A taxi pulled up. McCabe slowly walked Forrest to the closest door and opened it, and helped her in. 'Mind your head,' he told her. He closed her door and opened the front passenger door, resting his hand on the top of the door. He turned to Tanzy and nodded. 'Apart from the pizza shop, it's been a good night, Ori, speak tomorrow.'

'Will do,' Tanzy replied.

As McCabe lowered himself into the car, and closed the door, Tanzy frowned, confused. On McCabe's hand where he was holding the top of the door, he was sure he saw blood on his fingertips.

Tanzy thought back to what happened before. Beech was only bruised. There'd been no blood from his injuries. Unless it was someone else's blood.

58

June 14th, 2004
Darlington
15 years ago

The time was just before ten. Sarah was still down the bottom of the garden talking with Shez, sharing a laugh about something that happened at school a couple of years before. They'd been up a few times for refills, taking turns.

The music was still loud, and the party had got busier. People had sent texts out, inviting more people. The garden – as well as the downstairs inside the house – was almost full now.

'I'll just go check inside,' Shez said to Sarah, leaving her with two of their friends.

'Okay, don't be long.'

Shez wandered up the garden, mindful of her balance. God, them drinks have gone to her head faster than she'd have liked. After all, it was her party and she needed to keep some level of control. She'd told people to text anyone they liked, as long as they could vouch for them being decent and wouldn't wreck the place. The last thing she wanted was for her mother and father to come back from their weekend away and find the house totally upside down.

She passed Stuart and Ian on the decking and gave them a smile.

'Hey, you alright?' Porter said.

She nodded, then disappeared into the noise. There were two people sitting on the sofa in the conservatory, arms wrapped around each other, leaning back, indulging in a passionate kiss.

'Get a room,' Shez giggled, passing them. She knew the girl; used to be in the same class.

Inside the kitchen, the CD player was blaring, filling the space with 90's dance songs that would become classics in the future. She weaved around little groups, again, smiling and saying 'Hi' to people she knew. There were a couple of unfamiliar faces, but that was okay; she wanted this party to be the best ever so would sacrifice a couple of strangers in her parent's house. She wanted people to talk about it for ages. They'd say, remember that night at Shez's house…

After checking the house, finding a handful of people upstairs, two of which were lying on her parent's bed which she told to get out, she went back downstairs, topped up her wine and made it back outside. The sun had almost vanished now. The temporarily lighting she'd hung across the side of the garage and along the side and rear fence lit the garden up well, giving the space a warm glow which reflected the happy buzz on people smiling faces.

She stepped outside, the temperature dipping slightly than it was before she went in. On her right, she noticed Ian Porter and Stuart Richards still sitting on the bench, smoking and drinking, staring down into the garden. She suspected they were watching Sarah. It wasn't a secret that Sarah was desirable, in fact, it's safe to say she could have anyone she liked. She had her pick. And tonight, dozens of eyes were watching her, waiting to make their move, hoping it was them who'd be chosen. She had a figure that every man wanted and a figure which every woman envied.

Next to Stuart and Ian, was James Whittaker and Gregory Timms, who'd arrived a few minutes ago. They'd collected a drink from the collection of mixers on the kitchen worktop and made their way outside.

Stuart informed them both that him and Ian had a bet, that he could sleep with Sarah for twenty pounds. James and Gregory sided with Stuart and agreed that he had no chance. They reminded him that he'd tried before and failed so what made him think this would be different.

'I'm going to fuck her,' he expressed strongly.

'Not a chance!' Stuart almost laughed, and the others nodded in agreement.

'Watch me,' he said, standing up, making his way confidently across the decking, dressed in a crisp white shirt and dark jeans. He stepped down on to the path that led down to the bottom of the garden.

Stuart, James, and Gregory watched him.

'He does know he has no chance, right?' Gregory laughed.

On his approach, Sarah and Shez stopped talking and glanced his way. He kept solid eye contact until he stopped a few feet from them.

'Hi, Sarah,' he said.

'Hey.' Her smile was magnificent, her perfect white teeth reflecting the glare from the hanging lights around them. The music had developed to the 80's stuff now and everyone was loving it; some moving slow, some moving fast, some kissing, and some dancing alone with nothing but the words and rhythm beating through their relaxed, drunken bodies.

'Can I get you a drink?' he said, leaning forward, trying to get closer. He could smell her sweet perfume. It excited him. The thought of being on top of her, his face dug into her neck, the smell and touch of her skin, sent a rush down his body.

'If you like?'

He nodded like an eager dog. 'More wine?'

'How did you know I was drinking wine?'

'I can see in your cup…'

She mulled over his words for a moment, then finally nodded. 'Yeah okay, not too much though, I've had a lot already.'

'Okay, I won't be long.'

Ian Porter left them at the bottom of the garden and almost skipped back up. As he passed the boys, who were still on the bench, he gave them a wink.

'Where you going?' Stuart asked.

'Getting her a drink.'

'You have no chance, Ian!'

'We'll see,' Ian laughed but there was an underlining feeling of determination inside, something that he felt he needed to do. He'd failed in the past; it couldn't happen again. So far so good, though, she'd agreed to a drink, even if he wasn't buying, he was making the effort to go and get her one. Maybe that counted for something.

In the kitchen, where the collection of drinks were slowly disappearing, he found an empty cup and poured wine into it until it was half full. He placed the bottle back next to the other bottles. There were bottles of Wine, Vodka, Sambuca, Apple Sours, cans of cider, lager, and bottles of Brown Ale. Most of the food was gone, although a couple of slices of cold pizza sat with crumbs on plates.

Without making it obvious, he glanced around the kitchen, seeing who was there. A couple who'd been together for years were discussing an issue about her flirting with someone outside and he wasn't happy about it. They were occupied and wouldn't notice what Ian was about to do. The other people were too engrossed in their worlds to even care.

Ian put his hand deep into his pocket and pulled one of them out. Then placing it on the worktop, he used one of the wine bottles to crush the tablet into powder, then after placing the bottle back, he scraped the powder in to the plastic cup and mixed it with a spoon he'd found in a drawer to his right.

When it had fully dissolved, he left the kitchen, headed back outside.

'Go on, lad!' James teased him as he walked by them.

Stuart added, 'Twenty quid, mate, you giving me it now or later?'

'Fuck off, Stu!' he joked, then concentrated on not stepping on the empty beer bottles that people had carelessly dropped on the floor. Down at the bottom, he held out the plastic cup towards Sarah. 'There you go.'

'Thanks, Ian,' she said, taking it from him, then she abruptly turned her back on him and faced Shez who then laughed at what she'd done.

'Awkward,' joked one of her friends. He stood there for a moment, his face growing warm and cheeks on fire with humiliation, watching the back of her head as she continued to ignore him and talk to her friends. After a few embarrassing seconds, he slowly turned feeling the world was watching him, dying to break out into laughter.

He stepped up on to the decking and sheepishly angled back over to Stuart, James, and Gregory, who could barely contain their laughs. He felt so stupid.

He'd never felt so embarrassed in all of his life, even more than the time when Rupert Marllons pulled his trousers down in year seven chemistry and at least five girls saw his penis which was definitely nothing to write home about.

'Don't worry about it, mate, it's only twenty pound,' laughed Gregory, sliding along the bench making space for him to sit. 'Here, there's your drink.'

Ian took it quickly, his cheeks still warm, his blood boiling. 'The silly cow,' he said. 'The fucking bitch!' he muttered a little louder, then stared down at the floor, still feeling every persons' eyes on him. The reality was that only the three of them were watching, and now, seeing him staring at the floor so upset, realised how humiliated he felt.

'Hey, don't be daft mate,' Stuart said, 'we can't get them all.'

'Just means you owe him twenty quid, pal,' added James, smiling.

Ian half-smiled at them. 'The night is still young…'

'You still have time,' Stuart replied, encouragingly.

Ian glanced away and focused down at the bottom of the garden, the bright hanging lights illuminating Sarah's gorgeous figure which turned him on like nothing else had ever turned him on.

He'd keep an eye on her, because soon the tablet he'd mixed into her drink would start to take effect.

Then he would make his move.

59

Sunday Afternoon
Police Station

Hope was sitting at her computer in her lab coat. Underneath, she was wearing a dark red turtle neck jumper, blue jeans, and high black boots with zips at the sides. Often when they worked overtime on a weekend, the so-called dress code didn't matter as much, the management felt more relaxed about the formal wear.

She leaned forward reading the analysis of the hair sample found under the fingernail of Mary Richards, the brunette found hanging from the tree in Cemetery Lane, when the door to her left opened and in walked Paul Beech and Jacob Tallow.

'Ahh, here they come in…' she said, 'finally.'

'Give me a break, my head is pounding,' Tallow replied, squinting as his eyes adjusted to the lab's bright lighting. He went over to his desk and pulled a chair out, then dropped in it, as if his body weighed more than it did.

'Good night?' she asked, humouring him.

Beech pulled out a chair, took the seat next to him.

'Yeah… good laugh, these hangovers are getting harder, though.'

'I have no sympathy,' she told him, turning away and focusing back on the screen.

'Why didn't you come out?' Beech asked.

'I had plans,' she replied.

'What you got on there?' he said, pointing at her computer screen.

'Results from the hair found on the body of Mary Richards.' She slowly faced them both, their faces all puffy and red-eyed. 'Jesus, have you two even slept.'

'It doesn't feel like I've had any sleep at all,' Tallow joked, clamping his eyes shut.

'Barely,' Beech added. 'What does it say?' He asked, nodding towards the screen.

'Well… turns out the hair we found in the Qashqai and the hair found under her fingernail are a match. It's the same person.'

The news filled the room quickly and suddenly there was an energy around them. Tallow sat up straight, rubbed his eyes, and leaned forward. 'Really?'

'That's what the DNA properties suggest. If this is true, then the same person was involved in both of the murders. And if that is the case, it's likely we have a serial killer on our hands.'

Both Tallow and Beech stared wide-eyed at her, as if not quite absorbing the information fully.

'And if that's the case,' she added, 'it's the first time in a very long time that's happened in Darlington. We've had a couple of deranged killers, but this - this is something else…'

Tallow nodded slowly. 'I need a fucking coffee. Who wants one?'

Beech raised his arm. 'Please, put two in. I need it.'

'Yes, please,' Hope added.

Tallow padded away gingerly, the effects of the alcohol consumed hours earlier clearly weighing on his balance as he made his way to the door of the lab.

With his mouth still open, Beech leaned forward towards Hope, the scent of her perfume tinkering with his senses. It was a sexy, yet sophisticated kind of smell, one he hadn't smelt before.

'A serial killer?' he asked quietly, not quite believing what he'd heard.

'It seems so, Paul.'

'Jesus.'

'Is Amanda coming in today?' Hope asked, tapping away on her keyboard. 'Did she have a good night?'

'She had a lot to drink - *a lot* to drink. She was worse for wear when we were getting a pizza. McCabe took her home in a taxi last I heard. Tanzy texted me when he got in to let us know. Don't think she'll turn up today. I sent her a text an hour ago but don't expect her to be awake just yet.' He edged forward and winced.

'What's the matter?' Hope asked him.

'Some little shits in the pizza shop last night. Pushed me into the shelf and kicked me when I fell onto the floor.'

'What – why?' She angled her body towards him.

'You know what this town is like, I didn't even know him. Full of idiots!'

'What happened after that?'

'Tanzy came over, flipped the lad onto his back. Jesus, you should have heard the sound.' He winced at the pain that lad must have experienced. 'They backed off after that.'

'I can imagine.' She turned away, focused back on the screen, confirming the details of the DNA report. She reached for her phone on the desk, unlocked it, and found the number he needed, then put it to her ear.

'Who you ringing?' Beech asked.

'McCabe. Let him know about this.'

Tallow came back in, opening the door with his hip, still looking worse for wear, dark semi circles sitting under his eyes. In his hands, he carried three cups of strong coffee. It didn't take long for the smell to fill the lab as he placed them down on the wide desk where Beech was sitting. He walked around him and handed Hope her cup.

'Thanks,' she said, taking it with her free hand.

'Who's she on the phone to?' Tallow asked, taking a seat.

'She's trying to get hold of McCabe.'

After she tried three times, each time going to answer-phone, she hung up. 'He must be asleep.' She glanced down at her watch. It was nearly half ten. Through the window of the lab, the skies were dark and grey. Rain was imminent. Hope hadn't had chance to have any breakfast since she woke up, her stomach now grumbling. 'I need food now.'

'I'll get something delivered,' Tallow said, pulling out his phone. 'What do you want?'

Hope and Beech gave him their orders and he phoned the nearest café, which told him it would be ready in twenty minutes. He changed his mind and said he'd go pick it up, as it was only a two-minute walk, located on Victoria Road.

On Tallow's way back in, just before he opened the door to the building, he heard footsteps behind him. Dressed in a long coat was Byrd, his hands firmly in his pockets battling against the late-morning chill.

'We've just got sarnies in; wish I'd known you were coming, I'd have got you one.'

Tallow opened the door for him.

'Don't worry, I've had something already,' Byrd replied. They made their way through reception and down the corridor, back in the direction of the lab and there still sitting at the desk, was Hope and Beech, finishing their coffee.

'Look who showed up,' Tallow said.

Beech and Hope turned, saw Byrd walking behind Tallow, his hair all over the place. Tallow placed the bag of food down on the desk, the smell of bacon filling the air.

'Morning, Max,' Beech said. 'How's the head?'

'Sore,' he replied. 'I've felt better.' Byrd dropped down into a spare chair, sighing heavily. 'How's your back?'

'It hurts bad,' he winced, leaning forward, touching the area on his right side, a spot between his hip and lat muscle. 'If I wasn't drunk, I wouldn't have slept at all.'

'Is Tanzy here yet?' Byrd asked them.

'Haven't seen him yet, Max,' Hope said. 'Is he coming in?'

'He said he might, I'll ring him soon.' Byrd stood up. 'Who wants coffee?'

They shook their heads and watched him go in the direction of the canteen. 'Oh, Max…' Hope said quickly. He stopped before the door and turned. 'The results came back from the DNA of the hair found under Mary Richards fingernail. It's a match to the hair found in Julia Porter's car. The same person was involved in both murders, Max.'

For a second, he stood in silence, absorbing what she'd said. Then he nodded, turned, and made his way to the canteen, mulling over what had been discovered, thinking about the photograph that he'd seen at James Whittaker's house.

The same person.

A serial killer.

He had to tell Tanzy. At the canteen, he pulled out his phone, found his number and pressed CALL.

'Max,' he said.

'Ori, you coming in?'

Tanzy moaned something inaudible.

'Orion?'

'Sorry?' Tanzy said.

'Are you coming in?'

'My head is pounding, Max. I'll get a shower, I might come in later. I need to…' he trailed off.

'Need to what?'

'Ignore me, Max, I've just woke up. I'll get sorted. Be in later.'

'Before you go, mate…'

'What?' Tanzy said sharply.

'We've got the match back from the DNA. Both hairs at the separate crime scenes match up. We have a serial killer on our hands.' He paused a beat, flicking on the kettle in the canteen. 'Have you heard from Harrison?'

'She hasn't got back to me yet. Her husband hasn't got in touch, either. I think there's something seriously wrong here - I think she's in trouble.'

Byrd never replied.

'What you thinking, Max?' Tanzy asked in response to his silence. If Byrd never answered when he asked him a question, he knew he was thinking about something.

'What if she's in trouble, but a different kind of trouble?' Byrd asked.

'What you talking about, Max? Tanzy's tone turned sour, knowing what he was insinuating.

'What if she's done something seriously wrong and has disappeared because of it?'

Tanzy never replied, knowing what Byrd meant. Maybe she's committed some kind of crime and had gone missing? It was a possibility for sure. But the detectives knew her, especially Tanzy who'd known her for a couple of years.

'I don't know, Max, I…' he fell silent for a second, 'but there's something I need to speak to you about.'

60

June 14th, 2004
Darlington
(15 years ago)

At the bottom of the garden, Sarah wobbled a little on her feet.

'Easy, Sarah, easy,' muttered Shez, holding her up. 'The drink has gone to your head. Do you need to sit down?'

Sarah recklessly shook her head, then removed Shez's grip. 'No!' She moved away and started dancing to the sound of the music coming from the kitchen back inside the house.

'Okay, fine,' Shez said. There was no telling her. They'd often drink together at weekends, but she'd never seen her get so drunk so quickly, unless she had more than Shez had.

'Come on, let's go inside, Sarah,' Shez said to her.

Sarah, who was almost out of it, her state deteriorating rapidly, finally gave in and nodded, leaning on Shez's shoulder. 'I'm going to take her inside,' Shez told the other girls, 'I don't know what's wrong with her.' The atmosphere around them changed and suddenly they started to grow concerned as they watched Shez lead her across the decking and into the kitchen.

'Why she like that?' asked one of the girls. 'She hasn't had that much…'

Sarah took a step forward and stumbled, if not for Shez holding her weight up, she'd have hit her face on the floor.

'Jesus, Sarah, hold on…' Shez begged, struggling to keep her up right. 'Hey, Jess, give me a hand over here.'

'How many she fucking had?' one of the lads nearby shouted then laughed.

'Where we taking her?' Jessica asked, quickly helping Shez.

'We'll take her up to my room, lay her on the bed.'

They helped Sarah into the house and slowly up the stairs.

In Shez's bedroom, she turned on the light. On the floor next to the bed, there was a boy on top of a girl with his pants down around his ankles. It seemed they hadn't started what they were about to do.

'Get out now!' Shez demanded.

'Shit!' gasped the girl, 'sorry!'

'Just get out.'

Once they had left, Shez and Jessica lowered her onto Shez's double bed and placed her head carefully onto her pillow.

'Why's she like this, Shez?'

'God knows, she hasn't drunk any more than we have,' she replied. 'Must be…'

They stopped. 'What?'

'Has she taken anything?' Shez's eyes hardened at Jessie.

'You mean drugs?' Jessie raised her eyebrows.

'Yes! Have you given her any drugs?'

Jessie edged back. 'What! No, of course I haven't… why would I?'

'Because I've never fucking seen her like this before. She's never done this. And everyone knows you take drugs!'

'Well don't be blaming me,' Jessie snapped, 'whatever this is, it isn't my fucking doing!'

Jessie stormed off, stamping her feet until she disappeared through the open door. The sound of the music downstairs came through – sounded like someone had turned the cd player up. Shez would deal with that after she sorted Sarah out. The best thing for her was to go to sleep. She went over, closed the door and returned back to the bed.

'Aww Sarah, what's happened to you?'

Sarah didn't reply. She was out of it, somewhere between being semi-conscious and sleeping. Shez, doing the best she could, lifted her up and pulled the duvet covers back, then slowly lowered her back down on the bed again, and pulled the covers up over her.

Using the back of her hand, Shez felt her forehead. She was hot. She pulled the covers back down to her stomach to keep her cool.

'I'll get you some water, babe.'

Shez got up, left the room, padded along the landing to the bathroom, where she filled up an empty cup from the tap and returned to her room. When she got there, a man was standing in the middle of the room, staring down at Sarah.

Shez froze behind him. 'Hello?'

The man turned slowly towards Shez.

'What you doing in my room, Ian?'

Ian Porter shrugged. 'Is – is she okay?'

'No, she isn't, I think she's been drugged or something, she's out of it. I'm going to let her rest on her own for a while, so please, if you could go.'

'Do you need any—'

'Ian – go, please!'

Ian left the bedroom quickly, but instead of taking the right to head back downstairs, he took a left and hid in the bathroom. After a couple of minutes, staring through the slit in the door, he watched Shez step out of her bedroom and close the door, then went back downstairs.

He smiled.

Maybe he'll win his bet after all.

61

Monday Morning
Police Station

As Tanzy left the office, he could smell coffee drifting down the corridor from the canteen. From his team, he was the first to arrive, which wasn't unusual. It was almost an unwritten rule, for as long as he'd known, when managing a team, you should arrive earlier than them. When the team turned up, the manager needed to have an update and a plan for the day ahead. He or she needed to make the right decisions and that took preparation, patience, and time. At least thirty minutes of it, in Tanzy's opinion.

So at half seven when he pulled up and turned off his engine, the only car there belonged to DCI Thornton's. A brand-new black Range Rover.

Tanzy was sitting at his desk with a coffee. He turned on his computer and watched the morning traffic out of the window. He heard DCI Thornton on the phone in her office behind him. He turned slightly, seeing her door open half an inch. It sounded like she was on the phone to one of her friends, judging by the nature of the conversation, discussing possible plans for the weekend, he assumed.

He picked up his phone from the desk and tried the number for PC Harrison again. It had been three days now that she'd lost touch with him. Byrd told Tanzy he'd tried and yet again, he'd had no joy.

The phone call went straight to answerphone. Her phone battery was dead, Tanzy assumed. He found the number he had saved for her husband and dialled that. That, too, rang out but he received a text straight after saying:

Can't speak. Sill no sign of Kim yet. Thanks.

Deciding it was time, he pushed his chair back and stood up, took a few steps to DCI Thornton's office and rapped on the door.

'Come in,' she said.

'Morning,' he said, entering and closing the door half shut.

'Hey, Ori. Good weekend?'

'It was okay, was in here so wasn't the most exciting.'

'I saw the news,' she said, 'with the Jones'. You did well.'

'Thanks. Still nothing come in yet though.'

She smiled. 'Give it time. How can I help?'

Tanzy took a seat and composed himself. 'I'm worried about PC Harrison.'

'Have you not heard from her yet?'

He shook his head. 'No. I—'

'When did you last see her?'

'Friday afternoon. No one has heard from her after she left. Did she say who in the family had an emergency?'

'No, she didn't say much. But she seemed distracted, as if something was on her mind. Let me try her.' Thornton picked her phone from the desk and called her. She frowned after it went straight to voicemail and placed it back down on the desk.

'Voicemail?' Tanzy asked.

She nodded.

'When I went to see her husband on Friday night, he said he hadn't seen her either. I've just phoned him and he replied with a text now saying he still doesn't know where she is. I don't know, I think something's off here, Boss.'

Thornton thought in silence for a moment. 'I must say, knowing Kim, that is unusual. But what if, now hear me out, Orion, this isn't what I think, it's just a possible although unlikely scenario. What if she went away with someone, someone who wasn't her husband?'

Tanzy mulled over her words. 'Unlikely.'

'Why?'

'Because I know her, I know she wouldn't do that. She's happily married.'

'How do you know that?'

'Because she told me.'

'Ori… just because she told you, it doesn't mean it's the truth.'

'Fair enough.' Tanzy paused a beat. 'I think it's time to put a missing person's report in on her.'

'Yeah, maybe you're right, Ori. Leave it with me, okay. I'll sort it.'

'Thanks,' he said. He stood up and left her office. Back at his desk, he noticed Byrd was sitting on his chair, a mug of steaming coffee cupped in his right hand.

'Cosy talk with the boss?' Byrd joked, a grin lining his face. 'Always knew you wanted fast promotions…'

Tanzy smiled and took a seat. 'Expressing my concerns about Kim – I think there's something seriously, seriously wrong. I know she had an issue a few months back where she felt down, but I think it's something more. You remember when she was like that?'

Byrd nodded.

Tanzy went on: 'She changed, didn't she? We saw a difference in her and when I'd asked her, that's when she told us about her problems at home. But then she said things were fixed, and things were okay again. She was back to her usual happy self, wasn't she?'

'She was, I remember,' Byrd agreed.

They said nothing for the best part of two minutes whilst Byrd's computer booted up. The system, like it often did, was playing up today.

'What was the thing you wanted to talk about?' Byrd asked.

'Sorry?'

'You said to me on the phone there was something you wanted to talk about?'

Tanzy nodded, remembering what he'd said. He then leaned back and pointed upwards to the ceiling, reminding Byrd of the hidden microphone that he'd found. Byrd bobbed his head, understanding, and said, 'You want a coffee?'

'Yeah. I'll come with you.'

They both stood up and made their way through the office in the direction of the canteen.

'Morning, boss,' said PC Amy Weaver, who was sitting at her desk.

Byrd nodded. 'Good morning, Amy, you have a good weekend?'

She smiled. 'Yes, thanks. It was… very good.'

'Morning, Orion,' said a voice from their right. It was PC Cornty, who was sat bolt straight in his chair, his eyes peering over his glasses which were resting on the end of his nose.

The canteen was quiet. DS Stockdale had walked in as the kettle was boiling and kept his side of the conversation to a minimum. He seemed to be more interested in what was happening on his phone, which the detectives didn't mind, because they needed to speak in a place where they knew wasn't being tapped: where nobody was listening. He gave them a professional nod before leaving.

'So?' Byrd whispered.

They were standing side by side, inches apart, Tanzy's mouth close to Byrd's ear.

'You remember Saturday night?' Tanzy began. Byrd nodded. 'You remember McCabe getting a taxi with Amanda – I know you left before we did but he was taking her home, right?' Again, Byrd nodded. Tanzy went on: 'When the taxi pulled up, he put Amanda in the back and then opened the front door. He then put his hand on the top of the door and—' He stopped, as if possibly changing his mind about telling him.

'What is it?'

'As he said bye, I noticed something on his fingertips, Max.' His eyes narrowed. 'I'm sure it was blood. On the end of his fingers.'

'Blood?'

He nodded twice, his eyes serious.

'Was it not the trouble that Paul had, was he not hurt?' Byrd asked, frowning.

'Paul was hurt but he wasn't bleeding – I remember. And McCabe didn't once help him - he was stood with Amanda, making sure she didn't… fall over I guess.'

'Ahh and that's when you jumped in like Jackie Chan?'

'Don't judge me - I'd had a few drinks by then…'

As the kettle boiled and clicked off, Byrd gave him a smile then reached up, grabbed two fresh cups, placed them down on the worktop and put a spoonful of coffee in each of them.

'Perhaps it was dark, Ori, maybe you thought you saw something that wasn't there.' He turned fully to him after he stirred the coffees. 'Why would he have blood on the ends of his fingertips?'

Tanzy shrugged heavily.

'Maybe it was dark, and you imagined it?'

He shrugged again. 'I don't know, maybe…'

'You okay, Ori?'

'Yeah, mate, I'm… fine.' He nodded.

'You sure?'

Tanzy nodded again, this time, more confidently.

'Okay, good.' Byrd dropped some milk into the cups and stirred again. 'Did Jennifer Lucas find the man in the black fleece on the CCTV? You popped down there to see her, didn't you?'

'How do you know that?'

Byrd tapped his nose. 'I know everything. And because you told me.'

'We couldn't find him. Not on the cameras we were looking at anyway. She said she'll get in touch if she sees him again.'

'A needle in a haystack in a town like this.'

'Tell me about it,' Tanzy replied, deflated.

They made their way back to their desks. The office was filling a little now, a handful of people staggered at various desks around the room. Back at their desks, they noticed DCI Thornton's door was closed.

'You tried Harrison again?' Byrd asked, taking a seat.

'Yeah. Not answering. Even Thornton tried.' Tanzy slumped down, rubbing his palm over his tired face and sighed, then glanced up for a second at the ceiling, imagining the exact location of the listening device above the ceiling tile.

'Did you get chance to file the missing report on Janice Whittaker?'

Byrd nodded. 'Yeah, it's in the system, sent out to local services. I've updated Thornton on it.'

'Good.' He leaned forward, took a sip, then picked up his phone. 'I need to find a number and make a phone call.'

Byrd watched him. 'Who to?'

'Gregory Timms. He was the fourth on that photograph, Max. Two of the men's wives are dead. One of their wives is missing. We need to go see Gregory, let him know his wife, whoever she is, could be in danger.'

62

10 Days Ago
Junior School, Darlington

Evelyn Jones, after packing her bag, stood still whilst the other children were in the cloakroom collecting their coats.

Neil McMahon glanced up from his desk. 'Is everything okay, Evelyn?'

She pushed out her bottom lip as tears formed in her eyes. The teacher stood up and dashed over.

'Evelyn, dear, what's wrong?' He lowered to his knee. 'What's with the face?'

'I don't understand…'

'You don't understand what? He asked, frowning with concern.

'Bye, Evelyn!' a little voice shouted from the open door of the classroom. Evelyn faked a smile and waved to her friend who'd she usually walk home with.

'What don't you understand, Evelyn?' he asked again.

'The question.'

'The maths question?'

She nodded, then a tear fell down her cheek.

'Aww, Evelyn.' He placed a palm on the outside of her small arm. 'Don't worry about it. We'll go over it tomorrow okay, you're not alone, you know. Some of the others didn't fully understand it so we'll go over it again so everyone knows what to do. How does that sound?'

With her eyes still glassy, she sniffed and nodded positively. 'Yeah, okay.'

'Right, go on, get your coat on and catch up with your friends. You'll be the last out - it'll be getting dark soon.'

She slowly zipped up her coat and left the classroom. Neil McMahon was told that one of her friend's mothers lived around the corner from her house and usually walked her so far then Evelyn walked the extra thirty seconds. They walked down the street, crossed the road, went down the bank of grass, through the woods, and out on the other side. It was the same route they took every day.

Apart from when Evelyn got outside this time, her friend was gone. She was alone in the playground, the last of the parents shuffling out of the gates in the distance.

'Wait for me,' she shouted towards the gate that seemed a million miles away. She recognised the coat that Sophie's mother usually wore and ran along the path, her school bag bouncing side to side across her back. 'Wait!'

When she reached the gate, she took a left and looked down the street. Sophie and her mummy were gone. She froze, unsure what to do. She glanced the other way, hoping to see a familiar face.

There wasn't one.

Her mother always said if a parent wasn't there for whatever reason, to go back into school and ask her teacher what to do. So she turned around and ran back along the path to the school door she'd just left through.

The door was locked.

She knocked a few times, and after waiting for nearly a minute, she gave up.

'Are you okay?' she heard a voice behind her.

She turned quickly. 'Huh?'

'Sorry I scared you, honey,' said the man. She'd seen him before. It was the caretaker. 'Are you okay?'

She nodded, then shrunk into herself, as if she'd done something wrong by standing there after school had finished. 'I'm… okay.'

'Do you need to be back inside – have you forgot something?'

She shook her head. 'I was looking for my friend.'

'I think everyone's gone home, little one.' The man was of average height, average build, a little heavier around the middle, obvious he liked the odd beer every now and again. His dark, almost black eyes watched her closely.

'Okay, sorry.' She moved forward and angled to the right but stopped when he held up a palm. 'Are you okay walking home by yourself?'

She nodded several times. 'I can walk home.'

'You sure?'

'Yeah.'

'Which way do you walk?'

'It isn't far.'

The caretaker looked up to the sky, noticed darkness was creeping in. 'Are you sure? You're not very old.'

'I just have to go down the street and through the woods. It doesn't take long.'

'Okay.' The man stepped to the side, allowing her to pass, then as he walked towards the gate to lock it, he watched her run until she left the school grounds and disappeared to the left. When he reached the gate, he stepped out onto the path and glanced left. Evelyn was just turning the corner.

Evelyn knew where she was going. Would it matter that she wasn't walking with Sophie and her mummy? As long as she went the same way, she'd get home like she did any other night. After she turned the corner onto Barnes Road, she crossed over and took a right, then walked around the bend until she reached the grass.

After she'd walked down the grass bank, she stepped into the woods and hurried along the man-made path in the direction of her house. The sun was falling quickly in the distance.

She noticed it was different walking through there by herself. She felt vulnerable. Alone. But there was something she never noticed.

The figure walking behind her, watching her closely, closing the gap with each stride they took.

63

Monday Afternoon
Darlington

Once they'd got in touch with Gregory Timms, they learned he worked at Jewson's builders merchants on Valley Street in town. He said he wouldn't mind them coming down to have a word about something important.

Byrd walked through the door of the merchants where the pleasant smell of freshly-cut wood hung in the air. He passed an array of shelving and stopped at the counter.

'Is Gregory in?' he asked the thin guy looking down at the computer screen behind it. Byrd noticed a name tag fixed to his chest with the name Harry on as well as the word 'manager' printed underneath it.

The man looked up, peering up at Byrd over thin-framed stylish glasses. 'He is. Who's asking?'

'Tell him it's the police,' Byrd informed him. 'We spoke to him earlier.'

'You did – what's this about?'

'Can you just get him please?' Byrd said, avoiding any unnecessary small talk. The man with the glasses held his gaze on Byrd before he took out his phone, pressed some buttons and put it to his ear.

'Come to reception. Police are here for you.' He lowered the phone, put it back into his pocket. 'He's coming right out.'

A minute later, a small man that Byrd recognised from the group photo to be Gregory Timms walked through the open door, wearing a black fleece with a yellow Jewsons' logo sewn on to his chest.

'Did I speak to you earlier?' he asked Byrd.

'You spoke to my colleague, he asked if I could come and have a quick chat with you. I'm Detective Inspector Max Byrd.' He extended a hand.

Timms stopped dead, frowned, then cautiously took it, wondering what this could be about.

'It's not a massive concern, just something we're following up on, so don't be alarmed straight away.'

Timms' shoulders relaxed a little as he slowly nodded. 'How… can I help?'

Byrd reached into the inside of his pocket and pulled out the photograph, turned it around to face Timms, who glanced down at it. When he recognised the four teenagers on it, his eyebrows furrowed.

'Where's this from?'

'I got it from your friend, James Whittaker, two days ago.'

'Okay…'

They both stepped to one side to allow a man pulling a large trolley full of timber to slide past.

'Thanks,' the man said.

'I don't understand,' Whittaker stated, confusion enveloping his whole face.

'Well,' Byrd began, 'this man's wife'—he pointed at Ian Porter— 'was brutally murdered five days ago. You may have heard it on the news?'

Timms shook his head.

'She was found at their home, tied to a chair, with her eyes missing.'

'Jesus.' Timms raised a palm to his open mouth.

'And this guy'—he pointed to Stuart Richards— 'this guy's wife was found hanging from a tree with only one hand.'

Timms tried to say something but whatever it was, got stuck in his throat.

'And this man'—his finger now on James Whittaker— 'his wife was taken on Saturday morning in Aldi's car park by three men in a van.'

Timms found his voice but it came out weak. 'God…'

'So my interest in you and this photograph is what your connection is? Why has suddenly within five days has there been two brutal murders and a missing person?'

For a long moment, Timms stared at the photo, until he said, 'We were friends back in school. All in the same class, we kept in touch for a while then we kinda lost touch… these things happen.'

'Why did you lose touch? Something happened, didn't it?' Byrd asked.

'I worked more hours, I found a girlfriend, settled down.'

'Is that right?'

He nodded confidently. 'I'm still with her now.'

'True love, eh?' Byrd said.

'Guess so…'

'When was this photograph taken?' Byrd enquired.

'Erm…' Timms focused on the background behind them in the photo. 'At a party. It was at a party. Someone's birthday, I think.'

'Can you remember who?'

He expelled a sudden, hopeless pocket of air from his mouth. 'I have no idea. We went to all sorts of parties back then, I think – hang on… Shez someone, maybe?' he frowned, titled his head back, thinking hard, then nodded. 'Shez. Yeah.'

'Has Shez got a second name?'

'A girl from school. We weren't in her class, but she was in our year. I only knew her as Shez.'

Byrd nodded, making a mental note.

'The main reason for my visit here today is to potentially warn you to keep an eye on your wife.' He stabbed his finger at the photo. 'If this is anything to go by, with what's been happening, then there's a real possibility she could be in danger, Mr Timms.'

'Okay.'

'Can you think of a reason why anyone would want to cause harm to these men's wives? Or your own wife for that fact?'

'Like I said, I haven't spoken to them in years. I don't even know their wives. I – I…' he trailed off.

'What?' Byrd asked, tilting his head.

'I can't think of anything at all.'

'Well, keep an eye on your wife, Sir, because this is a very serious matter.'

'I will,' Timms exclaimed. 'Thanks for stopping by.'

Once Byrd was back inside his car, the heavens opened. Stone-sized droplets pounded the windscreen in a fast-rhythmic beat which made him feel relieved he was sheltered.

He plucked the photograph of the four from his pocket and stared at it for a long moment. 'What happened that night?'

64

Tuesday Morning
Neil McMahon's house

Judith flicked on the kettle and asked him if he wanted one.

'No, thank you,' Neil McMahon said to his wife. It was just after seven, and they'd both been awake for nearly an hour. It was their routine. Even on a weekend they'd get up early and make the most of the day.

McMahon was sitting at the table, looking at the local news.

'Have they heard anything yet?' she asked him.

'No, not yet. I spoke with her parents last night, but we're no further forward. The kids in the class almost see her as a distant memory now. It's awful. Upsetting. A couple of them, the ones who sit on her table, look almost lost next to the empty chair. Whenever the door opens, I pray to look up and see her walk back in.'

She padded over in her fluffy slippers and placed a hand on his back. She didn't say anything.

Then they heard something.

McMahon frowned, glanced up. As did his wife. The sound was coming from upstairs. It was like a cry – or a wail.

'What on earth is that?' McMahon said.

Judith frowned.

He stood up, looked up at the ceiling. 'What is it?'

The more they concentrated on it, the more it sounded like a cry. Like a child's cry. He left the kitchen, stepped into the hallway.

'Where you going, Neil?'

'It's coming from upstairs, I think.' He took the first step on the stairs and ascended them slowly, carefully listening for the sound he didn't understand. At the top of the stairs, he heard it again.

His wife was right behind him. 'Neil?'

'Shhhh.' He turned his head to listen. 'It's coming from in there…' He stepped up onto the landing and crept into the back bedroom. His wife followed, then stopped behind him when he came to a halt.

The cry broke out again. A helpless cry.

'It's coming from the cupboard I think?' McMahon said, edging forward towards the sound. He reached for the handle of the built-in cupboard and pulled it open. The crying suddenly came to a halt. Inside the cupboard was an array of shelves to the right and clothes hanging from a rail on the left.

He stared intently. Confusion took over him as he focused into the completely normal cupboard. 'I don't understand.'

'What's there?' she asked.

'Nothing. Just our wardrobe,' he said.

'I need to knock on next door, it'll be their daughter. She sounds upset.'

'Yeah, she does.'

McMahon moved past her, padded down the stairs and put his shoes on. If their daughter was that upset, the question was: why? He loved children and it was his job to look out for them, to guide them to better futures. It took him less than half a minute to knock on her door. Through the small piece of glass in the window, he saw Alex, the girl's father, appearing closer until the door opened.

'Hi, Neil?' he said, appearing flushed, his cheeks red. Sweat dripped from his brow.

'Hi, Alex…' he started. 'Strange one really… is your daughter okay?'

He glowered at McMahon. 'Yeah… why?'

'We heard crying upstairs in our house. Seems like it's coming from maybe your daughter's room?'

'So?'

'And… I'm just checking that she's okay, if you hadn't heard her crying?'

'I heard her. She was getting told off for something bad she did…'

McMahon stared at the man, wondering if any physical abuse had been used. 'Okay.'

'Is there anything else?' he said sternly.

'No,' Neil said, 'sorry to have bothered you.'

The man closed the door quickly, almost slamming it. McMahon stepped down, walked along the short driveway until he hit the path.

Outside of the house, he'd noticed the white van that Alex had been driving around in wasn't there anymore.

65

Tuesday morning
River Tees

Derek Pratt, like he did every day, parked up in the car park of Broken Scar, got out and opened the boot, allowing his dog, Jasper, to bounce out with excitement about his walk. A chill hung in the air, like it usually did this time of the morning.

'Come on, boy,' Derek said.

Jasper kept still long enough for Derek to attach the lead to the red collar around his neck. They strolled along the man-made path, heading along the side of the river.

It was quiet.

Occasionally, he passed familiar faces, but this morning it was almost derelict, as if the path had somehow been forgotten about, dog walkers and runners now using another spot.

In the distance, fifteen metres up in the sky, a flock of birds circled furiously, one of them occasionally scooping down for something. No doubt picking off the fish in the river, he assumed, waiting for the perfect time to catch their bait.

After stepping over the metal hop by the side of the closed gate – designed for keeping the sheep and cows inside – they continued, following the footpath by the wide area of grass. The floor was soggy and damp, the mud stuck to the bottom of his shoes like glue from the rain that hammered down the night before.

Suddenly, Jasper darted right, yanking on the lead which had extended to its full length. Derek struggled to keep a hold of it, slipping on the mud. 'Easy boy, easy!'

He angled in the direction that the dog wanted to go; it was desperate, as if it had picked up a scent of another canine nearby. But there was no sound, no barking, no noise – apart from the gushing flowing river beside them.

Jasper pulled Derek closer towards the river. There was an angled plane of grass with a ledge that led to a small area of stones, almost hidden by a small cluster of trees.

'Easy boy,' he said again, feeling the power of the dogs desperation as he was dragged down onto the stones. The dog slowed and started sniffing, his wet nose close to the ground, his head moving frantically.

Out of nowhere, a vulture flew up into the air and darted off into the sky. Jasper barked at it until it disappeared from their sight.

Jasper edged forward again, pulling on the lead. Then Derek heard the sound of buzzing. The closer he got, the continual buzzing sound overpowered the sound of the river. It sounded like a bees nest.

And then he saw what it was - it wasn't a bees nest.

At first, he wasn't sure if it was real. Somehow, it seemed… not right.

It was… it was unlike anything he'd ever seen.

'Jesus Christ.'

66

Tuesday Afternoon
Broken Scar, River Tees

Tanzy slowed the Golf and took a left into Broken Scar. Standing in front of the temporary tape that had been put up was PC Cornty. After he realised it was Tanzy, he moved and let them through.

As Tanzy stopped his car down in the bottom carpark, Byrd released his seat belt and opened the door. Tanzy did the same. The air outside the car was freezing as they stepped out and closed the doors. As they headed up the ramp, they could smell damp in the air, the way the trees and plants had soaked up the rain from the night before.

'Whittaker's wife?' Byrd asked.

'There's a good chance it is.'

Along the muddy path, not a word was spoken between them, until they reached a metal hop-up at the fence, where a familiar PC was standing, stopping any members of the public accessing the area. 'Afternoon,' said PC Amy Weaver.

'Hi, Amy,' Tanzy said, 'how you doing?'

She said she was okay.

'Are forensics here yet?'

She nodded. 'The full lot.'

'Tallow, Hope, Forrest, Beech?' Byrd asked.

'Even McCabe is here…' she said.

'Full show today, must be important for the Hollywood stars to show up, too.'

PC Weaver smiled at him.

The detectives made their way around the bend and came into view of another officer standing in the middle of the grass. It was DS Stockdale, pointing behind him, just off to the right. 'You wanna be down there.'

'Thanks. You been down?' Tanzy said, carefully stepping over the overgrown grass in his not-so-perfect-footwear.

Stockdale nodded. 'Yeah…' A look of sadness swept across his face.

'What is it?' Byrd asked.

'You should see for yourselves.'

Byrd and Tanzy passed him, carefully making their way down the wet, grassy decline, then stepped down on to the small area of stones. There, in front of them, were the forensic team. Hope was kneeling down in front of the body. Tallow was standing beyond her on the other side of it, taking photos, and Forrest and Beech each had a pen in their hands, scribbling down notes on their own separate notepads towards the right. To the left, stood McCabe, looking in the opposite direction of the body, staring at the river. He seemed to be in a trance.

'Tony?' Hope said, glancing in his direction. He turned around and nodded.

The detectives grew closer. They could see the legs of the body now, the wet fabric torn in several places, probably caught on the rocks as it floated down the river.

Tallow heard them approach and glanced their way, giving them a sad smile.

'Morning,' he said softly.

'Good morning, guys,' Byrd said.

Tanzy never spoke.

'What do we have?'

Hope stood up slowly, also giving a sad smile and allowed them room to step forward and have a look. The body in front of them was female, they could tell that by the matted, soaked blonde hair. There was a clump of entwined blood stuck to the back of the victims head, telling them she'd been hit by something hard, hard enough to damage the area of the head. Most likely, at a quick glance, the kind of damage that a baseball bat would do but it was difficult to tell. Her face was swelled with water and her skin had a hint of transparency to it. Her body looked a little overweight due to the water it had absorbed in the time in had been there. It was evident that little areas of skin on her face had been eaten by birds and fish, it seemed, the parts of draping flesh hanging loosely off her.

'Jesus.' Byrd edged forward some more then came to a halt, feeling a lump rising in his throat.

Tanzy followed suit, but a couple of steps behind, absorbing the scene, and the lifeless female in front of them. The smell that surrounded them changed from the damp plant life smell to something else, something—

'Oh, God.'

Tanzy's stomach flipped, then twisted inside out, forcing him to turn away, lean over, and be sick on the grass to their right. Hope winced in his direction but understood why.

'Why? He said, quietly at first, then: 'Why!' His voice echoed through the air, then he turned back to her. 'Why her?'

'How long has she been in the water for?' Byrd asked Hope.

Tallow answered. 'Hard to say. Judging by her skin, the way it's swelled… could be three to four days in my opinion.'

McCabe, who was now standing next to Tallow, the height of Tallow making McCabe look like a child, nodded, confirming Tallow's quick theory. Testing would be done to find out exactly what happened to her.

One of the things running through Tanzy's mind was how was he going to ring her husband to tell him that she was dead. *He* had to do it. Not Byrd, but him. It was his duty.

'I'll find whoever did this to you,' Tanzy whispered to her lifeless, swelled body. 'I promise you that… Kim Harrison.'

67

June 14th, 2004
Darlington
15 years ago

When Shez Barker had stepped out of her bedroom and closed the door, leaving Sarah to sleep off whatever had caused her to feel the way she did, she headed downstairs, her shadow dancing on the ceiling above her as she descended into the flashing lights of the party. The music was still borderline unbearable, but everyone was so drunk, they seemed to be enjoying it. Maybe too drunk to even care.

Ian Porter stepped out and stopped at the closed bedroom door, then glanced left. There was no one on the stairs. No one coming up. Quickly, he opened the door and slid in to the darkness, then closed the door behind him. The room would have been in total darkness if not for a dim lamp resting on the right side of the drawers near Sarah's face.

Even in the state of unconsciousness, she was still beautiful.

Ian padded over the white carpet carefully, finding his bearings of the room. Straight ahead was the window. To the right, a set of wide wardrobes that looked like they could be built in; Ian wasn't sure in the dark, nor did he care, as long as there was just them two in the room, that's all that mattered. He focused on Sarah. She was on her back, her head tipped to one side, her body slightly turned, her face angling towards the door.

It was a shame, Ian thought, the way she'd been put to bed. The covers were up over her stomach to keep her warm. That was no good.

'You don't need these on, dear, we don't want you getting too hot, do we?' he whispered, then he prudently pulled them off, dropped them to the carpet by his feet. He gasped and felt himself getting hard in his jeans after seeing her black underwear in between her tanned, muscular thighs.

'Wow,' he whispered.

Self-conscious of the time he had remaining, he unclipped his belt, let his jeans drop to the floor, then pulled down his red underwear and kicked them to one side. He dropped down onto the bed, leaned forward, and using one hand to hold his balance, he used the other to grab the thin strap of her underwear and yanked them down.

He climbed on top and inserted himself into her.

68

Tuesday Afternoon
Police Station

Tanzy walked back from his desk carrying the weight of responsibility on his shoulders. Somehow, he felt accountable for what had happened to PC Harrison, and felt angry about it. To see her on the stones less than an hour ago, was an image that wouldn't leave his head. He tried the best to block out the mental imprint, clamping his eyes tighter, but nothing seemed to work. The way her skin had lost its colour and appeared thinner, the way her body had swelled, making her appear like someone else entirely, but at the same time, obviously her.

Tanzy and Byrd had left the scene at the river to let the forensic team do their thing. They'd be there for a while, collecting evidence, taking samples, obtaining photographs etc.. Tallow tended to take a video of crime scenes, so the forensic team could refer back to it later when analysing.

When they reached the office, Tanzy had told Byrd to take a seat and that he'd get them some much-needed coffee.

'I'll have a pint of Coors Light if there's one…' he wished.

Tanzy headed for the canteen. Byrd took off his coat and sat down slowly, letting his weight fall into the chair. He felt numb. One of their own had died.

Did she drown? Did she accidently slip? Why was she there in the first place?

Judging by what he saw on the stones, it looked like she'd been struck over the head with something hard. Hard enough to draw blood anyway. He'd speak with Hope and Tallow later to get a better idea of exactly what happened.

Byrd turned on the computer, waited impatiently for the screen to come on, thinking about his mother and father, how helpless they both were lying there in comas at the hospital. It was horrible. One part of him wanted to go see them. When he felt shit, that's what he would do: he went to see his parents. They always picked him up, especially his father; he was a very positive kind of guy who saw the best in people and the situations he found himself in. Once, Byrd recalled, they were driving back from Scarborough when they got a flat tire. They'd just set off and Byrd, as a boy of nine, really wanted to get home to go to a party at his friend's house. He'd been looking forward to it for ages but then his father told him the recovery company couldn't come and fix the car in time, so they'd have to get a taxi back into Scarborough and stay at one of the hotels. It was the Lord Nelson hotel just above the bar located on the sea front. It was one of the only places that had a last-minute available room and was pleasant enough.

His father had told him that although he would miss the party, he had to change the way he looked at things. He told him that every cloud had a silver lining if he looked closely enough. And when Byrd had snuggled up to his parents that night in probably one of the smallest rooms he'd ever slept in, the sunrise on the sea front at six in the morning was the most beautiful thing he'd ever seen. That same morning, they got candy floss and went to the fairground again. Then they'd went on a speedboat that was docked the day before due to bad weather. So in a way, he was grateful for the car having a flat tire because that morning was so good, he'd never forget it.

Unfortunately, it was a difficult task looking for a silver lining regarding the condition of his parents. There simply wasn't one.

Tanzy returned with two cups of coffee and handed Byrd one of them. Taking a seat on his own chair, he sat back and sighed heavily. The office was quiet. The air felt different, as if the news of PC Kim Harrison was hanging, changing the density of it.

'Guna be some fucking day, mate,' Tanzy muttered.

'Yeah, I know.'

For a long moment, they both just sat, still and quiet, as if on standby mode, reserving their energy for the next thing. A lot had happened to them over the past few weeks. Darlington hadn't witnessed the kidnapping of a seven-year-old, three murders, and a missing person's enquiry within the time frame of ten days before.

It was all happening fast.

It was tiring.

Tanzy almost closed his eyes when he heard the door open behind them.

'Orion…'

He blinked a few times and turned to the voice, as did Byrd.

'Yeah?' said Tanzy.

'My office, please?'

He nodded, found his feet and went into DCI Thornton's office.

'Close the door, Orion.'

He did.

'Sit down.'

He did.

'How you doing – I heard the news about Kim…' she said.

'It's awful,' he began, 'she was a lovely girl with a brilliant future ahead of her. Always so pleasant to people. Hard working. Why would anyone ever do this to her, it's – it's…' he trailed off, dropping his face into his hands for a moment.

She gave a sad smile, observing and sympathising with his emotions. 'I know… but listen, Orion,' she said, 'we'll do everything we can to find out what happened to her, okay… we'll speak to McCabe when the forensics are finished and get a good idea.' She leaned forward, reached for his right hand, and squeezed it. 'We'll find whoever did this, I promise you that. It's hard enough when it's a member of the force, but when it's your own, it's…'

He glanced up and sighed, 'Yeah.'

'Will you be okay?' she asked.

Tanzy mulled over the question for a moment.

'You can take a day off, or a few days to yourself if you need it? We can handle things here, Orion?'

'I'll be fine… but thank you.'

'Okay. Well let me know if there's anything I can do for you.'

'Thanks,' he said, then he stood up, made his way back into the main office—

'Orion.'

Before he stepped through the door, he turned sluggishly.

'We'll get them, you know. Don't worry about it,' she said with determination in her focused eyes.

'I know we will,' he said. 'We always do, Boss.'

69

Tuesday Afternoon
Police Force Control Room

Mary Ellis had been the forefront of the Police control room for the best part of twenty-two years. Over that time, countless employees had come and gone, some on to better things, some, leaving the police force entirely.

On seven occasions, she'd been offered a promotion, but she'd declined every time. She loved the job as a call handler - loved every minute of it, in fact. One of the biggest reasons was, although the job mainly included answering emergency calls and allocating services to various locations, which seemed like a monotonous task, the causes for the calls were certainly diverse. They varied hugely from a girl being trapped inside a lift, to an old man who'd had a plant pot stolen. A few days ago, she answered the call from a lady who'd had her bra stolen by the man next door, then caught him sniffing it the day after on his front door step in front of her.

There's some weird – and wonderful – people out there, that's for sure.

The time had just gone three in the afternoon. She finished her coffee and placed the empty cup on the desk next to her keyboard. A call hadn't come in for twenty-four minutes, which was unusual for Mary. On average, there were one-hundred and seventy calls daily to the team which were handled by Mary, Jackie, Alan, and Peter. This number doubled on a bank holiday and the average usually increased during the summer months.

She sat back, waiting for the next call, then right on cue, the phone rang.

Raising her hand to her headset, she accepted the call.

'Emergency, what service?' Mary said into the headset.

'Erm… I – I…' the voice trailed away.

'Emergency, what service?'

'It's dead,' the voice said, 'I've haven't seen anything like it…'

'This is emergency response,' Mary said loud and clear, 'what service do you require?'

'Police – I need the police.' A few seconds of silence followed then: 'Or maybe an ambulance.'

She guessed it sounded like a male, most likely between the age of fifty to sixty, an ability she'd picked up over the years.

'You require the police?'

'Yes. It's not – it's just on its own…'

'Sir, where are you?'

'In a back alley. Back of Green - Greenbank Road… near the hospital,' replied the flustered man. 'I'm in front of the bin.'

Immediately, she put the address into the system, and waited for further information from him.

'What's in the bin?'

'It's a… oh God…'

'Sir, can you please tell me what's in the bin?' she said, calmly.

'A woman's head.'

For a split second, Mary was stuck for words, wondering if she'd heard him correctly. 'Can you confirm you told me you've have found a woman's head in the bin?'

'Yeah… it's a head.'

'Emergency response is being sent to your location right now, Sir.'

'Okay.'

'Can you please stay on the line until they get there. Is that okay, Sir?' she asked.

'Erm… yeah. Okay.'

'What is your name?'

'Patrick.'

'What's your second name?'

'Walton. My full name is Patrick Matthew Walton.'

'Okay, Patrick Walton, thank you for calling me today. Is it okay for me to call you Patrick?'

'Yeah,' he said, 'that's fine.'

'Okay, Patrick. Are you alone?'

'Yes – well no… I'm with my dog.'

'Your dog?'

'That's when we saw him,' he told her.

'Who did you see?'

'A man. He – he dropped something inside the bin, then he ran into the house through the back gate next to the bin.'

'What did the man look like?'

'Scared. He was panicking.'

'What was he wearing,' Mary asked.

'I only got a glimpse of him. He's wearing a red jumper I think. He had black hair. Or maybe brown. That's all I saw before he went inside the gate.'

'Okay, that's great. How old is the man?'

'I – I don't know. Maybe forty, could be fifty… it was hard to tell. Maybe older.'

'Emergency services should be there very, very soon, Patrick.'

Whilst holding the phone to his head, Patrick heard sirens somewhere in the air, growing louder by the second.

'I can hear them,' he told her.

'They're arriving right now, I can see their location on my screen. Thank you for your call, Mr Walton.'

A marked Astra flew around the corner of the alley and came to a sudden halt in front of Patrick and his dog. The brakes pinged, and the tyres squeaked on the damp cobbles. The lights on the top of the car span like a top in synchronisation to the almost deafening siren. The driver leaned forward, pressed something on the dash. As the blasting noise abruptly stopped, he threw the driver's door open and jumped out. The female officer sitting in the passenger seat did the same on the opposite side and closed her door.

'Mr Walton?' asked the male, dashing towards him.

'Yes, yes,' Patrick replied. His dog, a border terrier crouched down, gritted his teeth at the officer.

'I'm PC Cornty.' He pointed to his right when the female arrived in front of the hot bonnet. 'This is PC Weaver.'

'Hi,' he said.

The two PC's observed the bin to the man's right. Cornty took a step forward. 'Could you just take a step back from the bin please, Sir?'

'Sure.' Patrick and his dog moved back several paces as PC Cornty carefully placed a fingertip on the corner of the bin lid and lifted it up, then tipped his head forward to have a look.

The buzz of blow flies rushed out and inside, there must have been dozens and dozens of them around the woman's head which was inches below the top of the bin, facing upwards. Her eyes were wide open looking up to the sky, then at PC Cornty when he came in her line of vision. The head was severed three inches below her chin by what looked like a very clean cut, although strings of veins, arteries and God knows what else hung out the bottom of it, pooling the household black bin bags underneath it with thick blood. The skin of the head appeared white and pasty, several areas of the face blotchy from the way the blood had settled.

'Jesus,' he whispered, edging back. He faced Patrick. 'What happened?'

Patrick turned, pointing. 'I walked from down there,' then he turned back and lowered his arm, 'then I saw a man standing where you are looking inside the bin. He must have heard me or something because he looked right at me. Then he panicked and ran inside there.'

'Where?'

'Through that gate.' The man stepped forward, stabbing the air towards the dark blue gate just left of the bin. 'In there. In there.'

Cornty turned to Weaver. 'Get back up now. Ask for forensics too! Do it now!'

With urgency, she grabbed the radio from her belt and called for back-up, telling dispatch the situation and confirming they'd found a woman's head. She also said that the suspect had gone through the gate next to the bin and that they were going in.

Cornty told the man to take a step back, then turned towards the gate. On the step, he saw drops of blood. He pulled out his baton, and using his left hand, unlocked the catch of the gate and pushed it open. The concrete path on the other side of the gate was smeared in blood. Bright and red. It looked like a trail.

He followed the path with wide eyes, absorbing the direction of the trail until it veered to the right out of sight.

'Amy, I'm going in…'

'Right behind you,' she replied.

He stepped up onto the path, careful where he placed his feet and went through the doorway. The back yard was rectangular. Roughly ten metres back by four metres wide. On the left side of the yard, it was busy with plant pots and bright coloured flowers. The wall above was lined with trellis and wiry, thin stems that had arched and bent as they'd grown.

The right side of the yard was a different story. From his feet to about a third of the way down leading to the house, was a thick trail of blood. He gulped hard, his heartbeat pumping through his whole body as he slowly shifted forward.

'Hello!' he shouted. 'Hello, Police here…'

Weaver stepped up behind him with wide eyes. 'Can you see anything?'

'No.' Cornty scanned the window ahead of him, then along the windows of what seemed like a kitchen extension to the right.

On the floor, the trail veered off to the right down a thin narrow alley where a brick-built shed was located.

'What the fuck, Phillip,' Weaver muttered behind him, staying close.

'Shhhh…'

Level with the alley, Cornty noticed the shed door was half open to the right. Down on the floor, he saw the blood trail lead inside of it.

'Stay back,' he told her, edging around, following the messy trail.

Close by, sirens wailed in the air – back up was near. Cornty thought for a second about waiting but needed to see what was inside, needed to see where the blood was coming from.

Using his left hand, he pushed the door open and peered into the darkness.

70

Tuesday Afternoon
Greenbank Road, Darlington

At the back of the concrete shed, there was a naked body sitting upright against the brick wall. The legs were straight out resting on the floor in the shape of a thin V.

Blood ran down from where the head used to be down the body, smothering the stomach with thick, chunky trails. There was enough blood to fill a small pond.

'Fucking Christ,' he shouted, pulling back suddenly. 'What on earth!'

'What? What is it?' Weaver panted.

'Get back, get back – just get back.' He used his hand to edge her back. 'Come on, we need to find him now.'

He dashed around to the back door and tried the handle. Locked. Taking a step back, he lunged hard at it with his right boot; the shudder shot up his leg, causing an uncomfortable throbbing pain, but the door never budged.

'Fuck,' he screamed as he lowered his leg, suspending it off the floor for a second. He tried again, ignoring the pain and giving it everything he had. This time, the door gave way, the wood and lock mechanism sheering as the door swung open, pieces of wood flying off in all directions.

With a heightened pain in his ankle and shin, he hobbled into the kitchen. He quickly looked right, which was empty, then darted left out of the kitchen into a dining room. A smell of lavender hung in the air from a candle in the centre of the rectangular, wooden table in the middle of the room.

'Police here, come out right now!' he screamed, standing at the table, scanning the room frantically.

'Police, police!' Weaver said, overtaking him heading toward the hallway.

'Wait, Amy…' he begged, trying to pull her back but missing her. 'Wait!'

Down the corridor ahead of them, the front door smashed through as Byrd and Tanzy charged in. 'Police, Police!' They slowed when they spotted Weaver and Cornty. 'Where is he?' Tanzy asked.

'We don't know…'

Tanzy charged upstairs, Byrd a few steps behind him, both of them with their batons tightly in hands, ready for whatever they might come up against. Hanging on the wall of the stairs, they passed three medical certificates, but didn't stop to take the time to read them.

Cornty decided to stay downstairs – his ankle started to swell. Weaver followed them up, and at the top of the stairs, the two detectives took a right and reached the landing; Tanzy went left towards the bathroom and Byrd went straight ahead, pushing open a door into one of the rear bedrooms. Apart from a bed, bedside drawers, and a basic-looking wardrobe, the bedroom was empty.

'Hey, here, come here,' shouted Tanzy, standing outside the bathroom door. 'This is locked – it won't open. He's in here.' He banged five times on the door. 'Open the door, it's the police.'

There was no response from inside the locked bathroom.

He banged again with the outside of his clenched fist. 'Police, open the door!'

No response.

He moved back a few spaces, took a breath, then threw himself at the door, his foot colliding so hard into the wood, the door shot open with the loudest crack they'd ever heard, swinging around on its hinges until it banged into the wall with a thud great enough to shake the house.

In the corner of the bathroom, sitting on the floor, curled up in a ball, was someone Byrd recognised.

'Dr Ching?' he said, stepping into the large bathroom. Tanzy moved around him and stopped just before the doctor, who held his palms up in surrender.

'This is a mistake,' he blurted out. 'A mistake!'

Byrd's eyes widened. 'Dr Ching, what's going on here?'

'It's a mistake, it wasn't me…'

'We'll see about that down at the station, won't we?' replied Tanzy, grabbing his wrists and hauling him up like he weighed less than a bag of sugar. He turned him around one-eighty and cuffed him.

'My arm!' pleaded the doctor. 'Watch my arm…'

Tanzy, whilst holding both of Ching's hands behind his back, lifted them a few inches, sending a shooting pain up his arm. 'Is that any better?'

'Ahhhhh,' he cried out, wincing in pain.

'Ori, that's enough…' Byrd told him. 'Take him down stairs.'

Tanzy pretty much man-handled him back to the police van which had turned up a minute later. Cornty was standing at the rear of the van, the door open, watching him as he was brought forward. Tanzy handed him over to PC Cornty who took a firm hold of his arm and guided him up the step into the back of it. The doctor, who had tears in his eyes, took a seat on the white, flat plastic seat to the left and glared sadly at the cold, hard floor.

'I didn't do this – this is a mistake,' he whispered to himself.

Cornty stepped up into the cramped space, leaned forward, and with his mouth close to his ear, he whispered, 'Fucking sicko.'

Once the van doors were closed, Cornty banged twice on the back door, the metallic sound pinging in the street. Byrd and Tanzy, who were standing across the road, just in front of Dr Ching's house, watched the van edge forward, then pull out onto the road, and off it disappeared in the direction of the station.

'I don't fucking believe this…'

'What?' Tanzy asked Byrd, noticing the surprise on his face.

'It's the doctor that's looking after my parents, the doctor I'm dealing with about their progress.'

'Really?' Tanzy was surprised.

'Yes. Dr Ching.'

Tanzy was speechless, then noticed PC Cornty approaching them. 'Good work,' Tanzy said. 'Were you the first here?'

Cornty nodded. 'Yeah. We were close by when dispatch got the call from the man with the dog.'

'Where is he?' Byrd queried.

Cornty turned, spotted him across the street, sitting down a low brick wall belonging to the house opposite.

'Okay, thanks – we'll go speak to him.'

'Have you been inside?' Cornty asked. 'Have you seen what's in the shed and the bin?'

'No – we've been told,' Tanzy said.

A nod from Cornty. 'You should go see. But I must warn you that you'll need your strong stomachs.'

'Forensics are here already, we'll give them space,' Byrd added.

'Well, if what I think is true, if this has something to do with Julia Porter and Mary Richards, then I think it's safe to say we've found our serial killer.'

Byrd and Tanzy both absorbed his eager words, but Byrd didn't want to believe it, he didn't want to think the person who'd been caring for his unconscious parents was capable of doing something like this.

It just didn't add up to him.

Then Byrd said, 'Maybe… we'll see what he has to say down at the station.'

71

June 14th, 2004
Darlington
15 years ago

Ian Porter didn't last very long, although Sarah was practically unconsciously throughout the whole ordeal. She made the odd grunt, and Ian, being his drunken stupid self-absorbent self, took that as her feeling pleasure. She didn't even know what had happened.

But he did it – he finally did it. He'd now go downstairs with a half-smile on his face – not that he'd actually achieved anything apart from committing rape on a girl he'd fancy for longer than he could remember – and claim his twenty pound off Stuart Richards.

He slowly lifted himself off and stared at her. All of her. Then using sweaty trembling hands, he pulled up his jeans.

'I enjoyed that,' he whispered coldly.

The beat of the music was still drumming through the foundations of the house, although most of it was blocked out by the closed door, but the energy that bounced through the walls were felt inside the darkened room. He finished doing his belt and took a few steps back, glaring down at her naked body once more. He'd even managed to pull her top off without much of a struggle to feel her breasts. Oh, they were so perfect.

As he turned towards the door, it suddenly opened, a rush of dance music and a flashing lights flooded in.

He froze.

'Ian… what the fuck?'

Stuart, James, and Gregory all staggered in, absorbing the scene before them.

'Ian,' Stuart said, 'what's happened?'

'What's happened is you owe me twenty pounds…'

Gregory took a few steps forward, glared wide-eyed at him, then down at Sarah. 'You fucking raped her?'

Ian carelessly shrugged and glanced back at her. Gregory raced to the door and closed it, blocking out the brunt of the sounds, making the room private.

'Ian, you can't just go around fucking raping people you mad bastard!' Gregory shouted, appearing just before him. Rage filled his face; he was disgusted at what his friend had done.

'I said I'd fuck her. That's what I did,' he explained to them, shrugging without a care in the world.

'You say it so casually,' James added. 'You're going to fucking jail, mate!' James lunged forward, almost knocking Gregory out of the way, and threw his arms out at Ian's chest causing him to fumble back until he finally tripped and collided into the back wall. 'Fucking idiot!'

After Ian landed hard and fast, he screamed, 'What the fuck?' then rubbed the back of his head rigorously where he felt a lump forming. Ian then jumped up quickly, dashed over to James with his fist cocked behind his back.

'Calm the fuck down!' Stuart balled, grabbing him from the side. 'Chill the fuck out!'

Ian tried to shake him off, but Stuart was in a better position, pinning his arm around his back. 'Calm the fuck down.'

Ian eased off a little, shooting daggers at James with his eyes, who was standing in the middle of the bedroom ready for him with his fists clenched.

'Right, right,' Gregory said calmly. 'Everyone just take a second until we figure this fucking thing out!' He pointed around the room, then down at Sarah, who was shuffling slightly. 'What the fuck are we gonna do?'

Without answering, they all stared at each other. They didn't know. They had never been in a situation like this before. Gregory noticed Ian had calmed down a little and had a taken a few steps back to be by himself.

'I've raped her…' he muttered to himself, just loud enough for them to hear.

'Yeah, you fucking have,' James yelled. 'Fucking disgusting little man you are!'

Ian tensed up, darted towards him again. Stuart stepped across and pointed a firm finger in his face. 'Sit the fuck down or I'll put you on your arse, Porter!' He pushed hard on his chest and knocked him back a few steps.

Porter understood how serious he was and retreated to the corner of the room, muttering some inaudible drunken shit to himself. Stuart turned, glanced at the other two. 'The fuck we gonna do, boys?'

'We'll just leave…' James said. 'That's all we can do…'

The three of them stared down at Sarah, who was lying on her back, her legs open, her arms either side. Completely out of it.

'Unless…' Stuart whispered.

'What?' James asked, frowning. 'Unless what?'

Stuart's eyes widened. 'Unless we fuck her too?'

James' mouth opened. 'Are you out of your mind?'

'Yeah, go on… fuck her!' Ian shouted from the corner. 'Do it! She won't remember anyway. You're never gunna have this chance again. Not with her.' He paused a beat. 'Or - or are you all too scared… fucking virgins?'

'I'm no virgin!' James retorted. 'But I'm not—'

'I'm not scared,' Stuart replied, unbuckling his belt quickly. 'I'll do it!'

'Stu, come on man, don't do this…' James begged. 'It isn't right, man.'

'If you're too chicken shit, then leave!' he teased him, stepping forward with his penis hanging down. James and Gregory exchanged worried glances, then looked back at Stuart, who climbed on top of Sarah and inserted himself into her, holding her wrists down on the bed.

Over the next ten minutes, the four of them raped Sarah to the beat of the dance music seeping through the closed door. The stuffy air inside the room smelt of sweat, perfume, and a sense of false masculinity. After they all finished, they got dressed, high fived each other and snuck out the room, closed the door, and casually descended the stairs as if nothing had ever happened.

72

Tuesday Late Afternoon
Police Station

Doctor Ching sat in the interrogation room alone. Through the window to his right, although he wasn't aware, Byrd and Tanzy were watching him closely.

'What you thinking, Max?'

'I don't know, Ori,' he said, keeping his focus on the doctor through the one-way glass. 'It doesn't add up.'

'If he's involved in the other murders, he's one serious nut job – they're running his DNA now, to see there's a match with the hair found at the other scenes.'

Byrd glanced at Tanzy. 'When will we know?'

'ASAP, they're doing it right now.'

Byrd nodded, looking back through the glass.

'He looks an oddball though, Max, you have to admit?'

'You should never judge a book by its cover.'

Minutes later, they headed inside, leaving DCI June Thornton, PC Cornty, and PC Weaver on the viewing side of the glass, who'd just turned up.

The door opened. Tanzy went in first, then Byrd. They pulled their chairs out and sat down, not saying a word. The air in the small room was cool and ventilated, the AC unit in the top corner whirring away, but sweat lined the forehead of the doctor, who since the detectives came in, hadn't looked up from the table.

'Can I get you a coffee?' Byrd asked softly.

The doctor seemed surprised at the generous offer but shook his head.

'Then we'll make a start…' Tanzy said, leaning forward, turning on the recording equipment. 'It's 18.43,' he began, 'I'm Detective Inspector Orion Tanzy here with Detective Inspector Max Byrd of Durham Constabulary. We are interviewing Doctor Sion Ching, who's been arrested for first degree murder. Doctor Sion Ching has rejected the opportunity to seek representation from a lawyer or anyone associated with the criminal justice department. Can you confirm this is true, Dr Ching?'

'I can.' His voice was flat and quiet.

'Can you tell us why we found a headless woman inside your shed at the bottom of your yard, and why her head was inside of a bin at the rear of your property, outside in the alleyway?' Tanzy asked.

For a moment, the doctor stayed silent, as if almost forgetting why he was there, as if what he'd been told didn't resonate with him.

'Doctor?' Byrd said.

He coughed first, then: 'It's a mistake, I had nothing to do with this.'

Tanzy looked at Byrd, then back to the suspect. 'Interesting. What makes you believe that?'

'Believe what?' he replied.

'That you had nothing to do with it? It's your property, it's your bin. Please explain. Detective Byrd and I are very keen to hear…'

'I – I received a phone call…'

'From who?' Byrd this time.

'I don't know…' He gave a small shrug. 'It was a man. He asked me if I was Dr Ching. I said yes. Then he told me to look in the shed outside and then in the bin in the alley. I asked who it was, but he wouldn't tell me. He said it didn't matter who he was.'

Ching was very convincing – his body language told Byrd he was telling the truth. He knew this because he knew Dr Ching to a certain degree. He'd spoken with him at the hospital about his parents several times. Once you knew someone when they told the truth, you could distinguish them when they lied. Their facial expressions differed. Their tone of voice changed. Their body language altered. Byrd was confident the doctor didn't display anything different to what he'd seen before, therefore was confident the story he was telling the detective rang true, unless he was an Actor as well as a Doctor.

However, deep down, Byrd knew people were capable of things beyond their imagination. He'd been in this game as long as anyone, but he didn't want to believe the doctor was capable of what he'd been accused of.

'Then what happened?' Tanzy said, leaning forward, a frown lining his forehead.

'I was confused. Then I went outside, saw the blood in the yard near the shed. I looked inside and… Oh God!' He fell silent for a moment and threw his hand to his mouth, as if reliving the moment earlier in his mind. 'It was horrible. I then remembered what he said about the bin and looked outside and saw the…'

'The head?' Tanzy said.

He gave several short nods. 'Then a man was walking his dog and saw me. I panicked, came inside quickly. I didn't know what to do. I ran upstairs and hid in the bathroom.' His body sunk into the chair a little, embarrassed by what he'd said.

'Dr Ching, why didn't you ring the police?' Byrd asked, curiously.

'I—'

The door to the interrogation room opened, and in came PC Weaver with a sheet of A4 paper in her hand. Her face was flat, emotionless. She never smiled, nor frowned. After she placed the paper in front of the detectives, she nodded at them and left the room, closing the door behind her.

Byrd reached forward and picked up the paper.

Tanzy leaned in so they could both read it. On the other side of the desk, the doctor stared, wondering what was so important.

It was the DNA results.

After flicking through three pages over the next minute, the room stayed absolutely silent, even their breathing slowed down.

'Please, go on,' Byrd said finally, glancing up from the paper back to Ching.

'I didn't ring the police because like I said, I panicked. It would look like *I* did it for crying out loud!' His voice slapped off the back wall and back to him. He sighed heavily and stared back down at the table.

'No,' Tanzy said, 'you didn't ring the police because you murdered her. Using some form of sharp instrument, to cut her head off.'

'I – I… please listen to me, I—'

Tanzy raised a quick palm. 'What I don't understand is why you went to so much trouble covering your tracks with Julia Porter and Mary Richards.' Tanzy angled his head towards Byrd. 'It doesn't make any sense, does it, Detective?'

Byrd shook his head. 'It doesn't…'

'Who are they? Mary Richards and Julia Palmer. I've never heard of them?'

'Julia Porter actually… Ahh playing that card?' Tanzy muttered, a smirk lining his lips.

'What… card?' the doctor asked, confused.

'Making it appear like you never did it, that you—'

'Because I never fucking did it!' he shouted, his cheeks now glowing red, his eyes fixed on Tanzy, who matched his stare but lost the grin.

Tanzy, not reacting to the outburst, said, 'We have matched your DNA to other crime scenes. A sample of your hair was found in the passenger seat of Julia Porter's Nissan Qashqai, and then under the finger nails of Mary Richards when we found her body hanging from the tree you hung her from.'

The doctor edged back suddenly. 'Listen – you have me mixed up with someone else here, I can one-hundred percent guarantee you I don't know these women and one-thousand percent say I never did these awful things you're suggesting I did.'

'How did we get a sample of your DNA then?' Tanzy questioned.

He shrugged. 'I don't know. It wasn't me.'

'We have the proof here, doctor…' Byrd added, who'd been sitting in silence for a while.

'Mr Byrd, please listen to me, I've done nothing wrong here, you know me, you know I'm a doctor. A good doctor. That's all I've ever known. Do you think I'd be capable of doing these awful things?'

The doctor aimed the question at Byrd and Byrd only.

'I think people are capable of anything' he replied.

Ching sighed.

'Doctor Sion Ching,' Tanzy said, 'you're going to prison for a very, very long time.'

'I need a lawyer,' he demanded.

'Interview terminated at 18.56. The suspect in custody now requests legal representation.'

73

June 14th, 2004
Darlington
15 years ago

The time was approaching midnight. The music had been turned down a notch, a sign of respect to the neighbours, although it was still loud enough to wake the dead in the nearest cemetery. Shez Barker said bye to a couple of friends at the door, waved them off as they walked down the drive, then closed it. About half the people had left, jumping in the dozens of taxis that had pulled up at the house over the last thirty minutes. Some party-goers had work in the morning, others headed into town, whilst others had vomited their drink in the back garden or down the toilet and were put into a taxi and sent home.

Back inside the hallway, she looked around, felt a warm buzz about how the party had turned out. There were more people than she'd ever imagined and knew this was going to be news for a long time.

Before she went through the kitchen, she popped her head through into the living room. People were laid out on the sofas, watching the music channels on the television screen resting on the glass cabinet in the corner of the room. So far, nothing had been broken – nothing that she was aware of anyway. No doubt, she'd find out in the morning when it was empty and quiet. It would give her a full day to clean up and sort the house out before her parents returned.

Turning, she sauntered merrily into the kitchen. Most of the drink on the white worktop had been consumed, bar an inch left in a selection of the not-so-desirable drinks, one of which included Port, which she'd taken from the drink cabinet in the dining room. She'd locked it and hid the key, otherwise the whole lot would have gone within an hour.

'Hey, gorgeous!' she heard the slurred voice behind her.

She turned to see a boy called Ernie – it wasn't his real name, only a nickname – who was glaring at her through glassy eyes. 'Ernie.' She nodded politely. 'Hope you've had a good night.' She attempted to walk around him but he gripped her forearm, pulling her back a little. 'Hey, that hurts!' she shouted.

'Calm down, Shez…' He glanced up to the ceiling and hiccupped so hard, he winced at the pain. 'How about you and I go upstairs…'

Using her free hand, she loosened his grip and placed his hand back by his side. 'How about you go outside and go home?'

He smiled and swayed for a second, then leaned to the left, leaning on the breakfast bar that Shez hoped was solid enough to hold his weight. Moving past him, she stepped into the conservatory, then out on to the decking. The temperature had dipped, only a handful of people were out there smoking and chatting quieter than they were before, a sign of the night whittling down.

To the left of the decking, she noticed a ray of light seeping under the side gate, just a slither, but enough to catch her eye.

'Fuck's that?' she whispered to herself.

She opened the gate and stepped out onto the long driveway. The light inside the garage was on for some reason. Through the small window of the garage, which was located beside the door, she saw four people in there. She leaned closer to the glass, peering through it with her hands cupped at the side of the head to help her focus. She'd had a lot to drink and used the window to steady her balance.

Inside she saw Stuart, Ian, James, and Gregory.

'What the fuck are they doing in there?' she muttered. They were huddled close together, their arms wrapped around each other, talking quietly among themselves. Shez could hear the mumble of voices but couldn't make out what was being said.

'Shit,' she whispered, suddenly thinking about Sarah, who she'd left upstairs a while ago. She wondered what they were doing in her garage but there wasn't anything worth stealing so she'd check on Sarah first then come back to them.

After making her way through the house, she took a right at the base of the stairs and climbed them as quickly as she could whilst maintaining her balance. She opened her bedroom door and stepped into the dark room, glaring in the direction of her bed.

The bed was empty.

'Sarah?' Her eyes flitted around the room. 'Sarah, where are you?' In the corner, on the other side of the bed, she saw Sarah, crouched down, low to the carpet, sobbing quietly to herself, dressed in only a bra.

She dashed over to her.

'Sarah?'

Lowering to her knees, she gasped again, not understanding why her best friend was only wearing a bra and nothing else.

'Sarah, what's – what's happened?'

'They did it to me... I heard them,' she said, 'I felt them inside of me, one at a time...'

'Who did?' Shez demanded, now understanding the severity of the situation. 'What happened to you?'

'They raped me, Shez, they fucking raped me.'

Shez was down on her knees holding Sarah in her arms when Sarah broke into a ball of tears and clung on to Shez tightly.

'Who raped you?' Shez became very serious now.

'I – I think they were four of them... four different voices.'

Shez blinked hard and sighed. Four of them.

She'd just seen Stuart Richards, Ian Porter, James Whittaker, and Gregory Timms in the garage together discussing something that seemed very important.

'I think I know who it was,' Shez told her.

74

Wednesday Morning
Darlington Memorial Hospital

James Whittaker had been contacted yesterday about the suspicions that the body and the missing head found at the rear of the property in Greenbank road could well be his wife, Janice.

Butterflies circled and bounced off the inside of his stomach as he walked in through the hospital doors into the busy corridor. God, was there ever a quiet day in these places, he thought. He hadn't slept a wink and looked terrible. Felt even worse. He'd tried, but ever since he was asked to come in and was more aware what it was regarding, he'd imagined over and over in his head if it was going to be Janice.

The blonde woman in her fifties sitting behind the reception desk directed him to where he needed to be, which was the pathology department. It took him less than two minutes to find it, weaving around patients struggling along with the aid of family members.

After taking a left, he pushed open the double doors and went inside. To the right, there was a small desk with a woman sitting behind it.

'Can I help you?' she said. She was hitting on for sixty, James guessed. She had nice eyes and her skin was smooth, as if she'd been using moisturiser every day since she was born.

'Hi… I received a call yesterday. My wife… my wife went missing and they think it could be her…'

The woman gave a quick, sad smile, as if practised over the years, but James felt it was genuine. 'Just a second.' Her green eyes flitted across her computer screen for a long moment. 'Are you James Whittaker?'

'I am.'

'Okay.' She leaned forward an inch and raised her arm into the air, pointing to the double doors to her right. 'Go through there, then take a left. There's a room straight ahead. Someone is waiting for you, James.'

'Okay, thanks.'

Through the double doors, he went left, then straight ahead, and just as the receptionist had said, there was a man standing in a suit holding an A-4 sized envelope. He heard James' footsteps and half turned.

'Mr Whittaker?' the man said.

'Hi.'

The man offered his firm hand. 'I'm Dr Jason Lannark.'

'James Whittaker.'

'I'm the pathologist who's doing the post mortem for the female in question. Can you please follow me into this room?' The pathologist released his grip and turned, pointed to the small room a few metres from them. Whittaker nodded and went in first. Dr Lannark stepped through, and although the corridor was silent, he closed the door for further privacy.

As both men sat down, James observed the envelope in the pathologist's hand. He knew it would be the photographs. Often where possible, if someone had to identify a body, the pathologists will offer photos first, because sometimes that was all that was needed. It wouldn't be a photo of the whole deceased member, it would be something distinctive about them, like a tattoo or a close up of their face. The team would also be thoughtful on minimising the impact by not showing gory-filled images causing the person identifying the body any further unnecessary pain.

Dr Lannark leaned forward and placed the envelope onto the small, low circular table that split the two chairs they were sitting on, and clamped his hands together, interlocking his long fingers. He moved smoothly, almost methodical and thoughtfully.

'Okay, Mr Whittaker, what I'm about to show you are three photographs. One of them is of the female's face close up. I'm sure you have been told the nature of the body when it was discovered so our photographer has ensured that the image doesn't show below the chin. The second photo is of the female's hand, showing her wedding ring. The third image is of a tattoo located on her right forearm.' The pathologist allowed that to sink in. 'That okay, Mr Whittaker?'

'Yeah,' he replied, breathing heavily.

'Okay.' Dr Lannark grabbed the envelope and pulled the images out. 'All I need you to do is confirm if this is your wife, Janice Whittaker.' Whittaker nodded.

The first photo was of the tattoo, which James knew straight away belonged to his wife; she'd got it when they went away to Amsterdam nearly ten years ago. The pathologist showed him the next two images, but it wasn't really necessary.

'Yes, that's my wife,' Whittaker confessed to the following photographs. He hung his head, his lost stare finding the dull linoleum floor below them.

'I'm so, so very sorry, Mr Whittaker.'

James nodded solemnly, lost for words.

'What will happen now is there will be a full autopsy carried out by myself. I will work alongside the police forensic team who've been to the property on Greenbank Road. Then, we'll determine exactly how this happened.'

James nodded again. His focus was still down by his feet. 'Okay.'

'As you've just received some devastating news and I know the effects it has on loved ones. Can I order you a taxi to get home? I need to advise you, on a professional level, that you shouldn't drive. You may think you're fine, but something devastating has internal effects that often aren't recognised until it's too late. Do you understand what I'm saying?'

'I do, thanks.' He fell silent for a second, thinking. 'I'll be fine. I can drive.'

'You're absolutely sure?'

Whittaker's body went rigid. 'I'll be fine.'

'Can I call anyone on your behalf? Any family members that you need to immediately make aware?'

'My mother is looking after my daughter, so I'll tell her, but it isn't important to tell her right now – it makes no difference. There's no bringing my wife.'

The doctor offered a thin, heartfelt smile, then leaned to his right where there was a shelving unit located against the wall. On the middle shelf, he grabbed a thin pile of paperwork and placed it down on to the table.

'If possible, could I ask you to sign this document? It's a confirmation that you've come in and you have identified the female.'

'Yeah, that's fine.'

James Whittaker signed the document, stood up and left the hospital, feeling drained. The sky above the carpark was clear and blue, the sun low, but bright, it's light glistening off the car windscreens. Once he was back in his car, he dropped his head into his hands, and cried harder than he ever had.

75

Wednesday Morning
Darlington

Byrd made the coffees this time. While he was away, Tanzy was on the phone to Ray Jones, who'd rang asking if there'd been any developments on his daughter's whereabouts.

Today made it the twelve-day Evelyn Jones' had been missing. So far, there'd be nothing to go on, no clues or evidence that had given the police any idea where she was. Tanzy knew the Jones' were empty and had lost all hope. The only hope that ran through their emotional veins was that she hadn't been found dead yet. If she was still missing, it meant there was always a possibility that she could be alive.

'Thanks, man,' Tanzy said to Byrd when he placed the steaming coffee next to his keyboard.

Byrd sat down on his chair and pulled himself in.

There was an air of sadness hanging in the office from the news about PC Kim Harrison. It was always the same when something bad happened to their own. Some of the newer faces hadn't experienced this kind of loss and didn't quite know how to handle it. Instead, they mirrored the sadness of the other team members around them and rode out the storm until it got better.

Earlier in the morning, Byrd and Tanzy had been to see the forensic team about an update on Harrison. Had any pieces of evidence been found to give them anything to go on?

So far, all they knew, was that Harrison had received a major head injury – something hard had hit her head, causing a protrusion through the skin and damage to the rear of her skull. Could this have been done before she was in the river or had it happened when she was in the water. Was she placed at that exact point, or had she floated down river.

The forensics needed more time.

'Just spoke to Jason in the pathology department at the hospital,' Byrd said, taking a sip of his coffee, then lowering it. 'James Whittaker has just been in, confirming the female found at Greenbank Road was indeed his wife, Janice.'

'Fuck.'

'I know…'

'We need to find out what's going on here,' Tanzy stated, then looked down at the photograph of the four men on the table. Byrd also leaned over to have a look. 'Three of the four have been affected,' he continued, 'murdered in a brutal way that you wouldn't wish on anyone.'

'Maybe the link isn't between these men?'

Tanzy frowned. 'What do you mean?'

'Well so far'—Byrd turned towards him a little, rotating on his chair—'we have arrested Dr Ching, yeah?'

Tanzy nodded, listening intently.

'His DNA has been matched at the three sites where the bodies have either been found, or where the victim had been moments before, in the first case, his hair on the front seat of Julia Porter's Qashqai. It would make sense to presume that he was responsible, if not responsible, involved, in all three murders.'

'Go on…' Tanzy said.

'Well maybe this photo has nothing to do with it. We're looking at this photo as the link between these three woman, but maybe these men are totally innocent. Our original thoughts are – well, my original thoughts were that these men have done something and because of someone seeking revenge, something is happening to their loved ones. But perhaps that's just a coincidence that life wants us to believe?'

'I'm – I'm not following you here, mate?' Tanzy frowned at him. There were times – many times – when Byrd and Tanzy were singing off the same hymn sheet, but this wasn't one of them.

'Maybe the three woman are linked in their own way, or if not together, then linked individually to the doctor.'

'Will you just put it in layman's terms, please.'

Byrd smiled, nodded, then said, 'Maybe Dr Ching has treated them in the past?'

Tanzy pondered the idea for a moment. 'We need to check with the hospital to see if Mary Richards, Julia Porter, and Janice Whittaker have been one of his patients in the past.'

'Yes, we do.' Byrd leaned forward, picked up the pen and wrote it down as a task that needed to be done straight after their discussion. 'And we need to find out if Dr Ching has ever treated Samantha Timms?'

76

Wednesday Afternoon
Police Station

After several meetings, and a meal deal from the local Sainsburys for his dinner, Byrd returned to his desk. He found the number for the forensics department and put the phone to his ear, listened to it ring for three rings until it was answered.

'This is Paul Beech, Forensics department, how can I help?'

'Hi, Paul, it's Max.'

'Hi, Max, how you doing?'

'I'm good, I'm good. I was wondering have you guys looked over Janice Whittaker yet?'

'We have a little, but there's further work to do. You'll have to bear with me, Detective, if that's okay?'

'Yeah, sure, that's no problem. Just let me or Orion know.'

'Okay, will do.'

'Have you had the chance to look over Kimmy Harrison yet?'

'We have done some work on that. Would you like to speak to Tallow or Hope on this one?'

'No, it's okay,' Byrd said, 'if you can tell me, that's fine…'

'We have identified that her death has nothing to do with the other three. The way the body was intact – unlike the other three – and the way it was presented.'

'Elaborate please,' Byrd said.

'You're the detective here and I'm still training, so tell me if I'm talking shite. It's merely a thought.'

'Go on, Paul?'

'You see… Julia, Mary, and Janice,' Beech went on, 'were in positions that someone would see them. The body found in Porter's dining room was meant for her husband. The woman hanging from a tree was bound to be seen by the next person who walked down that lane. The woman's head in the bin would be noticed by the bin men. These are all situations where they'd be found.' He stopped for a moment, then: 'Harrison was found by luck. Her body wasn't on display in my opinion. There was no obvious hey-look-at-me aspect to hers. We found a substantial amount of water in her lungs, which tells us she could have drowned.'

'What about the damage to her head?'

'From the severity of the blow, in my opinion, and it's something I've discussed with Tallow and Hope, is that the likeliness that the damage was done whilst underwater is very slim. Underwater, the body moves slower even under the power of a strong moving current. I think this blow happened before she went into the water, where whatever caused it, travelled fast through air and not through water.'

'Okay, so she was attacked.

'It seems likely.'

Byrd said, 'What did you guys find at Dr Ching's house?'

'Now this is where we nail him. Firstly, his DNA was everywhere – it should be as it's his house, but we have that DNA match, putting him number one on the suspect list for the three murders, obviously from the strands of his hair being in Julia Porter's car and under the finger nail of Mary Richards. In one of the cupboards in the kitchen, there was a tool set containing an impressive display of surgical tools that we collected. After running analyses on the tools, we found three different bloods on them. I'll give you a guess whose blood it is?'

'Julia Porter, Mary Richards, and Janice Whittaker?'

'Correct. All evidence so far points to Dr Ching…'

'Jesus!'

'Yup!'

'What I don't understand is why the third kill was sloppy,' Byrd said.

'What do you mean?'

'Why at his own home? Why the other two so well thought out, so methodical, and clean. Then why the third one so obvious. Blood trails on the floor. Blood spatter all over. His surgical tools hidden in a cupboard that if someone was to search the house, would be found easily.' Byrd went quiet, thinking hard. 'I don't know, it just seems weird to me.'

'You know, Max, I'll be honest, I thought exactly the same. The third one is different. But there are undeniable similarities that can't be overlooked. The cut was as clean as the others. It was the layout that was messy. Either way, we have his DNA at three crime scenes and a case of tools hidden in his kitchen that contain the blood of the three victims. A coincidence… maybe, maybe not. We'll see what else we find.'

'So if Ching killed them three,' Byrd said, 'then who on earth would want to kill PC Harrison?'

77

Wednesday Night
Darlington

Gregory Timms walked into his living room and sat down on the sofa. He'd had a rough day. Every hour that passed had felt like two. But the day was nearly over and all he wanted to do was sit down and do nothing, apart from letting his eyes crawl across the screen of his new kindle until they were so heavy, he'd fell asleep.

Before he settled down to read, he checked his phone and social media updates. He didn't have any notifications of interest, but a post that someone had uploaded really caught his attention. He clicked on the article and scanned it, then scrolled back up to the top of the page and read it again, this time, much slower, absorbing the information like a sponge.

'Fuck,' he whispered.

He pulled his phone from the large pocket of his dressing gown, unlocked it, and searched through his contacts. He couldn't find the number he was looking for. After opening the social media app, he typed the man's name into the search bar and clicked enter, then watched the results come up almost instantly. He clicked on the man's name and briefly looked at his profile. Interesting. In the top right corner of the screen, he noticed an option to call him, so with is finger hovering over the 'Call' button, he decided to press it. The screen turned temporarily grey as the call was connected.

He waited.

'Hello?' the voice said.

'Hi, is this James Whittaker?'

'Yes. What do you want?' Whittaker replied. When the call came in, Whittaker would've been able to see who the caller was, as it worked like that when calling through media applications.

'James, I've just heard about what happened to your wife, I'm so sorry.'

'I don't want to talk to you, Gregory…'

'Wait, just hear me out, mate. I need—'

'We are not mates. I haven't seen you since—'

'I know, I know,' Gregory said, 'since *that night*. That's your wife, Ian's wife, Stuart's wife…' Gregory said.

Whittaker said nothing.

'Do you think it has something to do with that night?'

'I don't know, I…'

'What is it?' Gregory pushed.

'I don't know. What happened that night is something I don't want to think about ever again, let alone talk about. What we did to that girl was indescribable. It's better if we say nothing and put it behind us. No more bringing it back up.'

'I understand,' Gregory said. 'Do you think something will happen to my wife?'

'I don't know, I don't have a crystal ball, do I?'

'I know, I know. I just think someone has found out what we've done. After all these years. But why now? It was fifteen years ago, I can't believe that—'

'Listen, I need to go. Good luck to you. Don't call me again.' Whittaker hung up and the call ended.

Gregory sat still on the sofa, stunned. He lowered his phone and heard footsteps out in the hallway, growing louder.

Samantha ambled into the living room, dressed in a comfortable gown, wearing a smile on her tanned, thin face. She'd just got out of the bath and lathered herself in a moisturiser, her skin appearing smooth, glowing against the soft light from the lamp in the corner. 'Hey,' she said.

'Hey.' He forced a smile and decided not to mention the conversation he'd had with Whittaker

78

.June 14th, 2004
Darlington
15 years ago

Sarah frowned up at Shez. 'Who was it?' She started to come around, the drugs starting to wear off, but the feeling of grogginess still had a hold on her. 'Shez! Who was it?'

Rage filled her eyes. Shez was weary of the fire in them. Ever since they'd first met, Shez was aware of Sarah's temper, her ability to be completely normal, then at a flick of a switch, turn very, very nasty.

'The boys who did this are in my garage…' Shez explained.

Sarah, with rage in her face, got up as quickly as she could. She glanced around the room frantically searching for her top, dress and underwear, which had been thrown across the room like they were some kind of trophies.

'I'm going to fucking kill them!' she shouted.

'Sarah, Sarah, just calm down, please. We should call the police. We'll call the police and tell them what's happened.'

'I'm not ringing the police – I'm going to kill them.' She pulled her top over her head quickly, then bent down to grab her underwear and put them on. Her hands shook with rage, her body vibrated with an anger she'd never felt before. How dare they do this to her.

'Is your brother here, Sarah?' she asked.

'No, he isn't. Fuck my brother. I don't need my brother for this. I'll deal with them.'

Once Sarah had got her skirt on, she turned for the door and—

Shez grabbed her wrist. 'Wait, Sarah, please—'

'Get the fuck off me!' Sarah screamed, swivelling quickly and pushing Shez hard. Shez staggered across the room until she tripped over a plastic box and hit the back of her head against the wardrobe.

Shez fell to the floor and didn't move.

Sarah turned, left the room, charged down the stairs, went outside, and headed for the garage.

79

Thursday Morning
Darlington

Neil McMahon woke thirty minutes earlier this morning. He had some papers to mark for the children and did it with a strong cup of coffee in front of the television in the dining room.

He was feeling sad; he was missing Evelyn, but he knew life cracked on. He knew that the children in the class needed guidance and support. It would be hard to move on and forget about Evelyn, but until she was found, they still had hope.

After he marked the last paper, he placed it on top of the others and finished the last of his coffee. Along the hallway, he heard footstep approaching, and frowned down at his watch.

'She's up early,' he whispered, his eyes on the doorway leading to the hall. A moment later, Judith came into view and entered the room, rubbing her tired eyes.

'Hey,' she said.

'Morning,' he said, 'did I wake you?'

'No, I couldn't sleep. I haven't slept most of the night to be honest.'

'How come? What was wrong?'

'I couldn't stop thinking about the little girl next door, how upset she was the other day.' She gave a sad smile, padded across the fluffy carpet, and pulled a seat out at the table he was sitting at. 'Why was she so upset?'

'When I knocked, Alex had told me she'd done something wrong and that he'd told her off. Just being a parent I suppose. It's hard for some parents.'

She raised a silencing palm. 'I know it is, Neil, but I'm just wondering if there's something more, something a little sinister.'

Neil shrugged. 'You think?'

'Do you not?' she asked.

'I don't know. I do know that it isn't our business how parents bring up their children in the confines of their own home.'

'But if it's something more,' she said, 'if there's abuse involved?'

'We don't know that… we can't assume.'

She glanced away in the direction of next door, almost as if she could see through the brick wall, to see for herself if the little girl was okay, which of course she didn't know, because she couldn't see through the walls.

'What time are you going to the dentist?' Judith asked.

'Soon. I also need to pop into town before I go to work. One of the other teachers are covering until I get back. Is there anything you need in town?' he asked, standing up.

'No,' Judith said.

'Right, I need to get ready, won't be long.'

Upstairs, Neil took out his phone and stared at it for a while. He dialled the number and made the call. After he hung up, he thought hard, wondering if he'd done the right thing.

Time would tell.

Minutes later, Neil came back downstairs. Judith was sitting on the sofa in silence.

'I won't be going just yet,' he told her.

'Why?'

'I've – I've called the police.'

She frowned. 'The police – why?'

'I think there's something going on next door,' he explained. 'I think you're right. They're coming over now. I'll hang around, I have time to spare before the dentist.'

Judith glanced down at her watch. 'How long will they be?'

'The operator said ten minutes.'

'I don't think Alex will be happy, but we'll see what they say.'

Just over ten minutes later, there was a knock at the door. Neil opened it slowly, the rush of the cold morning uninvitedly crept in.

'Mr McMahon?' said the PC.

'Yes. Come on in,' he said.

The PC's stepped inside into the narrow hallway. 'I'm PC Cornty. This'—he pointed to his left—'is PC Weaver.'

'Can I get you a coffee?' Neil asked.

'We're good, thank you,' replied Cornty gratefully. 'We're following up on the conversation you had moments ago with the operator down at the station. Could you fill us in with the details?'

The sound of footsteps were heard on the stairs. Judith smiled at the PC's who glanced up at her for a brief moment.

Neil answered: 'We heard crying, sounded like it was coming from upstairs. Obviously it wasn't, we don't have children. Then I went next door. They have a young daughter you see. She sounded upset. I knocked and spoke with her father. He told me that she'd done something wrong and that she got smacked. I know when I was younger if I did something wrong I got a good smack for it. But…'

'But what, Sir?'

'We had a daughter,' Neil said. 'Sadly, she died at seven. I may have lost touch with being a parent, but I'm a teacher. I know what's right and what isn't. And I know I certainly wouldn't treat my children that way.'

'Very sorry to hear that,' PC Weaver said, taking over. 'Okay, well we'll give next door and knock a speak to her—'

They suddenly heard a cry from somewhere in the house.

'What was that?' Weaver said, tipping her head back, looking upstairs.

Neil sighed lightly. 'We heard it yesterday, and the day before.'

The PC's absorbed his words but were still listening to the cry.

'It sounds like it's in this house?' Cornty said, also glancing up the stairs.

'We thought the same. The girls room is against the wall,' Judith explained.

The cry got louder, almost like an animal in pain. Weaver and Cornty exchanged worried glances. 'We need to check it out,' Weaver told him.

He nodded firmly.

Neil stepped around them and opened his front door for them to leave but turned to see the PC's going up the stairs. 'Where – where are you going?'

'It's not this house,' Judith said, watching them dash up the stairs.

'Where the hell are you going?' Neil asked, frowning. 'You need to be going next door.' He closed the front door, turned, and followed them up the stairs quickly.

Weaver and Cornty reached the top of the stairs and took a right onto the landing.

'In there,' Weaver said, pointing to the back bedroom. She followed Cornty into the medium sized room where the curtains were closed but the dull morning light crept around the edges, giving them enough light to see. The crying was louder now.

'Where is that coming from?' Weaver whispered.

Neil stepped into the room behind them. 'What are you doing?'

'Shhhh!' demanded Cornty, turning his head to listen. 'There…' He pointed at the large cupboard. 'It's coming from there?'

'No, it's not. It sounds like it's in there, but it's next door,' said Neil, shrugging hopelessly.

'We'd like to see for ourselves,' Cornty told him matter-of-factly, stepping towards the cupboard in the corner.

80

June 14th, 2004
Darlington
15 years ago

Sarah barged into the garage, the door almost coming off its hinges. Stuart, James, Ian, and Gregory were huddled closely in the middle of the space. They suddenly stopped talking, split up and glared at the door.

The garage became dead quiet, albeit the music in the background coming from inside the house.

'You fucking bastards!' she screamed at them as she shut the door.

Stuart gasped, slightly turning towards her. 'What are you talking about, Sarah – what's wrong?' He raised both palms at her in a form of confusion.

'I know what you did to me!' she bellowed, now inches away from Stuart's face. 'I know what all of you did to me…' She glared at all of them, one at a time. They were separated in the shape of a semi-circle around her. 'You fucking sick, sick, little boys.'

'Hold on a second, Sarah. What do you mean?' Ian asked her.

She edged towards him, pointing, the tip of her finger close to his red face. 'You fucking know what. You put something in that drink, didn't you?' Her eyes narrowed at him.

'I – I…'

'You put something in the drink to knock me out, didn't you?'

He said nothing, just stared, absorbing her words.

'You couldn't fuck me for real, so you spiked me and raped me.'

The garage was as quiet as an empty church - Ian was speechless. He knew what she was saying was true, and he could feel his skin growing warm in embarrassment, his face reddening with each passing second.

'You're pathetic,' she told Ian, then she turned to Stuart. 'Then you got on top next didn't you?' She leaned close to him. He backed off, not knowing what she was going to do until she sniffed the air around him. 'I can smell your cheap aftershave. Yeah, you got on top. You dirty fucking bastard.'

She glared at Gregory and James with fire in her eyes for a long moment, then back to Ian. 'Whatever you gave me didn't knock me out, Ian, I couldn't move but I heard it all. I remember everything now.'

James and Gregory sighed heavily, glancing nervously at each other, their bodies physically deflating. They could see the worry in each other's eyes and what this could mean.

'Listen, Sarah,' Stuart said, his palms in the air, 'I think you have made a mistake. We haven't touched you. We've been down hear the whole time. I think you've had a little too much to drink and you're imagining this.' He looked for support from Ian. 'Ian, is she imagining this?'

A sudden slither of hope appeared on Ian's face. 'Yes, she is. Like you said, we've been out here and the garden the whole time.' He turned towards Sarah, meeting the burning rage in her eyes. 'Sarah, you've made a mistake.'

Sarah thought about that for a short moment and smiled. 'Okay…'

'Okay?' Ian asked.

'If that's how you want to play this,' she said.

'What do you mean?' Stuart asked, wondering about her intentions.

'All four of you came inside of me. The DNA from your sperm is in me. You're not only disgusting but fucking stupid too. The evidence is right fucking there!' Using her finger, she pointed to her skirt. 'I wonder what the police will say about this – hell, I'm more concerned about what my family will do to you. Just imagine my brother, just think what he'll do when he finds out…' she trailed off, smiling, tilting her head side to side slowly. 'So fucking stupid you are.'

She laughed hysterically then turned, took a step towards the door and—

'The fuck are you going?' Stuart said, grabbing her wrist and pulling her back.

'I'm going to tell the whole world what little pathetic boys you are. Everyone is going to know. Your lives are ruined,' she told them, then sniggered as she took a step away from him but his grip on her wrist was solid.

'Get the fuck off me!' she screamed at him, trying to pull her hand away, but Stuart was too strong for her and held on. Their bodies were against each other as she tried to wriggled free, but he wouldn't let her go, wouldn't let her leave. If she left, that would be the moment everyone would know what they'd done. She was right when she said about the sperm – they clearly hadn't given that any thought.

She was unconscious at the time. She wasn't meant to remember.

'Stuart, let her go,' begged Ian, standing to their right.

'No, Ian, she'll tell people. We can't let her leave here…'

Ian frowned at him. 'What – what do you mean?'

'She isn't leaving this garage!' he shouted at them.

She pulled her arm down, and yet again, his grip was too much for her. 'Fucking let me go, Stuart!' she screamed.

He pulled her closer, and swung her around, then shoved his free hand over her mouth, the ball of his palm bouncing off her lip, in an attempt to mute her anger.

'Shit, shit!' James gasped, his eyes flitting from Gregory to Ian then back to Sarah.

'Heeeeeeeemmmmm!' Sarah shouted through his rough palm. 'Heeeeeeeemmmmm!'

'Stuart, let her fucking go, man!' Ian said. 'You're making it worse.' Ian moved forward, tried to grab Stuart's forearm but he was too strong for him, and shrugged him off with ease. Sarah started to shout through his hand, her volume rising with the desperation to be free.

'Stuart!' Gregory begged. 'Come on man!'

Stuart adjusted his hand over her mouth and covered her nose too, blocking the oxygen, and squeezed as tight as he could. Thirty seconds later, he let go and she collapsed to the floor, unconscious.

'Stu, what the fuck have you done?' Ian gasped.

Stuart panted heavily, staring down at her, watching her still body all bent and distorted. He switched his focus to the wall to the left, which was full of tools and other garden-type accessories. He rushed over, grabbed something and came back to Sarah.

'What the fuck is that for?' Ian said. 'Stuart?'

'Pick her up boys…'

81

Thursday Late Morning
Darlington

PC Cornty leaned forward, grabbed the handle of the cupboard in the back bedroom of Neil McMahon's house and pulled it open quickly. He stared inside with wide eyes.

It was a large cupboard, built in to the corner of the room by the side of the chimney breast. From a design aspect, it had been purposefully built, strong and sturdy. To the right of the space inside, there were shelves stacked on top of each other with a gap of around ten inches between each one. Every shelf had something different on. Underwear. T-shirts. Jeans. Jogging bottoms. To the left, about head height, a pole was fixed across the top of it with a selection of hanging garments: dresses and shirts. It was a mix between his and her clothes and most likely the clothes they seldom wore.

The sound of the cry remained the same but there was no crying child in there.

'It sounds like it's coming from here,' Cornty said, confused. He glanced at Weaver. 'But there's nothing.'

'That's what I was telling you,' Neil said. 'The walls are paper thin. We've heard her many times.'

Cornty and Weaver never replied, instead they stood at the base of the wardrobe staring into it, side by side, their shoulders almost touching.

'We need to go next door,' Weaver told him.

He nodded but kept his attention on the back wall of the cupboard. He thought he saw something unusual.

'Come on, Phil…' she turned, tugging on his arm. 'Let's go.'

'Wait,' he said suddenly, removing her grip from him. 'What's that?'

'What's what?' She turned back, scowled into the dark space, seeing nothing but hanging clothes and folded jeans. Cornty moved forward a little, his body shrunk as he lowered, almost now fully inside the cupboard.

'What are you doing?' Judith asked. 'What is it?'

Cornty raised a silencing palm in her general direction and continued to move into the cupboard. 'What is… that?' he whispered to himself, his eyes up against the dim conditions inside. The rear wall of the cupboard was different to the side. He raised his hand and touched the surface of the side wall, then moved it across to the back. It had a different texture. The crying was so loud now, it was almost in his ear as he turned his head side on to listen.

'What have you found?' Weaver asked, leaning into him, only inches behind.

'Something's not right here…'

'What do you mean?' Weaver asked.

'The wall… there's something behind it. It isn't a part of the cupboard. Is that a screw sticking out?' He leaned closer. By this point, he was fully inside. Weaver had one foot in there, the other, back in the bedroom where Neil McMahon and his wife were standing behind them.

'Can you see this wall here?' Cornty asked her.

There was a sudden thud, and Cornty felt Weaver collide hard into the back of him as she collapsed into the cupboard, her weight crushing him against the wall.

'Jesus, Amy – what are you—'

The cupboard suddenly became pitch black, the sound of the door slamming closed. The sound of a barrel lock rattled inside the dark space, causing waves of confusion. Weaver was fully against Cornty, pinning him up against the back wall, his face hard up on the sheet of wood.

'Amy, I can't breathe, get off me,' he begged, gasping for breath. It didn't take long for him to feel hot, claustrophobic, his breathing now struggling to the point of panic. His body was twisted, his weight – and his partner's weight – caused a horrendous throbbing pain on his twisted leg, worsening by the second.

'Mr McMahon… what is going on?' he shouted, but it came out barely inaudible. 'Mr McMahon… please.'

No one answered his plea.

The weight of Weaver's body was unbearable now, her face digging hard into his neck, squeezing him into the wall at the back of the cupboard.

'Amy…'

He didn't know what'd happened to her but assumed she'd been attacked, then the door had been closed and locked.

'Amy,' he said again but she didn't reply.

His right hand was trapped between his thigh and the body of his partner, but he shifted his weight to the left allowing him enough room to pull it free. His phone was tucked tightly into his chest pocket which he knew he needed to get but would be a struggle. After a minute of frustration and his body overheating, he somehow managed to collect it.

'Mr McMahon?' he shouted, this time as loud as he could, the desperate sound of his voice showing his chest was under pressure. The crying near him had stopped now. At least the girl next door was okay, for the time being.

Why did Neil McMahon do this to them?

He didn't know, neither did Weaver, unless she'd seen anything.

All he could concentrate on was his breathing and trying not to panic. When he was fourteen, he was in his Dad's garage being nosy. There wasn't anything in particular he was looking for but he'll always remember pulling something off a shelf and knocking several boxes down on top of him, which kept him on the floor until his Dad came in. His chest felt the same then.

The air inside was hot, each breath was beyond difficult as the feeling of claustrophobia was taking over him. A certain smell seemed to be getting stronger as well, Cornty had noticed but he couldn't decide what it was; all he knew was it wasn't pleasant.

From the position he was in, he could barely see his phone screen but did his best to navigate to Tanzy's number. Without looking, he unlocked it using his number code, then found the call list and assumed Tanzy's number was his most recent call according to his foggy memory.

Straining his neck into an almost impossible position, he peered down, seeing Tanzy's number on the screen. Using the thumb on a hand that he felt soon going numb, he tapped the CALL button. The number was ringing.

82

Thursday Mid-Morning
Police Station

'Who's this now?' Tanzy sighed as his phone rang in his pocket. He'd been in meetings and answering calls all day, much of work heavily involving the forensics, going over the details about various pieces of evidence recorded.

He plucked it out.

It was Cornty.

He put it to his ear.

'Phil?' Tanzy answered.

Nothing from Cornty.

'Hello… Phil?'

'… herrmm.'

'Phil, I can't hear you,' Tanzy said, 'can you speak up a little?'

'He's got us.'

'Who has?'

'He's got us,' Cornty repeated.

'Yeah, I heard that part. Who has got you?' Tanzy straightened in his chair. Byrd was sitting next to him looking at some police procedure he'd been sent by another department, but stopped and glanced Tanzy's way with a sudden interest in the phone call.

'Neil McMahon,' Cornty said quietly. 'Evelyn Jones' teacher.'

'Neil what?' Tanzy became agitated.

'Neil McMahon – we're inside of a cupboard in his back bedroom. He's locked us in and closed the fucking door.' His voice was strained.

Tanzy frowned. 'For the record, are you saying, that Evelyn Jones' Teacher, Neil McMahon, has locked you inside of a cupboard.'

'Yes.'

'Why are you talking like that?'

'I can't move. I can barely breathe, Ori.'

'Where's Weaver?'

'She's up against me,' he said, 'she's knocked out.'

'Why are you in a cupboard?' Tanzy asked, frowning. He then glanced at Byrd for a second.

'Long story – you need to help us,' he told his superior.

'We're on our way. We know the address. Hold tight.' Tanzy hung up the phone.

'The hell was that?' Byrd asked.

'Come on… Cornty and Weaver are locked inside a cupboard in a bedroom at Neil McMahon's house. He's knocked Weaver out and has them trapped.'

'Neil McMahon – the primary school teacher?'

Tanzy nodded twice, then stood up quickly. 'Come on.'

'This town never ceases to amaze me,' said Byrd, finding his feet quickly.

He popped his head into DCI Thornton's office and told her what was happening. She told him to take a couple of the PC's with them for support, which Tanzy didn't see a problem with. Cornty hadn't said about any weapons, although Tanzy could probably handle the situation himself one-on-one but no one knew what the teacher had at his house. After they threw their coats on, they went outside, Byrd and Tanzy got into the golf, the other two PC's, who'd been briefed very quickly about the situation they'd been dragged into, took one of the marked Vauxhall Astra's.

It took them three minutes to turn off Woodlands Road into West Crescent. The house they were looking for was number ten. Tanzy slammed on the brakes outside of the white semi-detached house. Parked in front of them was the car Cornty and Weaver had drove there in. Tanzy pulled the handbrake on, unclipped his seat belt, jumped out of the car and dashed to the white door. Byrd was merely seconds behind as Tanzy tried the handle, but it was locked. Using the outside of a clenched fist, Tanzy banged on the door several times.

'Open the door! Police!' His voice echoed out on to the quiet street.

Byrd stopped just near him, panting hard. Behind them, the marked Astra pulled up, stopping over the driveway. The young male PC's, who told the detectives they were called Leonard and Grearer before they set off, opened their doors and took a few steps towards the house. They were unfamiliar new faces. Neither were in Byrd's or Tanzy's teams. They both appeared around the age of thirty and were hesitant as they moved towards the house.

Tanzy banged another three times, the side of his fist pounding off the wood.

'Police, open up!'

'There's no car on the drive,' Byrd noted.

'They're in there! We need to get inside.'

'Can I help you?' a voice said coming from their left. They both turned, saw an elderly woman standing on the driveway of number twelve, her face showing concern.

'Have you seen Neil McMahon?' Tanzy asked quickly.

She frowned, then shook her head. 'No, not today. Is he in trouble?'

Tanzy ignored her question. 'We need to see him right now. Do you know if there's anyone in?'

The grey-haired, frail woman turned towards the road for a moment before returning her focus on Tanzy. 'That's their car, so I assume they are,' she said, pointing to a dark blue Mondeo. Tanzy recalled seeing it when he met with Evelyn's parents for the media conference.

'We need to get in now!' Tanzy told Byrd.

'I'll go around the back,' Byrd said, stepping away from Tanzy, and focusing on the PC's. 'Which one is Leonard?'

PC Leonard nodded. 'Me, Sir.'

'You come with me,' Byrd said.

The PC eagerly moved forward. 'Okay. Where are we going?'

'Round the back, come on.' Byrd went to the side of the house, noticed a gap between the garage and house. At the end of the very short alley, a black gate stood firm and straight. It looked the type of gate that would need to be climbed if it was locked because of how solid it looked. Byrd tried the handle and—

'It's open!' Byrd glanced back at Leonard. 'Come on.'

The PC followed him through the gate towards the rear of the house.

Back at the front, Tanzy banged several times on the door again before PC Grearer appeared by his side, his body nervous but excited.

'Try kicking it,' Grearer said. 'Here, watch out the way.'

Tanzy moved aside. 'Do your thing.'

PC Grearer wasn't tall or small, but he was stocky; an obvious gym-goer who supported by legs as thick as tree trunks. He lifted his right leg and lunged forward, the bottom of his shoe colliding with the space just below the handle. The door cracked and swung open with a loud bang. Parts of the lock sheared off, falling on to the carpet inside the hallway.

Tanzy held his palm up, holding the PC back, so he went inside first. As he crossed over the step, he cocked his head back. 'Stay close,' he told Grearer, who nodded eagerly, following him inside. 'Hello! Police here! Make yourself known wherever you are,' he shouted, projecting his voice throughout the house.

Silence came from all directions.

Tanzy angled to the left towards the base of the stairs – they'd been told Cornty and Weaver were locked in a cupboard upstairs.

'Stay behind me,' Tanzy told Grearer, who nodded at his instruction, his hand gripped the baton attached to his belt.

Step by step, they climbed them, listening. Once they reached the top, they took a right up onto the landing, then came to a halt. 'Weaver? Cornty?' Tanzy shouted.

Nothing.

Byrd and Leonard rounded the corner at the rear of the house. There was a platform of decking six inches off the floor. It was rectangular. The back door was a few feet along the wall to their right. He tried the handle, which was locked, so Byrd peered through the window into the kitchen. A table was resting against the far wall, with a calendar hanging from a nail above it. Various squiggles of writing lined the dates of the month. There was no one there. Methodically, his eyes ran across the rest of it, the fridge, the freezer, the worktop. Near the sink, there was a set of knifes.

One of the knives were missing.

'See anything?' PC Leonard asked, a step behind him.

'No.' He pulled away from the window, lowered his arms and glanced along the back of the house, noticing a window further down. At the window, he did the same, making a visor with his hands to fight against the low winter sun, gazing through the dirty glass.

There was a circular wooden table in the centre of the room with four chairs tucked under it neatly. The far wall was filled with old drawings. Child's drawings. A plethora of colours that ruined the décor but at the same time, made it look beautiful. The left side of the room sported a wide chimney breast and an alcove either side. In the furthest alcove, sitting on the floor, with her knees up to her chest, was a woman.

Byrd gasped.

'What is it?' asked PC Leonard.

'There…' he whispered. 'There's a woman in the room. In the corner. Come on, let's go back around, through the front door.'

As Byrd pulled himself from the glass and moved, he saw the woman's head shoot towards him. Byrd froze as they made eye contact. The woman's eyes widened for a second before she pushed herself up off the floor and darted for the door.

Byrd pushed PC Leonard towards the side gate. 'Go, go now!'

83

Thursday Midday
West Crescent, Darlington

DI Tanzy and PC Grearer were standing on the narrow, silent landing.

'Cornty?' Tanzy looked into the back bedroom, took a step—

'Wait!' Grearer said, pulling him back, his hand cupped around his forearm.

'What – what?' Tanzy turned back. 'What is it?'

'Look.'

Tanzy followed Grearer's pointed finger down at the floor. Blood. Several drops of blood. A small trail, leading towards the front bedroom.

Tanzy took a slow measured step. 'This is the police, make yourself known!' He cautiously padded into the room first, his baton tucked tightly in his right hand. It felt familiar but strange, as if he hadn't handled it in a while. 'Police, make yourself known,' he repeated.

The room was brightly lit. As Tanzy edged around the door, he felt something in the room, something that altered the air molecules. The drops of blood on the floor got thicker. His eyes carefully followed a trail that angled around to the right out of sight.

'Stay close,' he told Grearer, who was inches behind him.

The room was square. It had a high ceiling and enough light coming through the window to be able to see everything clearly. The trail of blood swept around the foot of the bed all the way to a closed wardrobe in the far corner. There was nothing else in the room apart from a bed, bedside units either side of it, and an ottoman at the window supporting a brown soft blanket which was folded and placed on top.

Tanzy reached out, grabbed the handle of the wardrobe and pulled it open. Inside of the small space, was a man, his body curled up awkwardly.

Neil McMahon.

He was curled up, laying on his side, and still. His face was motionless as he stared out at Tanzy. Tanzy stared for a long moment at his stagnant eyes, which never moved an inch. His stomach was smothered in blood with deep cuts through a white shirt. The aged carpet below was soaked in crimson liquid, too. Under different circumstances, he would have thrown himself down and checked his pulse, but it was obvious he was dead.

'Jesus!' Grearer gasped, standing inches behind Tanzy, now seeing what was inside the wardrobe.

Tanzy edged back and took out his phone, pressed a couple of buttons and put it to his ear. The phone was answered.

'Yeah,' Tanzy said, 'ID DN522 we need back up and forensics here. We're at 10 West Crescent.'

He moved away from the wardrobe, leaving the door open and went over to the bay window. He needed a second to compose himself before finding Byrd. But there was something else that he needed to do.

Find Cornty and Weaver.

It was then he heard a rush of footsteps downstairs somewhere. Then he heard them outside on the hard concrete. He turned, glared out the window, where he saw a woman dash towards a car, then climb in. Within five seconds, she pulled away quickly, smoke whirring from the spinning tyres.

'Fuck!'

Then his phone rang.

84

Thursday
West Crescent, Darlington

Through the window, Byrd watched the woman bolt from the corner of the room towards the door then disappear into the hallway out of sight. Byrd and Leonard rounded the corner and passed through the open gate.

The sound of screeching tyres exploded in the air as they galloped down the driveway. When they reached the road, the dark blue Mondeo was off into the distance in a flash. He pulled out his phone and called Tanzy.

'Max!'

'Ori, she's gone, I've—'

'I know, Max, I can see. I'm - I'm upstairs in the window.'

Byrd turned and looked up, saw Tanzy in the bay window. 'We're going after her!' Byrd told him, then darted towards the marked Astra that Leonard and Grearer had arrived in. Leonard ran around the front of the bonnet, pulled the door open and dropped in. Byrd dived into the passenger seat and slammed the door shut.

'Go!' he told Leonard, who threw the gear in first and turned on the blues and twos, the wail of the siren bombarding the usually silent street, then slammed his foot down.

'We'll wait here for forensics,' Tanzy said.

'Forensics?' Byrd shouted over the sound of the siren.

'We found Neil McMahon in the wardrobe…'

'Jesus.' Byrd followed the road as PC Leonard guided it around the bend, approaching the junction at Woodlands

Road, and after he saw it was clear, he threw the car left, following the direction of the speeding car. If it was a few seconds later, they'd have missed the car turning.

'Keep me updated, Ori!' Byrd yelled.

'I will. I need to find Weaver and Cornty!' Tanzy hung up the phone.

Byrd held on to the phone but lowered it to his lap. As they weaved in and out of traffic towards the traffic lights, he saw the Mondeo drive on the other side of the road, narrowly missing an oncoming red Corsa, forcing the driver to beep several times. Leaning forward, Byrd placed his left palm onto the panel above the glove box to steady himself for the next turn, which was left onto Greenbank Road.

Leonard skilfully guided the car around the bend, careful not to lose control on the wet road surface from the earlier light drizzle.

The Mondeo was just ahead, maybe having a fifty metre start on them.

'Stay with her, I'm ringing dispatch,' Byrd told him, focusing down on his phone and finding the number. The blood was coursing through his body, his heart rate was pumped.

'We're in pursuit of a dark blue Mondeo on Greenbank Road, heading north, towards the Denes area of Darlington.'

'Officer I.D?'

'DN443,' said Byrd.

'License plate of the vehicle pursuing?' asked the operator.

Byrd told her as fast as he could.

'Who's the driver?'

'Female. Blonde hair. Around the age of forty to fifty. Likely suspect to murder and fled the scene.'

'Do you need additional units at the scene?'

'No, Detective Inspector Orion Tanzy – I.D DN522 – has called it in. We need support vehicles for now.'

'Okay, we'll send additional units and I'll contact the CCTV control room to track the vehicle down. Do you need NPAS?'

NPAS stood for National Police Air Service.

'Just hold off on that one, we're not far behind. We'll catch up.'

'Call me ASAP if you do, it'll take—'

'I know – I will do, thanks.' Byrd knew the nearest NPAS base was Newcastle, so it would be at least twenty minutes until they had air support.

Byrd hung up the phone as they hit the slight bend in the road at the Gladstone street junction, and placed it back down on to his lap, ready if needed. The Mondeo flew down Greenbank Road, heading towards the Dene's park.

'Steady driving. Good.'

PC Leonard nodded. 'We've had good training.'

Byrd liked PC Leonard.

At the bottom of Greenbank Road, the woman took the right on to Widdowfield Street. Seconds later, the Astra did the same, the wheels sliding a little on the wet tarmac, and for a moment, Byrd thought Leonard was going to lose it but his control was exceptional, quickly taking the corner. Up ahead, just as the Mondeo was angling around to the left, a black Civic pulled out of the Salisbury Terrace junction, colliding into the side of it, forcing it up on to the kerb into the metal railing causing a horrendous crunch.

The Mondeo came to an abrupt halt, the side of it smashed in.

'She's stopped, she's stopped!' PC Leonard shouted, slamming the brakes on forcing the Astra to come to a halt behind the Mondeo.

Byrd climbed out of the passenger seat, closed the door, and grabbed his radio from his hip. The civic was a metre away from it, diagonally across the road.

'This is D.I. Max Byrd in pursuit of the Mondeo,' he said into the radio. 'Suspect has stopped at the bottom of Salisbury Terrace due to an RTC. Approaching suspect with caution. Send back up to this location. Proceed with attention, members of the public present.' Byrd placed the radio back to his hip, and wandered over, watching the car closely. Through the rear windscreen, he could see the woman in the passenger seat with her hands resting on the top of her head, most likely nursing a blow from the collision.

PC Leonard came to Byrd's side but slowed, allowing him to control it; he had more experience, more know-how. As

Byrd approached the door, he heard the woman shouting inside the confines of the car, followed by a series of bangs as she tried to frantically attempt to open it, but the door was crushed and bent, seized in to the frame of the vehicle. The other side of the Mondeo was crushed into the metal railings covered in a sea of glass. Knowing she wasn't going anywhere, she tried to climb out of the broken driver's window.

Just as she dropped down on to the floor, Byrd placed a knee down on to her back, while PC Leonard grabbed the handcuffs from his belt and arrested her.

85

Thursday
West Crescent, Darlington

'Are you going to be sick?' Tanzy asked PC Grearer, who'd gone white, crouched by the bed near the bay window, doing his best not to look at the dead body of Neil McMahon.

Grearer moved his hand from his mouth, shook his head a few times. 'I'll be fine, boss.'

'Come on, we need to find Cornty and Weaver, they're in here somewhere.'

Tanzy moved away from the window and rounded the foot of the bed, returning to the landing. He took a right, entered the rear bedroom. The room wasn't big nor small. A set of closed curtains blocked the daylight from penetrating through, making it seem dark and depressing. In the corner of the room, there was a built-in cupboard.

He adjusted his grip on the baton and padded across the soft carpet towards it whilst Grearer steadied himself behind him near the door. Tanzy reached forward, pulled the handle, but the door wouldn't open. Trying again, harder this time. Again, nothing.

It was locked. Under the handle, he noticed a small keyhole.

'Fuck,' he muttered. Around the room over the next minute, he searched for a key but had no joy. Grearer had tried pulling the door open too but failed. Then they both tried together, but it still wouldn't budge.

'We need to prize it open, boss.'

Tanzy nodded, then frowned. 'Or…'

'Where you going?' Grearer asked Tanzy as he headed for the door and left the room. 'Orion?'

Tanzy went back into the front bedroom to the body of Neil McMahon. He leaned down and carefully padded his left pocket first. Nothing.

'What – what are you doing?'

Tanzy ignored the PC and continued to search him. Bending down to get himself in a better position, he ducked and managed to get his hand under Neil's right side, which was close to the base of the wardrobe. He didn't want to move the body, knowing he could potentially mess things up for forensics who were on their way. He found nothing.

'Fuck. Go get a crowbar – try the garage or something.'

Two minutes later, PC Grearer returned with a long bar. It had a point on the end. 'Here.'

'That should do,' Tanzy said, taking it. He pulled on the bar and the door cracked open.

'Jesus!' Grearer gasped, as PC Weaver fell back into the room, hard down on to the carpet with a thud, her head colliding with the floor. There was a quiet, raspy groan from inside the cupboard. Tanzy saw PC Cornty awkwardly bent, his face and chest against the back wall.

'Call an ambulance now!' Tanzy ordered. He dropped the bar on to the floor.

Grearer backed off into the centre of the room and took out his phone.

'Cornty,' Tanzy panted, reaching inside. Cornty groaned again, but didn't move, as if his body had frozen in stone in that position. Very carefully, Tanzy used his strength to slowly manoeuvre the PC out and lowered him on to the carpet near where Weaver was.

'Doesn't look like she's breathing,' Grearer said, glaring down at Weaver.

'Check her pulse,' Tanzy told him. He lowered himself down to her and placed two fingers on her throat.

'It's there, but only slightly. What's this?' There was a cut to the back of her head, her blonde hair matted with blood where it appeared she'd been hit. 'Hang on in there,' Grearer said quietly to her. He looked at Cornty. 'How's he doing?'

Cornty groaned a little more as Tanzy mechanically straightened him out on to the floor, using his hand to lower his head down gradually to the carpet.

'I don't know yet, I—'

Tanzy's phone rang in his pocket. He sighed, plucked it out, and answered it.

'Ori, we fucking got her,' Byrd shouted.

'Good.' Tanzy was concentrating on Cornty beneath him and said nothing more.

'What's happening there… have you found Cornty and Weaver?'

'We found them. Locked in a cupboard. Amy has a cut to the back of her head - she's in a bad way but breathing. Phil is a little more with it but isn't much better. Just called an ambulance now.' He glanced up at Grearer, who nodded for confirmation. 'Is back up taking her down to the station?'

'Yeah, she's in one of our cars. We don't know who it is yet – I'm assuming it's his wife?'

'It would make sense,' Tanzy commented.

'We need a recovery truck to move this old banger – it's blocking the road.'

Tanzy didn't respond.

'Ori?'

'What is it, Max?'

'How are they?' Byrd asked.

'Amy and Phil?'

'Yeah…'

'Yeah, I think they'll be okay. Phil is groaning. Amy is quiet but she has a pulse. You heading back over here?'

'Yeah, need to see the crime scene. Be with you in two minutes.'

Tanzy put the phone back into his pocket. Ever since he'd opened the cupboard in the back bedroom, there was a strange smell. Strangely enough, it had grown worse as the minutes ticked by. He looked away from Cornty, tipped his head back and glared into the cupboard wondering what it was.

Then he heard a little girl crying from somewhere very close.

86

Thursday
West Crescent, Darlington

Byrd and Leonard pulled up at number ten. The PC turned off the engine and applied the handbrake.

'That's the first chase I've done,' he said, 'I know it wasn't the most exciting, but it… was good, in a strange way.'

'You did good,' Byrd said, giving the PC an encouraging smile. 'Come on, let's go inside.' They both got out, headed through the open door, Leonard a little apprehensive about what he was about to see.

'Tanzy?' Byrd shouted, projecting his voice through the house.

'Up here, Max.' Tanzy's tone was flat.

Byrd and Leonard climbed the stairs. When they reached the top, they could see Tanzy and Grearer with Weaver and Cornty in the rear bedroom.

'Hey,' Byrd said, entering the room. He sniffed the air. 'What's that smell?'

'It's coming from in here,' Tanzy said, kneeling down, facing the cupboard.

'What's that sound? Who's crying?' PC Leonard asked, frowning.

'It's coming… I think it's coming from in here?' They all went silent, watching Tanzy. 'I don't understand though.'

'Understand what?' Byrd asked him, frowning.

'It – it must be next door. There's nothing in here apart from clothes, I can't see – hang on a minute.' Tanzy leaned into the cupboard.

'What?' Byrd edged forward, stopped just behind him, and lowered down to have a look.

'What's this?' Tanzy asked him pointing to a screw hanging out the wood a couple of millimetres on the left-hand side, about half way up. Tanzy tugged on it but it was solid. Above and below where the screw was, covering an area of around a foot, there were empty screw holes where a screw had been fixed, then removed time and time again.

'What the…'

'Hello!' Byrd shouted, nearly penetrating Tanzy's ear drum. 'Hello – is there anyone there?'

The crying stopped suddenly.

Tanzy and Byrd were silent. The PC's behinds were silent, too, watching, waiting.

'Help me,' they heard a quiet struggling voice. 'Help.'

'To get this out, we need a screwdriver, Max.'

Byrd shuffled out, found his feet, panned around the room. He went over to a chest of drawers and opened all of them until he found a Phillips screwdriver in the third drawer down. 'Got one, here, try this!' Byrd handed it to Tanzy, who took it, and turned back into the tight space.

'Shine a light on it, please, Max. I can barely see!'

Byrd pulled out his phone, turned on the torch function and leaned in, shining the phone light on top of Tanzy so he could see the screw to turn it. The screw, after half a minute of turning, popped out and dropped to the base of the cupboard with a ping.

They noticed the wooden panel at the back came away an inch from where it was originally seated.

'Help me…'

The voice was crystal clear.

'Move back, mate,' Tanzy told Byrd, who got up out of the way. Tanzy found his feet and dragged the rail of clothing to one side. He then dug his fingers down the side of the panel and pulled it towards the room. It opened a few inches.

A horrific smell seeped out and Tanzy cupped his nose. 'Jesus!'

It was human excrement.

'What on earth is that?' Byrd said, now smelling it too, standing a few feet back. He watched Tanzy pull the panel open as far as it could.

'Jesus fucking Christ!' Tanzy gasped.

'What – what is it, Ori?' Byrd frowned.

'It's Evelyn Jones.'

87

Thursday afternoon
West Crescent, Darlington

'Help me,' Evelyn said. Her voice was so weak, it was almost inaudible.

'Evelyn, you're safe now,' Tanzy said, stepping into the space, being mindful not to step on her feet. He looked around the cupboard. It had been man made, that's for sure. It went about two feet back, and was the width of the wardrobe, which was also roughly four feet. Evelyn laid on her side on a dirty blanket, facing down to the floor. Her little body raised and fell with her shallow breathing but only slightly. To the left back corner, there was a pile of faeces on the floor and it absolutely reeked. To the right, there was a handful of empty bottles and a wooden box, which was maybe a little bigger than a shoebox.

'Here, take my hand, Evelyn, please,' Tanzy told her, leaning down.

Evelyn moved so slowly, it was painful for Tanzy to watch. If she'd been in here for the whole time she'd been missing. It was a level of cruelty he'd never seen before. Ever. She was wearing her school uniform, the same one she had on the day she'd disappeared. Her cheek bones were prominent, her eyes sunken deeply into her face – the complete opposite of the photograph that her parents, Ray and Jane, had given him ten days ago.

Tanzy took hold of her slender wrists, and carefully pulled her up to a sitting position. Her body was floppy, her spine almost folding in two, but she was still breathing, albeit only slightly. Severe dehydration. Evelyn could barely sit up properly, as if her spine and muscles had lost the memory of how to.

Placing his hands under her arm pits, he cautiously lifted her up and placed his hand under her bony bum and wrapped her legs around him, then very carefully backed out of the space.

'You're safe now, Evelyn,' Tanzy whispered in her ear. She didn't have the energy to respond. Tanzy told Grearer to grab a blanket or something to lie her down on. Half a minute later, he came back with a blanket he'd found in the front bedroom.

'Here.' Grearer laid the blanket out neatly and stepped back, allowing Evelyn to be lowered on to it. 'The ambulance is on its way.'

Amy Weaver was on her side in the recovery position.

Phillip Cornty was on his back, groaning, but he seemed to be more with it now, finally opening his eyes.

Byrd looked away from them, and went to the cupboard, and peered inside the small space. He gagged physically because of the smell. His mind hurt on an emotional level thinking about what she must have endured. He noticed the wooden box in the corner, bent down and picked it up, then carried it out.

'What's that?' PC Leonard asked, curiously.

'I have no idea.'

There was a lock on the front of it. But no key.

'Pass me the screwdriver, please,' Byrd said to Leonard, who'd took it off Tanzy moments earlier and placed it on the window sill. He grabbed it. 'Here.'

Byrd prized the locked off after a few goes and it fell off on to the floor. He opened the lid and glared inside.

'Oh my God,' he bellowed. 'Come have a look at this.'

88

Thursday Afternoon
Police Station
Interrogation room

Byrd and Tanzy were both sitting on one side of the desk in silence. In the five minutes they'd been waiting, they'd nearly drained their coffees. They couldn't believe what Judith McMahon had done – she really was the last person in the world they'd guess would be capable of anything like this.

The door opened to their right.

Their focused glares fell on DS Stockdale when he entered who gave them a courteous nod then stood side on, allowing PC Cornty and PC Weaver to walk in with Judith, one either side, holding her arms.

'Sit,' Cornty told her, pushing her shoulder down until she hit the chair.

'Thank you,' Byrd said to the PC's, 'you can go.' They bobbed their heads, turned, and left the room.

Judith McMahon, dressed in a light grey jumper and dark grey jogging bottoms, never looked up at the detectives, instead she kept her focus down on the table between them. Next to their coffees, there was a jug of water, and a recording device that appeared older than modern-day technology.

The door to the room closed and there was a click, the lock sliding across.

Byrd leaned forward and pressed the button on the recording device. After he sat back and got comfortable, he told the recorder the date, the time, his own name, the name of his partner, and the name of the suspect they were interviewing. Then he told the recorder the reason they were interviewing Judith McMahon.

Judith didn't even raise an eyebrow at the allegations. She'd zoned out as if they weren't there, as if they weren't speaking and asking her questions.

'Judith…' Tanzy said.

Her eyes never left the table, but her skin started to sweat, becoming almost wax-like under the bright lights above them. Her slim body started to rock back and forth, only an inch; it was almost unnoticeable, but the detectives noticed.

'Judith?' Tanzy said, louder this time. She glared at Tanzy for at least ten seconds until she gave up and glanced away.

'I'm going to allow you to explain yourself…' Tanzy said.

She stayed silent.

'Judith?' Byrd this time.

Again, she ignored him, keeping her focus down at the table.

The detectives had played this game before and decided to stay silent until it became awkward enough for her to speak. So that's what they did. Byrd, in his head, counted forty-seven seconds until she finally spoke.

'Yeah…'

'We'd like some answers, Judith McMahon,' Tanzy said, then he turned to Byrd. 'Should we ask her a couple of questions? You never know, depending on her answers, it might be worth something. It could determine the sentence the judge will give her.'

That got her attention. She glanced up, finding the confidence to switch her focus between both of the detectives for a few seconds but naturally settled on Byrd.

'We'll start with Evelyn Jones, shall we?' Tanzy said. 'Why?'

Judith looked at Tanzy, offered a little shrug.

'Why not another seven-year-old? Why not a boy? Or a ten-year-old girl?' asked Tanzy. 'Why lock her up in a cupboard for over ten days? You know'—Tanzy leaned forward a little, his eyes narrowing—'what you've done is one of the worst things I've ever seen. And believe me, I've seen some terrible things. We've seen some terribly awful things, haven't we, Detective Inspector Byrd?'

Byrd nodded several times.

'So, Judith... the question is: Why?'

'I was protective over her,' she said quietly.

'Protective?'

She nodded at Tanzy.

'Why?'

'She reminded me of my own daughter, Casey.'

'Your daughter, Casey, who died at seven?'

She nodded again.

'So why protective over Evelyn Jones? She wasn't your daughter. She belonged to Ray and Jane Jones. Not you. What happened to Casey was horrendous, God, I couldn't comprehend that happening to my own children, and I won't sit here telling you I know how you feel, because I don't. But... what gives you the right to take someone else's child?'

'Everything she did, she reminded me of Casey. Neil used to come in after school and tell me about her. About how she used to write and draw these amazing pictures. He actually said Evelyn had reminded him of Casey.' She paused a second. 'I wanted her. I wanted to keep her safe.'

'By locking her in a cupboard, feeding her scraps and bottled water and letting her urinate and soil herself? Is that what you mean by safe?'

Her eyes got teary. 'I missed Casey so much. I couldn't stand the thought of some other parents having the pleasure of bringing up a daughter who always had a smile on her face. My God, the stories about her were infectious.'

The detectives absorbed her outrageous reasoning for a few moments.

'How did you do it?' Byrd asked.

'I knew I was going to do it for a while... I just didn't know when. I built the cupboard as a personal project six months ago. Then I waited for the right time. I told Neil about doing something with the cupboard, but I didn't really expand on it and he didn't really ask – he didn't need to know anyway. He had plenty of room for his clothes and I said it was for my bags and shoes. He always said he hated all of my shoes and bags on show.' She paused for breath. 'Anyway, I knew exactly which way Evelyn walked home and grabbed her before she reached home.'

'And Evelyn just happily went along with you?'

She nodded. 'I told her I was her teacher's wife and that he'd bought her a present for doing so well in her Maths, which Neil had told me about. She followed me straight home.'

'Easy as that?' Byrd replied.

'Yup. Pretty simple.'

'Then what?'

'I grabbed her and put her in the cupboard, then locked it. I fed her sandwiches and water. Kept the door to that room closed most of the time and Neil never really went in there. When she used to cry, I used to say about how the man next door must be abusing his own daughter. Neil never suspected a thing.'

'And just how long did you expect to do this for?' Tanzy this time.

She shrugged. 'I don't know. I was going to move her. The smell was getting horrendous in there.'

'I'm not surprised after ten days,' laughed Tanzy. 'Are you?'

'Why did you kill your husband, Neil McMahon?' asked Byrd.

'Since he made the stupid choice to ring the police asking you guys over about the guy next door, it was hard not to. Especially when the other two coppers were looking inside the cupboard. I pushed the woman in and locked it. Neil asked me what the hell I was doing. I then told him what I'd done. He couldn't believe it, he told me he was ringing the police. That's when I grabbed a screwdriver and stabbed him in the stomach with it over and over again.'

Tanzy and Byrd never moved through her story, keeping their eyes on her and listening, feeling deeply disturbed how calm she appeared to be. Tanzy leaned back a little, raised his palms and placed them on top of his head, whilst Byrd remained still, his eyes focused on Judith McMahon.

'Then what happened?' Byrd asked.

'He staggered into the bedroom and collapsed near the bed. I pulled him across the carpet and put him in the wardrobe.'

Tanzy smiled at her. 'Now… before we take you away for a very long time, we'd like to talk about something else… something very interesting…'

'I'm listening,' she said.

'What we found in the box inside the cupboard you hid Evelyn in, is something that is very disturbing. Can you confirm, for the recording, what the contents of that box are?'

'I think you know what's in the box, Detectives,' she whispered, glancing down at the table for a moment, then back up at them, switching her focus between Tanzy and Byrd.

The air inside the room suddenly felt cold to the detectives. Byrd angled his head, took a quick glance towards Tanzy who met his stare for a brief moment of concern.

Tanzy said, 'I have an idea, but for the purpose of this recording, can you confirm us?'

'The contents of the box you found were bones,' she said, matter-of-factly.

'Bones?'

'Yes, bones. Skeleton bones.'

'Who do they belong to?'

'They belong to my daughter, Casey McMahon.'

89

Thursday Evening
Police Station

'Close the door, Gents,' DCI June Thornton told them as they entered her office. Byrd and Tanzy sat down. Her office was warm and smelt of lavender coming from the scented sticks on the unit behind her, positioned underneath the framed certificates on the wall.

'It's been a rough fucking week,' she muttered quietly. She looked pale, her complexion a little deflated. The detectives couldn't argue with her: it had been a rough week, so nodded and said nothing.

'I've heard what's happened with Judith McMahon,' she told them. 'Is Evelyn safe with her parents now?'

'Evelyn was taken to the Memorial Hospital to be checked out,' Tanzy started, shaking his head, 'she's severely dehydrated and needs to be on IV fluids for a while until she's back to normal. I've contacted her parents, Ray and Jane, telling them we've found her. They are with her at the hospital now.'

'Do the parents know exactly what happened to her?' she asked.

Tanzy nodded. 'Yeah, I told them earlier. They didn't take it very well – as expected. They asked what's going to happen to Judith McMahon. I told them she'd be going away for a very, very long time.'

She glanced down at her desk. 'It's awful what she did, I don't believe it. Did she say much about her daughter's bones?'

'She admitted they belonged to her daughter. That was one of the reasons why she killed her husband, too, because he'd have found out what she'd done to her.'

'Why did he do that to his daughter?' she questioned, under furrowed brows.

'She told us she wanted to be in control, that she wanted to keep her safe from the world. She said she'd locked her in the cupboard, same way she did with Evelyn, but Casey had eventually died after seven days. Neil didn't have a clue and now that he's dead, he'll never know what his wife did to their daughter.'

'She'll rot inside – I'm sure the inmates will have a few things to say to her,' she said.

Tanzy gave a sad smile. 'No doubt. The world has gone mad.'

'The world has always been mad,' she said, 'the difference now is we are more aware of it nowadays.' She slumped down in the middle of her leather high-topped chair and sighed heavily. 'What's the latest developments with forensics? Any update with Kim Harrison?'

Tanzy readjusted himself, slid forward a fraction, and straightened his back. 'We popped in to speak to the team before. Got an update from the new forensic guys, Paul and Amanda. Said it was clear she'd been hit over the back of the head before she entered the water. They assume that blow more than likely killed her. Tallow and Hope were busy with Janice Whittaker's body, examining the scene at Dr Ching's house.'

'I see. Anything back from the pathologists about Janice Whittaker?'

'Another surgical cut, similar to Julia Porter and Mary Richards.'

The DCI absorbed his words and bobbed her head. 'How confident are you both that Dr Ching is our man?' Her words lingered in the office for a moment, and it was a question that Byrd and Tanzy would have to carefully consider before answering.

Often, in day to day running, there'll be information that may not reach Thornton or information that she didn't need to know, so it would be up to the detectives to take the appropriate action and decide the channels of communication.

'His DNA in the form of a hair strand was found at all crime scenes,' Byrd said. 'The third crime scene was at his house. It places him present at all locations where the murder was either instigated or the body was present. The issue we have – I wouldn't say an issue but - is that he's denying it.' He paused for a beat. 'He's denying all of it. The next steps, as you know, is putting him in front of a court and let a lawyer present his case. We can hit him with the evidence we have, and they can make the decision. I'm confident about this.'

Tanzy nodded at Byrd's short summary, then transferred his focus back to Thornton.

'Talk through Kim Harrison again?' DCI Thornton said with sad eyes. It was a given she cared for the general public; it was her job. But when it concerned one of her own, there was something more. They were like family.

'Paul and Amanda said she'd been attacked with a rock before she hit the water.'

'How do they know for sure?'

'Because she wouldn't have obtained an injury so severe under the water.'

'Why?' The DCI asked.

'According to Paul and Amanda, and then confirmed with Jason from the pathology department at the hospital, the severity of the damage is too great to happen under the water. Outside, in the atmospheric air, a rock could go as quickly as a human arm could swing it or throw it, obviously depending on the size and weight of it and the strength of the person throwing it. It seems whomever it was, they were strong. The same sized rock that weighed the same wouldn't cause that much damage in liquid. There'd be much more resistance because of the viscosity of the water.'

'That makes sense,' she said. 'We need this wrapping up soon, you two. They're breathing down my neck about this. Of course about Harrison, but also about Neil McMahon being murdered too. Finding Evelyn was brilliant but discovering the bones of Casey McMahon is a brand-new shit storm that we need to bring up from the past. The last couple of weeks haven't been the best for Darlington.'

90

Thursday Evening
Darlington

The man sitting at the desk had a smile on his face. Everything so far had gone to plan. Every little idea of how this would play out has played out to perfection, like an orchestra who'd practised over and over in preparation for a one-shot show and nailed it with flying colours in front of a sold-out crowd.

All the evidence had pointed to the doctor and he'd now been arrested, no doubt pending a court hearing based on the strength of that evidence.

The printer underneath the desk near his right leg whirred and out came a sheet of A4 paper. He leaned over, picked it up and placed it down on the wooden desk in front of him. His smile widened, and his eyes sparkled.

There she was.

The headless body of Janice Whittaker inside the shed. His eyes slowly trailed the blood across the bottom of the shed, and up her body to where her head once was.

'Wow,' he whispered, an excitement tingling through him.

To his right, the door to the room opened; he couldn't hear it but the way the air changed allowed him to sense it, the way the molecules had shifted slightly. He craned his focus to find his wife cautiously stepping in, her eyes staring down on him.

'Did he send it?' she asked.

The man nodded. 'Yeah. Come see.'

The woman stopped behind him and wrapped her arms over his shoulders and peered at the image on the desk. 'We're nearly there, aren't we?'

He nodded. 'Just one more.'

'When?'

'Tonight.'

She gasped with excitement. 'Really?'

'Yes,' he said coldly, raising a hand and gripping hers for a moment.

She bent down, kissed his cheek and squeezed him tightly. 'Are you in the clear? Do they think it was the doctor?'

'I've haven't been arrested yet,' the man replied, 'and he has, so I think so.'

Another kiss, this time, longer.

'When are you going?' she asked.

'Right now, I need to make a couple of calls. If anyone rings, just say I'm busy.'

The man stood up from the chair and passed his wife, heading for the wardrobe. He grabbed a set of different clothes – darker clothes – and got changed. The curtains behind him were drawn, blocking out the dark world outside. His wife waited in the room watching him nervously.

'What time will you be in?' she asked.

'Soon. This will all be over tonight.'

He approached her, held her close and kissed her passionately. He went towards the door, turning, and said, 'I'll see you soon.'

There was something in his tone that she felt was different, something not quite right in the way he said what he did. As if he knew it would be the last time he'd ever see her.

91

Thursday Night
Low Coniscliffe

Byrd pulled up on his driveway, turned off the engine and sat for a moment. He unclipped his seat belt and opened the door, a wall of cold air seeped in. It had been a hectic day; a day he'd never forget.

He needed a drink. Badly.

On his way to his front door, his stomach rumbled, reminding him he hadn't eaten for most of the day. It had been several days since he'd seen Claire, but after speaking on the phone earlier, she told him to give her a text when he got home if he fancied some company and a takeaway. He hadn't indulged in one of them in a while. A night on the sofa, eating shit and watching whatever film they – she – decided to watch, sounded good.

If he was being honest, he wasn't sure it was going well with Claire. The last eighteen months had been good, sometimes great, sometimes even amazing, but over the past few weeks, it hadn't felt the same. The spark that was usually present wasn't there. Was it because of what'd happened to his parents in the car crash, the extra demand at work, the higher stress levels?

He didn't know, maybe.

Either way, Claire wasn't going to hang around forever if it continued this way. She wouldn't just sit on the side lines and come on as a substitute when Byrd needed her or craved her attention. He'd either have to change and make more of an effort or decide to let her go.

He stopped thinking about it, stepped into the house and closed the front door. After he locked it, he put the keys on the key hooks to the wall on the right. The house was cold and felt emptier than usual, but he didn't know why. He turned the lamp on to his right, the space at the bottom of the stair coming alive with a warm glow, then he strutted down the hall towards the kitchen, the rhythmic sound of his shoes bringing the house alive with sounds.

His mind was doing overtime.

He couldn't stop thinking about things. About what had happened over the past few days and weeks. PC Harrison. Evelyn Jones. Judith McMahon (and her daughter). Julia Porter. Mary Richards. Janice Whittaker. And lastly, Doctor Ching. The person responsible for caring for his parents, the person whose job it was to give them the best fighting chance they'd have to wake up.

Something didn't feel right about Doctor Ching.

He needed a second opinion. He pulled his phone out, found the number he needed and pressed CALL, then put it to his ear. Something unusual happened – it went to voicemail. It never went to voicemail.

He tried again. Same result. Voicemail.

He'd never needed to, but he tried their house phone instead. After four rings, someone picked up: 'Hello.'

'Hi, Pip,' Byrd said. 'Is Orion there?'

'He… he was but he's gone out.'

'Where's he gone?'

'Like I give a shit?' she mused.

'It's really important. If you see him, can you ask him to call me?'

'Whatever.' She hung up the phone and the line went dead.

Byrd placed the phone down on the worktop and frowned, then he reached up for a glass and the bottle of Amaretto. He filled the glass to the halfway point, lifted it to his mouth and swallowed it in one.

He stood still in the kitchen, thinking, wondering. He checked his call list and rang his voicemail. There were no new messages. Standing at the worktop, leaning forward with his palms down on the surface to steady his weight, he thought about his parents, thought about how he'd do anything to be able to pop to their house for a cup of coffee. Just to sit with them, even in silence, to watch them absorbed in the programmes they loved to watch. He turned away, wondering if he'll ever get to see that again.

You never know when you'll last see someone. By then, it could be already too late.

He clicked on Tanzy's number again. It went straight to voicemail against.

'Ori, where the fuck are you?' he said, leaving him a message.

92

Thursday Evening
Leafield Road, Darlington

Samantha Timms picked up the phone and phoned her husband.

'Hey,' said Gregory.

'Hey, where are you? Are you close yet?'

'I'm just leaving, I'll be home in five minutes. It wasn't busy at all. Next time I come, I'm coming at this time. Straight through the tills.'

'Okay.' She folded the towels that had just been washed and dried, and neatly placed them into the airing cupboard at the top of the stairs. 'Hurry up, I'm starving!'

'I'm coming now – how's the boys been?'

'Ahh, you know, like boys. Reece was fighting with Jack, but that's nothing new.'

'They in bed?'

'Yeah, just put them down, why?'

'I have a special treat for you…' he whispered through the phone.

'You do,' she said, 'I hope it's flowers, it's been ages since I've had flowers.'

'It isn't flowers, but you'll love it,' he told her. 'Do you want me to tell you?'

'Erm… go on,' she said, folding a couple of t-shirts for the boys into an immaculate pile.

The sound of the front door opening shuffled through the house, then it was closed.

She smiled. 'You were quick…'

'I don't mess around, you know,' he replied.

She walked to the bedroom and took off her bath robe, allowing it to drop to the floor and stepped into the en-suite. She leaned over through the open shower door and switched on the shower.

'Can you make me a coffee please and bring it up?'

'Yeah, I will,' he said.

'Don't worry about before by the way. They don't mean it. They're just growing up and finding things hard. It's a difficult age for them.'

'Yeah, I know,' he said. 'I just feel distant from them sometimes. It's hard working long hours. I miss my boys.'

'They miss you, too,' she replied. 'What's that sound?'

'The radio. Can you not hear me?'

Frowning, she leaned over and turned the shower off. The en-suite dropped to a deafening silence for a few seconds.

'You there?' Gregory asked through the phone.

'The radio? What radio?'

'The car radio,' he said.

'But… you're already home?'

'I'm just turning on Victoria Road now, I'll be two minutes. I'll bring your coffee up when I get in.'

Samantha glanced towards the bedroom door. She could hear slow footsteps on the stairs.

'Greg – you're not home?'

'I'm on Victoria Road, I'll be—'

'Greg, there's someone in the house,' she gasped. 'They're walking up the stairs.'

'Don't fuck around, Sam…'

'I'm not fucking around, Greg.'

93

June 14th, 2004
Darlington
15 years ago

Shez opened her eyes slowly. It took a few seconds for them to adjust to the lighting in her dark bedroom. She was laying on her front, half side on, her left leg bent awkwardly, facing the bedroom door. Out on the landing, she could see flashing disco lights coming from the party downstairs.

Her head throbbed.

Why was she on the floor? Using her left hand, she touched the back of her head and felt something wet. She saw blood on her hand. It was where she'd collided with the wardrobe when Sarah had pushed her over.

'Fuck!' she shouted, trying to find her feet, but she was dazed, almost toppling back on to the floor but used a nearby set of drawers to aid her.

Dizzy, she staggered across the room, pulled her bedroom door open, and stepped out on to the landing, the music downstairs was becoming louder now, although not as loud as it was before. Carefully, she descended the stairs one by one, holding on to the handrail, her balance not quite right. The house was quieter, in terms of the amount of people still there. She had no clue of the time. It could be midnight, or it could be three in the morning. She pulled out her phone, which told her it was half one.

She staggered through the kitchen. It was a mess. Old crusts of pizza were everywhere, empty bottles, squashed cans, fag butts – the likely cause why the kitchen stunk of cigarette smoke. Barely sitting on the stool, hanging over the breakfast bar, she noticed the lad who'd tried to kiss her earlier, laid out, snoring heavily.

'Go home,' she said, shoving him but he didn't move.

She coughed as she passed through the kitchen and reached the conservatory, then stepped over a girl who'd passed out in the doorway between them. She veered around the left, out on to the decking outside.

It was much colder now.

'Sarah?' she shouted. There was no one out here now – everyone had retreated inside to enjoy the latter dregs of the night.

She reached the garage and tried the handle. The door was locked.

'Shit,' she whispered.

She angled to the left and went down the narrow dark alley to the side of the garage, between the brickwork and the external fence. There was a small window, approximately a foot by a foot, the light inside the garage weakly illuminating the narrow alley. She peered in.

'Oh my fucking God!' she shouted, throwing a hand up to her mouth. Her whole body started to shake.

Ian Porter, who was still inside with the other three, glanced towards the glass, noticing her peeping in and quickly pointed in her direction. As quickly as she could, Shez ducked down to the concrete floor, could feel the cold brick against her back and her heart beating through her chest which was so hard and fast, it felt like it was going to penetrate her rib cage.

She needed to get help. She needed the police. Pushing herself up off the floor, she felt dizzy and disorientated using her palm against the wall to steady herself. She stopped herself from gagging and throwing up. She needed to get away, now.

When she reached the end of the wall, she stumbled down the driveway and—

The garage door opened fast. Ian Porter and Stuart Richards ran out and grabbed her quickly, hauled her up, and carried her back into the garage. She kicked and scratched like a vicious cat, violently enough for them to drop her just before the garage door.

'Get her in here now!' Stuart shouted to Ian.

Then she let out a scream, but not quite loud enough to grab anyone's attention from inside but another scream might just do it. Before she had the chance, Porter forced his hand over her mouth and she tried to bite it.

'Ahh you little bitch!' he yelled, giving her a back hand to the face.

She cowered to the cold concrete, yelping in pain.

'Lads, we need to go now, come on, let's fuck off…' Stuart told them. 'Come on, go, go!'

James Whittaker and Gregory Timms stepped out of the garage through the door and ran down the driveway. Stuart then dashed down there too and took a left at the end on to the dark, quiet street.

Ian Porter stood over Shez, who was whimpering on the floor, holding her swollen face. He bent down and whispered in her ear: 'If you tell anyone this was us, we'll come back and do the same to you.' He then grabbed her tightly, nipping the outside of her arms. 'Do you fucking understand?'

She nodded at him.

'Not a fucking word,' he told her, leaving her to cry down on the cold, damp, ground.

Shez turned on to her back and threw a hand out towards the silent garage. 'Sarah…'

94

Thursday Night
Darlington

Tanzy was sitting in his Mercedes parked up in town near a bar called The Grange. The town itself wasn't that busy – it was only a Thursday. A few college kids were out in groups, some in twos, and some older couples who'd probably been out for a meal and wanted to enjoy a few drinks before heading for a taxi home.

The time on the Mercedes dashboard was 11.10 p.m..

He hadn't spoken to Pip all day. He couldn't be bothered with her at the moment. There was too much going on at work and all she did was drain him. He missed the kids like crazy but they were in safe hands with Pip's mother. She'd been an absolute rock over the past few months.

He turned his phone back on in case there'd been any important calls he'd missed. He turned it off to shut himself away from the world. Peace and quiet. The phone screen lit up and the loading icon span on the display. Glancing to the right out the window, he saw the entrance sign of Joe's bar down the road, tempted to go and have a few pints, feel some music, and escape from reality for half an hour. God, he needed—

Tanzy jumped a little when his phone rang on the seat. He picked it up, checked the screen. It was a number he hadn't saved or recognised, ending in four zero six. He pressed answer and raised it slowly to his ear.

'Hello?'

'Detective Tanzy?' the voice was fast, hurried.

'Speaking. Who is—'

'You need to help me – my wife,' the voice said. 'There's someone at our house. You were right.' The man was out of breath.

'Who is this?' Tanzy asked, confused.

'Your partner gave me your card, Orion, please! It's Gregory Timms. You were right. She's in danger. My wife is in danger right now – there's someone in the house.'

'Slow – slow down, Gregory, please, just take a breath,' Tanzy said calmly. 'Where are you?'

'I'm heading to my house now. There's someone there. I'm a minute away. Please help me?'

'What's your address?'

'Leafield Road,' Gregory panted, breathing heavily down the phone. 'Please.'

'What number?'

He told him.

Tanzy recalled the location of Leafield Road in relation to where he was and remembered where it was. 'Okay, okay, I'm heading there now.' Tanzy hung up the phone, then called Byrd as fast as his fingers could type.

He set the gear in first and set off sharpish, the tyres spinning on the cold tarmac. The phone rang through the speaker system.

'Pick up, pick up!' he shouted. Then there was a click.

'Orion, I've been trying to—'

'Max, listen, there's no time,' Tanzy said, 'get in your car and get to Leafield Road now!'

'Leafield Road? Why – what's—'

'Just fucking listen, Max, someone is at Gregory Timms' house about to kill his wife. Gregory is only a few minute away. I'm heading over now.'

'Jesus.' Byrd sounded flustered, as if he'd just woken up.

'Come on, Max.'

'I'll set off asap!'

'I'll see you there,' Tanzy told him.

95

June 14th, 2004
Darlington
15 years ago

The car pulled up outside the house where the music was coming from. It had just gone two in the morning. Through the large bay living room window, the young man could see flashing lights and people slowly dancing. Others were flaked out on sofas and others were laid on the floor.

He applied the handbrake and got out. The sound of the music coming from the house was loud enough to be heard through the closed windows and seep out into the cold, frosty air. He ambled slowly up the driveway, scanning the house and windows. He took his phone out, searched for her number, then pressed CALL.

It rang and rang until it went to voicemail.

He tried the front door, which opened, and stepped up into the warm hallway filled with a smell of perfume and stale smoke. Some dance anthem from the early 90's was blaring from somewhere. Down the hall, through the kitchen, he saw a lad sitting awkwardly on a stool bent over a breakfast bar.

At the door of the living room, he popped his head in. 'Anyone seen my sister?'

The ones who weren't completely out of it glared up at him with glassy eyes. 'Hey, you're here, hey man—'

'Have you seen my sister?'

Three of them shook their heads.

He then heard another conversation.

'Where?' he heard a girl say behind him to one of her friends. 'Where – in the garage?'

'Come see,' the other person said to her. The two of them went through the kitchen towards the back of the house.

'Hey, what's in the garage?' the lad shouted.

One of the girls turned. 'Someone has found something.'

He checked the rest of the living room and dining room, then went into the kitchen. Crisps, pizza crusts, and empty bottles lined the floor. Sandy shook his head. 'Kids man,' he mused. At the end of the kitchen, he took a right into the conservatory.

And that's when he heard the screams.

It was coming from outside.

He dashed out, and through the back gate, he saw a number of people standing at the door of the garage, the light inside illuminating their terrified faces. They seemed frozen, unable to move. One of the girls was standing with her hands clamped over her mouth. Another girl started to cry.

Sandy stepped off the decking, went through the open gate. 'What is it?' he asked, approaching the commotion.

One of the lads stopped him, holding his palm on to his chest. 'Mate, don't…'

Despite the lads plea, he frowned and moved around him. He moved the two girls out of the way and peered inside the garage.

The whole of his body froze and his whole world was held in suspension for what seemed like a long time. There she was. His sister. Sarah.

Hanging from one of the roof support beams by a rope around her neck.

Her face was purple and drained. Her eyes were open. He dashed in and grabbed her legs in an attempt to lift her up, a desperate way to free her.

'Help me! Fucking help me!' he begged the girls at the door, who'd decided they weren't going inside and started to cry instead. After realising he couldn't lift her high enough to loosen the rope around her neck, he frantically stared around the garage, and noticed a chair kicked over on its side a few feet away from where Sarah was hanging.

It took him nine seconds to find a pair of gardening sheers in a drawer to his left. Using the sheers, he snapped at the rope violently, screaming her name, until it gave way after the fourth attempt, then Sarah's body fell to the floor with a sickening thud.

He leaned over her, crying, holding her closely, trying to shake her awake.

There was nothing he could do.

It appeared she'd hung herself.

She was dead.

96

Thursday Night
Leafield Road, Darlington

D.I. Orion Tanzy pulled up outside of the house, slammed on the brakes causing the car to skid before it jerked to a halt in front of a white self-drive hire van.

'Son of a bitch – the stolen van!'

He took a mental note of it – no time for writing it down - and threw his car door open. He dashed over the damp road towards the Timms' house, sliding down the gap between two parked cars and stepped up onto the path towards the front door. At the door, he pushed down hard on the handle, barging into it with his strongest shoulder, causing it to fly open. He almost lost his balance, falling through into the hallway, but somehow managing to stay on his feet.

'Samantha!' he shouted, his voice tearing through the house and rebounding back at him. 'Gregory!'

No response from either of them. He must have beaten Gregory here but knew he wouldn't be far behind. He checked all the rooms downstairs, starting with the living room, then the dining room, then through to a narrow, low-ceilinged kitchen. He galloped to the end of it, finding a small toilet when he barged the door open, but it was empty.

No sign of anyone.

'Fuck!'

He went back through the house and took a cautious right, glaring up the stairs, which were in total darkness. He saw a switch, turned it on quickly, then started to climb them. At this point, he didn't care about being quiet. From what Timms had told him about the phone call with his wife, there was no time to enter without being noticed; he had to enter making as much noise as possible, hopefully deterring whatever danger Samantha Timms was in.

The door at the top of the stairs was shut. He pushed down on handle and threw it open. 'Samantha?' It was the bathroom. A pull-down cord was hanging to the left. He yanked on it, the bathroom filling with light.

No one in there.

Leaving the bathroom, he jumped up a couple of steps on to a higher landing, could feel his body starting to sweat under his long coat. Ahead of him, there were three doors.

One to the left, one further down on the left, and one straight ahead at the end of the landing.

'Gregory? Samantha?' he bellowed.

Pushing the first door open, he stepped into the darkness, instantly smelling the scent of metal in the air and something sweet. His eyes adjusted but not enough to get the full picture, the room filled with shadows. Frantically, he turned to the wall and hit the switch. As the room lit up, he swivelled his focus back to something in the corner.

Then he froze.

The smell he recognised was obvious now.

Blood.

The sweet scent was no doubt perfume. Perfume coming from Samantha Timms, who was slumped in the corner, naked and lifeless. Her eyes were open, staring up at the white ceiling, her head back against the wall, her body partly twisted.

Very slowly, he padded in, keeping his eyes on her, then looked around the room for anyone else. After a few seconds, his focus then fell to the floor around her. There was more blood than he'd ever seen. No wonder the smell of metal consumed the air so bad, the iron in her blood was almost sickening. The once-cream carpet had turned crimson and looking at her body, it was obvious she'd been stabbed over and over again in the stomach, chest, arms, legs, and feet. She had more holes than a used dart board.

'Jesus fucking Christ!' Tanzy cried, stopping just before her, immediately feeling sick at her torn figure. His heartrate pounded through his chest and the skin was damp with sweat under his clothes now.

Then he heard it.

A rush of footsteps out on the landing behind him. Hard, fast bangs, pounded the loose wooden floorboards as a figure in black whizzed past on the landing.

'Hey!' Tanzy screamed, glaring at the doorway. The figure reached the top of the stairs and started drumming down them, the desperate thuds shaking every beam and doorframe in the house. Tanzy pushed off on his left foot and dashed towards the door. If the trailing wire from the hoover hadn't been laid across the doorway, he'd have probably caught up with them before they reached the front door downstairs, but instead, his right foot looped under the wire and when he lifted his foot for his next stride, the cord became tight, causing him to trip and fall forward, stumbling onto the landing, his head colliding into a wooden spindle.

As he fell to the floor, the sound the pounding footsteps faded as his body became weak and his world became black.

97

Thursday Night
Leafield Road, Darlington

Tanzy's eyes flicked open.

The front of his forehead pinged with a throbbing pain that made him wince for a few seconds. The house around him was silent. What the fuck had happened?

He found his feet slowly, as if he was only half functioning, then steadied himself by holding on to the bannister handrail.

Then he remembered the figure running along the landing. A sudden wave of concentration took over and he darted down the stairs, two at a time, knowing one wrong step would send him tumbling but there was no time to waste. When he reached the bottom, he raced towards the front door that was left open and ran out into the dark cold night. The van that was parked in front of the house had gone.

'Fuck!' He slapped his thigh and roared into the air, first looking left, then looking right. He could see the van at the end of the road towards the right, the brake lights illuminating the road below it. Without indicating, it took a left onto Park Lane, narrowly missing an oncoming car that had to brake suddenly, its tyres screeching in the darkness.

Then the sound of an engine roared to Tanzy's left. It was Byrd in his X5. He stopped the car and Tanzy ran around the bonnet and climbed in.

'Go, go! The van's turned left. Go, Max!' Tanzy shouted.

'Ori, what happened? Why are you—'

'Max, fucking go! There's no time.' Tanzy shouted, pointing, stabbing the air in front of him.

'Okay, okay...'

Byrd put the gear in first and put his foot down, the wheels of the X5 taking a second to grip the damp road, then suddenly the car surged forward. They hit the quiet crossroads and ploughed straight over. Any oncoming cars would be seen by their headlights, but the road was still and dark. At the end at the junction on Park Lane, Byrd veered to the left, a little cautiously but got up to speed quickly as they passed the cattle market on their left.

The van was just up ahead.

Tanzy took out his phone and called it in, telling the operator what he'd found at the house on Leafield Road. The female operator told him she'd dispatch emergency services and notify forensics immediately.

'Jesus,' Byrd gasped, hearing what Tanzy had told her. He gripped the steering wheel tighter, his knuckles white. The van took a left at the corner of Hogan's pub, then disappeared out of sight. Byrd was maybe fifty or sixty metres behind but was going fast, a few seconds later, slowing the car and making the same turn.

'Come on, Max!'

'I am!'

He threw the car into third, planted his foot as he chased the van down Victoria Road, approaching the roundabout near the Vue cinema. The van took a right, going all the way around and pulled off on to St Cuthbert's way.

Byrd pulled off three seconds later, gaining comfortably. His training over the years had come in useful but it'd been a while since he'd done this except earlier when he was a passenger chasing Judith McMahon with PC Leonard.

Up ahead, standing by the traffic lights crossing, were two teenagers dressed in tracksuits. They were tall and slim. Byrd noticed them standing on the edge of the path, waiting to cross the road. The van approached them fast, but for some reason, they stepped down on to the tarmac, assuming they had more time, misjudging the vans speed.

'No, no, wait!' Byrd shouted.

'What—'

'The lads up there, don't go!'

The van hit one of them with the corner of the bumper, catapulting the lad in to the air over to the left, landing several metres across the other side of the road. The other teenager threw his hands on his head and screamed.

'Fuck!' Tanzy screamed.

The van didn't even slow down, continuing on its path.

Tanzy grabbed the radio. 'Dispatch. This is Tanzy, Orion, DN522, requesting immediate ambulance support on St. Cuthbert's Way at the bottom of Yarm road, teenager has been knocked down by the runaway suspect in the white van. Send medical assistance immediately!'

'Roger that DN522, emergency response being sent now.'

Byrd slowed a little, winding down his window, but kept the car rolling in second gear. The other teenager was crying and shaking. 'Listen, young man,' Byrd shouted quickly, 'help is coming now, help is coming now! We need to keep going, we need to catch them!'

The lad nodded several times, tears coming from his eyes, watching the black X5 pick up speed and disappear down the road.

'Fuck sake,' Tanzy muttered, looking forward. 'Fucking hate doing that… Max. There, there!' he shouted, pointing ahead.

The van took a right at the roundabout onto Haughton Road, finding speed up the slight incline, passing Halfords which was on the left. Byrd hit the roundabout seconds after, barely braking, the heavy coiled suspension keeping the X5 balanced and guided the car on the same path. They both glared at the self-drive van.

'Ori… this isn't going to end well.'

98

16th October 2018
(Nearly a year ago)
South of England

It was a sad day for the family. It was only a matter of time before it happened. She hadn't been well, and these things are, unfortunately, inevitable. Life didn't go on forever.

He picked up the envelope with his name on it, turned it over, and opened it.

It was a letter from his mother, who'd passed away a week earlier. He'd heard the news, but he didn't believe; he didn't want to believe it.

I want you to know that I love you with all my heart. What you're about to read is something I should have told you a long, long time ago, but I didn't have the courage. I didn't know what you would do. If you had found out what had really happened to your sister, Sarah, God rest her soul, you'd no doubt be in prison now, so I didn't want to tell you. I didn't want you to waste your life behind bars, although, whoever did it, truly did deserve it. Now I'm about to leave this world, it's time for you to know what really happened. I won't be here to see the consequences. Maybe that's selfish, but at the same time, these men can't get away with it forever, and I know you'll do everything you can to put things right. You will give these men what they deserve. They took our Sarah from us. What these men did to Sarah made

her hang herself. They humiliated her so much, she had no choice to end her life.
I love you forever, and always,
Your Mum
X

He re-read the words over and over until he was ready to read the other piece of paper. It was a pathology report, dated, June 16th, 2004, from Darlington Memorial Hospital. He read the following paragraph over and over and over again. Tears of anger filled his eyes.

Death report Paragraph four:
Sarah had died due to hanging herself in the garage of a property in Darlington. This was her main cause of death, there's no doubt, due to the bruising of her trachea and indentations on her skin. Due to further analysis of her deceased body, we found four counts of sperm inside of her posterior fornix, an area in the back of the vagina, yesterday, which was the day of 15th June 2004. It's evident there's bruising on the inside of her thighs and bruising on her wrists indicating she'd been held down in some form. From my experience, it's apparent that Sarah had been raped several times.

The man slammed his clenched fist on to the table and screamed.

His wife entered the room quickly. 'What's wrong, God, what's wrong?'

'Look!'

She took hold of the letter while the man dropped his face into his hands and cried hysterically. She read over the same paragraph several times. Then she took hold of him and said, 'We'll get them back, we'll get them back!'

99

Thursday Late Evening
Haughton Road, Darlington

Byrd, with his foot flat to the floor, reached fifty-five miles an hour. The van was just ahead, going up over the brow of the hill crossing the railway line. On the right, the Darlington College stood in darkness.

Tanzy's phone rang in his pocket. Quickly, he pulled it out, put it to his ear. 'Hello?'

'Orion, it's Jennifer Lucas from Darlington Control room…'

'Hey, Jen – kind of a bad time – Jesus!' A car pulled out, not looking and veered over the white line onto their side of the road for a second but Byrd swung around it.

'Look where you're going!' Byrd snapped, shaking his head.

'It isn't a good time, Jen, sorry, I'll—'

'You might want to hear this, Orion.'

'Go on…' Tanzy said, panting.

'I found your man. Remember the footage on High Row in town. The man in the black fleece?'

'Yeah?'

Byrd approached the temporary road works at the roundabout and angled round to the left, following the semi-circle then joined the road, heading in the direction of McMullen Road.

'I found a different angle from a shop. The EE shop just next to Burger King. It picked him up walking across the road. It had a good shot of him. I ran facial recognition on him.'

'What came back?'

'He's one of ours, Orion,' she said. 'It's one of the trainee forensics, Paul Beech.'

Tanzy's eyed widened. 'You sure?'

'Yes. I'm sure.'

Tanzy was speechless for a moment, then: 'We're chasing him now, he's on the run. I need to go, thank you for letting me know.'

Tanzy hung up before Jennifer replied and grabbed the radio again.

'What's happening?' Byrd asked, in the dark about the situation.

Tanzy held a silencing palm, and Byrd concentrated back on the road.

'Dispatch, this is Tanzy Orion DN522…'

'Go ahead DN522…' crackled the voice.

'Just had word on the very possible identity of the suspect in the van we're trailing. The name is Paul Beech. He's one of our own. A trainee Forensic.'

The operator never replied straight away.

'Did you get that?' Tanzy asked.

'Received loud and clear, DN522. What's the current situation?'

'Following the suspect at high speed passing through the intersection at McMullen Road, heading straight for the A66 bypass.'

'Roger that.' The line cut off.

Tanzy lowered the radio, glanced at Byrd.

'Paul fucking Beech?' Byrd shouted.

'Yeah.'

'Fuck.'

'We need to bring this fucker down now!' Tanzy screamed.

Byrd dropped it a gear and planted his foot, the sound of the engine screaming at him, but the acceleration threw them forward until they were just behind the van, trailing it by a few metres. The digital speed on the dash was eighty-nine miles an hour. The lane split in to two up ahead.

'What you gunna do?' Tanzy shouted, loud enough for Byrd to hear over the roaring engine.

'Wait till he slows at the bend up here and take him out.'

There was always a risk when doing anything like that, especially at high speeds but Byrd had been trained well in the art of high-speed driving – just as Tanzy had. It was always different when it happened in real time in a real situation. The adrenaline was there, the chances of an accident with fatal consequences always present, sometimes inevitable.

The van surged on, closing the distance to the roundabout. He'd either take a right, heading towards McDonalds or a left, heading for the A66. The van's brake lights flashed briefly for a split second and veered into the right-hand lane.

'He's going right!' Tanzy said.

'Just wait… wait.' Byrd knew better than that.

As the van slowed a touch in the right-hand lane, suddenly it shot off to the left, almost timing the gradual bend to perfection. Byrd had seen this in his mind; he knew this was coming, so instead of moving over to the right directly behind it, he waited in the left lane. When the van angled over, Byrd purposefully clipped the back quarter on the left side, sending the van sideways.

The air bags exploded and cushioned the detective's faces as they both screamed.

The rocking van, under its high-speed momentum, tipped on to its side, crashing in to the island, then after a high-screech of metal scraping against tarmac, the van crunched to a halt.

'Fucking hell!' Byrd shouted, feeling his nose broken. The air bag had hit him harder than he thought it would. He glanced left at Tanzy, who seemed a little out of it, blood running from his forehead.

'Ori?'

Tanzy grunted.

'He's down, he's down. The van tipped,' gasped Byrd, unclipping his seatbelt. His nose was running with blood, so he cupped it with his right hand feeling it fill with warm crimson liquid, then reached over with his left and open the door.

The cold air hit his skin as he stepped down carefully, light-headed, and unbalanced. There was a smell of burnt metal. He lowered his hand and let the blood seep on to his jacket. The van was on its side, motionless. Everything was quiet, as if the world had been turned on 'mute' mode. Byrd ambled painfully to the rear of it, then around to the front.

Through the smashed front windscreen, he bent down a little and peered in.

The seat was empty.

'Where the fuck is—'

Then he felt something hot on his leg, a burning sensation only growing hotter by the second. The pain became excruciating. He glared down to see a surgical knife sticking out the side of his thigh. He gasped loudly when it was removed and watched the blood spurting from the wound. Turning around, through foggy vision, he noticed Paul Beech on his knees just behind him, struggling up to his feet.

'Paul?' Byrd muttered but it was almost inaudible. 'Pa—'

Byrd fell back on to the floor, landing on his back.

Paul Beech climbed to his feet, holding his forehead with his right hand, stopping the blood coming from one of his temples. The knife rested in his other hand. After a few seconds, he composed himself, and wandered over to Byrd, who was almost to the point of passing out.

'I'm sorry things had to end this way,' Paul whispered, leaning over him. He raised the knife in the air and brought it—

An incredible force collided into the side of Beech, throwing him to the left. Tanzy landed hard on top of him, the knife flying up into the air, landing metres across the empty road. Tanzy mounted him, punching him in the face, relentless blows, over and over and over again until his knuckles became numb.

Paul Beech lost consciousness and passed out.

Then in the distance, the sound of police sirens filled the air.

Tanzy glared along the road they'd just came down and saw dozens of flashing blue lights heading their way.

100

22nd October 2018
(Almost a year ago)
Darlington

Paul Beech thought long and hard about that night. About what he saw when he arrived at the party. When he walked into the garage, he saw something he would never forget. His sister, Sarah, hanging from the roof beam, a blue rope wrapped around her neck. Her face was blue and puffy, her eyes were red and lost.

The feeling that she'd hung herself for no reason absolutely crushed him. Obviously now, there was a reason – she'd been raped. He needed to find out more. On the night, he remembered seeing Shez Barker… God, she was so upset. It was her best friend. She told Paul she'd found her in there after she went looking.

But after seeing the pathology report he read six days ago, about four counts of different sperm found inside of her, he needed more answers. He came back to Darlington, asked around and found out Shez lived at the house with the pink wall.

It was set back a little from the road with a well-installed paved driveway. A brand new dark green Vauxhall Corsa covered most of it, the paintwork glistening in the afternoon sun. He'd been watching her movements for a couple of days now. She worked late shift, usually leaving the house at four in the afternoon.

The time on the dash inside of Paul's Jaguar was 3.58 p.m..

He waited and watched.

The black door opened, and out stepped Shez Barker. It had been fifteen years since he'd seen her, but he recognised her features, the shape of her body that she'd done well to keep over the years. Shez closed the door, locked it, and climbed into the Corsa.

Paul stepped out of the Jaguar and closed his door. He checked the quiet road, and crossed it, keeping his eyes fixed on her. She hadn't noticed him; she was playing around with the radio. He stopped right in front of the car and stared at her through the windscreen.

She glanced up, shuddered, then a second later, raised her hands to her mouth and screamed, the sound of her wail creeping through the seals in the doors. She watched him with wide eyes. She knew exactly who it was.

Paul slowly walked around the side of the car and climbed in the passenger seat. She wanted to lock the door but she'd completely frozen in terror. Paul stared at her for a while before he said, 'Hi Shez. It's been a while.'

She was speechless, the silence was deafening.

'Lost your voice?' he asked her.

'Sandy…' she glared with wide, terrified eyes. 'What – what –'

'What am I doing here?'

She nodded quickly. Sandy was a nickname that his friends had given him from his surname, Beech.

'I need to know the truth, I need to know what happened, Shez?'

'What about?'

'You know what about… about that night.'

She sighed, tried to control her breathing. 'What do you mean, Sandy?'

'Here, look at this.' He handed her the pathology report that his mother had left him in her will.

Taking it with trembling hands, she unfolded the paper and started reading.

'Read that part…' He pointed at the bit about there being four counts of sperm inside of her.

A tear fell from her eye and she started to shake. When she finished reading, she placed it down on her thighs.

'What happened, Shez? You need to be honest with me?'

She took a very long breath. 'She was raped, Paul.'

'I know she was fucking raped!' he shouted, causing her to jump. 'By who?'

She sighed again, staying silent.

'Shez, you need to tell me, I can't settle until I find out. You were there, you were with her that night. You know what happened.'

'There were four of them… Ian Porter, Stuart Richards, James Whittaker, and Gregory Timms.'

Paul's skin grew hot, the anger he felt, he could have put his elbow through her passenger window, but he never. Instead, he simply asked, 'Why didn't you tell me? Or the police when they got there?'

'That wasn't everything…' she confessed.

'Go on…'

'She never hung herself, Sandy, she didn't do that to herself.'

Her words ran down his back like a shiver. He knew what was coming next, but he wanted her to say it.

'They said they would kill me if I said a word. I was petrified of them.'

'Say it… tell me…'

'They hung her, Paul. They did it.'

He clenched his fists so hard, the whole of his hands went white.

'Who said they'd kill you if you said anything?'

'Ian said it to me just before he left. I haven't seen any of them since.'

Paul sighed heavily and sat for a moment. 'You should have told me…'

'I'm – I'm sorry.'

He nodded and opened the door.

'Where are you going?'

'They think after all these years that they've got away with this,' he said. 'I'm going to prove they haven't.' He got out of the car, closed the door and walked over to his jaguar.

101

Friday Morning
Police Station

After Paul Beech had been interview by DI Byrd and DI Tanzy, he'd been taken back to his cell. It was fair to say that he would be going away for life. He told them he would do it all again in a heartbeat and that he regretted nothing.

Byrd and Tanzy waited in the interrogation room, sipping on coffee, and discussing something when the door opened.

PC Cornty guided Paul's wife, Grace, inside and directed her towards the chair. She took a nervous seat and glared at the table, not at the detectives.

Tanzy nodded at Cornty, who turned and left, closing the door on his way out.

Byrd leaned forward, pressed the button on the recording device.

'This is Detective Inspector Max Byrd with Detective Inspector Orion Tanzy. We are interviewing Grace Beech in the connection with her husband, Paul Beech, in relation to her involvement in the murders of Julia Porter, Mary Richards, Janice Whittaker, and Samantha Timms. The time is 10.34 a.m. on Friday 22nd November 2019.'

From the interview, the detectives were told that after Paul found out what had happened to his sister, he'd applied for a job as a trainee forensic at Darlington. He'd spent four years prior doing a degree in forensic science because he was obsessed with crime scenes.

'Obsessed?' Tanzy asked, frowning.

Grace nodded. 'When he found out what happened to his sister, he started doing research on crime scenes, what to look for, how to analyse it. He decided to do a degree in that subject and hoped get a job doing it.' She paused for a second. 'When he got the degree, he received a letter from his mother telling him what really happened to his sister. That she was raped. Then he spoke to one of her old friends and found out what really happened that night.'

'Which friend?' Byrd asked.

'I'd rather not say. When he'd been with you guys for a while, he found the confidence to get revenge. He learnt how you guys do things and did everything to make sure he wasn't found out.'

'That didn't work out too well for him though, did it?' Tanzy mused.

She raised her eyebrows for a moment. 'No, it never. But he certainly got them back, didn't he? Now they will feel pain forever without their wives, knowing they'd been tortured and murdered, just like his sister was.'

Byrd and Tanzy exchanged a quick glance.

She went on: 'When we grabbed Julia Porter last Wednesday night, our guys took her away in the van. Paul and I waited, out of sight. When Porter went back to his car, Paul attacked him from behind, knocking him out. We hid for over thirty minutes, and then when crowds gathered, we innocently went back. He was dazed, confused, unsure what had happened. Then we acted like caring civilians and asked him if he was okay. He didn't know who I was. And he never recognised Paul. He muttered something about his wife and child being taken, then got in his car and went home.'

'So,' Tanzy said, 'if you and Paul never killed Julia Porter, then… who did?'

'Oh we certainly played our parts. But Julia Porter… she was the first. We needed it done right. Paul knew a little about crime scenes and how to dismember bodies, but we needed some professional help.'

'Dr Ching?' Byrd asked.

Grace Beech wailed in laughter, rocking her head forward into her hands. Byrd and Tanzy sighed, watching for closely, waiting for an explanation.

'Aww, you guys are funny,' she laughed. Then she lost her smile. 'No, Doctor Ching played no part in this. If Paul was never caught, I'd have certainly gone along with the story that Doctor Ching was involved but seeing as Paul will be going to prison for a long time, there's no need in punishing a man for something he never did.'

Byrd frowned. 'The evidence we found placed Dr Ching at the scenes?'

'It did, I have to agree.' She nodded.

'What are you not telling us?'

'I took a job as a cleaner at his house and took some of his hairs from a brush in his bedroom. Once I got what we needed, I never went back. We then placed the hairs in Julia Porter's car and then under the finger nails of Mary Richards. Then obviously, we put the body of Janice Whittaker in his shed, then her head in the bin.'

Her words were so casual, so distant from any human feelings.

Byrd nodded.

'All of that is for nothing though. Paul is arrested. He's going to prison for life. You've been arrested. You're going to prison, too, for probably just as long.'

She nodded in understanding. 'And I'd do the same again, over and over. The people who raped and killed Paul's sister will suffer forever. As long as that's done, I'm not really bothered what happens to us now. Our mission is complete. If he goes down, I'll go down with him.'

'So… who helped you then? Paul can't have done this alone. You didn't just get help from anyone, you got help from someone who knew what they were doing, someone skilled, someone much more skilled than the level Paul is currently at.

'He was only training. I don't care how many books on forensics he'd read over the years. That level of skill takes years to develop.'

She smiled at them.

'Who helped you?'

'Now that, my detective friends, is something you'll just have to figure out for yourselves. Now take me away, I'm tired of this, I could do with a sleep.'

102

Friday Afternoon
Darlington Memorial Hospital

'You going on your dinner?' The young assistant asked him.

He nodded. 'Yeah. Gunna nip out to get some air.'

He left the room with his jacket on. He'd heard some of the patients talking about what they'd heard on the news, about the man responsible for the four murders had been caught, and that his wife helped him.

He dashed along the corridor, weaving in and out of visitors and patients and made it outside. The air was cool. The ground was covered with a fine layer of frost.

He pulled out his phone. He had a missed call and three text messages.

The call was from Grace Beech from her spare phone, as was one of the text messages.

The message from Grace read:

Paul has been caught and arrested. They're no doubt coming to take me in. I'll tell them everything about what Paul and I did, but I won't mention you and your involvement. You've been a massive help to us and your family is proud of you. You've been more of a brother to Paul than a cousin and we'll always remember that. We won't ever see you again, but we want you to know we'll be forever grateful for what you did. Look after your family. Lots of love, Grace and Paul xx

He put the phone back inside of his coat pocket and took a lungful of cold air, held it, and slowly breathed it out. He never replied to her because he knew she'd have destroyed the phone and got rid of it, so it couldn't be traced back to him. He stayed in the car park for another ten minutes before he went back inside.

'That was quick,' the young assistant said behind him.

He jumped. 'Jesus, you scared me…'

'Sorry,' she said, smiling.

'Yeah, I wasn't that hungry really. I just needed some air, that's all. Gets a bit too much in here sometimes.' He took his coat off, placed it on the back of the door inside the office.

'What's on this afternoon?' she asked him.

'We have a body coming in. A woman in her fifties. Suspicious death.'

'Okay, I need some pictures for my portfolio… if that's okay, Doctor?'

'That's fine,' he replied.

His phone rang in his pocket. 'Excuse me a second,' he said, stepping out of the office into the corridor. He answered it, 'Hello, Dr Jason Lannark speaking?'

103

Friday Afternoon
Police station

Tanzy brought Byrd a coffee over, placed it on his desk, and sat down.

'What a fucking day!' Tanzy sighed, allowing his weight to fill the padding of the chair.

'Tell me about it.' Byrd took his coffee, raised it to his mouth and sipped it.

'How's your mam and dad doing?'

'I don't know… I'm going to see them this afternoon. If anything had happened, they'd have phoned, so I assume things are as they were. I need to make a decision about them.'

'What do you mean?'

'If there's no signs of improving, then it's my decision to turn off the life support.'

'That's hard, I'm sorry.'

'It's just life.' Byrd angled his head, glanced out of the window. 'How's the kids? How's Pip?'

'Kids are fine. Both at school. I spoke with her mother half an hour ago. They're doing okay.'

'Good. How's Pip…?'

'We need to sit down and talk about things. I haven't had then chance over the past week or so, with what's been going on. I've left her to her own devices. She's probably home drunk.'

'Yeah. It's been a week from hell, that's for sure. Why don't you go home, Ori? Things are okay here. There's just reports to file. I can do that until I go to the hospital. Go home, sort your marriage out.'

'You know, I just might. I need to get out of here.'

'Good man.'

Tanzy stood up, grabbed his coat and went to DCI Thornton's office. He knocked before opening, then stepped inside.

'Hey, is it okay if I take the afternoon off? I know we're busy with what's happened this morning, but the interviews are done, and Max said he'll make a start on the reports. There's a couple of personal things I need to take care of.'

'That's fine, Ori, you take care of your business,' she said, peering over her glasses, sitting behind her desk.

'See you tomorrow,' he said.

'You certainly will. Hang in there, okay?'

Tanzy nodded at her and closed the door. He took a few steps towards Byrd and patted him on the shoulder. 'Catch you tomorrow, Chief.'

'Yeah man, take it easy.'

Tanzy left the office and went to his car, turned the engine on and headed for home.

104

Last Friday Afternoon
Police Station
6 days ago

PC Kim Harrison was concerned. She walked into the forensic lab and heard Paul Beech on the phone to his wife. Not wanting to interrupt, she stayed out of sight, but it was inevitable not to hear the conversation, although he was speaking quietly.

'Listen to me, Grace, they won't find out. Jason has done a fine job with the bodies… They won't have a clue it was us… honestly, you're being paranoid. I know how these things work… trust me, Grace… yeah, yeah… did you get the evidence from the doctor? … Good, everything is going to plan. They'll regret what they did.'

Paul Beech hung up the phone and frowned, glancing towards the door of the lab, sure he'd heard something. 'Hello?'

Harrison edged back slightly, staying out of sight, until she reached the door. As quietly as she could, she opened it and disappeared down the hall, immediately looking for DI Tanzy. One of the other PC's had said he was in a meeting so she didn't want to disturb him, although she was very concerned what Paul had said on the phone. She tried to find Byrd, but he wasn't at his desk. Instead, she knocked on the door of DCI June Thornton.

'Come in.'

Harrison opened the door gently. 'Hi, sorry to bother you.'

'It's no problem, what do I owe the pleasure, Kim?'

She ambled in nervously. 'I know I should go through the right paths, but I've tried to find DI Tanzy but he's in a meeting. Can I express my concerns with you, or should I wait for DI Tanzy?'

'It's fine – what's on your mind?' Thornton lowered the paperwork in her hand, placing it on her desk.

Harrison told Thornton about Paul's phone call, how she felt he was speaking inappropriately about things that disturbed her. Thornton listened to what she had to say, then said, 'This definitely happened, he mentioned about getting evidence and that people wouldn't find out?'

Harrison nodded confidently.

'Well,' Thornton said, standing to her feet, 'let's go speak with Paul and ask him what this is all about.'

DCI Thornton and PC Harrison headed towards the forensics lab. When they opened the door, Jacob Tallow was sitting on a stool, looking intently at his computer screen.

'Jacob,' DCI Thornton said, 'have you seen Paul?'

'He left a minute ago. He said he needed to go out for a little while.'

Thornton and Harrison left the lab, dashed down the corridor, went through the main door outside and scanned the car park. They saw Paul climb into his car and pull away.

'Have you got car keys?' DCI Thornton asked.

PC Harrison felt her pockets. 'Yeah, I've got them.'

'Pass them here, I'll drive. Come on, lets follow him,' she said, heading towards the marked Astra. They got in, buckled their seat belts and off they went, following Paul Beech cautiously.

'We'll keep well back, so he doesn't see us,' Thornton said.

They hit the roundabout at the top of Victoria Road and followed Beech on to Coniscliffe Road. 'Where's he going?' Harrison asked.

Thornton shrugged. 'As long as we stay on him, it doesn't matter.'

A few minutes later, Paul Beech slowed and took a left into Broken Scar picnic area. Ten seconds later, DCI Thornton slowed, indicated, and guided the car left.

Very slowly, she crawled up the ramp and stopped the car. 'He's gone down there…'

Thornton sat for a moment, thinking hard.

'What should we do?' Harrison asked.

'Why is he here?'

A shrug from Harrison.

'We'll go down, see what he's up to,' Thornton suggested.

She put the gear in first and slowly controlled the car down the steep descent, dabbing the brakes carefully, and angled left at the bottom. Paul's car was parked up on the right but there was no one inside of it.

'Where's he gone?' Harrison said, confused.

'We'll find him – he can't have gone far.'

She stopped the car, applied the handbrake and turned off the engine. She unclipped her belt and opened the door. PC Harrison did the same. They looked around. It was just them two.

'Come on, over here,' Thornton said, heading towards the top where she knew there was a path. 'We need to find him.'

'There!' Harrison said, pointing to the footpath on the right, seeing the back of him for a brief moment before he disappeared behind a tree. They angled in that direction and kept vigilant, stepping carefully over the wet, muddy trail. At the end, they could either go left, or straight up.

'Up there,' Harrison said, 'that way is up to the park, I don't know—'

A branch snapped towards their left, causing them both to freeze.

'Down there,' Harrison said, going first, being careful not to slip down the steady decline. They ducked under the awkward hanging branches on to a muddy area just before the water.

It was quiet.

No one was there.

'Where did he go?' Harrison asked, then turned towards—

A heavy rock, about the size of a shot put, came pummelling towards her head. She saw it for a split second, then felt the horrendous pain before she blacked out and fell forward into the river with a splash.

DCI Thornton lowered the rock and sighed heavily, panning left and right, seeing if anyone had noticed what'd just happened. After half a minute of silence, she sighed heavily watching PC Harrison floating on the water.

'You can come out now,' she said, turning behind her.

Paul stepped from behind a tree and smiled. 'Hey.'

They both turned towards the water, watched PC Kim Harrison's body on the surface, her face down and her body still. The underwater currents were tugging on her, easing her lifeless body over the centre of the river. Soon, she'd be washed away, no doubt found in a couple of days.

'I better head back, Paul, people will be wondering where I've got too. I need to take her car back, make it look like she left the station on foot.'

'Okay, I'll come back later. I told Tallow I was popping out for a little while.'

'You take care. Be careful. I'll sort everything out,' she told him.

'Thanks, Auntie June,' he said. They both walked back to the cars without saying anything. Paul climbed in his and DCI Thornton opened the door of the marked Astra. Paul set the gear in first and slowly climbed the hill and took a right onto Coniscliffe road. Thornton waited a few minutes and set off in the direction of the station.

105

Friday Early Evening
Police Station

Byrd glared at the computer, aiming to finish the reports so he could get out of there. What a crazy couple of weeks it had been. He had to concentrate on his parents now, hoping they'd pull through.

There was a ringing sound near him. He frowned. It was the office phone. Each desk had one. He leaned to the left, picked it up and said, 'Hello?'

But the ringing continued.

He placed it down and picked up Tanzy's phone.

'Hello?'

'Orion Tanzy?' the voice said.

'Eh, no, this is Detective Inspector Max Byrd, can I take a message for Orion?'

'It's Jennifer Lucas from the Town Hall in the control room,' she said.

'Hi, Jennifer,' Byrd said, 'how can I help?'

'I was hoping to speak to Orion, but maybe you can help me?'

'Yeah, go on, I'm listening.'

'When one of his colleagues, a PC Kim Harrison, went missing, Orion asked me to check the CCTV around the town, starting with the cameras closest to the station, you know, because of what happened.'

'What do you mean because of what happened?' Byrd said, frowning.

'On Friday when your colleague PC Harrison went missing, I checked the cameras at the station. Unfortunately, for some unknown reason, from 3 p.m. till 6 p.m., the cameras were down. I chased it up with the maintenance team, but they weren't aware of any planned work. I was hoping to see Kim Harrison on there – Orion had given me the registration of the Astra she normally uses. Maybe it was a system error. Sometimes, camera systems fail and rebooted after a certain length of time.'

'Okay,' Byrd said, deflated.

'But just before half past four, I spotted the car from a camera on Coniscliffe Road, heading west.'

'What time was it?'

'Half past four,' she said again.

'But she wasn't driving the car. From the still shot I have of it, she was sitting in the passenger seat.'

'Who was driving the car?' Byrd asked, edging forward.

'It appears to be your DCI, June Thornton.'

Her words ran over Byrd like a shiver. 'Thornton?'

'Yeah. I'll email you the still shot over asap so you can see for yourself.'

'If it is her,' Byrd said, 'then she was the last person to see Kim Harrison alive.' He hung up and waited nervously.

The email pinged through shortly after.

Byrd clicked it open. He gasped, glaring at the image. It was indeed DCI June Thornton driving the marked Astra.

'It can't be, it…'

He pulled his phone from his pocket and unlocked it, then found the number, and pressed CALL.

'Come on, pick up, pick up.'

'Hello?'

'Ori, listen to me, I've just had a call from Jennifer Lucas at the Town Hall control room.'

'Yeah?' Tanzy said.

'You really need to come in, you won't believe it over the phone. You need to see it with your own eyes, Orion.'

'Okay, I'll be there in fifteen minutes, Max.'

Byrd hung up and placed the phone down on the desk. Then he remembered something. The office was empty, but he hadn't seen DCI Thornton leave yet. She was still in her office. He stood up and quickly turned—

He never heard it, but he felt it, the heavy blow to the temple causing him to stagger for a moment, until his legs collapsed from underneath him, and he crashed to the floor with a loud thud, his head hitting the hard ground.

Then the world went black for DI Max Byrd.

106

Friday Early Evening
Police Station

Tanzy pulled up in his Golf, turned off the engine and stepped out of the car. Byrd's words played over and over in his mind, making him wonder what could be so important.

There were only three cars in the car park.

Byrd's X5.

Thornton's Range Rover.

And his Golf.

He stepped through the sliding double doors and walked briskly down the corridor towards the office. When Byrd had rang, he'd been talking to Pip, trying to have a serious conversation about their marriage. He told her whatever it was that Byrd wanted to show him, he'd be an hour at the most, and they'd continue with it when he returned.

The office was empty.

There wasn't a sound from anywhere.

He glanced along the rows of computers and frowned when he couldn't see Byrd, assuming he'd be at his desk, ready to show him whatever was so important.

Byrd's desk was empty, but his chair was pulled out. His coat was hanging on the back of it.

'Max?' he called, glancing around.

He plucked out his phone and called him.

Somewhere very quiet, he heard his ringtone. He turned around, staring at DCI Thornton's closed door. He recalled seeing her car in the carpark, figured whatever Byrd wanted to show him, he was discussing the matter with Thornton.

He padded to her closed door and—

'What's that?' he whispered, seeing something on the floor.

Drops of blood.

'Max?' he called out.

No answer.

He remembered Byrd's words on the phone: You need to see it with your own eyes, Orion.

See what, he wondered. He stopped still and thought hard, his mind doing overtime. Then he turned, tip-toed over to Byrd's computer screen, and leaned over. The screen was in sleep mode. He moved the mouse, causing the Log-in screen to appear. Byrd's username was already in; all he needed was the password.

Knowing it, he typed it in and pressed ENTER.

The screen came alive with an email from Jennifer Lucas from the Town Hall. The image of a still shot of the CCTV taken from Coniscliffe Road. The marked Astra. PC Kim Harrison in the passenger seat. DCI Thornton in the driver's seat.

His eyes widened when he noticed the time stamp in the top right corner. Calculating the last time anyone had ever seen Kim Harrison, he made the same assumption that Byrd had: Thornton was the last person to see Kim Harrison alive.

'Shit,' he whispered, then glanced down at the desk, noticing a little blood spatter at the far side just under the flat screen monitor. 'Max?'

His heart beat increased suddenly as he turned around to face her door. Very quietly, he padded over and stopped just outside of it. He took a couple of deep breaths.

'DCI Thornton?' he said.

There was no answer.

'If anyone can hear me, I'm opening the door now.'

He grabbed the handle, pushed it down, and in a sudden movement, he threw the door open and very quickly jumped back, just avoiding DCI Thornton's swinging arm as it brushed past his face. He saw something in her hand, something solid looking. After she missed the swing, she fell forward, losing her balance and collided into the open door. Tanzy took a few steps back, staying light on his feet.

Thornton found her balance and turned towards Tanzy, then charged out of her office towards him holding the object high above her head. It was a knife. When she was close enough, Tanzy decided to charge at her, an attempt to take her by surprise.

It did.

He went in hard and low with his right shoulder, crashing into her stomach and lifted her up, driving her back until he clattered her body off the stud wall of her office. The plaster dented under the huge impact causing her to wail out in pain and drop the knife, which landed on to the hard floor several paces from them. Tanzy let her go and watched her small frame crumble to the floor. He'd nearly bent her in two.

'Max?' he shouted, stepping away from her and darting into her office.

In the corner, near the window, Byrd was unconscious, lying on his front with his eyes closed. Blood had pooled around Byrd's head from the blow to the left side of his temple. Tanzy bent down and shook him a few times.

'Max? Fucking wake up!' He shook him again, this time harder. Finally Byrd grunted something but didn't move. 'Wake up, come on!' He let out another inaudible grunt, telling Tanzy he was alive at least. 'Wait here, I'll be back,' Tanzy told him.

He dashed back out of the office and looked to his right, glaring down at DCI June Thornton, who had been severely winded from the blow.

He grabbed his radio and called dispatch.

'DN522, Tanzy Orion, requesting emergency assistance.'

'Orion, what assistance do you require?'

'An ambulance and police assistance.' He stepped back and stared at Byrd who was still on the floor of DCI Thornton's office. 'We have an officer down, repeat, an officer down requiring emergency medical attention. Send immediately.'

'Location?'

'DCI Thornton's office at the station,' Tanzy told the operator.

'Can you – can you repeat that?'

He did.

'Copy that Orion Tanzy, requesting immediate assistance to you right now.'

Tanzy sighed heavily, glaring down at Thornton, her body folded inwards as she tried to catch her breath. As her eyes slowly opened, she squinted up at him.

Tanzy lifted the radio back to his mouth. 'Better make that two ambulances. The suspect will also require medical attention.'

'Copy that, DI Orion Tanzy. They'll be with you shortly.'

Tanzy lowered the radio from his mouth and leaned over Thornton. 'June Thornton, I'm arresting you on suspicion of murder. You do not have to say anything, but it may harm your defence if you do not mention, when questioned something you may later rely on it court. Anything you do say may be given in evidence.'

It wasn't long until he heard the sirens outside.

He went back into DCI Thornton's office and went over to Byrd and lowered himself to the floor. 'You okay, Max?' he asked, placing a palm on his back.

Byrd, finally conscious, opened his eyes and stared up at him.

'Hey,' Byrd said, his voice flat.

'How you doing, Max?' Tanzy asked. 'How's the head?'

'Feels like I've been hit with a hammer.' Byrd sighed. 'What a day it's been, Orion!'

'Never a dull day in Darlington, Max, you know that.' He helped him up to his feet and placed Byrd's arm over his shoulder, then slowly left DCI June Thornton's office, stepping around her.

The main entrance door opened and a handful of officers came storming in. Tanzy briefly told PC Cornty what had happened and pointed to the back wall. He went over, put the cuffs on Thornton and led her outside.

'Thanks for coming, Orion,' Byrd said, struggling along.

Tanzy smiled, holding him up. 'Come on, Max, let's get you fixed up.'

THE END

Acknowledgements

I hope you enjoyed 'That Night' as much as I did writing it. It took me around seven months to write and edit it, which was much quicker than my debut novel, Someone's There.

A big thank you goes to my family and friends. Their support in my passion is an eternal blessing, and I really appreciate it. From my experience, as many writers will know, it's very hard finding the time to write when you work fulltime and have a family, not to mention the day-to-day living, so a big thanks goes to them for their patience.

A special mention to several Facebook groups such as Crime Fiction Addict, Crime Book Club, Books on the Positive Side, and Skye's Mum and Books, for their support. There are many great individuals in these groups, some of them fellow writers, and almost every one of them are readers, who have supported me in one way or another. I have seen many book recommendations from their members and they know a thing or two about crime, so feel free to check them out. They are always looking for new members to share their passions for reading and crime.

My biggest thank you goes to my wife, Becky. An absolute superstar of a woman who holds our family together like glue, letting me hide away and write while she keeps the children in line.

My last thank you is to you, the reader. You make all of this possible.

Thank you.

About the Author

C. J. Grayson has self-published his second novel seven months after he released his debut novel, Someone's There. Writing will always be hard (if you write, you'll know what's involved), but it's a passion he's always loved and he'll continue to love it forever. He loves reading crime thrillers and watching horror films.

In his earlier days, he did an apprenticeship in Pipefitting and worked in Engineering and Construction. He completed his HND in Mechanical Engineering and a Level 6 Diploma in Business Management.

He's aged 30, lives in Darlington, in the North East of England. He's married to Becky, and has three boys, aged 8, 3, and 1.

He's currently writing his third novel, which will be the 2nd book of the DI Max Byrd and DI Orion Tanzy series.

If you can spare a few minutes, and enjoyed this book, he'd really appreciate some feedback on Amazon and / or Goodreads. Your thoughts and support are more valuable to him than you'll ever know. They keep him up till the early hours writing.

Keep up to date with his current work and updates regarding future novels through his website and following social profiles:

www.cjgraysonauthor.com
www.facebook.com/cjgraysonauthor/

www.goodreads.com/author/show/19642709.C_J_Grayson
www.instagram.com/cjgrayson_writer/
www.twitter.com/CJGrayson4

Printed in Great Britain
by Amazon

42333263R00246